FRACTURED KINGDOM

Book One

IN THE SHADOW
OF RUIN

Tony Debajo

ISBN 978-1-8383586-0-0

Published by De-Bajo
www.de-bajo.com/books.

Subscribe to my newsletter at www.de-bajo.com/books for updates, character artwork and sneak previews on the upcoming books in the Fractured Kingdom Series.

For Basil

GLOSSARY

Babalawo - Many names have been used to describe this group - witch doctors, medicine-men or women, and herbalists, to name a few. Their areas of expertise are often varied. Some are healers and purport to have the ability to cure any form of ailments, while others claim to possess the power to cast spells that can ward off evil spirits, create wealth or guarantee a positive outcome to any endeavour. However, their services tend to come at a cost, that is not always forthcoming or apparent at the onset.

Burukutu - An alcoholic beverage popular amongst the northern tribes. It is brewed from the grains of Guinea corn and millet.

Calabash - A fruit indigenous to many parts of Africa, that was also used traditionally for medicinal purposes or harvested mature and dried to be fashioned into utensils like cups, water bottles, plates and spoons.

Danshiki - Traditional west African attire. It tends to have varying designs and patterns around the neckline and sleeves and are usually colourful. The more elaborate the patterns, the wealthier the wearer is assumed to be. However, the northern tribes prefer more subtle designs and plain colours.

Iro and buba - Traditional attire worn by west Africa women, translated in the Yoruba tongue to mean wrapper (see description below) and blouse or upper clothing. These items are designed with a variety of materials ranging in colour and texture and are accessorised with matching headgear.

Iroko tree - A large tree of hardwood commonly found in west Africa and some species can live up to 500 years. The wood from this tree is favoured for crafting expensive furniture, spear shafts and sword handles.

Juju – Synonymous with black magic or dark arts, practiced by small groups in several African countries and other parts of the world. Juju can relate to minor incantations for protection, wealth and prowess, while other times it can be associated with much darker spells to inflict harm or summon evil spiritual beings.

Kabiyesi – A title given to Yoruba kings and said to be translated to mean, "He who cannot be questioned".

Kaftan – Similar to the danshiki, a kaftan is long flowing garment that is often accessorised by a belt at the waist. Commonly worn by men, however, they can be fashioned into women's clothing, having more elaborate designs and colours.

Kola nut – The kola nut is a fruit of the kola tree and grows in tropical African countries. It has a bitter taste and contains caffeine and is used as a flavouring in different types of beverages. The nuts also hold a traditional significance in west African countries, often used traditionally for celebratory purposes and a sign of friendship and respect, like the sharing of mead.

Marabu – Marabus are the Hausa equivalent to the Yoruba Babalawo.

Masquerade – These are long-standing traditions of Nigeria and span across the various tribes. It is essentially an elaborately designed mask and outfit worn by a tribesman that represents the essence of their tribe. Some are perceived as a manifestation of spirits, good or malevolent, while others are simply entertainers. They are usually accompanied by large processions, mostly musicians, who serve as their heralds. The ones who entertain tend to be acrobats, performing energetic dances, while others carry bamboo canes to lash those that would stand in their path.

Modakeke – These people are a sub-tribe of the Yoruba, who also claim to be descendants of Oduduwa, the Yoruba deity. They are a warrior-elite group whose loyalty lies solely with the Kingdom of Ife. They are the kingdoms deadliest military force and have no rivals to that claim.

Ncho – Also known as *ayo*, ncho is said to be one of the oldest board games known, dating back thousands of years. It is a pastime of the elders in Yorubaland and is fashioned from wood with pits carved in rows into the board. Stones or seeds are placed within the pits, and the aim is to move them around.

Oba – This is a title given to a Yoruba ruler, which is used as a form of address.

Ogogoro – An alcoholic beverage, which is indigenous to Nigerian. It is a spirit distilled from the fermented juice of a palm tree. It holds traditional value and is a typical drink of choice at ceremonies and gatherings, such as weddings.

Orisa – This is the collective name for the deities of the Yoruba people.

Palm wine – Similar to ogogoro, palm wine is another alcoholic beverage that is extracted, or tapped from the tallest section of a palm tree and is left to ferment with the yeast present in the air. This drink is a favourite of many of the Nigerian tribes and is also used traditionally like ogogoro.

Wrapper – This is a typical garment for west African women and in simple terms, is a length of cloth wrapped around the waist and tightened by several folds at the hip. Men also wear this attire, but have it tied in a knot over one shoulder and draped around their body, which is common in the Igbo tribes. The designs and texture often vary, some being heavy and coarse, while others could be light and fine.

TRIBES & CHARACTER LIST

YORUBA

Often referred to as the westerners, are homogeneous people made up of numerous sub-tribes that all speak the same language of Yoruba but with varying dialects. Some claim to trace their lineage directly to the gods that once roamed the earth. They consider themselves to be the most intellectual and progressive amongst the tribes, and they pride themselves for their great warriors and hunters.

Adeosi Adelani (ah-day-o-see / ah-day-la-nee) – Father of Jide and Olise, former king of Ile-Ife (e-lay-e-fe), also referred to as Ife, and all the provinces and tribes south of the rivers Niger and Benue.

Bunmi Adelani (boo-me) – Mother of Jide and Queen of Ile-Ife.

Enitan Adelani (eh-nee-ton) – Third child of Jide and prince of Ile-Ife.

Jide Adelani (je-day) – King of Ile-Ife and all the provinces and tribes south of the rivers Niger and Benue.

Kayode Adelani (ka-yor-day) – Father of Adeosi and grandfather of Jide. Fabled king of all the lands south and north of the rivers Niger and Benue (although he never completely conquered the north, but he claimed it as part of his dominion).

Lara Adelani – Queen of Ile-Ife, wife of Jide and mother to the three princes; Toju, Niran and Enitan.

Niran Adelani (ne-ron) – Second child of Jide and prince of Ile-Ife.

Olise Adelani (oh-lee-se) -Half-brother of Jide and son of Ekaete. He also has Igbo and Calabar heritage from his mother.

8

Toju Adelani (toe-ju) – First child of Jide and heir to the throne and southern kingdom.

Adebola (ah-day-bo-la) – Commander of the guard in the Ondo province under Olusegun.

Adedeji (ah-day-day-je) – Head of the Modakeke warriors (the royal family's personal army and warrior class of the tribes), and the council of ten (elders/ leaders of the Modakeke).

Akin (ah-kin) – Blood-guard (protector) to Jide and Modakeke warrior.

Ayo (ah-yor) – Blood-guard to Enitan and Modakeke warrior.

Bankole (Ban-ko-lay) – Citizen from Ile-Ife.

Dare (da-ray) – Chief of the island provinces (the islands that make up Lagos).

Dele (day-lay) – Ondo warrior / also a citizen of Ile-Ife.

Demola (day-mo-la) – Blood-guard to Adeosi and Modakeke warrior.

Dimeji (de-may-je) – Blood-guard to Olise.

Doyin (doe-yin) – Disgraced Modakeke warrior, father of Dimeji.

Eni (eh-nee) – Second in command of the Adelani royal guard.

Fadeke (Fa-day-ke) – Daughter to the chief of the Ekiti province. Unelected chieftain of the region.

Gbenga (ben-ga) – Elder from the Ilesha province.

Kola (kor-la) – Chief of the Ogun province, father of Lara and grandfather to the Adelani princes.

Leke (lay-kay) – Blood-guard to Toju and Modakeke warrior.

Ogie (o-ge) – Commander of Olise's army.

Ogogo (o-go-go) – Commander of the Adelani royal guard.

Olusegun (Segun) Lawal (oh-loo-sheer-goon / la-wal) – Chief of the Ondo province.

Remilekun (Re-mi-le-koon) – Head of the council of ten during the reign of King Adeosi. Father of Akin.

Rotimi Balogun (row-ti-mi / ba-low-goon) – Chief of the Owo province.

Seun (shay-un) – Blood-guard to Niran and Modakeke warrior.

Soji (saw-je) – Prominent citizen from the Ilesha province.

Taiwo (tie-wow) – Captain in the Adelani royal guard.

Wale (wa-lay) – Commander of the guard in Ogun province.

CALABAR

One of the tribes of the rivers and considered to be the most powerful across the River-lands. Located in the south east, their provinces are based around the many veins of water that feed into the two great rivers Niger and Benue that flow through the country. Fishing is their trade of choice, but they are also known to breed exceptional warriors.

Abasi (a-ba-see) – Renowned warrior. Captain in the Calabar army, father of Aniekan.

Achojah (ah-co-jah) – Councillor in Ile-Ife.

Akpan the just (ak-pan) – Chief of the Amoso province.

Aniekan – Daughter of Abasi, Jide's first love.

Edem the ugly (eh-dem) – Chief of the Akwa-Ibom province.

Efetobo (eh-feh-toe-bow) – Chief councillor in Ile-Ife and relative of Ekaete.

Ekaete (eh-ky-e-tay) – Second wife of Adeosi and mother of Olise. Claims Igbo heritage from her father.

Etido (eh-ti-doe) – Commander in Olise's army.

Mitaire (me-tie-ray) – Councillor in Ile-Ife.

Odafe (O-da-fay) – Commander in Olise's army.

IGBO

The Igbo also claim to be decedents of the gods and are perhaps the proudest people amongst the tribes. They dominate the eastern region of the country, with borders deep into the south that overlap the River-lands. They are a tribe of warriors and farmers and are known to be an amiable people.

Achike (ah-chi-kay) – Chief of one of the Igbo provinces.

Azuka (a-zu-ka) – Nsukka warrior.

Chidi Chidozie (chee-de / chee-do-ze-yay) – Former head of the Chidozie families and father of Ekaete.

Emeka (eh-maker) – Chief of the Nsukka province and distant relative of Zogo the black.

Iboro (e-boro) – Abia warrior and commander in Olise's army.

Ikenna (e-cain-ah) – Chief of one of the Igbo provinces.

Nnamdi (n-nam-de) – Cousin to Zogo, chief of the Anambra province.

Uche (u-chay) – Nsukka warrior.

Zogo the black (zo-go) – Renowned warrior and head of the Chidozie families, lord of all the Igbo provinces. Also, a relative of Ekaete through marriage.

HAUSA

The horse tribes dominate the northern lands beyond the great rivers. Little is known about this elusive tribe other than the fact that their provinces, which are mostly deserts, make up for half of the landmass of the country, which could easily make them the most populous amongst the tribes. They are expert horsemen, adapting this to their style of warfare, making them a formidable foe. They are mostly herdsmen by profession.

Abdul Abubaka (ab-dole; ah-boo-ba-ka) – Father of Suleman and grandfather of Mustafa. Emir (ruler) of several provinces immediately north of the rivers Niger and Benue during the reign of King Kayode.

Suleman Abubaka – (su-lay-mon) Father of Mustafa and emir of most provinces north of the rivers Niger and Benue during the reign of King Adeosi.

Mustafa Abubaka – (mus-ta-fa) Emir to all the lands north of the rivers Niger and Benue.

Danjuma Abubaka (dan-ju-ma) – First son of Mustafa and prince of the north, heir to the northern kingdom.

Habibah Abubaka (ha-bee-bah) – Second daughter of Mustafa and princess of the north.

Usman Abubaka – (us-man) Third son of Mustafa and prince of the north.

OTHER

Neguse Nirayu (ne-gu-se / ne-ri-you) – Ethiopian warrior who conquered most of East Africa.

THE GODS (ORISA)

Aganju (ah-gan-ju) – The god of the earth and often associated with volcanos. Also known to be close to the deity Shango, some claiming that they are brother gods.

Chineke (chi-nay-kay) – Is the king of the gods to the Igbo as Olorun (Olodumare) is to the Yoruba.

Esu (a-shoe) – The trickster god synonymous with misfortune, chaos and death. Once the messenger of all the orisa able to speak the language of every creation but later becoming forgetful and misconstruing the messages that led to chaos.

Obatala (o-ba-ta-la) – The god of the sky and rumoured to have been instrumental in the creation of the human form before life was blown into them by Olorun (Olodumare).

Oduduwa (o-do-do-wa) – A lesser god sent by Olorun to help with the creation of the Yoruba lands. He was also known to have created Ile-Ife and settled there as its first divine king. The Adelani family claim to trace their bloodline directly to him.

Ogun (o-goon) – The god of war. Depicted with a machete and a hammer. He was also known as the god of blacksmiths who forged all the metals used to create instruments of war.

Oko (o-ko) – The god of farming and agriculture. He is celebrated especially during the seasons of crop harvesting.

Olorun (o-lo-roon) – Also referred to as Olodumare (o-low-do-ma-ray) is the king of all the gods in the Yoruba tribe and the creator of everything.

Oshosi (o-show-she) – The god of hunting and all things associated with the forest. He is known for his cunning and astuteness and is said to favour the bow and arrow over the spear.

Shango (shon-go) – The god of thunder, often depicted as a bolt of lightning in human form. Considered to be the most feared of all the gods for his firery temper and known to shoot flaming arrows from his hands when angered.

Yemoja (yay-moe-ja) – The goddess of the rivers. Known as a protector of women and healer in matters regarding fertility and childbirth.

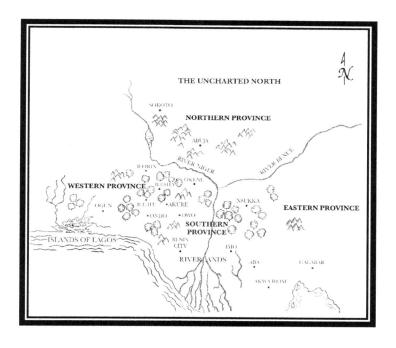

THE UNCHARTED NORTH

SOKOTO

NORTHERN PROVINCE

ABUJA

ILORIN

RIVER NIGER

RIVER BENUE

WESTERN PROVINCE

ILESHA

OKENE

OGUN

ILE-IFE

AKURE

NSUKKA

EASTERN PROVINCE

ONDO

OWO

SOUTHERN PROVINCE

ISLANDS OF LAGOS

BENIN CITY

IMO

RIVERLANDS

ABA

CALABAR

AKWA IBOM

15

RITUALS

The rain started just as Jide made his way through the forest. He travelled light to move quickly and unencumbered. His only items were a pouch strapped to his back containing the offerings he had been asked to bring and an ornate dagger sheathed at his hip. The blade had been carried by six generations of his line, the Adelanis. Passed from father to firstborn son. It had always been worn or within reach of the bearer and he was loath to leave it behind, despite the misgivings of his counsellors. He had been warned that weapons would be perceived as a threat by the seers, but the king did not relish the idea of being completely unarmed in the presence of such men. He had given way to every other concession requested of him, but this would not be one.

He continued to stalk through the thick shrubs and vegetation and wondered again if he was making the right decision to seek counsel from the seers. He knew there would be a price to pay for their aid, but he needed affirmation of success before he committed himself and his tribe to war, choosing not to rely solely on the protection of the gods. His half-brother, Olise, would certainly turn to the dark arts to secure his success in the battles to come and seize control of the tribes, especially if the rumours were true about Olise's mother and her affiliation with the occult. Jide would take every opportunity afforded him.

His thoughts flashed to his wife, Lara, and his three young sons, quickly sending a prayer to *Yemoja*, the Orisa of the rivers, his most beloved deity, to safeguard them in the days to come. He felt a moment of peace and decided to keep moving.

He spent the best part of an hour navigating the forest before he came upon a clearance with a mud hut in the centre, a few yards from where he stood. The area seemed desolate, devoid of any form of life, and a feeling of foreboding settled in him. He would not allow his doubts and fears to take root and force him to turn away, so he closed his eyes and took a deep breath to calm himself.

With his resolve restored, he quickly scanned the surrounding area and the line of trees around him before deciding to move towards the dwelling. He walked a few yards and came to a halt at the threshold of the forest. The constant patter of the rain against the leaves seemed to stop, although the rain still fell in thick torrents. Something didn't seem right. He looked around again but there was nothing there. He told himself that he was letting his imagination get the better of him, but his skin prickled and the hairs on his arms and neck had begun to rise. It felt like he was being watched, silently judged, and suddenly he heard his name whispered on the wind.

Did he imagine it? He was not sure, but he frantically swept his gaze around the forest. The only thing he noted was the gentle swaying of trees and the rustle of leaves all around him; then he heard his name again, this time louder and more urgent. Jide's hand moved unconsciously to the blade at his hip; the habit of an old warrior accustomed to meting out violence in the face of fear or danger.

He looked around again and, to his shock, saw a young girl standing as still as an old tree about ten paces behind him in the forest. She was of a fair caramel complexion, different to the darker skin of his people. Unnaturally beautiful, with long dark hair down to her elbows in fine braids, her dark unwavering eyes seemed to possess intelligence far beyond her years. She was dressed simply, in a length of cloth wrapped around her chest down to her knees tucked in under her arms. The cloth, or *wrapper,* as it was called, had vivid embroideries that seemed to shift and mimic the movement of the trees and leaves of the forest. She also wore a set of coral beads around her neck, another on her right wrist and one around each ankle.

There was something about the girl that unnerved Jide, but he could not place a finger on it. Those eyes, that appeared to see right through him, made him hesitate before he spoke.

'Who are you and what are you doing alone in a place like this?' She didn't seem to have heard him, so he tried again, 'Are you lost, child? Do you need help?' She only shook her head, almost imperceptibly. When she spoke, the voice that passed from her lips was not that of a girl but that of an elderly woman, haunting and deep.

'Turn away from here, King Jide; do not seek guidance from these seers, for they only wish to deceive you. *Yemoja* watches you, as she always has, but you risk her scorn seeking advice from charlatans.

These words troubled Jide to his core, but how could he turn back now, with the storm gathering towards his kingdom? He tried to resist challenging her comments, even though everything inside him screamed the contrary.

'How do you know who I am and why should I trust the words of a stranger? How can I be sure that you do not also wish to deceive me as you say the seers will?' She did not respond so he carried on, fear slowly gripping him but not willing to be cowed. 'By whose authority do you speak? I am beloved of *Yemoja*, but I cannot be turned away with an enemy at my door. If only you know–'

'Silence,' she said, interrupting him, 'you are beloved in truth, but your arrogance and desperation has blinded your judgement. You have been warned, but I see that you will do as you please.'

Jide stood aghast at her words and the confidence with which she spoke. *Who is this girl?* he thought; it was clear that she was no ordinary child, but he was the king, and he always commanded respect. To be spoken to in such a manner, he could not fathom. He closed his eyes to find his composure. Satisfied, he opened his eyes and turned towards the dwelling for a second, weighting his reply but as he looked back at the girl, she was gone, vanished into thin air. Jide rubbed his eyes and wondered whether he had imagined the whole encounter. He stayed in the same spot for a while, his eyes still searching the forest for her, but there was no sign.

He battled with his conscience, for the message from the girl had disturbed him deeply. *Will I truly displease* Yemoja *if I proceed?* He mused, then his thoughts turned to his half-brother and the armies he had amassed over the last year, the towns under Jide's rule that did not submit to Olise and were reduced to rubble, the deluge of displaced townspeople who had come in their hundreds to his capital city for refuge. He could not turn his back on his people, and he knew his forces alone could not stand against Olise.

Most of his allies who had not already been destroyed or displaced had already gone over to Olise through bribery, manipulation or even fear of witchcraft, he could not tell. He promised himself that he would see to it that all the turncoat vassals were paid in kind. Once Olise was defeated, Jide vowed to sweep through his kingdom and cleanse it of all the puppet rulers and establish new governments across the kingdom. It was time for a change, if anything, just to secure his legacy and the birth right of his sons. If his sons were to have any hope of ruling in his stead, he would need to enact this change soon, once he had dealt with his half-brother.

Jide made his decision, telling himself that it was the right choice for his family, his people, and his kingdom. His mind was set, and he tentatively moved towards the dwelling.

Suppressing a shudder, he stopped outside the door of the hut. He paused for a minute to observe his surroundings and make sure he wasn't being watched, just before he pushed open the door slowly.

It took a few seconds for his vision to adjust to the gloom, and then his eyes fixed on four figures huddled over a large cauldron. No one spoke until the king lost his patience and said, 'I have come a long way for your guidance, do I have to wait longer still to be acknowledged?' The first of the seers turned his head, a weathered face with long tribal marks running down his cheeks like the marks borne by some of the western tribes. The old seer's eyes scanned the king before him, and a hint of a sneer crossed his face before he spoke.

'You seek guidance from us, so do not presume to hold any authority here, King Jide.' Before Jide could respond, one of the others spoke without turning, 'Arrogance is one thing, but to come here with a blade is another; do you seek to threaten us?'

Jide's sense of authority and composure began to falter as he regarded them, so he spoke quickly to try and dispel the tension. 'Forgive my rudeness, the circumstances that has led me here robs me of the respect that is due to you. My predicament is a desperate one, but I come here humble, please forgive my impertinence, I beseech you'.

Another one of the old figures began to laugh, a horrible sound similar to a fowl being strangled. 'Sit my child, these old men are not accustomed to visitors and only seek to assert their seniority. Please sit, do not be frightened'.

The one who spoke turned slowly and Jide realised that this one was blind. His eyes gleamed white in a grizzled face. Finally, the last seer spoke. It was obvious that this one was the most revered amongst them; he turned, and the others seemed to shrink slightly as he fixed his cold dark eyes on the king, quietly appraising him. He seemed to sense Jide's thoughts, his innermost fears and doubts; all the while the seer's eyes bore deep into Jide's mind and even the depths of his soul. This almost unmanned him, but he reminded himself of who he was and what was at stake.

'Bring forth the contents of your pouch' he said without preamble. Jide hesitated for a second before reaching behind him and pulling the pouch free. He opened it and produced four kola nuts, a goat skin of palm wine tapped from the trees of his lands, a small clay vase containing blood taken from an untouched girl of his household and finally a bunch of his hair bound with leaves from an iroko tree grown from his gardens.

Jide had thought it strange that all the items he had been asked to bring by his councillors were things that had to be from his household, but he was past being cautious and just wanted the ritual to be done with. The blind seer shuffled over and picked up the contents as if he could see them as clear as day, and Jide noticed that half of the small finger on his left hand was missing. All of them had this deformity, which marked them as *Babalawo*, the ones who dabbled in the dark arts and were feared and respected in equal measures in the lands of the tribes.

The blind seer mumbled some words under his breath before passing the offerings to the lead *Babalawo*, who took them and expertly began to pour the contents of the vase and skin into the cauldron. He picked up the four kola nuts, passing one to each of his companions, which they all chewed noisily for a few seconds before spitting the moistened contents into the cauldron. Finally, the lead *Babalawo* took the hair wrapped in leaves. The leaves were split and the *Babalawo* began to separate the hairs between finger and thumb and slowly spread them around into the cauldron in a circular motion. All the while his lips moved, chanting an old incantation in the native Yoruba dialect of Ile-Ife. A dialect thought to have been long forgotten, but this was the tongue of the *Babalawo*, this was how they communicated with the ones who are not seen or spoken of aloud. This was the art of *juju*.

It was known that the only thing that separated the *Babalawo* from witches was that they only took a glimpse into the other side, the unseen world. They did not, however, allow themselves to become consumed by it, for there would be no return.

He chanted a few more incoherent words and, as if on cue, Jide heard the cauldron begin to bubble, and steam slowly started to rise from it. All the *Babalawo* began to rock back and forth and Jide thought it must have been some sort of trick.

He looked over his shoulder towards the entrance of the hut, the only opening that permitted sunlight into the dwelling, but something drew his eyes to the wall in front of him where all their shadows were cast. Suddenly he noticed that his shadow didn't quite move as he did. It seemed like nothing at first until he raised his hand and saw that his shadow did not do the same.

Right before his eyes, his shadow slowly rose and seemed to grow bigger, dominating the room. Jide shrank back at what he saw but the *Babalawo* didn't seem to have noticed. Fear rooted him to the spot, but he could not turn his eyes away from it.

The shadow was a terrifying sight and, at the same time, mesmerising. It almost appeared to communicate with him, with an outstretched arm that pointed towards the entrance – a silent warning only meant for his eyes. He looked around at the seers again and they were still transfixed on the cauldron and their ritual. How could they not see what was happening before them? It beggared belief, but suddenly the words of the girl from the forest come to Jide's mind. *Could this be something to do with her perhaps?* He did not know.

The shadow, his shadow, had now moved towards the entrance and lingered there for a while, then slowly went back to its original place opposite him. Just then, the lead *Babalawo* broke from his trance and dipped his hand into the cauldron, producing a small clay horn, immediately breaking the spell of what Jide saw, or what he thought he saw.

He gestured to Jide to come closer and handed him the horn, motioning him to drink from it. Jide hesitated for a moment and wondered whether he should drink from it after what he had just seen, but he relented. He put the horn to his lips and tried not to smell the liquid before swallowing the contents quickly. It felt warm and lumpy in his throat, and it was extremely bitter, but he forced it down and tried not to gag, making sure every drop of the unknown concoction was gone before handing back the empty horn.

The lead *Babalawo* looked pleased before he announced, 'It is done, I have seen your future and you will be triumphant in the days to come. When you return to your palace, sacrifice a white ram and burn its organs at the setting of the evening sun. Nothing will stand in your way, but be warned, King Jide. Do not heed the words of anyone claiming to be of a higher order to us. Only we can guarantee your salvation, any deviation from our words will see your kingdom turned to dust within a year.'

Jide nodded to himself, satisfied that he had done all that he could. He yearned to get out of that place and put as much distance between him and the seers. He rose slowly, forcing himself not to appear too eager to leave and cause further offence.

Gathering the pouch from the floor he thanked the *Babalawo*, bowing briefly as he turned towards the door. As he began to walk, one of the seers spoke: 'Do not stop or look back when you leave here and do not speak to anyone of what you have witnessed here today.' Without another word Jide left and began to make his way out of the clearing. As he reached the tree line of the forest he was tempted to stop and look back, but he forced himself to keep moving, slowly picking up pace as he made his way to the edge of the forest.

As he left, he did not see the dark figure of a woman shrouded in black from head to toe standing close to the hut. She watched him walk away deeper into the forest, hatred seeping out of her every pore, but as Jide moved further and further away, a wicked smile slowly started to spread across her face.

The rain began to fall heavily as dark clouds started to gather and sweep over the horizon. In the distance the sound of thunder rumbling could be faintly distinguished, a sign of what was surely to come.

TIDINGS OF WAR

Akin kept his eyes on the dark outline of the forest and occasionally glanced at the skies. He could tell a storm was coming, he smelt it in the air and saw it in the way the clouds moved. He relished the rain to come; it had a purity about it, as if it could wash away all his doubts, all his ill intentions and quell his sense of guilt when hard choices had to be made.

Cleansing would certainly be needed, he thought. He of all people knew what the days to come were likely to hold, and the blood that would be shed in the name of the king. He grimaced, not wanting to dwell on the struggle ahead. Regardless of the outcome, he would embrace it; after all, he was the king's sword hand, his strength, and he would follow him to the bowels of the underworld if he had to.

A man of muscular build and dark skin, borne from his years in the field waging war in the king's name, Akin was unmatched amongst the tribes in his skill with a sword. He stood in full armour, laden with not only his weapons but also those of the king. He clutched tightly on to the pommel of the king's sword in one hand; a fine sword forged from good iron, unlike the bronze swords more commonly used by soldiers, and a shield with a spear through the leather handle in the other hand.

The face of the shield held the crest of the king; a spear on a blue background, representing the river. The crest served as a tribute to *Yemoja*, the river deity, and, as with the king's dagger, the shield had been passed down through the generations. Akin's own sword was strapped to a belt by his side and his shield and spear lay at his feet. He was starting to feel weary from standing in the same position for hours now. The king's army was some 20 paces behind him, all loyal and ready to lay down their lives for the kingdom.

Akin surreptitiously looked back at the men standing stoutly in their ranks, all familiar faces he had known over the years. Veterans. These were the king's elite, men he had stood and fought with for years. *How many of them will soon become the faceless men of the dead, snatched away from their loved ones, never to be seen or heard from again?*

He could not dwell on these thoughts, but he promised himself that he would make a fitting sacrifice to the Orisa of the sky, *Obatala,* to protect him and give him strength. 'I will not fall,' he told himself, 'I will prevail no matter the obstacles put before me, as *Obatala* is my witness, I will protect the king and lead him to victory as I have always done.' A chant he had said many times over the years preceding every battle. He was adamant his course was just, and this thought empowered him. He had no fear.

Akin had known the king all his life; he was handpicked as the king's companion, a blood-guard from birth, chosen from the bloodline of the Modakeke, the warrior class of the people of Ile-Ife. This was the practice of all those born to royalty in the Yoruba land of old, a tradition steeped in history as far back as the first settlers of the southwestern kingdoms. A tradition sown from necessity to protect the male royal bloodline. The blood-guard's main purpose was to serve as a battle companion and tutor during the early years of the royal children. Each Modakeke warrior was ten years older than his charge and they were the most loyal subjects to the throne.

For the hundredth time, Akin went over his plans in his head, as he was trained to do; he knew the land intimately, and he thought again how he would use the terrain to his advantage. The impostor to the throne, Olise, would not stand a chance, no matter the numbers he brought with him. He was not from Ife; he did not know the land as Akin did. Even with his victories against the lesser tribes and vassal provinces, his triumphs would pale to insignificance once he set foot on Ile-Ife soil and faced the king's elite, not the goat herders and un-blooded warriors of the outer provinces. Olise would rue the day he decided to march on the king's capital city.

While he was lost in thought, the rain came down in thick droplets, already turning the leather of his breastplate dark brown. He almost missed the dark shape that began to take form in the forest. He narrowed his eyes and gripped the pommel of the king's sword tighter. He could feel the tension in the men behind him, ready to draw their swords and surge forward at his command. As the figure came closer, Akin recognised the silhouette of the king, the way he moved like a cat ready to pounce at any moment. This brought a smile to Akin's face, for he knew he had trained the king well. He could not imagine anyone ever getting the better of his king; it was unthinkable.

Jide finally emerged from the thicket of trees and bushes soaking wet from the rain. His face held no expression and, for a second, Akin wasn't sure if the king had received the response he had desired from the seers. Had he seen a bad omen or were the seers not pleased? He would soon find out.

'Kabiyesi,' Akin ventured, using the king's formal title, but Jide only walked forward and reached out for his sword. He took it and ran his hand along the leather scabbard affectionately, as if the action and the weight of iron in his hands gave him comfort. Finally, he looked up at Akin and held his stare for a second before he gave a curt nod and spoke. 'The prophecy was as expected, we will take to the field to confront my brother'.

Akin could not help but show his teeth, he craved a good battle and he knew the king would only move if he was confident. Jide, however, hid the conflict he felt. The words of the girl he saw in the forest and what he had witnessed in the hut of the seers still played on his mind, but he could not allow his half-brother to continue to scourge his lands with impunity. He would not allow it.

Akin sensed some of the king's apprehension but he assumed it was nerves preceding a battle, and the prospect of confronting his sibling. He knew the king had been close to his brother for a time and, no matter the circumstances, the king was a good man with a good heart, and he would be torn between his duty to his people and the blood-tie he shared with Olise.

Akin tried to make light of the situation. 'It gladdens me to know we will march, but hopefully it won't be too soon. My wife will be cooking goat meat stew tonight and I promised her that I would be back in time for supper'. Jide smiled at that and clasped his old companion on the shoulder. 'You are right, old friend, we had better head back to the city and summon the chiefs. There is a lot to prepare for.'

Just as Jide let his hand drop to collect his shield and spear, they were alerted to muttering coming from some of the men, and a few of them parted for a scout who came bounding in, looking strained and clearly struggling to catch his breath after what must have been a long sprint. The scout recovered surprisingly quickly when he saw the king. 'Kabiyesi, enemy warriors have been sighted a mile away from Benin Kingdom, I left the scouting party to observe their movement and came here in all haste to inform you,' he said while prostrating himself in front of the king.

Akin turned to the king, anticipating his reaction. Olise intended to take the Kingdom of Benin, which was one of the king's richest domains, producing vast amounts of gold, iron ore and other precious gems, all bringing great revenue to the kingdom.

Benin Kingdom also held strategic value as the main trading routes from the east passed through the city. Olise could cut off their supplies and any hope of reinforcements from the eastern and southern provinces.

'Your orders, Kabiyesi?' Akin asked, seeing that Jide had come to the same reasoning. Jide was taken aback at this; he had hoped that Olise would be slowed down by some of his allies and vassals, unless they had been destroyed or, worse, joined forces with him.

He realised that he had underestimated Olise; he was not the same man Jide had loved all those years ago. Jide had hoped to return to the palace to see Lara and his sons and feel the warmth of their embrace before the cold reality of confronting Olise. This news, however, had robbed him of that luxury, he would have to march immediately and gather his forces along the way to engage the invaders before they could reach Ile-Ife. It occurred to him that he wouldn't be able to complete the sacrifice he had been instructed to perform by the *Babalawo*, but he could not afford to lose any time. He would have to take the risk.

Although he had his personal guards with him, he had only intended for the day's march to be a light training exercise. This news had changed everything.

'It seems my brother will stop at nothing until he takes control of the kingdom. He leaves me no choice; we must meet him on the road before he can consolidate his forces and reach the capital. I would prefer not to fight him on Ile-Ife soil and inevitably spill blood on our sacred land. Ready the men to march.' Jide turned to the scout and added, 'You have done well. Send word back to Ile-Ife instructing Adedeji to gather the rest of the Modakeke, I will need them to accompany us. Then dispatch messengers to Ondo and Ekiti informing the chiefs that I have taken to the field and I require them to be armed and ready to join me when I arrive. Also, send the same message to the towns and provinces to the west; let them know that they are summoned to stand with their king to repel the threat to our kingdom.'

The scout responded 'Yes, Kabiyesi,' just before he rose from his position of reverence, turned and headed off in the direction he had come from, the feeling of fatigue dwarfed by the weight of the task bestowed on him.

Akin's eyes followed the scout and he said, 'Well, it seems I won't be having my wife's stew after all. No matter. I'm sure she will understand.' With that, Akin turned towards the soldiers standing in ranks and barked out an order. With the discipline of veterans, all the warriors began to check their weapons – spears, shields and swords.

Some of them brandished short axes and daggers. Akin could not help but smile at these men, like a proud father admiring his children, only that these "children" were born killers loyal to the land. Nothing could change that. Before long they all turned as one and began to march east. A short while later, the group of five hundred warriors were jogging lithely on the road to the province of Benin with the king at their head, flanked by Akin, as the rain continued to pour all around them.

BIRTH OF A KING

*K*ing Adeosi was content. His kingdom had not known war for seven years since he had come into power and all the cities under his rule prospered. Trade was good, food was plentiful, and the people thrived.

The only thing he lacked was an heir to the throne. For five years the queen had been unable to conceive a child and pressure was mounting from the scions and citizens of the land as the queen's fertility and ability to carry on the royal bloodline was continuously brought into question. This had rarely bothered Adeosi in the past. The love he held for Bunmi was all he ever needed, but he understood the significance of establishing his bloodline as his forebears had before him. He could not, however, turn a blind eye to the sadness he saw in Bunmi's eyes any time the subject of children was broached.

They had even been to several seers and all forms of fertility doctors, to Adeosi's displeasure, he hated the thought of feeling vulnerable around such men, all of which yielded the same result. This only increased the despair and desperation that had slowly begun to consume them and weigh heavily on their union.

Then, one day, queen Bunmi met a mysterious woman who appeared in the river near Ile-Ife claiming to be Yemoja, the deity of the river, who gifted fertility onto barren women. Yemoja had sought out the queen as she swam in the river, which she had done on the eve of every full moon ever since she was a child.

Bunmi's guards and servants had been sceptical of letting this strange woman close to their queen, but most had heard the tales of a demi-god who dwelled in the river, and the powers she possessed. The guards had drawn their swords and waded into the shallows, putting themselves between the queen and Yemoja. However, Bunmi did not sense any danger, and asked the guards to stand down. She came out of the river, dressed and permitted her guards to allow the woman to approach, letting her intrigue get the better of her, to the amusement of the demi-god.

Yemoja had revealed to her that she had felt Bunmi's sorrow and pain every time she came for a swim, which she observed from the depths of the river. Yemoja's council in her kingdom in the river had permitted that she should come to Bunmi's aid. Therefore, she had come to instruct her on what she must do to conceive a child. However, there would be a price to pay. Not only must the child be raised in honour of Yemoja, the deity of the river, but the child's life would come at the cost of another.

Bunmi's only concern was that the life to be taken was not that of the king; she could not bear to live without him, even if she had a child, her sorrow would be unbearable. However, Yemoja would not reveal the name of the life to be marked for death, and finally Bunmi accepted the offer, so profound was her desperation to fulfil her duty to her husband and king.

The prospect of a child filled her with great joy, as nothing she had tried previously had ever come to fruition, so she was prepared to try anything if it would give the kingdom the heir that the people so desperately desired.

Yemoja had instructed Bunmi on the sacrifices and offerings that were required to complete the ritual, but she had also mentioned that all of this should be done in absolute secrecy; not even the king was to have any knowledge of this mysterious visit.

Bunmi's entourage were to gather all that was required without delay and meet Yemoja the next day – the night of the full moon – at the same location where Yemoja had first appeared. The servants, three girls, were more than eager to help but the two royal guards were less trusting and openly showed their misgivings; however, they would not betray the queen's trust and swore to do what was required.

The next day, all the offerings were brought, including a white ram that was to be sacrificed in the river. Yemoja awaited them at the bank of the river dressed in a plain white wrapper that covered her from chest to just below the knees. Cowrie shells decorated her long-braided hair, which was tied up in a knot. She also had a sets of white coral beads around her neck, wrists and ankles.

She motioned for the ram to be brought to the bank of the river, which was done with some difficulty, as the ram protested and struggled against its bonds. Yemoja offered a prayer to the river gods before expertly slitting its throat. She produced a calabash bowl and collected most of the ram's life blood, allowing the rest to run clear and foul the river in which they stood. Yemoja then asked Bunmi to strip, and she poured the blood over her head, which tickled down her body. Yemoja chanted through the entire process.

Bunmi was warmed by the sensation of the blood flowing over her and immediately thought she felt a difference in her body. Yemoja announced that she was to wait an hour before washing away the blood, first from her hair then the rest of her body. She also instructed her to lie with the king as soon as she arrived back at the palace, which Bunmi had already contrived to do.

Yemoja mentioned that the child was to be brought back to this spot a year from now to bathe him in the river and give offerings to her, which Bunmi gladly agreed to do. After that, Yemoja waded further and deeper into the river, then a mist slowly started to rise and suddenly she was gone, vanished as she had first appeared the night before.

Bunmi was eager to return to the palace where the king awaited her. Adeosi was in the throne room when Bunmi arrived. He was pleased to see her and, somehow, he could tell that her spirit was lifted. Without words, Bunmi approached Adeosi, took him by the hand and guided him off the throne and towards the bedchamber. Adeosi looked puzzled, but he went along with her. As soon as they were alone, they fell into each other's arms and eagerly began to undress one another. There had always been a genuine love between them and an insatiable appetite to pleasure each other, but this was different. The urgency only adding to their desire, fuelling a passion that they could not comprehend. On that day, a king was conceived.

* * * *

31

Nine months passed and Adeosi stood on a hill overlooking Ile-Ife, his ancestral land, with his blood-guard Demola. They had jogged five miles through the forest and sparred with swords for an hour as he had done since he was old enough to take the weight of a sword. Now a man of thirty-three, he was just coming into his prime.

The queen was in labour at the palace and he could not bear her screams, feeling powerless to help the one he loved above all others, and this had driven him out into the wilderness to distract himself and await the news of his unborn child. He had ordered messengers to bring him the news as soon as the midwife emerged from the queen's quarters and, just like the king, the entire kingdom held its breath.

From Adeosi's vantage point on the hill, he suddenly noticed dark clouds creeping their way across the horizon. The clouds flashed with streaks of lighting and seemed to be rolling towards his kingdom.

It started off slow enough, but now Adeosi could see that the clouds seemed to gather momentum and move like a living thing. Suddenly Ile-Ife was plunged into darkness and strong winds and lashing rain began to pound the lands. Adeosi stood his ground, but it was becoming harder to stand still against the rain and howling wind that threatened to blow him off the hill. Demola struggled to the king's side and had to shout in his ear to be heard, telling him that they should head back to the safety of the city.

Adeosi relented and they made their way back to the palace. They did not come across any riders on the way; could that mean the queen was still in labour or did the messengers seek shelter in the palace? If it was the latter and his child had come into the world without his being informed, someone would answer for it, he thought.

The closer they got to the palace the stronger the storm seemed to get. Soon, they were within sight of the palace, and what they saw sent a cold feeling of dread down their spines. The eye of the storm appeared to be directly above the palace. This seemed *impossible to fathom and Adeosi had to blink a few times to make sure his sight did not deceive him. The storm remained.*

Heedless of his own safety and what he was witnessing, Adeosi charged across the field and headed straight to the entrance, closely followed by Demola. He could not bear to stand and watch the palace potentially get destroyed by the storm while his queen and unborn child were inside – he would either save them or suffer their fate, whatever that would be.

Miraculously, they made it to the palace without incident and Adeosi wasted no time in seeking out his queen. He made it to the queen's chambers through the chaos of servants running frantically around, and outside the door he could hear the queen's screams.

He pushed open the doors and saw several servants arrayed around the room. The midwife gave him a disapproving look, but he ignored her and walked to the queen's side. She was drenched in sweat, but she forced a smile on her face at the sight of him just before a spasm of pain contorted her features and she screamed even louder than before. The storm outside continued to intensify with every labour pain felt by the queen, then suddenly, the storm stopped, and an unnatural calm fell upon the room, only to be shattered by the sound of a baby crying. It was a boy.

As the storm stopped, the clouds receded, leaving a ray of sunlight that filtered through the windows of the room. Adeosi felt tears sting his eyes, but he felt no shame. 'I have a son,' he whispered, emotion gripping his chest as he knew that this was surely a gift from the gods. The royal bloodline was finally secure. Bunmi reached for the child that had been wiped clean, eager to wrap her arms around the tiny life that had eluded her for so long. She longed to bear the child in her arms if only to make sure that it was real and not a cruel dream.

The baby nestled in her arms and, in that instant, she was so relieved and overwhelmed with love that she felt her heart would burst. She turned to Adeosi with tears of joy streaming down her face and said, 'I want him to be called Oyejide,' – which meant the ancestral chieftaincy has returned, in their native Yoruba tongue. Adeosi smiled and said, 'It will be so.' Bunmi also told him that the child was to be taken and bathed in the river every year on this day in reverence to the deity of the river.

Although Adeosi reserved his reverence for Oduduwa – the deity of the people of Ile-Ife – he was so elated that he would have agreed to anything in that moment, so he acquiesced.

He looked down at his wife. She was so beautiful, and content, and he wished he could freeze the moment for ever. Bunmi seemed to sense his attention and turned her head upwards to gaze lovingly at him with a smile on her lips. He stroked her face and, as he did, her eyes closed for the last time.

FIRE AND ASHES

The scent of smoke was heavy in the air, punctuated by the screams of tortured men, women and children and the clash of iron and bronze. The scene was one of chaos, but it was all too familiar to Olise. His warriors had already taken several towns and cities, with more flocking to his standard along the way. He was not sure how his mother, Ekaete, had managed it, but she had promised that the smaller chiefs would come, and they had in their droves. Olise wondered what sort of influence she possessed for them to practically fall over themselves to win his favour, but he decided not to read too much into it and be grateful of her support.

The city in which he now stood; Benin City, in the heart of what was previously the Kingdom of Benin, now the jewel in the crown of the Kingdom of Ile-Ife, was yet another place that refused to pledge its fealty to him, so he would reduce it to ashes and rubble on his path to Ile-Ife.

As he watched the carnage before him, a deranged man with a broken sword came storming out of the mass of fighting figures, screaming a war cry and heading directly towards him. He had somehow managed to kill two of Olise's warriors in a frenzied attack and he seemed to be in a bloody rage, presumably at the sight of his city in flames. Olise wondered absently whether the man was someone important in the city; judging from the armour the man wore and the way he had skilfully killed the two guards, perhaps he was a minor chief or a warrior of some renown, but, as the man came closer, Olise's men cut him down before he could reach within striking distance of their prince. The man's shouts were cut short instantly as he was added to the growing piles of severed limbs and corpses that littered the streets.

Olise had yet to blood his own sword and he didn't intend to. Twenty of his guards had formed up around him, their swords drawn with blood dripping to their hilts. All the guards wore the distinctive dyed black leather armour Olise favoured. Not that he was ever in much danger, as the towering figure of his blood-guard was ever present at his side.

With dark ebony skin and webs of scars covering his face and arms, all telling a story of a lifetime of hardship and violence, Dimeji was without doubt the most feared warrior in all the lands and far beyond for his shear strength and ferocity. His presence struck terror into the hearts of any man who came across him, and the mere mention of his name had a similar effect. He was known by other names, but the one that was always whispered was '*ejo*' – serpent in the Yoruba tongue – for he was said to be unpredictable and could strike at a moment's notice. He walked beside Olise with utter indifference at the horrors unfolding all around, but he didn't speak. His preferred method of communication was with his sword or spear in the language of death, a language in which he was most fluent.

There were bodies everywhere and more corpses fell as the rest of Olise's men moved through the city methodically, clearing out every dwelling before setting fires and moving onto the next one, adding to the ruin of what was once a beautiful, prosperous and peaceful place. Olise was determined to leave nothing behind but a trail of ashes in his wake, provoking a response from his half-brother Jide. 'If this does not move my brother, I do not know what will. I find this business tedious and a waste of my time. Right now, we should be at his gates with the *king* at my feet'. He said the word king as if it tasted bad on his tongue.

'I think it is good practice for the men, it won't be as easy once we reach Ile-Ife,' Ogie, the commander of his guards, and a solider of some renown, said.

'That is true, but my patience is drawing thin and I'm tempted to leave a force behind to finish off here. They could catch up with us once they're done, after all we have the numbers at our disposal.'

Ogie rubbed his chin in thought. 'That may not be the best move, my prince, we don't know how many men will stand with the king but we know it will not be an insignificant number, especially if he manages to mobilise his allies from around the islands of Lagos and the surrounding towns in that region. I suspect that we will need every warrior if the king summons all his allies to his cause.'

Olise shot him a venomous look. 'I am the king! Well, I will be soon enough, at any rate'. He softened his tone and added 'But your words are wise, Ogie, as always. I will endure this... butchery a while longer. Make sure that anyone who resists is killed, I do not want the added burden of prisoners slowing us down once we leave here.'

At that, Ogie bowed his head, moved to the front of the guards surrounding Olise and began to issue orders to his officers to pick up the pace. A few of the guards detached from the main body of men and went off in different directions to pass on the orders to the ranks.

Ogie knew that the killing would be indiscriminate, but the warriors still needed to be reined in. He would prefer only hostile male combatants to be put to the sword and not the innocents, but he knew that Olise did not care for such details, so he would need to be the one to make the decision and give the order.

Ogie's keen eye could not help but take in the features of the city; the fortifications, the lands within the city limits reserved solely for cultivating crops and grazing from cattle, the vast number of supply stores, water sources and not to mention the strategic location of the city in relation to trading routes. It was obvious that holding such a location could prove advantageous, especially with the unpredictability of the outcome of the battles ahead.

He made a mental note to convince Olise of the benefits; even if he was to endure Olise's wrath, he would make him see sense in the proposal, surely. This was clearly a commercial hub and one that could serve Olise's purpose quite suitably, now and in the years to come. Maybe he wouldn't give the order to kill all the men after all. If he could convince Olise otherwise, they would require slaves to tend the fields and serve the ever-growing army of Olise. He smiled to himself at his own insight and acknowledged that he had earned Olise's trust and respect for a reason.

Olise turned to Dimeji as he heard the big man grunt. 'Don't worry, my friend, I know your sword arm itches, you'll get your share of blood soon enough.' Olise's words seems to satisfy Dimeji slightly and he settled back into his look of indifference verging on boredom. Olise looked back over the destruction and his hand found the amulet that hung from his neck, given to him by his mother, who said it would protect him from any weapon fashioned by the hands of man.

He thought again that he would sit on the throne of Ile-Ife even if he had to burn the whole kingdom to get to it. After all, it was his destiny. No longer would his line be regarded as illegitimate and despised by the other royals.

Growing up he was banished to a far-flung settlement to lord over goats and cattle. This was his long-awaited opportunity to end that chapter of his life. The thought of vengeance warmed him, and he felt excitement at the prospect of meeting his brother over the battlefield.

A minute part of him, perhaps his conscience, still tugged at him from time to time at the betrayal of his brother, who had once been the closest person to him, when they were growing up as children; but that was in the past. They were men now and each following a distinct path that would lead to war.

Now was the time for a new ruler, a strong king who would rule with a strong hand over the realm. Jide's rule had been too weak, too lenient. Trusting the citizens to govern themselves and appoint their own representatives. Goats do not dictate their path to the herder. Perhaps that was why it had been so easy for some of them to switch their allegiance.

He intended to be the only herder in the field when the day was at an end, and not a herder with a stick but one with a barbed whip, and plenty men willing to wield it for him.

THE SECOND

'I fear the time has come; start packing the supplies and send the riders out to the chiefs of the tribes, we can't afford to wait any longer.' Lara stood tall and confident as she instructed the three envoys. She was determined to discharge her duties as she had agreed three nights ago with Jide; although it pained her and broke her heart, her first duty was to protect her children, and she would not fail in that.

The envoys bowed briefly before setting off at a run to carry her messages with all haste to the tribal leaders, north, east and west of the kingdom. The chiefs of those lands would receive the king's children and protect them until it was safe for them to return home. Jide and Lara had both spent the last five years nurturing the necessary alliances for this very reason. They had decided long ago that if it came down to fleeing the capital, the children would be separated. Worst case scenario, one of them would live through the turmoil and Ile-Ife would rally around the rightful surviving heir. As long as the bloodline of the royal house of Ile-Ife survived, there would be hope.

It was known that Olise had spies in every city and it was hard to know who was in his employ even in the palace, so caution and secrecy was a necessity. Only the most trusted members of the royal household were privy to any useful information. Even the envoys did not possess knowledge of the travel arrangements of the royal family, only their intended destinations.

Lara had decided to go west with her youngest son, Enitan, where her father still ruled as chief in those lands. He would protect them, and it would be a welcome sight to see the lands of her childhood again after so many years. Besides, she couldn't bear leaving her youngest to travel alone; after all, he was only twelve, and she wasn't convinced that he understood the gravity of their family's predicament.

She walked briskly through the inner throne room and into the sleeping chambers of her second son, flanked by the commander of Jide's royal guard and his second-in-command, with her servant trailing behind, laden with packs of food wrapped in bundles of cloth brought from the kitchen.

Niran was sitting on his bed with his back turned and his blood-guard, Seun, stood beside him while they spoke in hushed voices. She saw that both men wore swords and her thoughts immediately went to her husband. 'I hope you are not planning to join your father in the fighting, it took me an age to convince your older brother to remain in the palace. You should be preparing to leave for the eastern lands,' Lara said, as she looked around the room.

Niran had his armour laid out on a couch next to the bed and she could see that he had already packed a leather sack bulging with an assortment of weapons and other items. Niran turned to face his mother, his hazel eyes rested on her. He gave her his warm mischievous smile as he always did, which broke Lara's heart as she knew the reality of the separation and the possibility of not seeing him again. 'I'm just taking precautions as father has always told me to,' he said, reading her thoughts, the smile never leaving his face. 'I can't afford to embark on such a journey unprepared, I would hate to disappoint anyone who would dare think of me as anything other than a war-hardened prince.'

This brought a smile to Lara's face, knowing that this was the type of thing Jide would say. Niran was the mirror image of his father, tall and well defined with the same confidence, compassion and intelligence. Though he lacked his older brother's natural athleticism and prowess, he made up for it in wits and his rational approach to all situations.

At sixteen, he was loved by everyone in the city and anyone who came across him. It was whispered that he was the favourite to inherit the throne, given his charm and temperament; firm but fair; but especially for his intellect.

'Where are your brothers?' Lara asked, unable to keep the agitation from her voice. Niran noticed this in an instant, nothing got past him, and he immediately rose to meet his mother. 'Father will not return in time to bid us farewell, will he?' A statement rather than a question, but before Lara could respond, Niran approached her and gave her a warm embrace. Lara closed her eyes against the tears that threatened to ruin her composure before gently pushing him away and pretending to smooth down her clothing. She could not meet his eyes, but she knew that he understood.

Niran regarded her for a second before turning to his blood-guard. 'Seun, please find my brothers and tell them to gather their essentials, we must leave here within the hour.' Lara was taken aback at how quickly her son had assessed the situation, even down to the length of time they had to safely leave the palace. Her pride in him swelled further.

Seun only nodded and walked out of the room to deliver the message. Niran turned back to his mother and asked, 'How many soldiers do we have to defend the palace and our retreat, Mother?' The commander of the guards answered the question; Ogogo, a gruff man but reliable and a good swordsman. 'We have twenty of the royal guards in the palace and another two hundred men in the barracks outside the palace walls.'

'Good,' said Niran, 'I think we should split the guards between the travelling parties and leave the soldiers in the barracks to protect the city; besides, Father may need the reinforcements if the fighting should reach the city proper.'

'Very good, my prince, it would be better to travel in smaller numbers to avoid suspicion. I will travel with the queen. The king instructed me not to leave her side,' Ogogo said.

'Excellent, ready the men to march'. Just as Niran was about to address his mother, three of the king's councillors walked in, interrupting his chain of thought. Niran despised them as he felt their only purpose in the royal court was to place themselves in a position of power, not really caring about the kingdom or its subjects.

In the past, all the policies they had proposed only seemed to benefit the elite of society; granting farming rights on the most fertile lands to the privileged, whilst the poor could only gain access

41

to sparse plots of rocky terrain that hardly yielded any crop. The ones who were lucky enough to own any half-decent land were hit with taxes so high that they often tended to work extra jobs, farming the lands of the rich for a pittance to make ends meet.

The councillors had recently persuaded Jide to grant a monopoly on fishing to the southern provinces, specifically the regions under the influence of Olise's branch of the family, in a bid to prevent war. This meant that local fishermen from Ile-Ife were now forced to sell their catch in secrecy to avoid being charged hefty taxes or risk their goods being confiscated if they were caught.

This was one of many policies that inflamed Niran. It threatened to cripple their already waning economy and undermine the king's authority. He had raised the point with his father on numerous occasions, but all the councillors were influential in their own way. Jide had no choice but to placate them, which he had done over the last two years for their continued support.

Jide had finally seen sense and had gradually started to take back Ile-Ife's sovereignty. This had led to discontent with Olise's line and what now culminated into the current civil war. It was, however, suspected that the seeds of discontent were sown by the councillors; particularly the chief councillor, Efetobo. The honourable Efetobo was a pompous and corrupt man, large in stature and with an insatiable appetite for power. He owned vast holdings in the south and was a close relation to Olise's mother.

His cronies, two other councillors, were equally influential and wielded similar powers in the southern lands. The councillors were made up of five, but the other two were simpler men with roots steeped in Ile-Ife; they tended to have a more measured and reasonable approach in matters concerning the kingdom. They at least were loyal to the crown and the interest of the kingdom, but they were almost always out manoeuvred or out voted by the three southern councillors.

'My queen,' Efetobo droned on in his southern accent, 'what is all the commotion about? Everywhere I look it seems that the palace is being evacuated. Surely there is no need for such haste?'

Like Niran, the queen loathed Efetobo and could only bear his insolence if she didn't have a choice. Luckily, Niran came to her rescue and answered on her behalf; 'Councillor, I do not recall inviting you to my chambers, nevertheless, you have nothing to worry about, my mother and I are preparing for a trip to one of the neighbouring towns to check on our family holdings. Do not concern yourself with our plans.'

Efetobo was clearly outraged at the tone at which he was being addressed, by this boy prince, no less. This one was even more arrogant than the father, he thought. He would remember the insult and pay him back once the kingdom was overthrown. 'Your Highness, apologies for barging in unannounced, but I was dreadfully afraid at what could have prompted so much chaos.'

Before he could continue, Niran spoke over him. 'In case you have not noticed, there is a war approaching and we need to ensure that our interests are protected. Please leave us now as we do not have the time to waste on small talk, there is plenty to prepare. If I were you, I would look to my own security, with everything that is happening.'

Efetobo was beyond livid at the way he was being dismissed. Was he not a man of considerable power and influence at the royal court? This treatment was totally unacceptable. He was about to give a sharp retort but he looked around at the stone expressions of Ogogo, the royal guard, and his second, who both had their hands on the pommels of their swords, and just then Seun appeared at the prince's side wearing a look of pure venom, as if daring the councillor to attempt an insult and give him reason to shed blood on the marble floor.

Sensing the tension, Achojah, one of the other councillors, quickly intervened, 'We do not mean to cause offence, our concern is only of the royal household's safety. We will take our leave.' Niran added, without preamble, 'You would do well to.' And, with that, he turned his back on the three miserable figures, ending the conversation. Efetobo could not help but put in a final word: 'Your Majesty would also do well to keep the royal councillors close, gods

43

forbid we are the last resort between a peaceful resolution and complete destruction if the king were to fail in his endeavours,' he said with a smug look on his face before bowing slightly and leaving the royal chamber.

Niran could not help but think that the shifty old councillor knew more than he let on, he could even be one of the architects behind the imminent invasion. When the royal party was alone, he turned to Ogogo. 'I do not trust them, have a man follow them and observe their movements. I want to be informed of all their dealings.'

The queen looked shocked. 'Surely you can't suspect that they have a hand in all this?' she said, unable to hide the concern in her voice.

'Do not forget, Mother, that Efetobo is a relative of our uncle, and Achojah and Mitaire both own large plots of land in the south; they only seek to gain if the worst happens here.' Ogogo seemed to agree. 'I will see it done'. His second-in-command did not need to be told and immediately walked out through another door towards the rear of the room to carry out these orders.

The urgency of their situation seemed to have amplified with the conversation, as it was now apparent that the palace was even less safe than they had thought. There was no turning back on the plans now. 'Did you find the princes?' Lara asked Seun, who gave a slight bow before he replied, 'Prince Toju was with the soldiers outside the gates and has gone to the armoury to gather a few items before he heads back to the palace.' 'And Enitan?' Lara asked, a feeling of dread rising in her. 'Prince Enitan...' Seun began, and then hesitated.

'The prince is not in the palace; I am told he went out with his blood-guard earlier this morning hunting. He has not since returned.' Lara went pale, how could he have left the palace at a time like this? Enitan did not have a sense for danger, always on one adventure after the other. How many times had he got himself in trouble because of his reckless and carefree behaviour?

Niran made the decision without hesitation 'I think we should have his things packed and ready to go. He will have to make do with whatever is chosen for him.' Lara just nodded and walked towards the entrance of the bed chamber, her servant taking up the rear. After a moment, Ogogo followed her out.

'I hope Father defeats my uncle, so much depends on it,' Niran said and Seun shot back mildly, 'When has the king ever lost a battle, even if it was against greater numbers?' Niran thought about that for a second before responding. 'It's not so much the battle I fear but the state of the kingdom afterwards, regardless of who wins. There has been so much betrayal and side swapping that it will be hard to know who can be trusted.'

'Like father used to say; "If all snakes slither and wriggle on the ground, how are you to know the one that has an itch on its stomach?"' The memory of his father's words brought a smile to his face momentarily. 'In the end,' he continued, 'the kingdom will suffer, perhaps for a generation or more.'

The reality of his words dawned on Seun and he lost some of his confidence. Niran could see the future implications of the war with a clarity that spoke volumes of his intelligence, which for the time, seemed incomprehensible to the warring factions, including his father.

'There is little you can do about it, even the queen's influence wouldn't make a difference at this stage. Once the marching starts the only thing that can stop it is when one side falls and blood flows. You know how our people are, there has been war between the tribes for centuries, it is our way. Besides, your uncle has gone too far now with all the cities he has taken. Your father's honour, more than anything, is now at stake if he does not quench the flames of this rebellion. Who knows, before long, there may be another brave fool who thinks he can take control of the tribes without repercussions,' Seun said.

'And therein lies the problem,' Niran interjected, 'this whole war is driven by bruised egos, so-called honour and greed, what about the hundreds of displaced, and worse, killed innocents caught up in between this unnecessary power struggle? They have no part or say in the matter, but are forced to accept the fate that has been forced on them by men who are chosen to be their superiors.' It was a miserable affair, they both knew that, but the only option was to adapt and survive or become devoured in the whirlwind that swept everything away.

Niran made a decision 'I will have to be the one to make a difference. I will travel east as intended, but I will not cower in the shadows and wait for the war to be over, I'll unite all the tribes there to me and sweep across the south in strength. I will make sure that my father's kingdom remains in his name, I swear it.' Seun was touched by Niran's loyalty to his father, his people and the kingdom, he felt the conviction in his words. 'And I will be at your side, as I am sure your brothers will,' he said. The prospect of travelling east suddenly became more appealing to Niran and he relished the opportunity of building this army to preserve his father's kingdom.

WITH DAWN COMES DARKNESS

Exhaustion had finally caught up with Olise. Despite his plan to cover as much ground as possible to confront his brother, he could no longer ignore the fatigue he felt. Benin City had been much larger than he had expected, and securing the town was no easy feat. The city's inhabitants had fought valiantly and refused to give in as willingly as the other towns and settlements he had conquered. It had taken most of the day and night to finally crush the resistance and this had taken its toll on the army. Coupled with the fact that he had marched his men for over two weeks nonstop without a moment's rest, if he had tried to push them any further, he risked having a mutiny on his hands.

His soldiers had so far been unable to enjoy the spoils of war, which they were by right entitled to. There had been some displeasure voiced in the ranks, but the culprits were quickly singled out and hanged to serve as a deterrent to anyone who would dare question Olise's authority. After that, the soldiers carried on in grim silence.

Once the city had fallen, Olise had made the decision – with the advice of his captains – to halt the army and grant his troops the well-deserved rest they yearned. Sitting in the great hall of the city palace he had commandeered, he thought again how fortunate he had been to delay his advance and replenish the army's supplies.

The city was extremely wealthy, which was not immediately apparent, but after they had captured and tortured a few of the city officials, they had quickly discovered a vast reserve of gold in the palace treasury. Enough gold to finance the war for a decade, not to mention the stockpiles of iron ore mined from the surrounding quarries for improved weapons, and food that was so vital if they were to remain in the field for a prolonged period.

Furnaces across the city had been fired up for hours, smelting the ore and casting new iron swords and spear heads to supply the men, replacing the damaged bronze weapons that had won them their victories. Blacksmiths from the city had been working through the night, eager to please their new overlords. It was better to work rather than take their chance in the street and possibly run into the sharp end of a spear in the hands of a drunken soldier. The smart ones had even managed to convince Olise's men that their wives and children were needed to assist them with their work, even though most of them had rarely set foot in the blacksmiths' workshops. This had given them another chance at life, even if it was not guaranteed a long one.

Olise sat idly toying with a leg of roasted goat meat. He was too agitated to eat, even though his stomach rumbled, and he hadn't eaten for hours. He had reluctantly dismissed his personal guards, even Ogie was out somewhere in the city, no doubt participating in the night's debauchery. Olise tried to enjoy the quiet of the palace, but his mind could not rest with all the details of the campaign and the men under his control playing over in his head. The room he sat in was sparsely lit with only two torches, one at either side of the vast hall, and areas of the room were deep in shadow. Across from him, the room was dominated by a large window that didn't do much to illuminate the room but provided a good view of the city, and he could make out the lights of the furnaces snaking their way along the city's thoroughfare.

As he remained deep in thought, he was suddenly alerted to what sounded like footsteps over a carpet of eggshells; crunching with every step, somewhere over his right shoulder. The sound seemed to be getting closer, and he looked over in its direction, but it was too dark there to make out anything. A split second later, he heard the unmistakable rasp of a sword leaving a scabbard on the opposite side of him and Dimeji emerged from the gloom, sword in hand in a slightly crouched position, ready to spring forward and protect his prince. Suddenly a look of fear crossed Dimeji's face and instantly

Olise knew the reason. There was only one thing on the face of the earth that scared the massive warrior, Olise thought. Mother.

Ekaete sauntered out of the shadows dressed in all black as she often did; a matching iro and buba, which was a fitted blouse and tightly wrapped cloth, also called a wrapper, around her waist down to her ankles. Her skin radiated with youth; her age could only be discerned from her short grey hair plaited in small braids tight to her scalp, which was hidden under a black head-tie.

When she came closer, Dimeji instinctively took a step back but did not lower his sword, the muscles in his arm tensing. 'You should really announce yourself, Mother, before you decide to materialise out of thin air, it still baffles me how you are able to do that,' Olise said.

'Do not ask the questions that you are not prepared to know the answers to. Some things are better unknown,' Ekaete responded.

'Perhaps you are right,' Olise said. 'Maybe I don't want to know. Anyway, what brings you here to this place of good tidings, or are you here to claim your portion of the wealth I have discovered? I can still hardly believe it, the fact that Jide has managed to keep this place secret after all this time!' Ekaete had a disappointed look on her face, 'Do you really think I care for such things? You have much to learn, my child. I am here to guide you, as always.'

Olise turned to Dimeji, who was still standing awkwardly with his sword only lowered a fraction. 'You may leave my friend; I am quite safe with Mother.' Without a word, Dimeji backed away without turning around until he was lost in the shadows of the large room. A few seconds later, they heard the door to the hall open and close with a soft thud, indicating that they were alone.

Olise looked over at his mother with an amused expression. 'You know you are the only person who unnerves him. I have seen him wrestle a leopard with his bare hands and kill it, but in your presence, he is unmanned.'

Ekaete only shrugged. 'He is wise to fear me, as do most people, and if you were not my son, you would too.'

'Maybe, but one cannot fear what one loves more than any earthly possession,' Olise said smoothly.

Ekaete was not charmed but responded patiently as she always did with him, 'Save it for your bed warmers, there is much for us to discuss'.

Olise's expression hardened subtly. 'I'm guessing you have news of my brother,' he said expectantly. 'Half-brother,' Ekaete corrected him before continuing, 'and yes, it is news concerning him that I wish to discuss with you. Jide has taken the field and he is, this moment, marching his forces here with all haste. He has about five hundred men who march with him and he has summoned his vassals to him, including the island tribes. He will certainly be at full strength when he gets here.'

Olise was furious at this news; he had chosen to delay his march north against his better judgement, granting Jide precious time to rally his men and consolidate his forces. This could prove disastrous to his ambitions, even if he held all the wealth of the kingdom and an area of strategic importance.

He was not overly concerned with the number of men Jide had managed to amass, but he quickly realised that Jide's presence may play on the loyalty of the tribes who had betrayed him and now followed Olise. Bringing all his vassals and allies could shame the betrayers into going back on their decision to fight for Olise, especially if they were to face united forces under the rightful king. This could be a short war after all, he thought miserably, causing him to grip the armrests of his chair until his knuckles turned white.

Ekaete saw how her words had troubled him and, as always, her maternal instincts to protect him kicked in. 'Don't despair, have I not always gotten you out of trouble? This is nothing but a slight setback, and we will need to bring some of our plans forward, nothing more.'

A glimmer of hope came into Olise's eyes as he regarded his mother. 'What have you got planned, are you thinking of seeking help from...' he stopped himself before he uttered the words, but she knew what he had intended to say.

'No, I do not need to call on... them. Not now, anyway. We still have options. Did you send a faction of your men north like I told you before you marched?'

Olise's mood slowly began to brighten as soon as she mentioned this, as he had forgotten the plan they had set in motion even before he had taken the first city. 'You are truly wise mother. Surely Jide will not put his pride before his family. I think we will win this war after all.'

THE LOYAL ARE A DYING BREED

Jide had marched his men hard for three days and as the sun set in the west they came upon Ondo. Word had already reached the chief of the region of Olise's progress thus far and the fall of Benin, which filled the inhabitants of Akure and Owo with great fear. Before Jide's arrival, the city officials and the elders had met. It was even suggested by a small minority that a messenger should be dispatched to Olise proclaiming their fealty to him, to avoid a similar fate to that of Benin City. Those who had made this recommendation had quickly been ostracised and banished with their families, never to return to the city again. It was clear that the people of Ondo did not intend to turn their back on their king, even if their loyalty came at the cost of condemning the city to ruin.

Ondo remained an unyielding vassal state to Jide, and the inhabitants were notoriously loyal. In the past, Jide had come to the aid of the city on several occasions. He had provided vast supplies of food from his own lands to replenish the communities in times of famine; resources for the city to thrive including the expertise to develop irrigation systems, tools for farming and hunting, and the knowledge to cultivate and harvest crops. This had seen the city flourish, and it only increased the debt of gratitude the people felt towards him.

As Jide's party arrived at the gates of Akure, a delegation of dignitaries and city guards had been sent out to receive him and guide his entourage through the city. Despite the late hour, the streets were filled with people hoping to catch a glimpse of their king. Children sat on the shoulders of their fathers and women danced in jubilation for the king who had once again come to their aid.

Jide smiled and waved amicably to the crowds; in truth, he was exhausted and wanted nothing more than to fall into a dreamless slumber but, as always, his duty to the people came first. He would continue to show his appreciation for their loyalty, even though his title demanded it. Besides, he admired them, for they all knew the dangers that they faced and the possibility of losing everything, and yet they were undeterred and unwavering in their love and support for him.

Following the procession of delegates and soldiers, they approached the chief's house, an impressive building that was raised in the centre of the city. Most of the citizens had been discreetly held back by the city guards and the closer they came to the chief's residence, the more the crowd thinned out to a trickle of people. Jide walked briskly towards the house, where the chief stood at the entrance with the city elders, with a long line of his royal guard trailing behind him.

'You are most welcome my king,' the chief said, bowing deeply as Jide approached. He was a man in his early seventies with a shock of white receding hair but when he stood, he was erect; his back was not bent from old age, and he was strong, which was a trait in the people of Ondo.

'Segun, I am glad to find you in good health, I only wish this meeting could be in better times,' Jide said. Olusegun had a sad expression, but responded to the king defiantly, 'Kabiyesi, it is unfortunate, especially as the last few years have been prosperous. I can only hope that this conflict will be resolved without too much damage to our nations. Please forgive me, do come in, I have refreshments ready.'

'You have my thanks. Please see that my men are fed and sheltered; we have come a long way and I will have them ready to march again tomorrow.' Jide went into the building followed by Akin, whilst his royal guards formed into ranks like the disciplined veterans that they were, awaiting further instructions. The king's men were directed to the local barracks, which was a short distance from the chief's house. They would be well fed, and most would take the opportunity to rest. However, it was highly likely that a few of them would discreetly venture out of the barracks, to see what the night life of the city had to offer.

Once Jide and Akin had eaten and dispelled some of their weariness, the chief was summoned to give a report on the city defences. 'We have about eight hundred soldiers in the city and can raise another one thousand from Owo and the surrounding villages. Word has already been sent informing them to gather on the road to Ore and await your forces. They will be ready once you arrive.' This news pleased Jide but he still needed all his allies to pacify the threat to the kingdom. 'I need to know every shred of information about Olise and his forces. At this point, any advantage to be had will be welcome.'

Olusegun beckoned the commander of the city guard, who prostrated himself to the king in the old style of greeting. Jide waved him up and noticed that he was a young man in his twenties with strong athletic features. Jide appraised him approvingly before asking him to report. 'What is your name young man', asked Jide. The warrior bowed deeply 'My name is Adebola, Kabiyesi,' he replied. 'Please Adebola, give me your report' said the king.

Adebola began to relay the reports from the scouts he had sent out to observe Olise's progress. He described in some detail how Benin had been taken and most of the city put to the torch and the citizens put to the sword. He also confirmed that Olise and his army had not moved from the city, presumably using the opportunity to replenish their supplies and consolidate their forces.

This made perfect sense as the city, after all, was situated in a strategic location and was said to be rich in provisions all year round, specifically for a siege. How ironic that the same supplies would be used to restore an invading army. This news did not do much to reduce Jide's concerns.

'So, it appears that we will not be relieved by our allies in the east and the River-lands,' Akin said.

'At this point, we have to assume that either those regions have been taken or we have been betrayed. Either way, the east and south are lost to us,' said Jide. He was annoyed at himself once again at the reminder of allowing the revolt to get this far. He had clearly underestimated Olise's resolve and chosen to trust that he could appeal to his better nature and the love they had once held, but he was wrong.

'Besides, Olise is no fool,' Jide continued. 'He would never risk fighting a battle on two fronts, our upbringing taught us that much. He would have made sure to nullify any threat to his rear before he started to push west with his forces. This leaves me no doubt, all the lands beyond Benin are taken. I will have them know that their lands are now forfeit and I will declare them all enemies to the throne,' said Jide, his anger slowly rising as he spoke. Akin nodded his agreement, however, Olusegun looked troubled. 'Kabiyesi, if you promote a policy of retribution and punishment, your subjects in those lands will most certainly be forced to stay with Olise, if they truly have been turned against you. They will believe that all hopes of receiving a pardon are already lost, so why would they then stay loyal and suffer further injustice by Olise and his army, when they could simply join him and line their pouches in the interim? Especially knowing that no mercy awaits them either way.'

'That may be certain for the River tribesmen, but the lords of the east? I would wager that they fell in battle opposing your brother, Kabiyesi,' said Adebola. They all looked over at the young guard. In Yorubaland it was tradition that the younger or lesser subjects of the realm only address their elders or, in this case, royalty when given leave to do so, but these were very different and desperate times.

'Forgive me, Kabiyesi,' he said, lowering his head in supplication; however, the king motioned for him to continue. Adebola felt more relaxed and carried on, 'There has been an enmity between the nobilities in the east and the south for generations. It is true that they both tried for peace when the marriage between the Chidozie and the Ukeme families was brokered during the reign of King Adeosi, your father, but that only slowed the eruption of the chasm that later drove the two regions into instability. The easterners would use any opportunity to oppose the south. You are aware of the raids and skirmishes that have been fought over the last few years.'

Jide had a pensive expression when he spoke, 'You are quite wise for your age and well-studied in our history, young man. This does you much credit.' Adebola took the compliment as an opportunity to prove himself further. 'If you approve, Kabiyesi, let me lead a party of scouts east; I will take them via the northern route, following the paths close to the river Benue. Olise would not risk taking his forces that far north.'

'A good plan,' said Akin, 'but what if you are taken by the horse tribes of the north? If there is truth in the rumours, they roam those parts and could easily use the opportunity to capture southerners to gain more information on the affairs south of their borders. Who knows, they may have plans of their own to take advantage of the situation. Let us not forget, it wasn't that long ago that we were almost at war with them.'

Jide dismissed this notion: 'I have no quarrels with the emirs in the north. The pact they made with my forebears still holds firm. They will not break their oaths to the throne, I am sure of it. Besides, once the island tribes join the march, the tides of any battle to come will most certainly shift.'

'For all our sakes, I hope you are right, my king,' Akin said with a slight inclination of his head towards the king. 'You and me both, my friend,' said Jide.

He then turned to Adebola. 'You have my blessings to go east, young man, provided your chief is agreeable and a capable captain can be appointed as the city guard in your stead?'

The last sentence was directed at Olusegun, who simply bowed his head, 'All I can wish for at this point is a quick end to the conflict, and if it means that I must part with one of my best warriors to achieve that end then I agree,' Olusegun said before turning to Adebola. 'You have my permission to go, but you must nominate someone to replace you.'

Adebola beamed, smiling from ear to ear; he would finally get the chance to prove himself not only to his chieftain and the people of Ondo, but also to the king himself. He prostrated himself again at the feet of the king. 'Kabiyesi, I will not fail you. You have my word. I will take four good men to move quickly and unnoticed and I will raise an army of easterners in your name,' he said before rising to his knee to address his chief. 'I'll see to it that the best man stands in my place at the head of the guard, my chief.'

'Very well' said Olusegun, 'make haste, we don't have any time to lose. May Oduduwa guide and protect you.' Adebola stood immediately and made his way out of the hall.

'He is a brave warrior,' Jide remarked. 'You have raised good men here; I am glad you, for one, have not forsaken me. Once this is over, I will see to it that you are greatly rewarded, Segun.' Olusegun waved a hand dismissively. 'There is no need for that my king, I am always a servant of the crown and you know how much I loved your father. My only desire is to right the wrong that Olise has brought upon the royal household. The smirch on the Adelanis' honour must not go unanswered; Olise must face his crimes.'

It was the king who now had a sad expression and he suddenly felt weary, the pressure of the days to come weighing heavily on him. Akin noticed and made an excuse on Jide's behalf. 'Perhaps you should get some rest, Kabiyesi, we have marched a long way and we have many more miles and battles ahead. Allow me to make any remaining preparations and see to the men. We need your strength, my king.' Jide was quietly grateful for Akin's perceptiveness as always. 'Thank you, my friend. We will resume our discussions in the morning. Segun, please show me to where I can rest these weary bones.' Olusegun beckoned two servants who had been waiting like statues in the wings. 'At once, my king,' he said and followed the king out of the room to the sleeping chambers.

Akin watched them go and couldn't help but think of his wife and child in Ile-Ife. He yearned to see them, to hold them both in his arms and tell them how much he loved them. He most certainly missed his wife's cooking and her humour, but he pushed those thoughts deep down. He chose to dwell on more pressing matters like the battles to come. He was confident in the ability of the soldiers from Ile-Ife, but he worried about the many others that would be joining the king's ranks, especially now with the question of loyalty weighing silently above them like dark clouds over a horizon before the rain.

The warriors of the other tribes were not bred for war like himself and the Modakekes, nor did they have the discipline of the warriors of Ile-Ife. He hoped that they would not become a hindrance. He was slightly consoled by the fact that most of Olise's army were reluctant civilians at best, but Olise did possess a good number of renowned fighting men who made up his personal guard, not to mention the one known as '*ejo*' – Dimeji, one of the most feared men in all the lands. He had always known that his path would one day lead him to stand before Dimeji in battle, but he somehow looked forward to it, relished it in fact.

Akin smiled to himself at the thought of fighting a true warrior. He was not concerned with the rumours of witchcraft and the dark arts that surrounded Olise, for he knew that Dimeji would have no man talk ill of his renown. That warmed Akin's heart. 'I truly cannot wait for the time to come,' he said to himself.

He heard voices outside and stood from the table to see what was happening. He reached the door just in time to see Adebola and four other warriors race off on horseback to start their mission, leaving a cloud of dust that swirled around in the night sky illuminated by the many torches that lit the townhouse. 'I wish you every success, young warrior,' he called out as the dust trail grew further away out of sight.

THE FIRST

Efetobo left the palace in a rage. He was still fuming at the reception he had received at the hands of the young prince and the queen. 'I will see to it that they all regret this insult,' he said, more to himself than to his companions. The other two councillors, Achojah and Mitaire could not meet his eye and hurried along taking interest in anything other than Efetobo.

'It may be a good idea for us to retire to our estates in the south for a while, at least until the unrest has settled. Besides, if the rumours are true and Olise's army are on the road to Benin, I would like to make sure that my village wasn't pillaged along with the rest of the south,' Achojah mentioned. He was looking at Mitaire and silently urging him for support. 'Your properties are safe enough, don't forget that my own estate is not far from yours. I stand to lose just as much as you if the villages fall, but you need not worry. We have already declared our fealty; besides, Ekaete is a relative of mine and I have her word,' Efetobo said with a shrug.

Mitaire looked thoughtfully at Efetobo, then turned to Achojah and said, 'I will travel with you. After all, my family is there too, and I should be with them, especially now.'

Efetobo grunted in approval but added, 'I think I'll stay in the city a while longer. If the royal family plan to depart, someone must be the face of authority in the city. Please go ahead, I will catch up with you in a day or two. Be safe, my friends, and may the gods go with you.' That was all the prompting they needed, so they both gave slight bows and started to make their way towards their quarters west of the palace.

Efetobo stood for a short while and watched them go before heading in the opposite direction. He walked with his hands behind his back confidently, while the palace inhabitants scurried all around him. His face was blank of emotion and he held his head high as if he owned the place, which was what he intended if the events to come were to go in his favour. The thought brought a smile to his face and he felt satisfied at the thought of the smug young prince's face when the realisation of what awaited him was understood.

* * * *

Ogogo's second-in-command, Eni, moved from cover to cover, embracing the darkness created by the buildings within the vast courtyard. He moved like a snake and it was easy to see that he had done this type of work many times. The only difference was that he was accustomed to doing this kind of work out in the open, not in a densely populated city. Although, the palace offered some advantage; he could remain hidden close to his quarry, blending perfectly into a crowd of people and remain unobserved.

So, he continued to follow Efetobo, remaining far behind but close enough not to lose him. He noticed that Efetobo stopped a few times, but he did nothing suspicious, merely observing what appeared to be one triviality or another. Efetobo then started towards the eastern quadrant of the palace grounds. This area had very few people and a lot of cover – it was a perfect location to spy.

Eni thought how easy his task was and he began to enjoy himself, until he noted a few men gathered some yards away from where Efetobo was heading. There was something out of place about these men. Although they looked ragged, they all had black lengths of cloth wrapped around themselves concealing their upper bodies, as if trying, quite poorly, to conceal weapons. To the eye of a keen soldier, the tell-tale signs were there; the bulge of a pommel, the way the men stood and shifted their weight, but most of all, the flat emotionless look in their eyes. The eyes of experienced killers.

Eni could tell that this information could prove useful to the prince, but he cautiously loosened the dagger in its sheath by his hip. He remained low and out of sight as Efetobo moved closer to the group of men. He tried to get closer so he could make out the words, he needed to be sure of what he was seeing and hearing. Once this news reached Niran, he knew that no quarter would be given, so he had to be certain of what he reported.

Efetobo appeared to raise a hand as if in greeting and a hushed and urgent conversation ensued with the men. Eni was crouched behind an upturned cart now, only a few paces away, but he still strained to hear what was being said.

He wondered to himself whether he should risk moving closer, as he could barely make out any words. He made his choice and pulled out his dagger before slowly moving towards a stack of boxes closer to the men.

He made it to the next cover without incident, felt triumphant and settled down to concentrate on the discussion. 'One of the princes is there with the queen, the others have been summoned but the youngest is out in the forest to the north,' he heard Efetobo say. 'That shouldn't be a problem, I have more men covering the north and south approaches to the city. They will be picked up or killed, maybe both. After all, Olise wants them all dead,' said a deep voice.

The voice was heavily accented and sounded southern. Eni understood in a second. The royal family were truly in danger and they needed to be warned. The young princes' intuitions were confirmed, Efetobo was a traitor. Eni gripped the handle of the blade in his hand tighter, he wanted to break cover and kill the treacherous bastard, but he had to get back to the palace and inform the prince of what he had discovered.

Just as he was about to leave, he heard a sound behind him. Eni began to turn just as a powerful hand grabbed his wrist that held the dagger and another yanked his head upwards, exposing his neck. He suddenly felt a sharp pain across his throat and his breath was cut short. It took him a split second to realise that his throat had been slit, and he sank to the floor gasping for air with his hand pressed to his neck to stem the blood that flowed out of him. His vision started to blur before the darkness took him. He never saw his attackers.

* * * *

A torch lit the armoury, reflecting off the ancient tools of warfare that adorned the walls. The weapons here had not been touched in years, and it was visible from the cobwebs and dust that had settled on them. Prince Toju stood in the centre of the room, holding the torch high above his head, admiring the history of the room.

This room had once been the pride of his grandfather Adeosi and his father before him. Every detail of the room, from the bronze statues, the positioning of each item hung to create a dramatic effect, to the intricate design of the tapestries and woven hangings along the walls; all of this spoke of the wealth of the royal family. The arrangement of weapons was an ostentatious display of the family's military history; every sword, spear, axe and shield in the room held secrets of a lifetime of blood. This was visible from the chipped and notched edges and scarred handle grips. It was a sobering thought of the number of souls that had been sent to the underworld by the items here, which now only served as decorations, telling a tale of glories long gone between the warring tribes.

Toju could not help the mixed feelings of pride and regret, as he knew that all of these invaluable items would need to be abandoned, free to be looted by the first soldier that stumbles upon them. After all, who would be foolish enough to pass up the opportunity of owning a piece of Ile-Ife's history?

His blood boiled at the thought of these precious weapons in the hands of common soldiers, running their fingers over his birth right, and their jubilation at discovering such a horde. He clenched his fists and swallowed the bitter taste he felt at the back of his throat. There was nothing he could do, but he was determined to take as much as he could carry with him to deny Olise and his men the satisfaction of getting their hands on the family's most prized possessions.

'My Prince, we must leave now. The queen has summoned us, and I am told that your father's enemies are only a few days' march from here. It is the command of the king that we are away before the city is overrun.' Leke, Toju's blood-guard, stood at the entrance of the armoury nervously peering over his shoulder at the chaos within the walls of the palace. 'So, you believe the king will be defeated?' Toju asked, half expecting Leke to talk of defiance and the faith he had in the king's army and allies, but what he saw in Leke's eyes was resignation to the fact that all hope was lost.

Toju did not want to hear the words spoken; if he did the reality of his father's predicament would be all but too much for him to bear. Knowing that he had been denied the choice of fighting by his father's side in battle still filled him with immeasurable anger. The duty of the first child born to the king was to serve as the king's right-hand when he became of age. His mother had robbed him of that, convincing the king that Toju's place was with his siblings; the royal bloodline, and heirs to the kingdom.

They needed to be protected if the worst was to happen. He could not forgive her that, but he pushed the thought away and tried to concentrate on the matter at hand. As his father often said, "once the waterfall runs down the hill, it cannot go backwards". Toju could not afford to dwell on past decisions and he was determined to carry out his duty as his father, or mother in this case, intended.

'I only need a minute to take my ancestors' sword and spear, it would be much quicker if you helped me rather than stand there with that expression as if we have already been defeated!' Toju snapped angrily. His patience was already frayed from the constant instructions he had endured from his mother and younger brother, when all he really wanted to do was to fight and prove his worth. Toju was a warrior born, as his great grandfather, Kayode, had been before him.

At the age of ten, Toju had killed a great wild boar that had charged him and his younger brother, Niran, while they were out playing in the forest. Their blood-guards had been distracted and Toju had thrown the spear as soon as he saw the animal coming. The spear pierced the heart of the boar and it died instantly, while still in motion. A near-impossible throw for a skilled hunter, let alone a child. By the time their blood-guards had arrived, the beast lay dead at Toju's feet. That day he had been marked for greatness and was said to be blessed by *Ogun*, the Orisa of war.

Leke reluctantly walked towards Toju and helped him to heft a spear from its hold on the wall. It was beautifully crafted, a weapon of no equal in the kingdom, and Leke could not help but stare wide eyed at the details etched into the wooden shaft of the spear. He turned it around in his palms and marvelled at the balance of it and the skill of the workmanship, which must have taken many hours to complete. There was an inscription in an old dialect of Yoruba near the spearhead, but the words were too faded to make out. 'Magnificent, isn't it?' Toju said, breaking the trance that held Leke. 'I am told that this spear was a gift from my great grandfather to my grandfather on his fifteenth birthday. If the stories are to be believed, grandfather carried this spear into his first battle, where he was first blooded as a warrior.'

'I have heard the story,' Leke said, 'it truly is a wonderful spear; I completely understand your reluctance to leave these here, but the royal bloodline comes first, especially before anything of material value.' Toju regraded Leke for a few seconds before nodding and collecting what he could and quickly making his way towards the entrance. He had settled on taking his great grandfather's spear, his grandfather's sword and his father's axe; three generations of weapons, which he tucked into his belt. Leke had taken a handful of items, which he folded in some dried cow hide they had brought along and bound with leather straps.

They both emerged from the royal armoury, which was a solitary building set near the southern wall of the vast courtyard, and started making their way towards the palace, but it seemed that the courtyard was unusually full of people. Everywhere they looked, the townsfolk seemed to be gathering their possessions and supplies, rounding up livestock and ushering children and the elderly on to any means of transportation available to them, from horses, cattle and goats to carts and even crudely designed wheelbarrows, which were really a few pieces of wood hastily banged together.

By now, most of the town's inhabitants had discerned that war was on the horizon, and, like the royal family, everyone was planning to flee the capital.

The soldiers, on the other hand, were busy arming themselves, with some cool-headed captains organising the palace's defences. It was obvious that most of the soldiers within the walls were preparing themselves for a siege, water was being brought in through the gates in large clay pots and guards were being stationed at the food stores to ensure that some over-enthusiastic citizens didn't get the bright idea of raiding the stores in their desperation. That could easily get ugly, and a riot could potentially end the battle before it had even begun.

Some of the soldiers looked nervous, and all the guards had their spears poised to fend off attackers at the mere whiff of a threat. All this was good, as Toju was confident that they were prepared for whatever was to come. He had earlier inspected the garrison just outside the walls and was reassured of the men's mettle.

Some of the guards who recognised Toju saluted him as he made his way towards the palace; he could tell that at least these men were not afraid. However, some could not meet his eye and preferred to feint being busy. Provided they carried out their duties when the time came, Toju was not concerned.

Toju had been sceptical of his father's kindness in letting so many refugees flood the capital, and with good reason. It was impossible to tell genuine victims of the recent sacking of cities from potential spies and threats to the family.

Toju had always had trouble trusting people, and he felt that both the king and his brother Niran were too kind-hearted and empathetic to the struggles of the common man. He, on the other hand, was a hardened warrior prepared to do what was necessary to protect his family, almost to the point of ruthlessness. If it was left to him, for one, he would have had his uncle executed the moment word of a rebellion began to filter through the kingdoms, and he certainly wouldn't have left the gates wide open to serve as a haven for so many commoners.

Suddenly, there was a commotion towards the eastern side of the grounds. People appeared to be trying to escape the area, and some of the soldiers were pointing, when the movement around the court became even more frantic. Toju ordered a company of soldiers not too far from where he stood to investigate the disturbance. It was a fire, and smoke had started to rise behind some buildings to his right.

'I can't believe this,' Toju exclaimed. 'I'm sure some fool knocked over a torch and started that fire. Find me the culprits, I'll have them flogged in the square!' he bellowed.

Leke raised a hand to Toju's shoulder and wanted to tell him that they should keep moving to the palace when he saw movement in the corner of his eye. Far to his left, he saw a group of men, perhaps ten to twelve, all seeming to move in unison towards the palace.

At first glance, they appeared harmless, all in peasant clothing and wrapped in threadbare lengths of black cloth. But something seemed odd. Leke studied them closer and noticed that the men all seemed to move with purpose, an immediacy not like the other people around them. A sense of foreboding took him, and he immediately understood the significance.

The fire must have been a distraction and these men, who he could now see were pulling out swords and axes, were probably sent by Olise to murder the royal family in the chaos. 'My prince, the palace is breached!' he shouted, pointing towards the group of men, some of whom were now scaling the walls of the palace. Others had already gained entry through an open window, with the efficiency of seasoned assassins.

Toju snapped round to see the last of the men pass through the window and he immediately sprang into action. 'Sound the alarm! The queen and princes are in danger.' He pointed at a captain who was standing still, puzzled at the prince's words. 'You, gather a squadron and carry out a sweep of the palace now, your queen is in danger, do you understand me?' To the captain's credit, he quickly grasped the situation, his training taking control and, within minutes, he had eight men with him and more were running towards the palace; soldiers who had been in earshot of the prince and presumably saw the last of the intruders disappear through the window.

By then, Toju was already pacing towards the palace with Leke right behind him. As Toju ran, he shouted over his shoulder 'Kill them all, but spare one or two for interrogation.' All the weapons they had gathered from the royal armoury were forgotten, but Toju had his great grandfather's spear in his hands and an axe hanging from his belt. His own sword and shield were in his bedchamber in the palace, so he'd have to make do with what he had.

Leke, however, never went anywhere without his sword, as did all the other blood-guards. Their swords were like an extra limb; only death, or lack of an arm, could part them from their weapons. So, Leke now had his hand on the hilt as he ran, to stop the scabbard from bouncing off his leg.

Toju burst through the front doors like a deranged man, startling one of the maids, who was holding a vase full of vegetable oil. The vase dropped to the ground and shattered, causing the maid to let out a shriek, but Toju ignored her and was already past her, headed for the upper level.

His mother and Enitan's rooms were up there, and he hoped the guards would be fighting to protect his family; he knew the palace guards were of a different calibre to the soldiers outside, and they, at least, would defend the royal blood as if it were their own.

Toju continued to run through a series of corridors, and all the while his heartbeat was steady; as he tried to remain calm, he barely registered that Leke was right behind him, matching him step for step.

Suddenly, he turned a corner and there they were. About six men were in the corridor and Toju could hear fighting further behind.

He came to a stop a few paces in front of the men and levelled his grandfather's spear at the foremost intruder. 'Surely, you didn't expect to storm the palace and leave here with your lives, did you?' Toju asked, with a smile like a viper spreading across his face.

67

The man closest to Toju returned the smile and spoke over his shoulder; 'Find the queen and the other princes, I'll take care of this–' Before he could finish his sentence, Toju sprang forward and thrust his spear into the man's open mouth. The rest of the assassins gaped in shock at the speed of the prince's attack. They had expected this to be easy, but they would soon learn.

The assassin standing next to the first was also slow to react, and Toju withdrew the spear, spinning it horizontally and striking him in the face with the heavy bronze base of the spear. The man's nose exploded in a crimson ruin, but before he could even scream, Toju reversed the spear point again and buried it in his stomach.

Leke was already moving and struck with an overhand thrust that took the next man through the eye. The sight of three of their numbers dead inflamed the remaining three assassins, and they all came forward at once to avenge their fallen comrades.

Leke had not stopped moving from his initial strike, and now he was driving forward into the three men before him. He parried a swing that was aimed for his head and had enough time to reverse his sword and sweep aside a thrust that was aimed at his torso.

But Toju was with him – his spear darted out like a viper, striking one of their opponents in the thigh, causing him to stumble, obstructing an attack from one of the other men. Leke took advantage and stabbed the man in the side of his neck, while Toju took the next man with a feint and a stab to the ribs but, as he fell, the spear was wrenched from Toju's hands, so he pulled the axe from his belt and threw it at the last man, catching him in the centre of his head.

Toju, barely winded, bent to retrieve his spear and his axe before he flashed Leke a smile, then they both ran past the cooling corpses to the next room, where the sounds of fighting were still audible. They came to see Lara, holding a bloody dagger, crouched next to a wardrobe with a fallen table in front of her. There were two dead assassins near the entrance of the room and Ogogo was struggling to fend off three more assailants, clearly losing the fight.

Toju impaled one of the men in the back and Leke beheaded another with a single backhanded swing of his sword. The

68

third turned for a split second, just before Ogogo severed the man's sword arm below the elbow, causing the man to scream out in agony. Ogogo was about to finish him off but Toju asked him to halt. 'I will have answers from this one. Make sure he doesn't die.'

Toju moved to his mother, who he now saw was bleeding. His heart tightened in his chest, but he tried to remain calm. 'Where are you hurt, Mother?' he said. She gave him a warm smile and reached for his face, leaving a trail of blood from her fingers on his cheek. 'It is nothing, my child, are you ok? Where is your brother? You must protect him.' He looked at her and back at Ogogo standing over the prisoner. 'I cannot leave you alone here with one of the enemy!' he protested, but Ogogo answered, 'She'll be safe enough with me, my prince. I trust you raised the alarm. Reinforcements should be here soon; you must go and help your brother.'

Toju thought for a second, then stepped forward and cracked the base of the spear against the head of the prisoner, knocking him out cold. 'Bind him and try and stem the bleeding. I will go to my brother. Lock the door behind us and do not open it until the guards are here.' Ogogo nodded and Toju turned to look at his mother for a second before racing towards the door to seek his brother Niran.

A GATHERING OF HYENAS

*T*wo years had passed, and the kingdom still mourned the loss of Queen Bunmi. The king had remained out of the public eye just as long, and it was whispered that the tribes were vying for control over the kingdom.

The horse tribes of the north, the Hausa, were said to be gathering an army, which was growing in strength every year, and they continued to sweep across the lands beyond the southern border, leaving a trail of ruin. Their boldness was becoming more evident as they had started to raid ever closer to the domains of the south, taking every village, town and city that stood in their path, slaughtering or enslaving their inhabitants. Fear of an invasion in the southern kingdom was a constant threat and with the absence of the king, more pressure was mounting for the chiefs of the land to take matters into their own hands, confront the Hausa and remind them of the power of the Yoruba.

An aggressive show of power was the best deterrent. The kingdom did not want to spark a war, but the mere thought of capitulating to the Hausa caused a lot of anger and division within the proud ruling classes of the south, especially as the last king, Kayode – Adeosi's father – had conquered those lands two decades ago, visiting fire and death upon them. He had reduced the north to a desolate wasteland and scattered all the surviving tribes and warriors to the wind. Only for them to now gather like hyenas that smell a wounded prey, with the knowledge that a weaker man now sat on the throne in the south.

The councillors of Ile-Ife had pleaded with the king to remarry and form new alliances to deter any potential threats, but Adeosi would not hear of it. He had lost his one true love and was a broken man for it. The only reason he had not been thrown into absolute despair was the child his queen had birthed, Jide, the only part of Bunmi that remained to him.

The king saw Bunmi's face whenever he looked upon his son, filling him with great joy and sadness in equal measures. Each moment he spent with the boy chipped away at him until he was a shadow of the man he once was. Before long, he had unknowingly begun to distance himself from the child, the constant reminder of his queen cutting too deep.

The boy, however, continued to grow in strength, and his joyful disposition seemed unaffected by the lack of regard from his father. His laughter was the only sound of life that echoed through the cold halls of the palace. The members of the Modakeke who lived in Ile-Ife had however, taken Jide under their tutelage. They had taken the opportunity to instil the discipline and education required of a future monarch. They assign a blood-guard to the child, which was normally the duty of the king, who schooled him in the art of warfare and served as a companion for the boy to look up to. This was yet another example of the responsibilities that had been neglected over the past two years.

The blood-guard chosen for Jide was one of some promise. His father, Remilekun, had been the head of the council of ten in the Modakeke tribe for many years and was said to be undefeated in single combat. At just twelve, Akin was already showing signs of his father's stature and strength, so the council of ten had been pleased to place young Jide under Akin's protection; the oaths required of the guard were given, and hence the beginning of a bond that would last until death.

Despite the constant air of melancholy around the king, his subjects, including the nobles, soldiers and servants, remained loyal to him, perhaps even more so than before, as the kingdom had loved the queen just as much as Adeosi had. This, however, had frustrated some of the members of the royal council, as they could not get close enough to the king to influence his decisions. Some had begun to plot to offer their fealty to the lords of the north, but amongst their number, many of them still had a debt owed to the king, whether it was a debt of blood or some other favour that the king had granted them in the past. This alone would not allow them to betray him so, the majority always voted in the best interests of the king.

But loyalties had been stretched to breaking point as the northern tribes continued to raid closer to the borders. Reports from the outer realms of the kingdom claimed that villages on the outskirts had been attacked. In one incident, a poor farming village was allegedly raided by a small force of horse tribesmen, who had kidnapped children between the ages of ten and sixteen; the boys would be groomed to either become warriors, adding to the ranks of the Hausa, or slaves, and the girls would be made into wives to breed more warriors to further swell their ranks.

This of course, could all be speculation, but the threat was real enough for the southerners to raise their voices in protest, which spurred the royal council into action.

The council had eventually decided to take it upon themselves to force a new alliance with the great house of the Adelanis, and sent word to all the nobilities of the south that the king was to be remarried. The word spread like wildfire, and even the nobilities from as far north east as Taraba and across the River-lands, down to Calabar answered the call. Before long, many royals were gathered in the capital to offer the hand of their daughter in marriage to the king of the tribes.

One such family were the Chidozies, from the Igbo tribe, a respected family from Imo in the east that had ties with the Calabar nobility. The head of the family, Chidi, had married the daughter of the chief of Calabar, uniting the two houses and giving them tremendous wealth and warriors.

It was, however, rumoured that the Calabar branch of that family practiced the dark arts and worshipped the deity of the underworld; Esu, as he was known in the tongue of the Yoruba, which was the source of their great wealth. Whilst most people dismissed this notion, many around the kingdom saw truth in it, which had only reinforced the fear and mystique surrounding the family.

Chidi's first daughter, however, was rumoured to be one of the most beautiful girls in all the land. She was seldom seen around the city or during the day, but it was said that, in the dead of night, she was known to walk the forests of her father's lands without an escort. She was, however, in Ile-Ife that year – although no one had seen her face, which was always hidden beneath a veil away from prying eyes – at the insistence of her father, to join the hundreds of girls hoping to be the next queen.

Even though the king had finally agreed to the proposal of an alliance, he was still uncomfortable with the required nuptials. He took counsel with his advisors on the appropriate and most beneficial families to consider, which narrowed it down to six. Three of the families were from the western tribes, one from the far eastern tribes and two from the River-lands of the south. One of these being the Chidozie girl.

The six girls were called into a large meticulously furnished room to attend the king, who was preparing to receive them in an adjoining room. He intended to speak to all the girls separately to gauge their suitability, before making a final decision. The girls were exceptionally beautiful and would have made a perfect match for the king, all being of noble birth from powerful and wealthy families.

Each girl passed through into the next room to speak with the king for a few minutes, some slightly longer than others, until finally it was the turn of the Chidozie girl.

She had entered the king's room veiled; her face had remained hidden for as long as she had been in Ile-Ife. The king was immediately intrigued and drawn to her. He asked her to remove the veil, to which she replied, 'To gaze upon me would be to accept me and the darkness that has become of me.' On hearing this, Adeosi called on his blood-guard Demola and commanded him to dismiss the rest of the girls.

Once Demola had left and the only movement was the shadow of the flames from the candles dancing on the walls, he asked the girl her name and she told him it was Ekaete. The king then asked her to remove her veil for the second time. She did so and from that moment onwards, Adeosi was lost; his happiness would be fleeting, after which he would know only darkness.

73

A CITY WILL FALL

Niran had never been in a real fight before but he was oddly unafraid and had welcomed the danger as easily as any lesson he had ever received in the past.

He had noticed the glow of the fire from his window and saw the thick plumes of smoke that rose into the night sky. He had heard the chaos in the courtyard below followed by the clash of arms within the palace. He knew what was coming, but he had remained calm through it all. He had anticipated this.

The sons of Jide had been prepared well for this very moment. Jide had tutored them in the art of fighting as soon as they were strong enough to wield a sword and spear. So, it was no surprise that when the time had come for Niran to put his years of training in the dance of *Ogun* - the Orisa of war - to use, he would not shy away.

The only thought that gave him pause was that Enitan was somewhere out there with no idea of what was ensuing within the city walls. He knew his younger brother was resourceful and smart but nonetheless, he gave a quick prayer to Oshosi the Orisa of hunting, to give his brother cunning to evade any threat from beyond the walls of the city. For Niran knew that this was only the beginning of the threat to the Adelani bloodline.

Seun was of a similar composition. He had simply sat opposite the door to the room and sharpened his sword over his lap, while Niran had finished lacing his armour. No words needed to be spoken. Seun and Niran possessed a bond and understanding that none of his brothers or his forebears had ever had with their bloodguards. They were alike despite the age gap of ten years, each complementing the other forming a perfect balance of intellect and skill at arms.

Niran finished putting on his leather armour and pulled his sword a few inches free from the scabbard to loosen it. It was a beautiful sword made of good iron, with an ornate cross guard and a handle wrapped in thick crocodile hide. The sword had not been used in a fight, but that was about to change. When he was ready, he turned his hazel eyes on Seun. 'Let's not keep them waiting. Shall we?' He indicated towards the door. Seun stood up and responded with a curt nod. Together they left the room and walked into the hallway.

The sound of screaming could be heard all around the palace. This meant that there were several intruders, presumably splitting up to get the work done quickly. Whoever they were, it seemed that they had begun to slaughter the household servants. This only enraged Niran, knowing that most would be helpless to prevent their demise.

They walked cautiously through the palace hallways to the lower level, into a large open room, which Jide had occasionally used to entertain ambassadors, and suddenly came upon a group of men in black ragged cloaks. It was obvious that these men were the source of all the misery and broken peace of the palace, for they brandished bloodstained swords and knives.

Niran discerned that their weapons were of good quality, confirming his suspicions that they must have been sent by his uncle. The thought saddened him momentarily, knowing that his own blood relative would wish them ill, but he quickly pushed his emotions to the back of his mind, remembering the words of his father – "Lions born of the same mother are still lions and will kill their own kin for survival and dominance in the pride."

One of the men held a female servant who was hysterical, while another had his arm around the throat of a child with a dagger point pressed against the child's temple. Niran recognised the servants; a mother and child. Other men were in the background. They appeared to have been looting; some had pieces of cloth improvised into sacks bulging with bronze and gold artefacts from around the palace. A few more of them looked as if they were trying to start a fire, piling up broken pieces of wooden furniture and other small flammable items.

'If it's the prince you seek, you have found him. Let the woman and child go, they are no threat to you,' Niran said, causing all the men to stop what they were doing and stare in shocked silence at the new arrivals. Niran remained expressionless as he spoke to the men before him in an even and unwavering tone. Seun slowly started to circle the men to cut off their retreat, not that they were planning to escape without doing what they had come to do, but Seun's nature was always to seek to use his surroundings to his advantage, whilst Niran tried to distract them with reasoning.

'At this very moment the soldiers from the barracks will be on their way here sweeping through the palace, there is no escape for you. Why not give up now and, you have my word, I will grant you mercy.'

The man holding the child looked scared and conflicted. He lowered the dagger he held to the child by a fraction, however, the other man who held the woman was undeterred. 'Do you think we care for your mercy? We serve only one man and we will die doing his bidding. Besides, how do you know that we have not already taken the city?' he said with an evil grin. He did not wait for a reply, but instead turned to his companion, saying 'Kill the child and the prince!'

That was all the warning Seun and Niran needed. Before the man with the child could change his resolve and push the dagger deep into the temple of the child, Seun drew a small blade from his belt and threw it, catching the man in his arm and causing him to drop his dagger with a yell.

Almost at the same moment, Niran had also pulled out a blade and had the same idea, but he had aimed for the man holding the woman. His blade spun through the air with lethal intent, not simply to disarm his target. It went straight into the eye of the second man, down to the hilt. The assassin's lifeless body was already falling backwards by the time Niran and Seun had started to move.

Seun made it close to the other side of the hall and immediately moved to intercept the men who were trying to start a fire, now scrambling to raise their weapons. They didn't stand a chance and Seun showed them the reason the blood-guards had been chosen to protect the princes.

Niran was now engaging two other men, one being the wounded man who had held the child, and for a few minutes the only sound to be heard was the clash of iron and the desperate grunts of men fighting for their lives.

Niran was a more than competent swordsman, which his foes quickly realised to their peril. He stepped in between the two men in a crouched position, dodging a wild slash meant for his head. When he came up, he swung his sword in an upward arc at the man who had missed him, slicing through his chest, neck and chin. Such was the edge of the sword and the ferocity of his counterattack.

On his downward stroke, he passed his sword backwards, catching the other man in the chest and finding his heart. The man opened his mouth to scream but no sound came out, and his eyes rolled back as he fell away from Niran's sword.

The speed at which Niran had dispatched the two assailants surprised even him, but he did not get distracted and moved forward to join Seun, who required no assistance. By the time he was close, Seun had already killed three men, with a fourth trying to crawl away to the closest exit with a mortal wound to his lower back that partly exposed his entrails.

Seun took no pleasure in this work but he was a solider, a warrior born, and he carried out his duty with ruthless efficiency. He plunged his sword into the base of the skull of the crawling man, silencing his cries and pleading.

'We must get to my mother now, I fear for her. If the words of the intruders are true about already taking the city, we may be in for a real fight for survival.'

Seun took his eyes away from the mess he had created and looked at Niran. 'You are right, my prince, but your brother and the palace guards will hold until reinforcements arrive, I'm certain of it. Nonetheless, we should move now. We have wasted too much time as it is.'

Niran gave a series of urgent instructions to the servant and her child they had just saved, and she immediately took her child by the arm and disappeared in the opposite direction, towards Niran's quarters.

'We must hurry,' Niran said, and they both headed for the exit. In the hallway, the sounds of jogging men were heard and Seun cautiously pressed his palm against Niran's chest, pushing him into a recess in the walls, concealing both from view. However, they need not have hidden, as the footsteps were from some of the soldiers of the palace.

Niran called out to them in relief. 'Who commands here?' he asked. The soldiers all spun around with their swords held high, but a grizzled captain stepped from their midst with his sword still in its sheath. 'My prince, I am glad you are safe. We followed your brother, prince Toju, into the palace when the alarm was raised. There are more guards coming behind us to secure the grounds. We shall root out the threat and eliminate them.'

Niran regarded the captain for a second; he had made it his business to know each of the senior soldiers in the palace and the barracks by name, as his father had taught him. 'Tayo, is it?' he asked. 'Taiwo, my prince,' the guard replied. 'Apologies, Taiwo, it has been a hard day,' Niran said with a half-smile, only then realising the blood staining his hands and arms.

'Where is my brother now? And my mother, is she safe?' he asked.

'I have sent men to the queen's quarters, but I lost your brother when we entered the palace. He cannot be far, my prince. Please come with us, we shall find them together,' Taiwo said, and he had already started to turn to his men to order them to continue their advance through the palace. Niran and Seun fell in amongst the men without missing a step.

* * * *

Toju had so far killed eight men, and Leke almost twice as many. The intruders didn't appear to be reducing, and the reality of

78

the palace truly being overrun slowly dawned on them with every encounter.

After a while Toju and Leke had decided to abandon the search for Niran and get the queen clear of the palace, as several small fires had started, and had begun to spread slowly through the halls, the ancient interior timber features igniting easily.

Leke then spotted a group of men moving towards them from the opposite side of a long hallway and, once again, they prepared themselves to engage the new threat. However, there was no denying that the previous skirmishes had slowly began to eat away at their energy, and the weapons they held were becoming heavier and slippery in their hands, slick with the blood of their enemies.

Just as Toju was about to charge the approaching threat head-on, he noticed the familiar features of the captain he had spoken to earlier that evening and, close behind him, his brother with his blood-guard.

His muscles screamed in protest as relief flooded him, but he would never show weakness, as he had been trained, and managed to crack a strained smile.

'I was beginning to think that you had been taken, or worse, struck down, little brother. I see that your books haven't robbed you completely of your training,' Toju called out.

'This is not the time for jibes, brother, I think the city is under siege. We need to get as far away from here as possible,' Niran said, poorly concealing his anxiety.

'What makes you think that? I was just out there, and all seemed as quiet as usual before the disturbance in the palace,' Toju remarked. He was not in the mood to be lectured, but he suspected that Niran was not far wrong.

He turned to the captain, not looking to push the point further with his brother in front of the men. 'You, where are the reinforcements? I see only eight men here'.

The captain met Toju's eye and answered calmly, 'I gave the order for the men to secure the palace, but I fear prince Niran may have the truth of it; we have not come across any of our soldiers. I fear the worst... my prince,' he answered, after a slight pause. Niran interjected 'This is a waste of time, where is Mother? We should get her to safety first and then consolidate what forces we have afterwards.'

He looked pleadingly at his brother, who acquiesced, and told them where their mother was barricaded. Without preamble, Niran started off in the direction he was told, closely followed by Seun and the rest of the palace guards. Toju had no choice but to follow in their footsteps, which gave him some respite, as he was so exhausted, and preferred not to make any decisions, but allow someone else to take charge. And who better than his younger brother, who was a natural leader of men?

As luck would have it, they reached the chambers of the queen without incident and Niran immediately pounded on the door demanding access. After some hesitation, the door opened a crack and the wary face of Ogogo came into view, clearly overwhelmed at the safety of the prince and the welcome support of more men.

The captain of the guards wasted no time in ordering the soldiers to form a defensive perimeter around the entrance to the queen's chamber ready to repel any surprise attack from the intruders. They all went about their tasks like the professionals they were, but it was clear that they were all nervous, with the fires spreading in the halls potentially preventing their escape.

Niran went to his mother's side, and he noted the small pool of blood next to her. His eyes went wide at the sight of the blood, but she raised a shaky hand before he could speak, showing a glimpse of the silent authority she had always possessed, despite clearly being weakened from the heavy blood loss. Without a word, Niran started to search for a wound, moving her with such tenderness that it brought the sting of tears to her eyes. He finally came across bloodied wrappings around her right thigh and knew immediately that a major artery must have been severed.

Ogogo had clearly attempted to staunch the bleeding as best as he could, which was evident from the shear number of bloody rags close by, but it was of no use. The queen was not long for this world.

Niran succumbed to his emotions and muffled a cry before burying his head in the folds of his mother's buba, not caring if the men around him saw, or what they thought. She patted his head, leaving clumps of dried blood in his coarse, curly hair, and whispered gently into his ear, 'It will all be well, my son, do not despair. You must look to your brothers for strength. My life is in the hands of the gods now. Niran was at a loss, he loved his mother above life itself, and the cruel reality of losing her would be unbearable. In that moment he cared not for securing the throne or the kingdom, nor for the fate of the people. All he cared about was his mother.

Toju was oblivious to all this and was in the middle of questioning the assassin they had captured earlier. Ogogo had clearly been working on him from the mass of bruises and swelling about his face, despite the man already missing half an arm. One eye was swollen shut and he had lost several teeth. That did not stop Toju from drawing his dagger to make small incisions along the man's chest, causing him to whimper under his breath. Toju intended to let him understand that no games were being played here.

'So, my friend, you will tell me, as you have told my good captain here, everything I need to know. Leave anything out and I will hurt you the more. You will not leave here alive, but how quickly you depart from this world is entirely up to you. The gods may still receive you with favour if you atone for your crimes, but if you choose loyalty to the traitor, *Esu* will have your soul,' Toju said as he stopped to inspect the edge on his knife and the work he had done.

The prisoner began to spill out all the information he knew in a torrent of strained words. He told them about the soldiers amassed with the coin of Olise's mother and how they had slipped into the city with all the refugees, seamlessly integrating into Ile-Ife for weeks, some even months, just waiting for the signal to start the slaughter of the city. He talked about the assassins who had been handpicked to take the palace and the help they had received from the councillor Efetobo in planning the foiled assassinations. He even mentioned the outriders, who at this very moment would be closing in around the city, tightening the noose, ensuring that no one left the city alive.

He gave them everything and more, even though he knew his time on earth was soon to end. He just wanted the pain to stop. Toju listened to it all in grim silence, taking in every detail. Everyone in the room who heard the prisoner's account looked on stunned.

It was as if they all held their breath, and only in the uncomfortable silence that followed did Toju seem to become aware of his surroundings once again and look upon each of the faces around him. His gaze finally fell upon the crouched figure of his brother next to the queen. He shot a glance at Ogogo, who slowly shook his head and struggled to meet his eye. Realisation began to settle.

He turned once again to the prisoner. 'I believe your words to be truth, and for that I will grant you a swift death.' In one smooth motion, he stepped forward and plunged the dagger into the temple of the prisoner's head, leaving the dagger there but keeping his word in granting a quick end to his pains. He then walked over to his mother and brother and went on one knee.

'We can try to break free with her,' he said to Niran, but not taking his eyes away from his mother. 'It is too late; she has lost too much blood. Moving her would only cause more distress,' Niran said in almost a whisper. 'Your brother is right,' said Lara, 'plus I will only slow you down. You must both leave here while you can. There is a tunnel in the next room behind the stack of clay vases. It will lead you to the forest behind the palace. Use it and find your brother, Enitan. I am of no consequence now, what is important is that the sons of Jide live. The people will rally around you, but if you are killed here today all will be lost.'

For once, neither Toju nor Niran protested. They both knew that Lara's words were true. More tears began to stream down Niran's face, but he quickly mastered himself. Toju, on the other hand, had an expression of stone; he was tormented by the thought of leaving his mother but at that moment all he wanted was to kill all the people responsible for this betrayal. For that reason alone, he was determined to survive, his anger and hatred for his uncle and all his followers and the memory of this moment would be the sustenance that would keep him for a lifetime if necessary.

Ogogo was talking at Toju's shoulder and it took a minute for him to comprehend his words. 'My place is at the queen's side; take what guards we have and leave here, but you must leave now. I don't know how long it will be before they figure out where to look or the palace is completely engulfed in flames. Either way, there is little time.'

'My children,' Lara raised her voice now with the urgency of the situation. 'Remember who you are, kingdom first. Go now, find your brother and live. Stick to our plan, go east, west and north and gather our strengths. Return to take what is ours, as our name, Adelani, tells it. Please, my sons, I will be with the gods.'

As she spoke, they could hear raised voices behind the door. The captain came running over finally drawing his sword. 'They are here, we must either stand and fight or leave now; what is your command?' He said that to no one in particular as he stared between the princes and the queen, sweat running down his face and glistening over the cords of muscle around his arms.

It was Niran who finally spoke, summoning the courage to do what was necessary given the circumstance. 'Taiwo, my mother... the queen will not be joining us. We will steal away through a hidden passage in the next room. Ready the men to move.' As he spoke the last words, he turned to look at his mother, who gave him a warm smile, which did little to lessen the burden of his decision. Taiwo looked beyond him at the queen on the ground behind. He then looked at Ogogo and understood that he was also planning to stay at the queen's side, giving his last strength in the service of the crown.

Suddenly they were all alerted to a loud pounding on the other side of the door, which increased in rhythm and frequency. The intruders were putting their axes to the door. Even though it was made of six inches of thick wood from an iroko tree, eventually it would give under the pressure. The guards around the entrance all tensed but didn't move from their positions, awaiting the Inevitable.

83

Taiwo turned back to the royal family. 'What are my orders?' he asked as if resigned to the fact that he would not be leaving that room.

Niran took his gaze away from the direction of the entrance and fixed his hazel eyes on Taiwo. 'The guards are to retreat with Toju and I. We will leave through the next room.'

'My prince-' one of the guards closest to them interjected; this was a break in protocol for soldiers to address their betters, but none of that mattered now, so the soldier pressed on before he could be silenced. 'My prince, I request to stay with the queen, I will gladly give my life to protect the queen and cover your retreat.' Before Niran or Taiwo could respond another guard echoed the same sentiment. 'I also wish to stay behind, my prince, if it is your will.' Crack! The door had now started showing signs of stress on the interior, slowly splintering with every blow that fell.

Ogogo now stepped forward, putting his hand on Niran's shoulder. 'Let these brave men stay, my prince, but take the remaining guards and leave now, we have run out of time. I know your heart bleeds but there is no help for it now.'

He turned to Toju. 'Go with the gods, my prince, we shall feast with *Olodumare* presently.' With that he hefted a spear that was lying close by and addressed the remaining guards at the entrance. 'Men of Ile-Ife, protect your princes with your lives and do not forget the sacrifices of these two brave warriors before you,' he said, glancing at the two who had agreed to stay behind. The men immediately left their posts and moved closer to the princes. Ogogo outranked all the soldiers in the room and his tone brooked no argument.

Taiwo nodded and turned to the six guards that would accompany the princes. 'Do as you have been commanded, make sure the tunnel is clear, and I want two of you to go through and secure the exit.'

Yes, sir,' said one of the guards before moving to the adjoining room. Taiwo turned back to Ogogo and met his eye. 'I will also stay to protect the queen; I can think of no better way to serve.

84

My sword is yours.' He inclined his head in the direction of the queen, who returned the gesture. Ogogo smiled, 'it is settled, then.'

Niran knelt again beside his mother and held her close for the last time. It took all his will not to burst into tears and, finally, Toju had to gently pull him away from her as the pounding on the door became more urgent. Toju bent to kiss his mother on the forehead, he held her stare for a moment and then headed for the next room, followed closely by Leke. Niran stood rooted to the ground until Ogogo stood between him and his mother and assured him that he would see to it that the queen would not suffer or be taken. Niran nodded, thanking him silently for the promise. He then made his way to the next room to join his brother and the other soldiers. He had never imagined that it would come to this, that the sons of the greatest king of the Yoruba people would have to flee from their home, their kingdom. He vowed to himself that all those responsible would pay dearly, just as he ducked into the tunnel that would lead him to safety.

* * * *

Bankole had just put his son to sleep. He lovingly stroked his hair and watched the gentle rise and fall of his chest. He had never known joy better than the sight of his child. His wife was in the next room warming him a meal and he thought to himself how lucky he was to be blessed with such a wonderful family, giving glory to *Oduduwa*, the deity of the people of Ile-Ife. He rose from the side of his son's bed and went into the next room to spend what was left of the evening with his wife, the most precious time of the day for him.

His wife gave him a warm smile as she handed him a bowl of pepper soup that she had just dished for the two of them. He took it thankfully and savoured the fragrant aroma of the steaming bowl that warmed his hands.

'What more can a man want, eh? I am blessed with a beautiful wife who knows my heart better than any, I don't deserve you,' he said. His wife just laughed, 'You always know the right things to say, my dear,' as she settled beside him to tuck into their meal. Just then, they were both distracted by the sounds of people screaming.

Bankole put his bowl down, his appetite forgotten, and walked over to the window to see what all the noise was about, taking a tentative look in the next room as he walked past, where his son was fast asleep. 'What is all this commotion? I hope the boy doesn't wake,' he said as he reached the window. He opened a shutter and peered outside.

What he saw made his blood run cold in his veins. People were running in all directions shouting at the top of their lungs, women carried children in their arms and some of the men appeared to have blood on their cloths. Many were carrying sticks and others had farm instruments, such as hoes and wood axes.

Bankole recognised one of his neighbours and called out to him. 'Dele, by the gods, what is happening?' Dele barely acknowledged him and continued to run, a look of pure horror in his eyes. As he passed the window from which Bankole was calling to him, Dele shouted over his shoulder, 'Save yourself and your family, we are being attacked!' Bankole only gaped in shocked horror at Dele's back as he receded into the night and was claimed by the darkness, then looked back in the direction of fleeing people. He could now discern men, scores of them, covered in black cloaks and brandishing swords and knives.

As he watched, a man was hacked down by one of the black clad men and another woman was impaled through the back with a spear as she ran, still clutching onto a child, who just cried and cried until the spear was retrieved from the woman and the child was silenced. Further back, Bankole could now see various fires around the dwellings, and the strong scent of burning wood tinged with the sweet smell of burning flesh reached his nostrils. He understood then what was happening.

He immediately closed the shutter and turned to his wife, who was now standing close behind him. He saw the fear in her eyes, which mirrored the feeling he felt in that instance. 'Take the boy and leave through the back door, hurry my love, and do not look back until you have reached the forest. Keep running until you get to the next town!' he said in a voice laced with fear.

To her credit, she asked no questions and ran for the next room to take her child to safety. Just then, the door was kicked open with such force that the bottom half broke off and was sent flying into the small room.

Behind it, two men in black stepped into the room, splattered in blood. Bankole did not hesitate. 'Run, my love!' he shouted as he sprang towards the men. Bankole had intended to grant his wife enough time to escape, but he need not have even tried.

Before he could reach them, the closest man brought down his sword, catching Bankole in the side of the neck, spraying blood all over the ceiling. The momentum of Bankole's lunge still carried him forward and he fell on his attacker and desperately tried to wrestle him to the ground. However, he was already dying, and his attacker simply knocked him aside to fall on the floor and bleed out into the straw that had once been lovingly spread.

Bankole's wife just stood where she was at the entrance to their child's room and began to scream hysterically as the two intruders walked over to her with smiles on their faces, covered in the blood of her husband. Bankole had fallen on his back and, as he watched the ceiling dripping with his blood, the last sound he heard was the cries of his son.

Outside, the chaos continued. The citizens were massacred indiscriminately in the streets and in their homes and the city burned. Ile-Ife had fallen.

THE THIRD

'**T**ry and keep up, old man!' More playful laughter and the distant sound of someone in pursuit. Enitan moved like a jaguar through the trees. He ran at almost full speed and still managed to avoid every stray branch, protruding tree root and all other obstacles presented by the forest with the ease of a child accustomed to the wild.

He had played in these parts as soon as he could walk, and knew every inch of the forest. This place had been his and Niran's sanctuary away from the royal court and the responsibilities that came with being a prince of Ile-Ife. Although the same responsibilities had finally caught up with Niran as they had with Toju before him. Now Enitan's only source of entertainment was with his blood-guard Ayo, who always seemed to allow him to win at every game they played.

'Just wait till I catch you. You'll see what this old man can do!' Ayo shouted back with a hint of amusement in his voice, but in truth he was finding it more and more difficult to keep up with the young prince, who seemed as agile as a cat with a boundless supply of energy, even though it had been Ayo who had taught the young prince how to blend and move in this terrain.

Ayo knew that Enitan was a special child, but no one else could see or acknowledged what he saw. Because of Enitan's age, he was often dismissed as too talkative, argumentative and playful, where Ayo saw inquisitiveness, sharpness of mind and an eagerness to discover the limits of his physical abilities, which by all accounts were considerably superior to his peers and some of the younger warriors of the tribe.

As Enitan was the third child, his position in the hierarchy of the royal family was of less importance compaired to his older siblings, who would naturally acend the throne before him. So, he was often overlooked. Ayo considered himself blessed with the wisdom and insight of the gods and saw what most did not. One thing he was certain of was that Enitan was guided by the hand of one of the gods, but which one, was yet to be revealed.

Ayo's thoughts were cut short by movement in the corner of his eye, somewhere off to his left side. Whether Ayo was blessed with divine insight was debatable, but he was blessed, however, with a heightened awareness and intuition. His senses of smell and hearing were like no other's, certainly not amongst the Modakeke. He slowed his pace and pretended to tie the straps of his sandals, all the while listening and assessing his options. There were at least six of them, lightly armoured for they made little noise, but he could sense them, almost feel their vibrations through the soil under his feet.

He was first fearful for the young prince, but realised that the men appeared to be gathering around him and not advancing towards the prince. They must have assumed that the prince was no threat. Take out the greater danger first, that's what he would have done.

But they underestimated him. Little did they know of the skill of the blood-guards. Soon they would find out. He could choose to catch up with Enitan and lose the men in the forest, but where was the fun in that? He was always eager to test his skill and push boundaries, after all, that is what true warriors did and what he encouraged Enitan to do daily. Besides, he didn't want to risk putting the prince in harm's way. He had to take them, quickly and quietly.

Once he was satisfied on the proximity of the men who watched him, he slowly rose from his crouched position and started to jog again, this time slightly off course from where the prince had gone, drawing the men away. Without warning he sped up and began to sprint, leaping shrubs and tree stumps until he was out of sight of his pursuers. He had climbed a sturdy low hanging branch and leaped to a taller tree, which he scrambled up, and perched on a large branch to observe the men who followed in a reversal of roles. The hunted had become the hunter.

He lay flat on the branch motionless and waited until three men came stalking through the bushes into view. 'Where did he go?' one of them hissed urgently. 'He was just in front of us a minute ago!

We cannot lose him.' More men joined until six stood below Ayo. 'Spread out, find him and kill him. Two of us should re-join the other outriders. I saw the signal so I'm expecting the citizens to start fleeing the city and the men might need some help.'

This news troubled Ayo but he remained still. 'Why must you be the one to go?' asked one of the other men. 'Because I'm in charge!' snapped the first. 'Says who?' The other responded, until another man dispelled the argument. 'All this talk you are talking is wasting time. I don't care who is in charge, but do you think Olise will let us off lightly if we have nothing to show, eh?' Olise. At the mention of that name all became clear to Ayo. He needed to get to Enitan.

'Ok, you two go back and re-join the outriders, the rest of us will find him, bring back his head and win Olise's favour in the form of a young female slave at the very least!' They all laughed at that. Two of the men detached from the main group and started off in the direction of the city, while the other four began to fan out into the bushes.

Ayo had to act fast. He needed more information but also felt his duty to eliminate the threat to the prince. He made his decision.

Climbing from one branch to the next, stalking the men like a leopard on the prowl, he got close to one man, dropped to the ground behind him silently and drew his blade across the man's neck. It was done effortlessly. Ayo was well known for his stealth, a skill he had extended to his young charge. He pulled the body to the ground and hastily covered it as best he could with fallen leaves and sticks.

Without delay, he moved towards the next man and cut him in the same fashion as soon as he was within reach. This man also died without a sound. Now Ayo crept slowly towards the last two, who, unlike the first two were not too far away from each other.

He soon caught up with one of the men and moved to cut his throat as he had just done, but at the last second, he stepped on a twig, which snapped audibly, drawing the attention of Ayo's victim. The man whipped his head round and his eyes went wide at the sight of Ayo moving towards him with a blade in hand.

The man was just about to cry out, forcing Ayo to quickly change his tact and jam one hand in the man's mouth and the other hand that held the blade, deep in the man's chest seeking his heart. The man let out a half muffled, half choked scream as he bit down on Ayo's hand, but the sound still carried across the forest. His companion turned around, startled, just in time to see Ayo drag his comrade to the ground.

Ayo had anticipated this. He left the blade in the man's chest and reached behind his back to pull out a short throwing axe, perfectly balanced to be used just for this type of situation. As he went down with the body, his left hand still in the dead man's mouth, he drew the axe and threw it underhand towards the last man, who had started to charge towards him shouting a war cry.

The throw was perfect, the axe spun through the air and caught the man in the centre of his chest, shattering his sternum. The impact lifted the man off his feet, and he fell backwards. Ayo hoped it wasn't a fatal wound, as he wanted to gather more information from the man.

Ayo moved quickly before the man could regain his feet, if he still could, and had a blade at his throat in seconds. 'I wouldn't make any sudden moves if I were you.' Ayo spoke inches from the man's face, which was twisted in a snarl, whether from pain or defiance, Ayo could not tell – but he cared little for the set of the man's face, he had him.

The man refused to speak, so Ayo encouraged him by pressing down on the axe handle, prompting the man to release a hiss of pain through gritted teeth. 'You are a brave man, but you will give me the information I seek, or I will leave you for the hyenas.' As if in answer to Ayo's threat, the howls of hyenas could be heard somewhere in the distance. 'Ah, they can probably smell the blood in the air. You don't have much time, thirty maybe forty beats of the heart before they track your scent. Why not save yourself, eh?'

The man's resolve crumbled, probably at the prospect of feeding the animals that roamed the forest. 'Ok, please don't leave me like this. We were sent by Olise to kill everyone in the city.' Ayo's suspicions were confirmed, so he pressed for more answers. 'I heard one of your number talking about outriders and a signal. Explain.'

The man looked pained, but he babbled on heedless of the pain. 'There are soldiers in the city, there have been for weeks. Once the killing started, the men were instructed to burn the city. The smoke was the signal, all the outriders would then advance and take out anyone trying to leave. No one lives, that is everything,' he rasped. Ayo's dread started to rise; what would become of the queen and the princes? He had to warn them somehow, but how would he get past the outriders? It was too much of a risk.

'Please', the man crocked 'help me!' Ayo looked down at his wound and knew he would never make it; the man had lost too much blood, not to mention the internal damage from the impact of the axe. 'I am sorry,' he said, then he stood and sprinted off to find Enitan. The sounds of the man's pitiful pleading faded with the sounds of the forest.

Enitan came to a halt when he couldn't hear Ayo in the background. He took a knee in the shrubs and listened but heard nothing. A gentle breeze started to blow, ruffling the foliage in front of him. The wind seemed to possess a life of its own, following a path through the trees as leaves and branches shifted before it. Enitan's eyes followed the direction of the disturbed vegetation mesmerised, until it stopped at two muscular legs.

Enitan's gaze immediately went up to the rest of the man who stood some paces away from him and he whipped out the short sword at his hip with the reflexes of a cat. For some reason unknown to him, he was unafraid. Instead, he felt a sense of familiarity, but he still brought his blade up and in front of him protectively as he scrutinised the stranger before him.

The stranger was heavily built as if sculpted from marble. Cords of muscle twisted around his arms and legs and his chest stood out like thick slabs of granite. He had deep dark skin and was roughly of middle age, but he was clearly a warrior from his posture and attire – exquisitely detailed leather chest plate, straps of leather and beaten bronze around his wrists and the pelt of a black jaguar resting on his powerful shoulders.

A thick set of coral beads hung from his neck down to his immense chest, giving him a sense of nobility. Enitan now saw that the stranger was a very handsome man, despite having a jagged scar that snaked from his left cheek ending, in his eye. An eye that was milky white and seemed to glow in the shifting light of the moon. The air around him seemed to shimmer with heat, and Enitan's nostrils were filled with the scent of burning grass; then he noticed that the ground the stranger stood on was clear as if burned away with a torch.

'Put away your weapon, child, I mean you no harm. I have watched over you for some time now and you have grown well.' The stranger spoke in an old Yoruba dialect not known to Enitan with a deep and rich voice. Enitan couldn't comprehend how he somehow understood the dialect, every word, every syllable, as if it was a tongue born to him. He lowered his blade slowly but did not put it back in its sheath.

'Who are you?' he asked without fear. A ghost of a smile crossed the stranger's face, which was quickly replaced with what Enitan thought was sadness, sympathy almost. 'I have come to give you tidings, my child. I do not deliver this news lightly, but I share your pain, I share your fear, and when you come into your own, I will share your strength, my child.' On hearing the stranger's words, Enitan was suddenly overwhelmed by emotion and began to cry.

* * * *

Ayo finally caught up with Enitan standing silently amongst the trees, peering into the gloom of the densely populated forest. The vegetation around Enitan swayed gently in the night air but the temperature around him was strangely warmer than the rest of the forest when he got closer. Ayo could not sense anyone around, but he felt a presence that he had never felt before, something profound that sent a chill through his bones. *Something has happened here*, he thought, and he walked cautiously towards the boy who stood in contrast to the swaying trees and shrubs arrayed in their natural splendour.

Somehow, Enitan appeared to stand taller, like a man grown, from the set of his shoulders and his stance; his legs were set apart as if ready to fight, and he saw that Enitan had his sword in his hand, held casually but firmly by his side.

Ayo's fear started to mount, but he forced himself to walk forward and gently touch Enitan on the shoulder. It took a few seconds for Enitan's eyes to focus, pulling him away from some distant place, and he turned his head to look at Ayo. 'My prince, we cannot stay here, soldiers are hunting us and I fear–' Enitan cut him off. 'Ile-Ife is under attack.'

Ayo was perplexed that Enitan knew what was happening; however, he chose not to use this time to ask questions. 'So, you know that we must leave here at once if we are to avoid capture. I think we should take the route next to the stream back to the palace and warn the queen and your brothers.'

Enitan stood still for a moment looking into the darkness, then he spoke. 'I think my family is lost to me. I must take my own path now, the path which the gods have set before me. But I cannot go until I see Ile-Ife with my own eyes. Will you stay by my side? I'm afraid of what I will find back home.'

This seemed a very strange request from Enitan, as Ayo would never imagine leaving him, now even more so. He looked into Enitan's eyes and saw the eyes of a child desperately seeking the reassurance only an adult could provide. But he also saw something else in those eyes, something that had not been there before, and he could not ignore it.

Breaking protocol, he knelt in front of Enitan, rested his arms on his shoulders and addressed him directly by name. 'Enitan, I am sworn to you till the day the gods decide to steal the breath from my lungs. I will never depart you nor let any harm befall you as long as I have my life and my spear. But something has happened in this forest. I feel that the mark of a god is upon you, I can sense it, but we do not need to speak about it if you are unwilling. Let us make haste to the city, we may yet be able to reach your family.'

Enitan turned his head in the direction of the city before he spoke. 'Thank you, Ayo. I will follow your lead.'

An hour later they had reached within a few miles of the city, taking a shortcut close to the stream for speed and to hide their tracks. They had miraculously avoided the outriders converging on the city, but several times the sound of men could be heard in the distance talking in low voices and moving through the forest.

There were many of them, at least a few hundred, and they were heavily armed from the sounds of their equipment. It had been to Ayo and Enitan's advantage that they knew the forest so well and the men who hunted them were obviously foreigners, unacquainted with the various tracks leading to the city.

The route close to the stream was beside a small hill, which overlooked part of the forest and the city, and Ayo had suggested scaling the hill to get a better view. They ascended the hill and crawled the final yards to the top on their hands and knees to stay out of sight.

What they saw when they reached the summit brought tears to both their eyes. Ile-Ife was in flames. Several large fires had broken out across the city and they could hear the faint sounds of a city being sacked. The helpless sounds of women and children in terror carried on the wind along with the dreadful sound of murder.

'His words were true,' Enitan suddenly said, and he began to sob. 'I didn't want to believe him, but he told me the truth.' Enitan buried his head in his hands and broke down. Ayo, on the other hand, could not tear his gaze away from what he saw. Was this a bad dream? Ile-Ife was the strongest nation in the south; how could this be? Everyone he knew and loved was down there but, with the number of soldiers in the town and the outriders slowly making their way to the city, any hope of survival was surely doomed.

'We have to leave, Enitan. We can't risk going down there now. If your brothers...' He trailed off before finishing. 'You must be protected. Nothing is more important right now.'

'West. We must go west,' Enitan said between sobs. 'My grandfather rules those lands and that is the only safe option we have.' The fire around the city was spreading rapidly and they now saw a line of men making a final stand near one of the city gates. Perhaps some of the remaining guards from the city barracks. It was a brave attempt, but a futile one, for they were quickly swallowed up by the tide of the enemy that fell upon then like waves on a beach, continuing its course through the city.

Enitan took one last look at the home he had known all his life. The fires in the city had now spread to more than half of the dwellings and they could see that the men with the swords were now making their way towards the gates of the palace.

The heat from the fires was now carried by the wind in the warm night air, which was heavy with the scent of burning buildings and the faint smell of burning flesh. The warmth in the air slowly began to dry the tears on Enitan's face. He had now mastered his emotions and his face took on a mask of resignation and then acceptance.

The image of the city in flames would forever be burnt into his mind's eye and he would carry this memory with him always, until he was strong enough to enact his revenge on those responsible.

He looked on for a few minutes more, not ever wanting to forget the moment. Ayo moved close to him and gently turned him away from the nightmare and eventually got him to descend the hill away from Ile-Ife.

FRACTURED KINGDOM

*E*ver since the announcement of the king's betrothal there had been a marked improvement from within the royal court. Adeosi was seen in public more, and he genuinely appeared to be happy, and seemingly over the loss of his beloved queen, Bunmi.

There was, however, still some dissent amongst the lesser lords and chiefs within the realm. Perhaps it was because some of them felt spurned that it had not been their daughter's hand that was chosen to wed the king, or their enmity for the Calabar tribe and the rumours that the queen had bewitched Adeosi.

The king was unperturbed by the animosity directed at his new bride and, despite the judgement and condemnation from some of his advisors and the people of Ile-Ife alike, he was determined to proceed with the impending nuptials.

The kingdom could not, however, dispute or disregard the advantage of this new alliance and the bolstered military support now afforded to the king's army with the joining of the Igbo and Calabar families to the Yoruba empire.

Prior to the engagement, the Igbo and Calabar royal families would only have come to the aid of the Yoruba if their own interests were threatened, but now, their interests were vested and aligned with that of the kingdom of Ile-Ife, and they would answer any summons to defend those interests with the full extent of the might of the two nations.

To further strengthen Adeosi's position, he had sent out an emissary to the emir of the northern lands with hopes of establishing a truce following the years of segregation brought on by the invasion of the north led by his father, King Kayode, years ago. Adeosi knew that the horse lords' pride had been shattered into many pieces and spread across the vast and barren north like the grains of sands that dominated those lands, as King Kayode had left it.

This was a new day, however, and it was time to placate the northerners. He would use this opportunity to welcome them back into the folds of a peaceful and unified country. What better way to do so than with a royal wedding in which all could come together and celebrate? This would be the perfect opportunity to renew old vows that predated his father's invasion, and create new alliances.

In one fell swoop Adeosi would secure his boarders to the north, putting an end to the raids in the south and, in time, give the people a new heir from his union with Ekaete. Both outcomes would ensure peace and a prosperous future for the kingdom in addition to a continuity to the royal bloodline, pleasing the chiefs and people alike and unifying the fractured kingdom. This would be a feat even his great father, in part, had failed to achieve without the force of arms.

Several months later, delegations from the south and the north converged on the quiet town of Okene, neutral ground between the two kingdoms. The king and the emir had chosen to come in person to show each other the respect due them and both contingents were attended by their household guards, councillors and their children. The emir had brought all his six children; four boys and two girls, from three wives. This slightly offended Adeosi who had only sired one child – prince Jide – and had only truly loved one woman – Bunmi.

This did not, however, dampen the air of genuine camaraderie discovered between the two leaders. Through their councillors, who translated the Yoruba spoken by the king and the Hausa spoken by the emir, they were both happy to renew old vows and pledge to come to each other's aid if the circumstance arose.

These vows would be extended to future generations; their children; and even though some of them were too young to understand the significance of the truce, they all followed suit in announcing the pledges and exchanging gifts of perpetual friendship. There was even talk of a betrothal between the children to forever seal their alliance, but this was only suggested light-heartedly with no hint of hidden agendas or veiled threats.

Both contingents parted in high spirits laden with gifts, and from that day forth, there was peace between the north and the south.

Adeosi's bride Ekaete did not attend the meeting, choosing to stay behind the closed doors and softer comforts of the palace.

There was more and more talk of her around the palace recently, mainly regarding her mysterious and frequent disappearance from her chambers at night-time. She would often retire to her room in the evening and, despite her door being guarded, the maids would find the room empty when they came to bring her water and ensure she was comfortable. Ekaete would be nowhere to be seen.

The guards would always swear that no one had passed through the doors, but in the morning Ekaete would emerge from the room as if she had been there all along.

A few local farmers had also claimed to have seen on numerous occasions a lone figure, supposedly a woman, walking into the forest at night holding a torch, often followed by the sounds of strange animals coming from deep within the bushes. These accounts, however, were often discounted, as the locals were known for their exaggerated and unfounded stories.

The rumours only added to the growing fear and suspicion towards Ekaete, which spread around the royal court and most of the surrounding villages. Whenever the subject was broached with the king, he would dismiss it out of hand and threaten to punish any such rumourmongers if caught.

Following the king's decree, all talk of the subject ceased in public, but it was still whispered in quiet corners of the kingdom and it was reflected in the way the new queen was viewed and treated by all the people she encountered.

The wedding was set a few months after the dance of two kings, as the meeting was later known, and surprisingly, all went according to plan. It was a lavish event and a banquet was held under the shadow of the palace gates on the threshold of the city, open to all the subjects of Ile-Ife and attended by nobles and vassals from across the realm.

The emir was by far the most talked-about guest. His recent alliance with the king was still viewed with suspicion by most of the lords and vassals, but they all afforded him the respect his station demanded.

The emir's gifts were also the most extravagant, putting all the others to shame. He had brought a horse drawn cart piled with an assortment of solid gold items including figurines of varying sizes, crockery, jewellery and weapons of all sorts – ceremonial daggers, swords and spears, all inlaid with precious metal and gems, and ingots of gold in their purest form worth a fortune.

In addition, the emir also gifted the new queen horses, cattle and bolts of tanned leather hides. This display of wealth and generosity astonished the guests and the king alike, as it was thought that the north was a barren kingdom, following its sack and destruction almost three decades ago, but they had clearly rebuilt and prospered ever since.

Later that evening, when the palm wine flowed freely and most of the attendants had lost some of their inhibitions, the emir, through his translator, disclosed to Adeosi that his father, King Kayode, had not struck a fatal blow to the Hausa after all. When word had spread of the invasion, the horse tribesmen had simply moved the then ruling emir, together with his most senior and trusted lords along with all the wealth of their cities, further north.

The armies King Kayode had faced and destroyed were only a fraction, albeit a large one, of the true force of the Hausa. They had anticipated the king's move and had masterfully outwitted him. The emir said, however, that no glory could be taken away from the old king, as the north had lost most of their best warriors and their magnificent and powerful cities, including their capital city Sokoto; the life and pride of the north had been destroyed. All had been reduced to ruins, and this had never been done before or since by any other ruler in their history.

Adeosi was surprised to learn this news and conveniently chose to overlook the conversation as the story of his father's triumph had been woven into the fabric of Ile-Ife's history. Changing the narrative now would only take away from his family's lustre.

As the festivities drew to a close and the sun began to set, casting an orange hue over the city, the guests gathered and waited patiently in line to bless the royal couple before they returned to their homes and their lands with full stomachs and a tale on their tongues of the event of the year.

East of the city, approximately two miles away, stood a hill that jutted out of the surrounding forest affording a view of the vista that Ile-Ife was known for. On the top of the hill six figures stood solemnly and observed the ceremony below them, framed by the fading light of the sun.

No one had noticed them, but it was clear that they were all dressed in black covering every inch of their skin. Just before Adeosi and Ekaete withdrew into the palace for the evening, the king intoxicated from the excitement of the day and too much palm wine, Ekaete stopped and gazed into the distance.

Adeosi was pulling on her arm gently, eager to retire into the privacy of the palace to consummate their marriage, and his blood-guard, Demola, waited patiently in the wings with the rest of the royal guards ready to escort them back to their chambers. Noticing her reluctance to move, Adeosi followed her line of sight and noticed the eerie figures in the distance. He could tell that they were all women from their silhouettes and the curves of their robes. He was about to question her when she suddenly announced that she was with child.

Adeosi turned to face her and was momentarily shocked and overwhelmed with emotions he could not quite comprehend – joy, confusion, betrayal – as he had not been intimate with her.

A hundred questions swam around in his mind but, before he could interrogate her, she said it was a boy and that he had come to her one night when he was drunk. Adeosi did not recall such a night, but he felt she would not deceive him, surely.

He was suddenly excited at the prospect of being a father again. He then remembered the people he had just seen on the hill and turned back to look, but there was no one there. He was sure he *hadn't imagined it, but he decided to put it out of his mind and focus on the news he had just received.*

Ekaete was no longer looking at the hill and, eventually, she turned away from the east and slowly began to walk towards the palace.

UNFORGIVING

Olise was incandescent with rage. After all his careful planning, coercion of the chiefs and their armies and his mother's influence, Jide had still managed to rally half of the kingdom to his cause.

According to his spies, Jide was marching towards Benin City with over two thousand warriors, the largest unified army known to the tribes, and it was said that almost double that number were likely to join him from the southwest; elite warriors from regions and islands around Lagos. The only consolation was that, unbeknownst to Jide, Olise now held Ile-Ife, the capital city and seat of power for the tribes, without compromising his own current position.

He held sway over the two most powerful cities in the realm and intended to hold them and use them to his benefit, waging his war from the comfort of the city's fortification.

It still amazed him how easily Ile-Ife had fallen, without much of a fight – so his men told him – but to his disappointment there was no confirmation that the princes had been captured or killed during the storming action. None of his spies had reported that any of the princes had been sighted but it was said that several bodies burnt beyond recognition had been recovered from the ruins of the palace.

He could only hope that his nephews were amongst the dead, as the people would never recognise him as the true heir to the throne if another Adelani still breathed, threatening his authority. The sooner he dealt with Jide and asserted himself as the rightful king the better, as everything was still up for grabs.

In a bid to hamper the advance of Jide's army, Olise had sent his men out to scorch the earth for 100 miles in every direction from the walls of Benin City, putting the flame to all the crops and grasslands, depriving Jide's army, horses and cattle of the much-needed nourishment required to sustain them in the field. In addition, all sources of water outside of that radius had been poisoned – streams, rivers and wells alike.

This did nothing to hurt Olise's position, as Benin City boasted an ingenious series of deep excavations that served as wells, sufficient to sustain the city for years. The water extracted from the wells also fed the numerous irrigation systems dotted around the city designed to cultivate crops, making the city a self-sufficient institution.

Olise, with the gentle persuasion of Ogie, had wisely spared the lives of most of the farmers and field hands who continued to toil the land – under armed guard – within the walls, generating enough produce to comfortably feed Olise's gathered forces.

Olise had also taken a personal interest in the city's defences, reinforcing weak sections of the walls and introducing new features, such as a vast trench around the perimeter of the wall complete with fire-hardened spikes that would deter even the hardiest of warriors.

Now all he could do was to wait patiently for Jide's army to arrive, expecting them to be half-starved and demoralised by the time they reached the city limits.

He sat in the main hall of the palace surrounded by his generals, or rather, the chiefs who had pledged their allegiance to avoid their own destruction. At his right shoulder as always stood Dimeji, with his arms crossed, wearing his usual look of indifference, and Ogie to his left.

'I believe the best course of action is to meet Jide head-on before he receives reinforcements from the southwest,' one of the chiefs was saying. 'I heard that the tribes of that region are fierce and I'm worried that their presence could cause some of our weaker allies to waver,' he finished.

Olise had his eyes focused on a map, which was an illustrative depiction of the realm south of the great river that divided the country, etched on a dried hide of cow leather.

'You need not worry yourself with the south,' he said without taking his eyes off the map, 'As it happens, I have taken Ile-Ife.' This drew gasps of shock and bewildered expressions from some of the men present, except Olise's shadows – Dimeji and Ogie, and a select few of his trusted chiefs who had agreed to send their warriors to aid in this conquest. Olise went on unheeded, 'When our dear friend King Jide learns of the fate of his precious city, I'm certain he'll send a great many of his army back to recapture his ancestral seat. Once his army splits, this is when we'll take the fight to him. I have men already in the field who will report the moment this inevitable event occurs. As you are all aware, I have also burnt all the crops on the road to the city, so if he chooses to bring his whole army here, they will starve before long. Either way I have his measure.'

The chief who had spoken earlier shook his head slowly in disbelief or in awe. 'I did not imagine that you would actually succeed... so quickly,' he added. 'I believe we have all made the right choice in supporting you,' said another man, prompting nods and grunts of agreement from all the other men in the room. This pleased Olise. He had almost doubted himself but, as his mother had promised, everything seemed to be falling into place.

One of the chiefs, however, sat solemnly in a corner staring into his wine horn as if waiting for its contents to reveal a message to him. 'What of the princes?' he asked in heavily accented Yoruba, bringing the clamour in the room to a sudden halt. This chief was known as Zogo the black – named for his unusual dark skin compared to the light skin of the people in his tribe, the Igbo. Zogo was a renowned warrior and chief from the eastern territories and a distant relative to the Chidozie family and, in turn, Olise.

Zogo's family and supporters still felt uncomfortable with the usurpation of Jide, as the Chidozies had always prided themselves on their loyalty and honour but, most of all, the preservation of the ancient rule of succession.

It was not too long ago – during the reign of King Kayode – that the Chidozie family had been at the receiving end of a similar family revolt, which saw many of their number needlessly slaughtered in a power struggle that forever shaped the hierarchy of the Igbo noble families. Zogo's support of Olise went against everything his ancestry held dear, but withholding his support from Olise would have come at too high a price.

Ekaete still had influence in the Chidozie family and for assurance of the family's support she had taken a number of the senior family members' children as hostages. This included her own cousins and Zogo's first son and heir to his titles and wealth.

The children were rumoured to be held in a town called Aba, a territory of Olise's that was fiercely loyal to him and him alone. Aba was the town which Olise had been exiled to, and where he had begun to fan the flames of his rebellion.

Aba was a heavily fortified town situated on the top of a rise with views for miles of the surrounding jungles and marshes. The jungles around Aba boasted a plethora of predators from an array of venomous snakes to wild boars, leopards and unnaturally massive man-eating crocodiles. The town also had a full complement of barracks with enough men to hold off an invasion of any size for several months due to its strategic location.

Needless to say, there was no chance of the children ever escaping or being rescued, so Zogo and a few other Igbo chiefs were held to ransom.

Olise slowly looked up from his map and regarded Zogo for a few seconds before he replied. He knew that his answer would be judged by the men in the room and he needed their continued support, respect and fear if he was to have a chance at seizing the throne.

'The princes are dead. Their bones and those of the queen are still smouldering in the fires that consumed the palace. Jide is the only Adelani who still lives and his time in this world is coming to an end, I will see to that. Come, let us not dwell on the details of Ile-Ife but start to look towards the governances of a new realm. Our realm. A realm that we will carve up between ourselves as we see fit, without being told how best to govern our lands.'

Zogo's face held no emotion and an awkward silence stretched between the two men. Dimeji slowly unfolded his arms, dropping his right hand on the pommel of the great sword sheathed at his hip. This gesture was not lost on Zogo and he raised an eyebrow slowly, whilst never breaking eye contact with Olise.

Finally, Olise cracked a broad smile and raised his arms with his palms turned outwards in a gesture of peace. He knew that he couldn't afford to shed blood in this place as it would only drive a wedge between him and the other Igbo chiefs present.

'Zogo, I understand your misgivings, but you have my word, your honour will never be questioned, and you should know how much I value your counsel and appreciate the army you have brought here. Let us look to the future, together.' This seemed to satisfy Zogo – for now – and he raised his horn and inclined his head slightly to show that he bore no ill intentions.

The other men in the room visibly relaxed and the atmosphere, which a minute ago had been suffused with sudden and unbridled violence, slowly receded as the murmur between the men returned.

Olise turned to the other chiefs, sweeping the room with a flourish and his charismatic smile. 'My chiefs, please see to your men, I hope you have every comfort here, but know that we may need to join the field at any time, so don't let your men get too comfortable. I intend for us to march swiftly to meet Jide's army once they are in range of the city, and your support is needed now more than ever. In the meantime, let me know if you need anything,' he said, with emphasis on the last word.

'Ultimately, I am responsible for the welfare of our armies and the responsibility of this task is not taken lightly. We can only succeed if we are as one unit and I most certainly will not act without your consent. Well, most of your consent.' This brought about some nervous laughter from the men, but Olise continued, taking on an air of seriousness.

'Please do not be mistaken, Jide is a formidable king and, above all else, a survivor. He cannot be allowed to live. Rest now, as I will call on your counsel soon.' With that, all the men began to leave the room, one after the other, until Olise was left with the only men he trusted, Dimeji and Ogie.

'Can you believe the nerve of Zogo? To undermine my authority in front of all the chiefs!' Olise exclaimed. 'He will suffer for such an affront.' Ogie was stroking his chin pensively. 'I feel you must stay your sword for a time, at least until we have defeated Jide's army. You probably don't want to hear it but we need Zogo's men and his influence with the other Igbo chiefs. Without their support, we stand little chance of success.'

Olise's earlier mask of arrogant confidence had been replaced with a raw fury that threatened to boil to the surface. The bitterness of the insult could only be sated with blood, but he knew better than to act irrationally. Besides, Zogo would remain his puppet for as long as his child was a prisoner at Aba.

'I hate to admit it but you are right, Ogie,' Olise finally conceded. 'But I want you to observe him closely. If any of the chiefs are to turn against me, it will start with him, I am sure. The minute this business with Jide is over, I will take his head. Zogo the headless would be a much more fitting name...' Olise mused.

Dimeji produced a rare smile at that, which was nothing more than a twitch of a scar next to his mouth that did nothing to soften his hideous features, but it was enough to prompt a reaction from the two men present.

'I would never have believed that stone could crack if I had not just seen it with my own eyes,' said Ogie.

'Indeed. Maybe he is excited at the prospect of carrying out the deed himself,' Olise remarked but didn't get a response from the warrior. 'To more serious matters, I need to know Jide's position and the minute he sets foot on the road east. I have planted some spies in his ranks but they cannot leave the army without arousing suspicion so they have been instructed to leave coded messages with information that can help us along the route.'

'That sounds complicated and risky,' said Ogie.

'Not really, all the locations were predetermined. I have village boys, children really, who will find the information, passing it from hand to hand ahead of the army. It's quite a network of spies, if

I say so myself. But I cannot take all the credit, it was mainly my mother's idea.'

'Ah, I see,' said Ogie, still stroking his chin. 'The information should serve us well then. We still have enough food stock to last us at least twelve turns of the moon, and the rate of weapons being churned out by the blacksmiths is better than I could have expected,' Ogie finished.

'That is because they use their whole families in the process. You see, the threat of death can do wonders for motivation and efficiency.' Olise laughed, only half joking. 'But I suppose I have you to thank for not slaughtering all the inhabitants. After all, they have proven themselves most useful.'

Ogie inclined his head at the praise. 'I will see to our men, my prince. There have been more incidents of rape amongst the locals recently. I fear I may have to hang one or two of the bastards to get the point across.'

'Be my guest.' Olise waved with a dismissive gesture. Ogie left the room, but Dimeji stayed by Olise's side as always and both men slipped into the comfortable silence they had always shared, then Olise turned back to his map.

* * * *

Jide's dreams were haunted by fleeting images of Ile-Ife in flames. So vivid were the scenes of chaos; screaming women and children crying over the bodies of their slain husbands and brothers and some being dragged away into the darkness by laughing soldiers with feral features like rabid dogs.

He saw scenes of men in the city fighting desperately to hold off tides of the same feral-faced soldiers, who were eventually engulfed and left behind as bloodied and broken bones.

The next moment, he was standing amongst the ruins of what was once the greatest nation in the west. Everything he touched instantly turned to ash that flowed through his fingers and was blown away by a soft breeze.

He saw his palace, which stood pristine and seemingly unaffected by the fires that consumed the rest of the city around him, but when he pushed open the thick double timber doors, all he saw was blood; it was everywhere. It was smeared all over the walls of the palace and thick droplets of semi-congealed blood hung from the ceiling like stalactites. There was no sign of his family, but he frantically searched from room to room.

He finally came to the throne room and, sitting in his chair on a raised dais was his brother, with his usual arrogant half smile, surrounded by a pool of what appeared to be more foul-smelling blood. Jide stepped closer but was unable to talk, his voice was stolen by some unseen force, and the closer he got to the throne the more he sank deeper into the fetid fluid, which clung to his legs like grasping hands, pulling him deeper still.

The blood was up to his neck now, and he reached out to grab hold of Olise's foot, which was only inches away from the tips of his extended fingers. Suddenly, a figure stepped out from behind the throne.

It was the girl he had seen in the forest. All she wore was a plain white wrapper around her slim body in stark contrast to the surroundings. She had blood on her open palms and a sad expression on her face, one of deep sorrow, but her eyes were cold. They were the eyes of one that had seen both what is yet to come and what had gone before.

Jide tried to plead with her for help, but no words passed his lips, until he was completely submerged in the pool of blood with whatever lurked below the surface.

Jide woke up with a start, covered in sweat that had soaked through to the linen and rushes on which he lay. He looked around him, at a space which slowly took on the familiar shape of the tent that had been erected for him on the field.

His sword and shield were by his side and Akin was huddled in a corner of the tent snoring softly and embracing his own sword as if it were a lover.

Jide had had the same dream every night since he had been on the march from Ondo, which only added to the concern he felt for his family's wellbeing. So, to reassure himself, he had sent out several riders with messages to the palace. None of them had returned.

After the first few weeks without word from Ile-Ife, he had convinced himself that the riders must have been slowed by the advancing tribesmen marching to join his army, finding safety in travelling with greater numbers. Time passed and his allies had eventually joined him on the road, but no one had come across his messengers bound for or coming from Ile-Ife.

This had only increased his anxiety, and he was continuously tempted to abandon the whole affair and march back home just to learn the fate of his family.

He hoped that if the worst had in fact happened and Olise had somehow managed to slip a raiding party past him to attack the city, Lara would stick to their plans and send his boys across the realm to their relatives and supporters.

With a sinking feeling, he had come to the realisation that he had travelled too far and gathered too many to his cause to simply abandon the campaign now. What would his subjects and vassals think of their king if he were to leave?

He had confided in Akin and voiced his deepest fears, acknowledging that a rash decision could cost him dear – the respect and honour of the family name, and possibly the kingdom. Akin had suggested sending a company of trusted soldiers back home to investigate; this would at least give the king the peace of mind to forge on and see his plans through.

This would be the sensible hand to play, but Jide was torn. He couldn't leave his family to whatever fate the gods had in store for them if he could influence the situation. At the same time, they were only days' march away from Benin City. The revolt could be brought to a swift conclusion if he was to commit all his resources to this one endeavour.

He decided that, before the day's march, he would table these options with his most trusted allies; a small council including Olusegun, Dare – the oba or chief of the island tribes, Rotimi – the chief of Owo and Adedeji – the head of the council of ten of the Modakeke.

After deciding, Jide rose from his bed, slipped on his leather breastplate and sheathed his dagger by his hip before making his way across the tent towards the entrance. Akin stirred and opened one eye suddenly. 'You weren't thinking of walking the camp without an escort, Kabiyesi?' he asked, and slowly stood and stretched his neck.

'It's fine, Akin, I would like to gauge the morale of the men. You do not need to accompany me.'

'Nonsense. Besides I'm up now. What better way to start the day than to stroll amongst fighting men, eh?' Jide smiled at that and made a gesture with his hands to signify that he did not object to the company.

Akin also put on his breastplate and picked up his sword before announcing that he was ready, then both men walked into the glorious dawn light that promised a bright and warm day.

The camp was spread across miles of land in a haphazard pattern. To an unskilled eye, it appeared to be disorganised, but there was order written into the detail of the layout; the earthworks dug around the entrance to the camp, the locations of the tents in order of rank and status – the common soldiers' tents were towards the front and rear, while the officers' tents were erected on the flanks and the chiefs and high-ranking commanders surrounded the tent of the king in the very centre. Each night the king's tent would be erected first and all the other tents would be raised around his.

There were many fires with wisps of black smoke coming from various spots around the camp, followed by the sweet aroma of roasting meat and fish wafting through the breeze and bringing a growl to Jide's stomach.

Some of the soldiers noticed their king and bowed deeply as a show of respect, while others simply prostrated themselves at his feet and called his name with reverence, as if a god walked amongst them.

Jide eventually found his way to Olusegun's tent and noticed that the old man was already up, sitting outside his tent of fine tanned leather chewing on a piece of tree bark, with a wrapper around his torso tied at his right shoulder.

'Ah, it was said that the king never sleeps, and I am beginning to believe the rumours,' Olusegun said with a warm smile. Jide dismissed his comment. 'Bah, and what are you doing up so early? I would have imagined that you'd need at least a couple of hours of massage to get those old bones to work every day.'

'I'm sure I can still keep up with you, my king,' Olusegun said with a wink.

Jide sat down on a stool that was brought by a waiting servant and leaned in close to Olusegun so as not to be overheard. 'Segun, I need your counsel. There is a grave matter that concerns me deeply and needs to be discussed. I will also summon Dare and Adedeji, but no one else. This matter is somewhat too sensitive for the other commanders just yet'.

'Of course, my king. I am at your service,' Olusegun said with a slight bow of his head.

They were interrupted by a commotion coming from a distance far off to the front of the camp, and Jide could just about make out a crowd of soldiers gathering. It sounded as if there was a message that was being conveyed between the mass of soldiers to the rest of the camp, but the words were too faint to be discerned.

Jide decided to see what the disturbance was about and Akin quickly moved to his front to clear a path while Olusegun took up the rear with three of his guards, all brandishing spears.

As soon as they were a little closer, they made out some of the words that were being shouted by the men. 'Message for the king, message for the king!!' echoed through the ranks of men.

Jide's blood went cold on hearing the words and the hairs on the back of his neck stood up. He had a feeling that whatever news awaited him would not be good. He raised his arm and shouted, 'I am here, make way for the messenger!'

A few minutes later a scout was on one knee in front of him panting heavily. Jide looked at the man before him and recognition slowly began to form. This was one of the scouts he had sent out weeks ago.

The man appeared to have taken a wound as one of his arms was bandaged, dry blood soiling the dusty cloth. He had several smaller cuts on both arms and the king had noticed that the man had limped before he took a knee. There was more dried blood staining the pommel of the sword at his waist, all of which were tell-tale signs that the scout had been involved in a fierce fight for survival.

As soon as the scout found his breath, he had difficulty in meeting the king's eyes. Jide was impatient and eager to learn the news the man carried but he composed himself as a king should and waited for the soldier to speak.

There was a deadly silence as everyone around the scene held their breath, and finally the soldier spoke.

'My king... Ile-Ife... is no more...' he whispered. This drew sharp gasps and exclamations of horror from the men within earshot. The scout, clearly uncomfortable at delivering this news, went on. 'There were soldiers all over the forest, it was almost as if they had expected us to come and had planned an ambush. We managed to fight off a few of them before deciding to separate, to avoid all of us getting captured. I can only talk of what I witnessed...'

The solider faltered and tears threatened to obscure his vision. So visibly profound was his sorrow that many of the soldiers around began to mutter angrily between themselves, and some were crying openly, already anticipating the fate of their loved ones.

The scout's voice cracked as he continued, 'I approached the city from the north, travelling an extra day to avoid capture. When I came upon the city, the first thing I saw were the flames. Then I heard the screams of our people. But worst of all, I saw the piles of bodies stacked high outside the gates; women, children and the elderly, mixed together without a shred of dignity, left to feed the hyenas and vultures.

I had to know what had become of the rest of the city, so I bade my time and eventually managed to kill one of the soldiers, disguising myself to gain access to the gates, but all I saw was ruins. Everything was destroyed and there was blood, on the streets, on the walls that were still standing and more corpses... everywhere.'

'And what of the royal family?' Jide interrupted. His face remaining blank without a hint of emotion.

'The palace had been razed to the ground, Kabiyesi. No stone stood unturned or timber left unburnt, nothing remained on the plot of the palace besides ashes and rubble. I am deeply sorry, Kabiyesi. After that I was discovered and had to fight my way out. I nearly didn't make it out alive, if not for the grace of *Olodumare*.'

Some of the men began to talk louder now, their voices pitching in anger, all demanding retribution. Some were asking what had become of their own families, but their voices were drowned in the tide of the blood lust that had taken control.

Jide held up his hands for silence; all the while his mind raced. His nightmares had come to pass. His deepest fears crawling out of the darkest corners of his dreams to manifest into reality.

He had always known the risks and planned for them accordingly, but to have the words confirmed was something entirely different, which he was in no way prepared for. He felt sick in his stomach and suddenly tasted bile in the back of his throat, which he had to force back down. He couldn't afford to appear weak in the presence of his men. He reminded himself of who he was, and it dawned on him that he could potentially be the last of his bloodline still alive. He would carry himself with dignity no matter the circumstances.

These acts could no longer be forgiven. He had harboured a hope deep down that all could be resolved without bloodshed once he met with his brother, but not any more. His men and the soldiers of Ile-Ife would want nothing but blood now. It had all gone too far.

Akin was gripping the pommel of his sword so tightly that all his knuckles were almost white. 'This cannot go unanswered,' he said through gritted teeth. Olusegun voiced his opinion too, as if echoing the king's thoughts. 'It has gone too far to be reconciled now. Our only response now should be in blood,' he said.

Jide was quiet for a few minutes and all eyes were on him, waiting to hear what their king would say in response to the destruction of their city, their home. The only true course of action was to respond in kind as Olusegun had stated. No procrastinating. No mercy. No forgiveness.

'I want a thousand of our best soldiers armed, armoured and ready to move to Ile-Ife to take back the city. The rest of us will strike for Benin within the hour, we can delay no longer.' With that Jide turned and started heading towards his tent. Men were already moving to carry out the king's orders and the camp came alive with men rushing to prepare themselves to march and enact their vengeance on Olise.

Akin and Olusegun flanked the king as he walked with a grim expression. Neither of them knew what to say to the king as he was clearly battling with his emotions and struggling to maintain his composure.

Akin was also reeling at the news as he contemplated the fate of his own family in Ile-Ife, but he would have time to mourn later. Now was the time for vengeance. The thought fuelled his rage and he suppressed his emotions as was required for a man of his repute.

Olusegun accompanied Jide in silence back to his tent with his own guards following close behind. When they reached the entrance of the tent, Jide turned to address his blood-guard and closest ally.

'I need some time to process all of this alone. Akin, I trust you will talk to our tribesmen; we have all lost a great deal, but they must be sure of their purpose now in memory of their loved ones, who we will be fighting for. See to it that they are focused. Segun, prepare your own men, the time has come to put their loyalty to the test.'

116

Olusegun stepped forward and placed his hand on Jide's shoulder. 'Kabiyesi, my men are yours and we will follow you on whatever road you lead us, always.' Jide nodded stiffly and turned towards his tent. He stood with his back to them for a split second and then ducked into the tent, closing the flap behind him.

When Jide had gone, Akin turned to Olusegun and said in a sad voice, 'Olise does not know what he has done. Jide will be without mercy, whereas he would not have been if this atrocity had never been committed. Olise has not only destroyed the city but he has destroyed the heart of the man who calls the city home. May *Obatala* protect us all.' With that he walked away to seek his countrymen to share in their sorrow.

Behind the tent entrance, Jide stood by the bed and silently shed tears for the family and home he had loved beyond life and had lost.

BLOOD IS THICKER THAN WATER

*T*he birth of a child can be described in many words –
joyous, celebratory, euphoric – none of which rang true
with the arrival of Ekaete's first and only child. Olise's
birth would henceforth be attributed to the single moment the destiny
of the tribes was irrefutably altered.

The events that precluded and followed the birth marked
the course of many lives in Ile-Ife, but none more so than that of
Adeosi. He had been overjoyed to discover the news of another son
but as the months passed and Ekaete's stomach grew in size, the king's
health steadily declined.

As always, rumours ran high across the realm and it was said
that the occult – to which Ekaete was always believed to belong –
demanded a life as her dowry. It was widely thought that the king's
life was slowly being sacrificed as an offering for the life of Ekaete's
unborn child.

In any event, Ekaete rarely left Adeosi's side throughout her
pregnancy, and gradually but undeniably, she became the voice of the
king. Even Adeosi's blood-guard, Demola, had gradually been
pushed out of the king's confidence and it was said that the strange
ailment that possessed the king made him irrational and lash out
unexpectedly, constantly dismissing the people who surrounded him,
except for Ekaete.

Adeosi's councillors had not been silent in their displeasure
of witnessing the change in their king, the shift in power in favour of
Ekaete and their diminishing influence in the city. They attempted to
wrest some of the king's powers back from her grasp, but with every
turn of the moon, she gained more influence, and the king faded
further into the background.

Shortly after, Ekaete gave birth to her child, which happened
in absolute secrecy. No one other than her own hand-picked staff

were permitted anywhere near her chambers, so no one outside of her circle knew the exact day of the birth. The date was, however, largely speculated, as Ile-Ife experienced three days of highly unusual events.

On the morning of the first day, the domestic animals in the city mysteriously disappeared; all the dogs and cats. It was not taken too seriously at first, but the following day, a mysterious sickness took most of the livestock and the farmers lamented the loss of their goats and cows, which had to be burnt in great heaps outside the city walls to prevent the sickness spreading and wiping out all sources of meat in the city.

On the third day, the city was visited by hundreds of snakes, slithering through the thoroughfare and the houses of the residents. Several people were bitten, some fatally, and it took another day before the people could rid the city of the serpents.

On the morning of the fourth day, it was announced that the queen had given birth to a healthy boy who was named Olise.

The elected councillors were infuriated with the news, mainly at the fact that the king had not made the announcement in person, as it was the custom for the king to hold a ceremony giving thanks to the gods and displaying the child to the masses. This gave them the impression that the king himself did not recognise the child as his own.

Unperturbed by Ekaete, they demanded an audience with the king, with support from several of the chiefs of the kingdom, who all rallied and were just as desperate to see their king first hand and not have a repeat of the king's absence, as had happened following the death of the former queen some years ago.

Several months had passed before their request was finally granted and a large contingent of noble lords, chiefs and supplicants gathered in the great throne room in Ile-Ife, all awaiting the arrival of their king. The morning stretched on and hours passed with no sign of the king. By the time the late afternoon sun began to cast long shadows in the hallways, Ekaete emerged with several of her soldiers clad in black armour, followed by the king, who was wheeled into the room on a makeshift chair draped with furs over his legs covering his lower body.

There were sharp intakes of breath at the sight of the king, who appeared to have aged by a decade. His skin was stretched loosely over his bones and saliva dripped from his open mouth. He had a vacant stare in his eyes and his arms rested limply in his laps.

The king's councillors rushed towards their beloved king on the dais, only to be barred by Ekaete's soldiers who crossed spears in their path.

All the men present began to shout their shock at the king's appearance and Ekaete raised her hands to silence them before speaking. 'The king is suffering from a grave illness that has robbed him of his voice but, before his tongue was stolen, he asked me to rule as regent in his name until my son is old enough to sit on the throne.'

This brought about a fresh wave of protest from the gathered dignitaries. Some called out treachery and witchcraft, while others called for Jide, the true heir to the throne. Ekaete's soldiers tensed, moving their hands to their weapons ready to strike down any man at the order of their queen but Ekaete only smiled to the men spewing unconcealed hatred towards her.

She raised her hands again for silence and gradually the chatter subsided enough for her to get her words across. 'I understand your displeasure in this message from the king,' she glanced over at Adeosi before continuing, 'but the king's words are final. He has chosen my child as his heir and declared death to any man who refuses to recognise his... now my authority.' The last word was all but shouted, dripping self-importance.

Some of the chiefs discreetly left the hall, presumably to spread word across the realm of what had just transpired, but most just stood in shocked silence and stared at the king as if waiting for him to suddenly spring to his feet and declare the whole event a charade. But this was no joke, the queen's words were as real as the setting of the sun and the fading light in the great king's eyes.

Demola, who stood among the dignitaries, almost had to be forcefully restrained by some of the senior members of the Modakeke who were also present, from drawing his sword and killing Ekaete where she stood, which would have surely been the end of his own life and possibly the king's.

His voice had been the loudest during the protests and all the while the queen had observed him with a steely expression. He had made a grave enemy that day and he knew it.

After some more heated exchanges, the remaining dignitaries had started to disperse, no doubt to contemplate their future in the realm. This was not the case for Demola, nor was it for the Modakeke and a handful of council members. They would create their own fate and take matters into their hands.

No sooner had they left the palace than they planned to reconvene in secrecy to plot the queen's displacement and restore Ile-Ife to the rightful heir; Jide, who, at three years of age, was oblivious to the power struggles and plots being designed in his name. Akin, on the other hand, was thirteen years old and was well aware of the situation and the heightened responsibility of ensuring the prince was kept safe.

Unfortunately, Adeosi did not live the year out and died some months after the meeting. Ekaete had announced to the senior members of the realm that she planned to cremate the body with no ceremony. This would not be accepted by the people. Adeosi was a descendant of Ile-Ife, as had been his forebears, and would be buried as such in the soil that gave rise to the great nation. No alternative would suffice. This was demanded by the realm and Ekaete had no choice but to relent.

Adeosi was beloved by all and the funeral was planned over several days to accommodate the volume of people expected to attend the king for the last time. People from all reaches of the kingdom made the pilgrimage to say their farewells. The kingdom was clearly devastated by the loss but surprisingly, none more broken than the emir from the north.

The emir was so stricken with grief that he made the trip on the day the news broke with his royal guards, running their mounts to exhaustion. On arrival, he went straight to the shrine where Adeosi had been laid to rest and wept at his feet.

As if intuiting the mysterious circumstances behind the king's passing, he had also brought along his marabu – the northerners' equivalent to the Babalawo in Yorubaland, presumably for his own protection against evil, but mainly to appeal to the spirit of the late king to rest peacefully and not to wander the underworld as a malevolent spirit seeking retribution, as was done in the custom of his own clan during burials.

Once he had paid his respects, he sought out Jide and his protectors – the Modakeke – and told them through a translator that Adeosi had been one of the greatest men the realm had seen. Through his humility, selflessness and vision of a unified country, he had won a lifelong respect from the north. He also mentioned that the king's pact of peace with the north would remain honoured so as long as a descendant of Adeosi sat on the throne.

His parting words were that Jide and the generations that followed him would always be welcome in the north. With that he departed the city and made the arduous journey back to the north on the same day without setting eyes on Ekaete.

The years that followed Adeosi's death were mostly uneventful, but Ekaete gradually consolidated her power. She did not have much influence over the other cities within the kingdom, as most of the chiefs had chosen not to recognise her as their monarch, but slowly her influence began to gain traction, albeit through unconventional and questionable methods; bribery, coercion and witchcraft.

She had managed to replace most of the councillors in Ile-Ife with people from her home tribe, granting her the majority rule in matters concerning Ile-Ife, with the exception of any matters relating to the wider kingdom or the Modakeke. They had remained outside of her influence, to her frustration, and they shielded Jide from her for fear that she would make an attempt on his life, legitimising Olise's claim to the throne.

Despite the tension between Ekaete's faction and the Modakeke, Jide and Olise had unexpectedly and despite all odds, established a bond. When Olise turned four years old and started lessons with the tutors of the palace, there had been a chance meeting with Jide, who also used the same tutors for his studies, as was customary for the royal children.

Normally, the princes' schedules were meticulously planned so they would never cross paths but on this occasion one of the classes had been delayed by several hours, causing a conflict in scheduling. Olise had just finished his classes and, on departing, ran into Jide and his escorts.

Both parties that guarded the princes were caught completely unaware, but it was too late, and both children came face to face for the first time. There was an immediate recognition, perhaps because they did not have much interaction with the other children in the palace, who were mostly servants, or because they shared the same blood; whatever it was they took to each other instantly and so began their friendship.

This had not gone down well with Ekaete or the Modakeke and despite their misgivings about the children's new-found friendship, the princes were determined to remain acquaintances regardless of the demands of their elders.

On discovering that they were actually brothers, their bond became even stronger, and there was no dissuading them. Eventually, Ekaete and the Modakeke gave in and consented to the princes' having a relationship, happy for the siblings to find common ground.

Some members of the council welcomed the friendship, which they assumed would be the first step in mending the broken ties in the kingdom, easing the tensions and bringing an end to the power struggle. But the question of who would ascend the throne still remained.

During these troubled times, Demola was, as always, a constant figure in Jide's and Akin's lives, almost taking on the role of father to the prince and his blood-guard, in addition to main advisor and chief protector. In turn, Jide loved and respected him above all.

Demola, however, had not been disarmed by Ekaete's change of heart and continued to criticise her both publicly and in secret. He had vehemently protested against the princes' developing friendship, claiming that it was a plot by Ekaete to get them to lower their guard and pull them into a false sense of security. He did capitulate but was always cautious, personally overseeing to Jide's safety.

The council of ten, however, did not see it the same way, but granted that precautions would need to be maintained in case Demola's suspicions should bear fruit.

More years went by without incident and the princes continued to grow closer, eventually becoming inseparable. They did everything together, from studying to hunting and training with arms. The Modakeke had refused to assign a blood-guard to Olise when he was born but Ekaete had taken it upon herself to find her son a suitable protector.

She had sought out a warrior who had been rejected by the council of ten because of his brutality in past conflicts – murdering scores of soldiers who had already yielded, putting entire settlements to the sword, against the express orders of the council and countless other atrocities. The warrior was also rumoured to claim that he was a disciple of the trickster god Esu, which earned him banishment from the council. The warrior's name was Doyin.

He had a son who had a reputation similar to his father's and, despite his young age, had already been in several skirmishes between bordering tribes. This young warrior was a social outcast and hardly ever spoke except with his hands and his skill at arms and it was obvious that he would grow to be a monstrous warrior both in stature and skill. Dimeji was his name. Olise was thrilled to have a blood-guard like his brother and he would later come to depend on him.

The kingdom had a period of peace until one morning, Demola was found dead in his quarters. His tongue and eyes had been removed, along with other vital organs. Once again speculations ran high in the capital, and it was said that his missing parts had been harvested to perform rituals since he had been a warrior of pure blood.

His death sent tremors through the kingdom and suspicion was directed at one person only, but nothing could be proved and despite the outcry of the council of ten and other senior figures in the kingdom. Nothing was done and the death remained unsolved and unpunished. For the second time in his young life, prince Jide had lost the closest person to him.

THE DESTITUTE

By what could only be described as sheer luck and the divine mercy of the gods, Niran, Toju, their blood-guards and the miserable remains of the royal guard managed to escape the raging fires and bloodthirsty soldiers that plagued the city.

They had to squirm like rodents through the half-submerged tunnels that ran underneath the palace and emerged in the forest north of the city, tunnels of which had not been used in decades and were infested with all kinds of unpleasant creatures. On leaving the tunnels, they had the treacherous task of circumventing the teams of soldiers still scouting the forests for anyone who managed to survive the sack of the city.

Several hours had passed, and by noon of the following day, the small party had managed to traverse a large area of the forest several miles away from the city with smoke still rising to the sky in the distance.

They agreed to use some of the less travelled routes; mainly dirt tracks, that were familiar to the princes, in the hopes of finding Enitan, but there had been no trace of the young prince. With every passing hour, filled with arguments and indecisions, their hopes of finding their brother alive, or at all, slowly diminished.

'I hate to say it, brother, but we can't linger in these parts much more than we already have,' said Toju. 'As much as I want to find Enitan, I for one am not willing to risk capture or worse, before I get the chance to show Olise the error of his ways for betraying his family.'

His voice cracked at the last words and carried so much naked emotion that it stopped Niran in his tracks. He was also struggling with his emotions and the prospect of choosing between finding his brother and survival, but he was not naïve to the reality of how precarious their position was. By all the gods, he burned with the desire to visit hell upon his uncle for all his family had endured.

But he couldn't deny that he was a little surprised at how much their predicament had affected Toju, who was in all regards the epitome of a warrior; always in control of his emotions whatever situation the gods presented to him. Maybe now that they were hungry, homeless and hunted – a position a prince of the land would never have contemplated – he finally understood that beyond the trappings of high birth, he was but a man and acknowledged his vulnerability and susceptibility to harm from those that would wish harm on him.

Niran moved closer to Toju and placed his hands on his shoulders. 'Brother,' he said softly, 'I know you're right, but I could not live with myself if we didn't try. Maybe he managed to get away, you know how cunning Enitan can be, and Ayo is more than capable of protecting him.' Niran said these words as much to convince himself as his brother.

Toju looked away, but Niran didn't fail to see the sorrow in his brother's eyes. It only lasted a second, though, and Toju's air of confidence and defiance returned.

'Let's go, I want to reach the next town before nightfall, if we can help it. The further away we are the better.' Niran nodded and, with that, the small party continued their journey north.

On the evening of the fourth night, they reached the town of Ilesha and decided to camp on the outskirts and reconnoitre the town before proceeding. They had to assume that all the surrounding towns of note close to Ife had been conquered and were hostile, so every precaution had to be taken.

Once they had settled in their makeshift camp, Toju sent an advance party of their guards to get a closer look at the town under the cover of darkness. The remaining guards took up watch around the camp. They had all formed a routine over the past days, alternating between keeping watch, hunting and cooking. Both princes took to these tasks naturally. Their father had taught them long ago that if they were to lead men, they needed to learn to live and endure just like them and adapt to their surroundings.

127

They decided against building a fire for fear of being discovered, and settled on eating a cold meal of charred bushmeat that they had trapped the night before. Toju and Niran were huddled close together looking at the distant lights of the town. They had grown closer and found comfort in their shared grief, but they feared to broach the subject that they may be the last remaining members of the royal house of Adelani.

'I still can't believe it has come to this. Not so long ago the kingdom was at peace and now our family is torn apart and we are hunted like animals, forced to live off scraps like scavengers. Who would have thought...' Niran whispered into the darkness. He could hardly make out Toju's features in the dark, but he sensed the tension in his brother's silhouette. 'There is no point dwelling over that now, little brother, what's most important is that we make it across our boarders, rally our allies and come back in force to reclaim what has been taken from us. Olise is like a pestilence that needs to be eradicated.'

'But I'll tell you one thing, never did I think I'd be looking forward to eating rat for dinner!' Toju joked, trying to lighten the mood. Niran let out a muffled laugh just as he was stuffing more of the meat in his mouth. 'It's not a rat, you idiot, it's a grass-cutter.'

'It's a rodent, isn't it? Same thing,' Toju said.

Niran's thoughts suddenly turned to his parents. 'What about father?' Niran asked, 'I very much doubt he was defeated so easily, not with his army and the Modakeke.' Toju was silent for a while before responding. 'That is my hope, but we must prepare for the worst and assume that, right now, we are the only hope of liberating our people,' he said eventually.

'I still can't help thinking how much we've been betrayed. To think that we had snakes amongst us for so long. I know you had your doubts about father letting in all those refugees but who would have thought?'

'What is done is done. No point dwelling over it. All we can do now is plan for the future and survive,' said Toju, trying to be positive.

'Yes, I know,' replied Niran, but he pressed on. 'Also, I think there was no way those men could have gained access to the city or the palace unchallenged without assistance from more than just Efetobo, it just doesn't make sense. We all know his appetite for power, but who would have thought his reach and influence was that strong? I suspect some of the city guards had a hand in this. I'd wager my sword on it.'

Toju was amused. 'Well, I hope you're right, because how will you defend yourself without your sword, little brother?' he asked. 'That's exactly why I have you,' Niran said with a smile, even though Toju couldn't have seen his expression in the darkness of the forest.

Toju was stroking the shaft of their great grandfathers' spear unconsciously. That and the axe he had taken from the palace armoury were the only items he had managed to save from Ife, the only connection he had to his bloodline. The thought put him in a dark mood, and they sat in silence for a while until they heard a low whistle from one of the guards on watch alerting them to movement in the bushes coming from the direction of the town.

They immediately went for cover and held their weapons tighter ready to defend themselves. Leke and Seun instinctively moved closer to the sides of their princes, until a similar whistle was heard in response to the first indicating that it was one of the royal guards Toju had sent to scout earlier.

'Well?' Toju asked expectantly once the three guards had made it into the camp.

'My prince, it appears to be a quiet place, no sign of soldiers or recent activity of a large host. Perhaps, the events in the south have not made it here,' said one of the scouts. He seemed confident and capable, so Toju decided to follow the man's instincts.

'Good work,' he said, 'Let's get some rest and carry out one final sweep in the morning. If all appears well, we'll reveal ourselves and pray to the gods that we are not taken.' The prospect of rest was a welcome one, as everyone was visibly travel weary. The watch was decided to be rotated every few hours and the princes settled down to what would be another restless night in the wild.

As dawn broke, Toju and Niran scouted the town themselves and decided it was safe enough; however, Niran, Seun and two of the guards would stay behind. If Toju did not return within the hour, he had left strict instructions for Niran to travel east in all haste.

The princes embraced each other and Toju made his way to the town with four guards at his back and Leke by his side. It was a relatively small town, made up mostly of small timber dwellings, but they could see a few stone buildings further along what must have been the main thoroughfare, presumably where more affluent townspeople resided.

The people they passed didn't really pay them much attention, other than the children who curiously trailed along in a ragged line. The men and women they saw didn't appear afraid at seeing armed men walking through their town, and Toju assumed that they had not been the first soldiers to visit.

After what had seemed to be a quarter of the way through the town, an elderly man dressed in a fine kaftan richly embroidered with flowing patterns intercepted them. His arms were extended with his palms open outwards – a gesture of peace – as he slowly walked towards the strangers.

'Good morning, friends,' he said pleasantly to the prince in the dialect of Yoruba common in this region. Toju acknowledged the greeting, responding in the same dialect. 'Good morning, baba, we have travelled a long way and were hoping to replenish our supplies and speak to the chief of this town. There are events in the south that we would like to bring to his attention.'

The man looked slightly bewildered but responded, 'There is no chief in this town but a group of elders. I am one of them and my name is Gbenga. I would be happy to take you to see the others, but I fear that the sight of you and your men may be a cause for concern. What is your name, young man?'

Toju thought for a second and decided to respond with a question of his own. 'I assure you that we mean you no harm, baba, but if you would, which king do you serve?' Again, a look of befuddlement crossed Gbenga's face, but he responded, nonetheless.

'There is only one king, is there not? We are all his subjects and serve at his pleasure. King Jide is his name. Are you from abroad young man? Do you wish to have an audience with the king? I'm afraid you are in the wrong place, it is Ile-Ife you seek, a few days south of here.'

Niran let out a breath of air and only just then realised that he had been holding his breath while Gbenga spoke. Leke and the guards by his side also showed subtle signs of relief.

'I had to be sure, baba, I am prince Toju, first son of king Jide and heir to the kingdom. I need to speak to the elders urgently, for you may all be in peril.' Gbenga narrowed his eyes and scrutinised the prince as if seeing him anew.

He took in the dirty but exquisitely designed leather armour interspersed with small gold discs about the chest, the ornate spear in his hands, the small tribal mark on each of Leke's cheeks, marking him out as Modakeke, and the seal of the Adelani house embroidered into the breast armour of the guards. His eyes went wide in realisation and he immediately dropped to his knees and prostrated himself before Toju.

'My prince, forgive me I did not realise it was you!' he lamented.

'Please, baba, stand up, it is ok. I was glad you did not recognise me for fear that you might be an enemy to the throne.'

Gbenga stood up and began to call to the people standing around curiously. 'Summon the elders, a crowned prince of Ile-Ife is among us. We must prepare a befitting welcome to honour him.' Most people had rarely seen the town elders, let alone a prince of the realm, and they were practically falling over each other to get close to him. So much so that the royal guards had to form a protective ring around Toju.

After making slow progress through the town, Toju was led to a big stone house that must have served as the town hall and was greeted by the remaining elders. There turned out to be three of them, including Gbenga, each of who equally and fairly ruled over the three quarters that made up Ilesha. There was almost a sense of democracy as there were several other wealthy townsmen present, presumably the representatives of the traders in the town – farmers, tailors, tanners and so on.

Toju was greeted warmly and he felt comfortable enough to send for his brother, to the astonishment of the town people. They could barely believe their luck of having the privilege of meeting two princes on the same day, a story that would surely be told for generations to come.

Once all the formalities were over and the princes and their group were fed and refreshed, Niran relayed to them the tragedies that had befallen Ile-Ife and the plight of the kingdom. All the elders and prominent citizens present listened fearfully as Toju made it known that there was a possibility that Olise's soldiers would eventually find their way to Ilesha.

'You are certain of this?' asked Gbenga. 'There could be a chance that Olise's men might not come this far to find you?'

'That is a possibility but, as long as we are alive, the people will not accept him as king. He has already shown that he'll stop at nothing to claim the throne,' Niran pointed out.

'Then we must hide you until we can gain some allies to challenge him. King Jide may yet defeat him in the field, then it would only be a matter of time before he marches back to the capital to take back the city,' said one of the other elders, a comment which was met by agreement from some of the other men present.

'But what if the king is defeated? What then? Are we willing to stake the lives of the people of Ilesha on this hope? We are but a small town with no army or walls to defend us. The only way we have survived is by giving our unwavering support to whoever is seated on the throne. I wouldn't want to gamble our future on falsehood.' This was mentioned by a wealthy looking man who turned out to be the head of commerce. He was clearly only interested in self-preservation and lining his own pouches.

'What is your name?' asked Toju. The man looked irritated, but he responded, 'My name is Soji. I only state the obvious.'

'You, Soji, are nothing but a fool,' Toju said, cutting him off. 'You think Olise would simply allow you to go about your life without demanding his pound of flesh? He will fall upon this town with spear and fire, more so for any township that has supported my father in the past, no matter how large or small,' Toju sneered.

Niran, as always, tried to play the diplomat. 'Look, we do not mean to spread fear, but what my brother says is true. We only seek to prepare you for what is to come and give you a chance at survival,' he said.

'Why should we listen to you?' Soji asked, and looked to the other men of Ilesha gathered in the room. None of them met his eye, showing that he wasn't a popular man, but he rambled on regardless.

'Why should we have to suffer because of a royal squabble that has nothing to do with us? We could simply hold you here until Olise's army arrive and trade you for our peace.' Soji realised too late that he had strayed over the threshold of arrogant posturing into open threats.

Toju smiled like a wolf that had picked up the scent of its prey and Niran shook his head sadly. 'You would dare to threaten a crowned prince of Ile-Ife? Toju asked. Soji's smug expression vanished in a second as the realisation hit him like a blow to the face. Again, he looked at his peers hoping that someone would speak up for him, but they all seemed extremely interested in anything else in the room; a lizard scurrying across the floor, a fly buzzing lazily in the room, anything but Soji.

He swallowed hard and dropped to his knees before the prince. 'My prince, please forgive me; I was speaking out of fear. I implore you.'

'Enough,' Toju said, and raised an eyebrow at Leke, who immediately drew his sword and brought it down in the gap between Soji's neck and shoulder blade, spraying blood all over the floor and the stone walls.

The men of Ilesha all cried out in unison, but the men of Ife hardly even blinked at the sudden act of violence. Soji had died almost instantly, without a sound. He slumped face first to the ground and Leke had to place his foot upon the dead man's shoulder to pry his sword free.

133

'This fool is not worthy to die by my hand. The coward,' Toju said. 'I didn't wish to spill blood here as you have welcomed us and shown us every courtesy, but I will not have men talk to me or any member of the royal blood in that fashion.'

Niran stood and addressed the elders, who visibly shrank back before him. 'We do not wish to bring you harm,' he said. 'But you must understand our position, we cannot simply allow remarks like that to go unanswered. You would do the same if you were threatened as we are. Do you know what it's like to have to flee your home for fear of assassination? Or to witness the deaths of people you know, people you love?' He glanced at Toju who gave him an almost imperceptible nod.

When he turned back to the men before him, his soft features and hazel brown eyes had taken on a hard edge. 'So, you can understand that we must root out any threat to the royal blood line.'

Gbenga was the first of the elders to speak and he did so with grace and courtesy. 'My prince, I cannot claim to understand your plight, but this town is also now in danger and may very well share the same fate as Ile-Ife. I still elect to keep you safe, as is our duty to the royal household.'

'Thank you, baba, but no,' said Toju. 'We do not wish to inconvenience you any more than we already have. If you can spare food, fresh water and some clean clothing, we will be on our way.'

'Where would you go?' asked one of the other elders. Niran, reluctant to provide much information said, 'It is better if you don't know, baba, that way you are protected if you are ever questioned. Besides, we wouldn't want to burden you with such details.'

The elders generously provided enough horses for all of them, which was probably half of the horses in the town, and as the sun began to set in the west, the ten men left the town with enough provisions to last them a week or more.

When they were a few miles out from Ilesha, Toju brought the party to a halt and ordered everyone to dismount and walk their horses further into the forest and away from the main road. When he

134

was satisfied that they were out of sight, they made camp just as the moon rose to illuminate their surroundings.

'Niran, I think we should stick to father's plan and split up. You should take half of the men and travel east to Imo and the Riverlands. I am sure you will find support there with the chiefs of those regions. They will keep you safe until we are ready to return in greater numbers,' Toju said.

Niran had been dreading this conversation, but he knew that the time would come when he would need to part ways with his brother. It was not safe to travel together lest they were captured, and all hopes of reclaiming the kingdom would be lost. If at least one of them were to make it, that would ensure that Olise would never be accepted as the rightful king.

He looked at his brother in the moonlight for a long time and Toju waited patiently as he could sense his brother's trepidation. Finally, Niran nodded and asked, 'So, you will go north, brother?'

'Yes, I will. I'm certain I will find refuge with the emir, and he would surely support our cause. Within a year, I suspect that, between us, we could raise an army of considerable power, but for now we must stay alive. That is what father and mother would have wanted.'

Tears came to Niran's eyes unbidden as he contemplated Toju's words. He agreed with everything he had said but it didn't make the decision any easier. Leke, who was sitting close by, spoke up.

'That is the safest course of action. One year will pass quickly, and you will both be reunited in strength. These men will give their lives to protect you and see your inheritance restored.' He gestured to the soldiers arrayed about the camp. 'And the gods will protect us all.'

As dawn broke, they chose their men, dividing their party into two, and said their farewells. Toju and Niran embraced for a long time, each not wanting to let the other go, but they had talked it through in length and were resigned to what needed to be done. When they finally broke their embrace, Toju took Niran's face in his hands, looking into his brother's hazel eyes, determined to sear the vision of this moment into the fabric of his memory. 'Stay safe, little brother, *Olodumare* protect you,' he said.

Niran held back tears as he said the same. '*Ogun* protect you, brother.' They parted ways with heavy hearts, not knowing if they would ever see each other again, Toju setting off towards the relatively unknown north and Niran to the east.

* * * *

Enitan and Ayo had been travelling nonstop for a week since leaving Ile-Ife. They had cut a course southwest through forests that gave way to dense jungle. They hunted as they travelled and made good progress across the vast uninhabited landscape.

The jungle they travelled was known to be home to numerous deadly predators and Ayo was at first sceptical of travelling through it, however, they were left with little choice but to brave the wilderness, or take their chances with the soldiers that still hunted them, who wouldn't dare to cross the threshold of the forest. And yet by some miracle, they were never in any danger.

It was almost as if they were guided by some unseen hand; they had lost count of seeing packs of hyenas or lone cheetahs or leopards stalk away from them as they approached. The same could be said about the snakes and crocodiles as they would only catch a glimpse of their tails as they slithered away in the undergrowth or swamps.

This only went further to confirming Ayo's suspicions about the child he travelled with and the change that had been wrought in him in the forests of Ife.

Men rarely ventured into these parts. In the past, scores of hunters and poachers had entered the jungles with aspirations of great adventure and fame, only never to return, leaving behind grieving families. This would not, so it seemed, be the fate of the young prince.

Hunting was also unnaturally easy for them; wild boar would suddenly appear and offer no resistance to being caught and slain for food and over the past week, they had never been wanting for nourishment.

Enitan had been solemn for most of the journey, hardly talking, and he cried himself to sleep most nights, but the boy was strong and rose every morning to face the day with the same grim determination as facing a wall of spears.

They eventually crossed Ile-Ife's borders, bringing them closer to the lands of his mother, Lara, and within reach of civilisation. It was comforting to be away from the so-called perils of the jungle and into the relative safety of the forest, but they now had new threats to contend with. Man.

Care was taken to avoid large groups of travellers and anyone looking suspicious, but the young men inevitably attracted attention and curious looks, despite Ayo's efforts to blend into their surroundings – begriming themselves with dirt, wearing ragged cloaks over their armour - presumably it was the swords and daggers they carried that were poorly concealed.

Despite Enitan's age, it was easy to tell that he wasn't the typical village child. He carried himself with a certain poise that made him stand apart from children his age, or older, in fact, and Ayo constantly had to remind him to change his gait and shuffle along less purposefully like most of the people they encountered.

They saw a few poverty-stricken settlements, hovels made from mud and tree branches with thatched roofs and the people spoke the broken Yoruba of the poor and uneducated.

Some were friendly and offered them food and water in exchange for other items. Enitan gave away a silver pin attached to his leather armour to one of the villagers for an assortment of food stock freshly harvested that very day, water and a donkey to bear the load. The villager was so happy at receiving such a "treasure" that he also offered the hand of his daughter, which they politely declined.

One particular village that they came upon was more peculiar than the rest. They had been travelling for several weeks now and noticed the settlement nestled in a small grove, so they followed the path leading to the village with the intention of gathering information from the locals, now that they felt safe enough not to be recognised. This had been what they had done for the last few stops they made.

On approaching the village, they heard a cacophony of noise and saw a crowd of people waving sticks and palm leaves around ecstatically. 'It might be better to avoid this one, Enitan. The people seem quite excitable and it's probably not the best idea to give them a reason to turn that sort of enthusiasm on us,' said Ayo, but Enitan, ever the curious child, only became more intrigued.

'I want a see what's happening. It's been weeks since we've seen anything more exciting than a village girl balancing coconuts on her head, so I want to know what all the commotion is about.' Ayo rolled his eyes but checked his weapons all the same and secured the donkey's harness to a tree before agreeing to investigate further.

'Stay alert, my prince, you can never really trust the common people, they would sooner sell you for food if given half the chance.'

Enitan smiled his innocent smile showing a glimpse of mischief like the child he had been before their ordeal. 'Come, don't be an old woman, besides, you're here to protect me and I'm sure you can handle a few villagers.' He barely waited for a response before he set off towards the crowd and Ayo took a final look at the donkey before following.

The closer they got to the crowd, the more they noticed that things weren't as jovial as they had appeared to be from a distance; the people in the crowd were shouting, but not with jubilance. No. The tone was unmistakeable, it was one of anger mixed with fear.

Ayo reached out to hold Enitan back, but the young prince had also sensed the difference in the atmosphere and had practically slowed to a halt. The crowd, now only a few yards away from them, seemed to be concentrating on something in their centre; a ring was formed around it and, on closer inspection, the people were all taking turns to strike down with their sticks and canes at whatever was within the circle.

Enitan took a closer look, with Ayo right behind him, and just about made out the prone figure of a young girl, who didn't seem

138

much older than him, through the legs of the angry mob. Without a second thought, he let out a command that rang loud and clear.

'Stop hitting that child now!' he roared, the tone of his voice so harsh that it took even Ayo by surprise, never had he heard the young prince speak with such authority and conviction.

Everyone froze and scanned the area for the source of the voice, finally resting on the two young individuals. There must have been about twenty people, men and women, and they had slightly parted, revealing the battered girl covered in bruises and dirt now in a fetal position.

'What is the meaning of this? How dare you all, grown as you are, attack a defenceless child? I demand an answer now!' Enitan seethed. Ayo had never seen the prince like this in all the years he had known him. He was like a boy possessed. His hands were balled up by his side and he was breathing very hard from the rise and fall of his shoulders.

Ayo glanced at the crowd and saw that there were looks of disbelief mingled with astonishment plastered on their faces, which was now slowly giving way to anger and indignation.

The villagers, however, just stood there transfixed at the child before them until Enitan demanded a response for the second time. 'Speak up, you cowards! Have you all lost your tongues?'

The spell was broken. One of the male villagers spoke up in broken Yoruba, clearly outraged by the manner at which the prince had addressed them. 'Who does this boy think he is talking to like that? He has no respect for his elders, eh?' he asked the crowd. 'You better disappear from our sight before we teach you a lesson like this witch!' said another and more of them agreed.

'This doesn't concern you child,' a woman in the crowd said. 'You better leave before you upset these people, you don't want the same fate as this one.' Indicating the girl.

'I will only say it once more. Leave her alone!' Enitan said in a low and threatening voice.

By this time all the attention was directed at him and the crowd began to turn towards him bearing their sticks and canes. 'We will show you pepper today, you spoilt little rat!' someone said and in smaller groups they began to walk towards the prince.

There was no turning back now. They were committed. So, Ayo did the only thing left to do, he let his ragged clock fall to the ground and drew his sword and dagger, allowing the lengths of iron in his hands to reflect in the waning sunlight. 'I must warn you,' Ayo said, speaking loud enough for his voice to carry, 'if any of you lay a hand on this young man, be prepared to lose that hand.' He finished with a wicked smile on his face. In truth, Ayo was a little excited at the prospect of a fight; he always was, especially after weeks of relative quiet.

Enitan had not moved from where he stood and he showed no sign of fear as he concentrated on the crowd and suddenly, what little sunlight remained of the day vanished under dark clouds. The wind around them picked up and the sound of thunder could be heard rumbling in the distance.

The crowd only faltered for a moment before focusing back on Enitan until someone, just beyond the crowd, shouted 'Stop!' causing everyone including Enitan and Ayo to turn around or strain their necks.

The crowd parted and a balding old man with a white beard leaning on a walking stick hobbled forward, he paused for a split second to look at the girl still on the ground now slowly rising on her elbow, before walking past the crowd to stand close to Enitan.

Ayo had already placed himself between the crowd and Enitan. 'That is far enough, old man, unless you want to be the first to see the gods.'

White beard didn't seem to have heard Ayo as all his attention was directed to Enitan. He looked on fearfully and extended a shaky, accusing finger at Enitan, who noticed that half of his small finger was missing. 'You have the mark on you! Leave this place, we do not wish to provoke his wrath!'

His words caused everyone in the crowd to look at each other in confusion, prompting more chatter amongst them.

Ayo never took his eyes away from white beard but now he looked over his shoulder at Enitan, who had not so much as moved from where he stood. Enitan's expression was still one of anger, but he wasn't as tense as he had been a few minutes ago.

'What will you have from us?' white beard asked, clearly trying his best to diffuse the tension. 'Give me the girl,' Enitan said and some people in the crowed immediately started to protest. 'But she is a witch, we can't just let her go!' one exclaimed. 'She deserves jungle justice, what if she comes back to lay a curse on us and our children?' cried another fearfully.

White beard only raised his hand to the crowd silencing them instantly. 'If this is the price we pay for our lives, it is one that I can live with. Leave at once,' he said, turning to the girl, who rose unsteadily to her feet and began to limp off towards Enitan and Ayo.

'Do not think of following us; if you value your lives, it is best you forget about us, but more to the point, forget about what has happened here today,' said Ayo as he sheathed his dagger and used his free hand to help the wounded girl.

Only when the girl was close enough to Enitan and out of danger did he unclench his fists and the dark clouds seemed to recede, revealing the last light of dusk. Enitan simply turned his back and began to walk towards their tethered donkey.

When they were away from the village and into the relative safety of the forest, Ayo turned to Enitan as he put away his sword. 'Are you going to tell me what just happened back there?' he asked with a raised eyebrow. Enitan only shrugged his shoulders like the child he was, and said, 'I don't know what came over me. It was as if someone else spoke in my place and I watched from a distance. I can't explain it.'

'And the girl? Do you think she really is a witch?' Ayo asked, gesturing towards the girl who stood solemnly looking at her bare feet. 'Is it true what the villagers said about you?' Enitan asked her.

She briefly looked up but avoided meeting any of their eyes. 'It is all lies. I have always been an outcast there. I'm from one of the neighbouring villages but my people along with my parents were killed in a dispute over some land with these villagers some years ago. One of the elders took pity on me and took me in, but he died a week ago. Since then, most of the villagers have looked for an excuse to get rid of me. Calling me a witch was the easiest way.'

Both Ayo and Enitan were moved by her story, but Ayo, ever the sceptic, suggested escorting her only to the next village.

Enitan disagreed. 'We can't just leave her there. What if the same fate befalls her? Then it's back to square one. She will travel with us.'

'But my pri-' Ayo had to catch himself before the words escaped his lips. 'Enitan, she can't travel with us, you know the dangers involved.'

Enitan was having none of it. 'Father always said realm and people before self, we have to protect her and if that means taking her with us, then that's what we must do'. Ayo inclined his head in acceptance, seeing the wisdom in the prince's words. 'We need to find a suitable place to make camp, it will be dark soon,' he said and began to gather their things. Before long they were travelling west.

They found a suitable place to lay their ragged cloaks, which doubled as blankets for them to sleep on. Enitan offered his own to the girl, who had still not told them her name, but he was content that he was keeping her safe.

'In the morning, we will find a stream or river for you to wash your wounds and clean up.' Enitan said and the girl just nodded and rolled over in his rags, falling asleep almost instantly. Enitan watched her for a few minutes then went to sleep himself with Ayo sitting on the ground against a rock next to him.

Enitan woke up a few hours later with a start. Although he didn't recall the details, he knew he had had a troubled dream filled with mysteries.

Ayo was still next to him, snoring softly with his sword between his legs and his hand on the hilt. This brought a smile to Enitan's face as he regarded his lifelong protector. The sun had already started to rise and pale fingers of light illuminated their surroundings.

Then he remembered the girl from the day before and turned around to look at her, but she was not there. In her place was a black dog, sitting with its front paws crossed. There was something familiar about the dog, then he realised, it was the eyes. Suddenly the dog rose and ran off deeper into the forest while Enitan looked on.

HE WHO HOLDS THE SPEAR

The earth was blackened for as far as the eye could see in every direction. Nothing had been left to grow; not a blade of grass nor sheaf of wheat remained in the many miles of open fields Jide's army had travelled. All that was left was ashes under their sandals and the dust that proceeded every footfall.

As if that was not bad enough, every source of water they came across had been poisoned; decaying carcasses of livestock, bloated with corruption, floated in the streams and rivers, and every well they happened to come across was filled with human excrement when the pails were drawn from deep below the ground.

This had done no good for the morale of the men, as supplies had continued to dwindle to meagre rations and discontent was rife amongst the ranks. The strength of the army was depleting; almost a third of Jide's army had been sent back to reclaim Ile-Ife after learning the fate of the city and out of the remaining forces, a quarter had either been lost to dysentery from drinking the tainted waters, or desertion.

Despite all these setbacks, Jide pressed on, determined to stop at nothing until he was at the gates of Benin City. His staunch supporters were with him and would sooner drop dead on the march before they turned their backs on the king. That was all the reassurance Jide needed, along with the blessings of the gods and the strength of his right arm.

The army stopped a day out from Benin to gather what was left of their strength before the final confrontation, and Jide called all his generals to his tent for their last council before the drums of war changed the course of their lives forever.

Akin and Olusegun were there as well as Dare, Adedeji and Rotimi – the chief of Owo. There were also several lesser vassal lords and captains present. The men in the tent stood around stone-faced. Everyone knew that the scale of odds had tipped against them and the nightmare that would succeed the dawn. Despite this reality, every one of them was determined to fulfil their duties to their king and kingdom.

'My generals, the hour is almost upon us. It has been a long journey fraught with hardship and tomorrow will be no easier, but I don't need to tell you that.' Jide looked at each man in the eye as he spoke.

'We have lost men and we are but a fraction of the strength we were when we marched proudly out of our villages, towns and cities, but this cannot be a deterrent for true children of Ile-Ife.'

'Olise is not one of us, he doesn't have our values or our honour. He is a man who wages war on innocent women and children, slaughtering and burning them in their homes. This is no warrior. Tomorrow we will right the wrong he has done to the families. To those he has left orphaned or destitute. To all of our people who have suffered at his hands.'

'When the blood has spilt, the dust settled and the god of war, *Ogun*, has had his fill of fallen souls from the battle, what will they say of the men of Ile-Ife? What will they say of your king? I may have lost everything. My sons, my wife...' Jide faltered for a second at the thought of his beautiful wife. Her smile. Her touch...

'But I will not lose my dignity or my honour. And if the goddess *Yemoja* should have it that the Adelani bloodline would end tomorrow, then I intend to go to her willingly with Olise to accompany me on the journey.'

Adedeji, the head of the council of ten, was the first to speak up. 'Kabiyesi, do not for a minute think you are alone in this. The Modakeke will be at your side wherever you choose to place your feet. If, as you say, the gods have deemed it is your time to fall, it will be on top of our broken bodies, and we will walk with you to the underworld.'

Every man in the tent held Jide's eye and nodded or repeated the words "it will be so". The love and pride he felt in that instant threatened to burst his heart where he stood and end the war before it even started. He glanced over his shoulder at Akin, who wore a smile on the side of his face. He knew the old warrior was undoubtedly excited about the prospect of a great battle at dawn. This comforted him further. If he was to cast the stones, he could not imagine better men to stand with.

Olusegun seemed distracted. He kept looking towards the entrance of the tent and Jide noticed it, he saw everything. Jide walked over to his old friend. 'This is a lot to ask of you, old man, I know. If you wish to take your leave I will understand. You do not have to fight this battle.

Olusegun looked truly hurt by these words and Jide had a flashback of the wily old warrior he had been. 'Kabiyesi, with all due respect, do not insult me. I swore my oath to you and your father before you to give my spear when it is needed, and I have answered the summons. My place is with you, I will speak no more on this subject.'

'Something does bother me, though. The camp is unnaturally quiet, do you not think? It felt as if half of the camp fell silent suddenly.' Jide had not noticed the drop in the noise, but now he strained his ears for sounds of an active camp with over three thousand men.

He gestured for quiet in the tent and the men around him seemed to sense the change in mood immediately. 'What is the problem, my king?' asked Dare. 'It sounds like a peaceful camp,' he finished.

'That is exactly the problem, it should not be this quiet,' said Olusegun.

Akin stood and stepped towards the entrance of the tent. 'Guards!' He bellowed, the flap instantly parted and two soldiers stepped into the empty space.

'My chiefs?' one of them asked expectantly.

'Have you seen anything suspicious?' Adedeji asked, beginning to flex his shoulder.

'Nothing, chief.' The same guard responded with a small bow.

'I will see for myself. Please return to your tents and see to your men,' Jide said as he picked up his sword and headed for the open flaps held by the two guards. Everyone in the tent followed behind the king into the warm evening breeze.

There were a few soldiers around busying themselves with their evening chores, but something was off. Some of the men in sight moved sluggishly and others were asleep in random places and positions; sprawled out on the ground, against a tree, and one appeared to have fallen asleep over a bush and seemed to be as comfortable as if he lay upon a bed of reeds.

Suddenly, a fog appeared overhead moving slowly through the air and spreading out over the camp. Olusegun noticed it first and sniffed the air briefly before yelling at the top of his voice. 'This is witchcraft! Cover your nose, do not inhale!'

Everyone in earshot looked over to where Segun was pointing and now saw what was giving the old warrior concern. They all began to hurriedly cover their faces with parts of their clothing. One of the captains stripped down to his loin cloth, wrapping his attire around his whole head, only leaving his eyes visible, and many of the soldiers followed suit.

'My king, please take shelter in your tent until the fog passes, we will try to divert it,' said Dare, and men were already gathering large pieces of cloth or any flat object to hand and starting to beat the air frantically in a bid to fan away whatever this thing was.

Their efforts seemed to be paying off as the fog began to disperse and thin out against the fanning motions of all the men who laboured as if their lives depended on it. The king had not fled, instead had stood by his men and helped as a good king would.

Luckily, the fog had only come from one direction, leaving the rest of the camp unscathed; however, everyone in its path had succumbed to whatever black magic – or *juju* as it was referred to by the Yoruba tribes – it was.

'I somehow doubt that this was a random act or one without purpose,' said Akin, and Jide was thinking the same.

'Guards, summon twenty of the Modakeke here now, I believe our camp has been infiltrated,' Adedeji said as he looked in the direction of the fog.

All the men around followed Adedeji's gaze and as they watched, men started to emerge from the camp behind. At first, there seemed to be only a handful of men, and then ten, twenty, thirty men stood yards away from the men of Ile-Ife, the king's tent being the only object between them.

The newcomers all wore the distinctive black dyed leather armour Olise favoured, and as they advanced, they were dispatching soldiers asleep in their path with quick sword or spear thrusts to their heart.

One of the king's guards set off without any further prompting, deep into the unaffected section of the camp to rouse the king's troops, but it might be too late. Jide and his generals were too few and would easily be overwhelmed. The only advantage they possessed was that together, they were probably the best fighting force ever assembled, all veterans of over sixty actions between them.

Jide and those around him drew their swords or hefted their spears almost in unison, piercing the air around. 'I see I have underestimated Olise once again,' said Jide.

'A good plan,' Adedeji conceded, 'if a treacherous one. Remind me to tell Olise when we cross spears with him in the morning.'

'And what makes you so sure you'll live long enough to see him?' Akin asked with a smile on his face.

'I will, O, I'm not destined to die in this wasteland, but old and grey with all my sons and wives about me.' Adedeji responded returning Akin's smile.

'You're already old and grey!' said Dare, and all the men who stood by the king laughed even in the face of imminent death.

All the king's men formed a protective wedge around him as if this was a dance they were all too more familiar with. Akin stood at his right shoulder as always, with Olusegun at his left, and Adedeji stood at the head of the spear grinning as if he was about to receive a great gift.

The newcomers came in closer but seemed to hesitate for a moment at the sight of the soldiers arrayed before them. They were expecting the unopposed slaughter of sleeping men, and only now realised that they faced the best fighting men in the realm, but their confidence was restored by their numbers, and some of the hardier warriors amongst them let out war cries and surged forward.

Instinctively, the soldiers either side of Adedeji who bore the traditional oval shaped shields of the tribes, brought them forward, and Jide roared out a command to ready spears. Just before Olise's men crossed the threshold of the king's tent, twelve spears were cast at the attackers, cutting the air like the wings of black ravens and delivering death at their tips.

Twelve men fell instantly, the unlucky ones screaming and fouling the advance of the men behind, causing them to stumble and trample on their fallen comrades. Seconds later the first line of running men came into contact with the men of Ile-Ife.

Adedeji's sword moved like a living thing, and men fell at his feet with every flick of his wrist. All the while he laughed nonchalantly as though he was merely in a training session, as he sent men screaming into the afterlife.

One of the shield bearers at his side suddenly fell with a spear in his guts and the wedge of men surrounding the king momentarily lost some of its cohesion before another one of Jide's captains moved forward to fill the gap.

The fighting was fierce for a few heartbeats as Jide's men fought off wave after wave of men and somehow, despite their lesser numbers, seemed to have the advantage.

Olise's men soon began to approach the fight more tactically and started to spread out towards the flanks, but they had lost their momentum and half of their number were dead or pouring their lifeblood into the soil. Jide's small force had only lost three men so far, and now started to press their opponents back, maintaining good order.

Adedeji was still at the spearhead of the men, now covered in blood and gore as he continued to wreak havoc in the ranks of men before him like an avenging angel. Suddenly, there was a growing rumble of voices coming from behind Jide. He dispatched a large soldier with an overhead strike to the throat and took a quick glance over his shoulder in time to see some of the Modakeke and other soldiers of Ile-Ife racing to the aid of their king.

Jide felt the tide of war change instantly as if the fight had flowed out of their opponents like sand through a sieve. At that moment, Jide gave the order to break formation and now he and Akin could finally let loose and enact some of their vengeance on Olise.

No one could stand against the king as he struck blow after blow, each strike deadlier than the last, and Olise's men soon broke and began to retreat as the rest of the camp came to life and ran down the enemy.

Jide addressed two captains, 'Bring me prisoners to question and kill the rest. I will not have men sending word back to Olise. The only message he will receive will be one of my choosing. And report back on our casualties.' 'Yes, Kabiyesi,' the men answered before setting off to carry out the king's orders.

Still panting from the fight, Jide turned to the men who had stood by his side; Akin, Adedeji, Dare, Rotimi, Olusegun and a handful of lesser chiefs and captains. None of them appeared to have taken any wounds and he sent a silent prayer to *Yemoja*, thankful for her protection.

'Do you now see the lengths Olise is willing to go to to ensure a clear path to the throne? This is exactly why he is not fit to rule. For him, the end certainly justifies the means, and he will use any opportunity to reach his goal. No honour, no warrior code, just deceit and treachery,' Jide said sadly.

'Well, at least we know it will be a dirty fight, so we should plan for it accordingly. If you ask me, I say we fight fire with fire.' Olusegun said looking at the bodies of Olise's men littering the floor.

'Please, Segun, speak plainly. At this point, I am open to any suggestions,' Jide finished. The other generals were also intrigued to know what the old chief had in mind.

'We could disguise some of our men as Olise's soldiers to infiltrate the city. Once they are inside the walls, they could open the gates to the rest of the army lying in wait,' he said.

'Not a bad idea, but I doubt we could move the army close enough without being discovered. Besides, he's probably cleared all the surrounding bushes, so he has clear visibility for miles beyond the walls,' Akin put in.

'There may be some merit in this plan,' Jide interjected. 'Olise probably won't suspect it, but I'm sure he didn't expect these men to succeed either, only to deal a crippling blow to our army.'

At that moment, one of the captains he had spoken to earlier returned to give Jide the report. 'Kabiyesi, we have lost close to forty men, maybe more. It is hard to know exactly, but we have also managed to capture thirteen of the intruders. The rest were killed.'

Jide was disheartened by the heavy death toll. He needed all the men he had if he was to have a chance at winning this war. 'Thank you. Bring the prisoners to me, I will have my answers now.'

'Yes, Kabiyesi,' said the captain as he sent for the captured men to be brought forward.

Within moments, thirteen men were frogmarched to the king with their hands bound, looking despondent. They were a miserable looking bunch, most of them bore marks and bruises that they had received courtesy of the king's men and on behalf of the soldiers they had killed in their sleep.

It was obvious they were all resigned to the fact that there was no tomorrow for them.

Jide walked in between the kneeling men, staring down each of them in turn as he went past. 'You all must know that your lives are now forfeit since you dared to attempt to assassinate your king, but you have the chance to choose the manner of your death if you tell me what I need to hear. Deny me this and I will make what is left of your lives a slow and agonising one.'

Some of the men started to plead for mercy and a swift end, but there were a few amongst them who appeared defiant and fearless. Those were the men that Jide singled out. He turned to the captain. 'These men show no sign of remorse, but I will have them begging for the mercy of the blade before we march in the morning.'

151

'Yes, Kabiyesi,' said the soldier understanding the king's meaning.

Those men would be tortured until they pleaded for the peace only death could offer. The rest of the captives told Jide everything he needed to know about Olise's plans and his strength. They were executed cleanly and quickly, as Jide had promised, along with receiving the king's forgiveness for betraying the throne and the realm.

The agonised and tortured screams of the remaining prisoners could be heard long into the night. In the end, they all pleaded for the sword just as Jide had foretold. They were denied this peace. It was only granted when they were beyond pain, beyond sanity, unable to voice their anguish.

Hardly anyone slept in the camp that night, choosing instead to stay up to watch the beauty of the sunrise, as they knew that for most, this would be the last time.

SEEDS OF DECEIT

Zogo gazed into the darkness over the fields beyond the walls of the city. He had been in Benin for over a month now and couldn't help but think of the family he had left behind in his home state.

He missed his wife and daughter; the scent of palm trees carried by the morning breeze; the warmth of his own bed, but most of all he missed his firstborn son, who was probably languishing in a cell in Aba, one of Olise's strongholds somewhere in the southeast. The thought alone made his blood boil and he was still tormented by not having foreseen the heavy price he had paid to ensure his continued support of Olise's campaign.

The memory of the day he had been summoned to Benin under false pretences, along with the other River tribesmen, still burned. His son, along with countless others, had been taken when the chiefs of the east and the River-lands had answered the call to arms, leaving only the elderly, women and children to fend for themselves, unable to stop Olise's men as they swept through the towns and villages rounding up hostages.

Some of the mothers protested and put up a good fight, only to be struck down with spear shafts and threatened with the sharp ends if further resistance was offered. The children were eventually ripped from their grasps, leaving many households empty.

The affront had not been forgotten, and couldn't go unanswered. One way or another, Zogo and a few other River tribesmen had vowed to visit the same fate on Olise and his family. The wheels of their plan for retribution had now been set in motion.

Secrecy could never be entirely assured, as Olise had spies all over the city, but Zogo had gone to great lengths to ensure that he was not followed as he stood on the battlements surrounding the city. Looking out with his arms folded, at his back stood three of his most loyal captains; men who would gladly give their lives before they betrayed their liege lord.

As they waited in silence, more men began to appear on the ramparts slowly making their way towards Zogo. These were hard men; the scars they bore told stories of violence and war. They were the Igbos and River tribe. When they reached within earshot, Zogo addressed them with his back still turned.

'I trust you were not followed?' he asked in their native tongue of Igbo. The first man to speak was Nnamdi, a big man, and a strong warrior. He was a cousin of Zogo's and they both had love, respect, and trust for each other. 'I'm sure of it, but if we were, I wouldn't worry too much about it. We are simply checking the defences and anticipating which direction King Jide will attack from, right?'

'Indeed,' said one of the other men, a River chief from Akwa-Ibom named Edem the ugly, for the scars across his face and the darkness in his heart. 'But I'm not concerned with Olise's spies; don't forget that without our combined power, his great army is nothing. Our men outnumber his by at least two to one.'

'That may be the case, but he holds our children. Do you think he will hesitate to slit their throats if he suspects we are plotting against him? I'm not willing to gamble the lives of my daughters to find out,' said another River chief called Akpan the just.

'Always the cautious one, Akpan. Your wife is young, she can still bear you more children. My pride, however, can only be restored with Olise's blood on my sword and his name removed from our history,' Edem sneered.

Zogo turned around to face the men for the first time. He had a fierce look in his eyes, one that Nnamdi had seen before. Zogo regarded each of the chiefs before him, finally settling on his cousin, favouring him with an almost imperceptible nod, before turning back to the one known as the ugly.

'Edem, I hear your words and there is some truth in them, but Akpan speaks wisdom; the lives of our children cannot be thrown away needlessly if it can be avoided. I propose we keep him close as we have done, until an opportunity presents itself. Besides, I'd like the fighting to have started before we reveal our hand.'

Edem spat over the battlements showing his disgust. 'I'm tired of playing the good soldier. We've been sitting on our hands for over one moon now when we could easily slaughter Olise and all his men in their sleep. Zogo, the time for waiting is over. Let's end this now.'

Akpan shook his head and Nnamdi looked over at his cousin expectantly, knowing that he would be the voice of reason. He trusted Zogo's instincts unreservedly. His word had always proven right in the past and his guidance was needed now more than ever.

'I think that would be a mistake,' said Zogo. 'Now is the time to exercise caution. There is too much at stake; not just the fate of our families but also that of the entire kingdom. We all agree that Olise cannot ascend the throne. It would spell the end of everything we hold dear; our traditions, our beliefs and our sovereignty. King Jide has always given us a free hand to rule over our respective lands as we see fit, provided we maintain his peace. That concession will be lost with Olise.'

'So, we are in agreement that Olise must die? Then why wait when we could end this war before we all lose good men?' snapped Edem.

'It is not that simple; he is guarded day and night by his trusted men. Besides, if the rumours are to be believed, he is protected by his mother's witchcraft. Don't tell me you're so naïve as to think she doesn't wield some sort of *juju* and have a hand in all of this?' Nnamdi added, drawing nods from some of the other men present.

'Plus, we can't deny the king his justice. He alone has the right to enact whatever punishment he deems suitable on Olise after everything that has happened in Ile-Ife,' said Akpan.

'By the gods!' Edem blasphemed, 'Why wait for the king when we can do his work for him? Are you telling me he won't be grateful if we present Olise's head to him, rather than wait for a pitched battle? Who knows how this will all end if we stay our swords?' he asked, looking at all the men around him in turn, but no one seemed to agree with him.

155

'I think you are all cowards. If I must be the one to wet my blade with Olise's blood, so be it. I'll end this war before it has a chance to sprout wings,' Edem said determinately.

'I cannot stop you, but I would advise you against it. Think about the rest of us, your tribesmen. If you fail, we all fail. Do you at least understand that?' asked Zogo, trying to appeal to Edem.

'I cannot fail!' he snapped. 'Olise is no match for me, neither is his dog, Dimeji. I will have both their heads before the sun rises.'

Zogo relented. 'Do as you will, and may the gods be with you whatever your choice is. But the rest of us will not be a part of this plan lest our plot is discovered, and all is lost. The only thing I would ask of you is that if the worst were to happen and everything fails, as a contingency, please leave instructions for your men to follow me or one of the other chiefs here.'

Edem glared at his tribesman. 'Now why would I do a thing like that? Do you wish me ill and truly believe I will fall? Has this been your plan all along, to take control of my domain? Why would I just hand you Akwa-Ibom on a plate? With my men, any one of you would easily have the biggest force in the east, and what would stop you then from claiming my lands for your own, denying my bloodline?'

'If your plan fails you won't have a bloodline!' Akpan exclaimed. 'Olise has your firstborn and I'm told your second son is a sickly child unable to master his coughing fits, let alone your lands!'

'You dare insult me!' Edem reached for the dagger at his hip, but Nnamdi stepped between the two chiefs before things could escalate further.

'Don't be a fool, Edem, do you really think we would wish your downfall, especially when so much is at stake? I know you are a cold-hearted bastard, but you're still of the River-lands, as are we,' said Nnamdi calmly.

'You have my word, Edem, I have no ambitions to rule over your people. If anything, I'd want to ensure that your lands and the townspeople are provided for if the worst should happen. But, like I said, you don't have to go through with your plan. Let's all be reasonable and wait for a better opportunity, one that will guarantee all our safety and success,' Zogo said, diffusing the tension slightly.

Edem stared at Zogo for a long moment, then finally cracked a broad smile; it was a terrible sight – as if *Esu*, the trickster god or devil, himself, turned all his attention on him.

'Very well. I will heed your counsel and wait a while longer. But know this, the first clear opportunity I get with Olise I aim to take it regardless of the consequences,' he said, removing his hand from the hilt of his dagger.

'That is fair enough, and thank you for reasoning with us. I'm told that the king is not long from the wall of the city, so our wait may soon be over. Let us all rest, for who knows what the day ahead brings?' Zogo griped the forearm of each of the chiefs in turn as was the way in their tribe, before all the men dispersed leaving him alone once again with his captains.

He turned back to the horizon as the first sign of dawn slowly crept over the vast land surrounding the walls. Lands that would eventually be saturated with the blood of many a brave man. Lands that would no longer bear crops for many years to come.

* * * *

'Jide yet lives. I am beginning to think that the gods have not forsaken him after all. No matter. He will not live to see another moon, so you have nothing to fear, my son,' said Ekaete as she peered into a calabash, which appeared to reveal to her the message she relayed to Olise.

They both sat in the great hall of the palace in Benin surrounded by his guards, who stood silently in the shadows like statues overlooking their prince. Since the gathering of Olise's commanders, Ekaete had persuaded him to increase the number of trusted men around him for fear that, as the battle loomed, some of the chiefs may still harbour a kindling of doubt in their hearts that could easily be stoked into a raging fire of guilt. The guilt of abandoning their true king, Jide. A guilt that may yet tempt them to forsake their vows to Olise and change sides yet again.

Olise sat beside his mother sipping on a horn of palm wine, trying and failing to restrain himself from speaking his mind. 'That is remarkable,' Olise said, his words dripping with poorly veiled sarcasm. 'I poured myself this very horn of palm wine from the same calabash a minute ago. If only I had known that it could show me my future I would have asked if there was a chance of me getting drunk tonight,' he said while he examined his horn.

'You would do well not to mock the things you cannot begin to comprehend. How can you even drink at a time like this, when Jide is almost at your gates? You should keep a clear head, now more than ever. Is this the image you would have your chiefs draw inspiration from?' Ekaete asked.

'How can I inspire men when I lack inspiration myself?' he snapped. 'You foretold that he would ride back to Ile-Ife once he learned the fate of the city, leaving the road clear for me to pursue and trap him. It was your idea to send men out to assassinate him in his camp, and now I learn that he still lives, and I have lost valuable men! This conflict tires me!'

'Did you expect it to be easy? Did you really think the kingdom would welcome you to the throne with open arms? No, Olise, it must be taken. I have spent my life raising you for this purpose, and now you act the child after a few minor setbacks? You had better get a hold of yourself, child. This is no way to act like a king!' Ekaete spat, with the authority of a mother.

Olise at least had the good sense to appear abashed. He knew he was being ungrateful. After all, Ekaete's aid had granted him the fealties of the chiefs and made his dream of taking the throne a reality. She had been the one to move all the pieces into place like the pieces on the Ncho board game. She alone had risked all and sacrificed more than he could imagine, so his humility was necessary. He put his horn down and wiped his face before he addressed her.

'Forgive me, Mother. I spoke out of turn; my impudence is spawned from the drink. I know you only act to preserve us both and place me in my rightful seat. But the waiting frustrates me. I wish Jide would soon knock on the gates, just to see an end to all the vying for power.'

'You may get your wish sooner than you expect. For now, keep your head and preserve your strength, you will need it. Let us not speak any further on the matter till you are rested,' Ekaete said, turning back to her calabash.

'Very well. I will call on you in the morning.' With that, Olise stood, somewhat unsteady on his feet, and left the hall with four of his guards in tow. He knew his mother was angry still, but he would see to her in the morning, right now he needed to lie his head down and settle the weariness in his bones and the pain behind his eyes.

He walked slowly through the halls of the palace to his chambers down a long corridor that was shrouded in darkness. The torches that clung to the walls along the passage and usually burned through the night were not lit. This was odd, but dawn was gradually approaching. Perhaps an overenthusiastic servant had thought to save the wicks to avoid replacing them the following night. Olise thought no more of the matter and continued to stumble towards his room, savouring the thought of the comfortable bed that awaited him. Maybe he would send for one of the serving girls to keep him warm tonight. Yes. There were still a few he had not bedded, and he favoured something different.

His thoughts were suddenly drawn to the sounds of running feet, followed by muffled struggling and gurgling noises. He spun round just in time to see his guards drop to the floor with their throats slit or a knife wound to the heart. From behind them stepped men he did not recognise, brandishing bloody blades with the unmistakable look of determination to do him harm. Olise immediately reached for the sword at his hip and grasped thin air, realising too late that he had not carried it when he had left his chamber earlier that night. In that moment he made a mental note never to leave his chambers unarmed.

His mother's fears had not been without good reason. She had warned him that his life was in danger, and he had dismissed her notions, believing them to be the paranoia of a protective mother. Surely no man would dare raise a hand against him while he remained within the confines of the city, but he was mistaken.

He thought bitterly of Jide. Never had he viewed his half-brother as one to fight from the shadows and send daggers in the dark, but as a man that would stand before his enemies and face them fairly. This was ironic, considering he had used deceit and cunning himself to gain the advantage, but these had been at his mother's insistence. If it were left to him, he would sooner face Jide in single combat to determine the true heir to their father's kingdom.

'It seems I am at a loss; you have found me without my sword,' Olise said, showing the assassins his empty hands. 'How about you allow me to fetch my sword so that it is not entirely a one-sided fight, eh?' he said with a smirk.

'Move aside, my sword will be the one to drink the blood of the traitor prince,' came a harsh voice that Olise vaguely recognised. The four men stepped aside, revealing Edem, one of the River chiefs. Realisation immediately dawned on Olise and, for a fleeting second, he felt a begrudging respect, love even, mixed with a tinge of guilt for his brother Jide for ever doubting he was a man of honour.

'Now I see it. If I am honest, I would have expected to see Chief Zogo standing in your place. I had my coin on him being the first, the only one in fact, to wish me dead. I would not have thought you would have the liver to cross me. I suppose the clue was always in the name, Edem the ugly,' Olise said, all but spitting Edem's name. This inflamed Edem, who drew a long blade from his belt that was as ugly as the man who wielded it. It was serrated on both sides with an additional hooked blade extending from the bottom of the grip. This weapon was clearly used for more than just killing.

'Brave words from a dead man. I have waited long for the moment to part the skin from your face and remove the tongue of the man who thinks himself above the River chiefs. You, traitor, are nothing but a mere bastard child of a witch. Unlike Zogo and the rest of your so-called commanders, I am no one's puppet. I will do the realm a favour and rid it of the pestilence that has plagued these lands for so long,' Edem said, wearing a smile that would even give the gods pause, as he began to walk slowly towards Olise.

'Are you afraid, bastard? I hope you are, because your time in this life is over. And where are your dogs? A pity they are not here to protect you. I would have liked to carve up that brute Dimeji and show him that a name means nothing to a greater man.'

'You may yet get the opportunity,' Olise said, indicating with a flick of his head, then suddenly one of Edem's men screamed as he was snatched by the neck and dashed against the wall head first with a sickening thud that silenced him the second he hit the wall. The remaining three of Edem's men spun around just in time to see Ogie leap from the shadows and plunge his spear into the nearest soldier, who fell to the floor clutching the spear shaft in his chest. Ogie stepped forward and placed his foot on the dying man's stomach to retrieve his spear before striking again in the man's throat to silence his death cries.

Dimeji now shouldered his way passed Ogie, his hands wet with the blood and brain matter of the man he had just crushed against the wall. He seemed to dominate the corridor with his bulk and the darkness only made him look the more menacing. He moved like a panther ready to pounce on its prey, which made the two remaining soldiers take a step backwards and take up fighting positions.

The soldiers of the River-lands did not scare easily and it was obvious that this would be a bloody struggle. All the while, Edem's smile never left his face and grew wider still. 'Ah, I should have known that your dogs would not be far behind. At least this makes it all the more interesting,' Edem said, looking between the new arrivals and the prince.

Without warning, he spun towards Olise and leaped at him with his blade slashing high, aiming at his throat, intending to kill him quickly before turning his full attention on Dimeji and Ogie. Olise, however, was no amateur and instinctively moved backwards to avoid the blow but ended up colliding with the wall behind him. There was no room to manoeuvre and he knew that Edem would have him. He raised his arm to shield his neck against the blade and the serrated edge sliced across his forearm with enough force to sever bone. Edem drew his arm back to strike the fatal blow, but paused, and slowly dropped his sword arm in shock. The smile he wore earlier vanished as quickly as it had come as he looked at Olise dumbfounded.

Olise's arm was still raised across his face, but there was no sign of blood. There wasn't as much as a scratch or bruise, and Olise began to laugh. Quietly at first, but then the sound rose in his chest and resonated in the confines of the corridor. Edem now saw that Olise's other hand gripped an amulet that hung from a thread around his neck and, suddenly, he came to the realisation that all the rumours that surrounded the prince may be true after all.

No one in the corridor moved or said a word as they all watched, as if waiting for Olise to explain to them what they had all just witnessed. And he did just that after he managed to stop laughing. 'I must admit, even I had my doubts when mother told me I could not be harmed, but now I see the wisdom in her words. Unfortunately for you, Edem, I will not be the one dying today.'

To Edem's credit, he recovered himself quickly and immediately sprang into action. He knew that any further attack on Olise would be futile, so the only sensible course of action would be self-preservation. There was a small chance that he could still fight his way out of the palace and join Jide's army beyond the fields, warning him of the danger he faced in Olise. This would be his last act of loyalty to the true king.

He turned and fled in the other direction and called for his men to stand and fight to cover his retreat. They obeyed, knowing that only death awaited them, but accepted this last request from their chief willingly enough. The two guards shouted their last war cries before throwing themselves at Ogie and Dimeji. They put up a good fight, and both Dimeji and Ogie were hard pressed against the skills of the two soldiers, who fought like men who knew that this would be their last stand. The first soldier parried a thrust from Ogie's spear and pressed his attack further, driving Ogie towards the wall. He swung his sword recklessly, hoping to make a quick kill and aid his companion, who wouldn't stand much of a chance against the terrifying figure he faced, Dimeji, who had now drawn his great sword and had already wounded his opponent.

Within a few minutes the fighting was over, with both soldiers from the River-lands bleeding their last into the stone paving slabs that lined the palace floors.

'Raise the guard!' Olise shouted, 'That traitor must not get away!' Without another word both men raced off after Edem. Olise feared that he would rouse his soldiers, which could embolden the other River warriors, causing a mutiny within the walls. This could not happen. Edem needed to be dealt with swiftly before the situation got out of hand. Too much depended on it.

* * * *

Edem had somehow made it out of the palace without being challenged and sprinted towards the barracks where his men resided, dripping sweat as he ran. He was still in a daze at what he had just witnessed. Olise's skin had not yielded under his blade! This was impossible, even though he had seen it with his own eyes. How could such a man be stopped? If this was true, then everything he had ever heard about him and his cursed mother would also be true. The thought alone sent a shiver down his spine. Jide must be warned of this, for he had no idea what he was up against.

Suddenly, a shock of pain burst through his leg and he cried out in agony, falling to one knee. He looked down and saw a spear through his calf and a pool of dark blood on the floor from his wound. The pain was nothing like he had ever felt before and he screamed as he tried to drag himself up to his feet.

'And just how far did you think you could run, chief? You didn't believe you would actually make it to your men, did you?' Ogie asked as he strolled out of the shadows followed closely by Dimeji. Edem only bared his teeth.

There comes a time when every man must stand and fight, discarding all his fears and embracing his fate. This was Edem's time.

He knew then that his plan had failed and that he would never be able to warn Jide. Zogo's voice of warning also came to mind, but there was no changing his destiny now.

He would at least die on his own terms, with a blade in his hand as any true warrior would hope for. He didn't give Ogie the satisfaction of a reply but simply steeled himself and pulled the spear from his calf, letting out a cry as the broad head ripped through even more ligaments and tissue causing further damage. More blood gushed out of the wound and he knew then that even if he could beat the two men, he would surely bleed to death. He looked up to the stars and beseeched the gods to grant him the strength to die well. Then he looked down at his opponents and smiled invitingly, 'Don't keep me waiting, dogs,' he said, with saliva dribbling from his mouth.

'Oh, I don't intend to,' Ogie replied as he now moved towards the wounded chief. Ogie then drew a long blade and lunged at Edem who, surprisingly, deflected the blow and sidestepped simultaneously, leaving Ogie to rush past him with his back exposed. With the skill of a natural killer of men, Edem brought his own blade up and used the hooked end to slice Ogie's exposed back, ripping through the soft fabric of Ogie's kaftan and leaving a deep gash in its place. Ogie cried out in pain, shocked at the swift movement of the wounded man. He had thought this would be an easy kill, but he was highly mistaken.

Now Dimeji came in, bringing his great sword down at an angle intending to cleave Edem in half. Edem tried to sidestep again but, as he placed his weight on his wounded leg, it collapsed underneath him causing him to cry out in agony and drop to his knee to take the full force of Dimeji's sword on his blade.

The force of the blow sent a ripple of pain through Edem's arm, which immediately went numb. In all his time as a warrior, never had he felt such force, such raw power. Dimeji raised the blade again for a second blow, but this time Edem chose to deflect the edge, as his waning strength could not withstand another direct blow. He did so expertly and rolled to the side, all the while trying to restore the feeling in his arm.

Ogie was now on his feet again and came in for another stab at Edem, who spun past the thrust and once again scored a slash on Ogie's shoulder. But he quickly began to slow. He had lost too much blood, which still pumped from the wound in his leg, and he knew that another attack from Dimeji would be the end of him. He tried to force himself up and limp away, but he faltered and fell flat on his face, striking a rock as he landed. Momentarily blinded by the blow to his head and the sand in his eyes, he rolled onto his back just in time to see Dimeji swing his sword down in an arc. There was a brief moment of pain, then darkness and nothing else.

As the sun rose, Olise summoned all the chiefs to the gates. Everyone was curious to know what was happening. There had been talk around the barracks of an attack in the palace, but some thought that Jide had somehow gained the walls in the dead of night and started the war from the shadows.

As the chiefs gathered they were greeted with the gruesome sight of five heads placed on spears adorning the ramparts above the gates of the city.

One of the heads was deformed and did not appear to be human; crushed beyond all recognition; and there in the centre stood the head of Edem the ugly, placed prominently above the others. He was even uglier in death than he had been in life.

'Let these heads be a reminder to those that would seek to betray me. I intend to root out any such men and visit the same fate upon them,' said Olise as he addressed his men. 'That is all,' he said before he turned and walked away, leaving the grizzly sight in his wake for all to see.

Zogo, Nnamdi, Akpan and the other men from the Igbo and River-land tribes looked on saddened and sickened at their old allies as the flies began to settle on what remained of a feared but nonetheless great warrior.

DIVIDED WE FALL

*D*espite the friction that threatened to divide the royal household, Jide and Olise's friendship and love for each other had endured the test of time.

The royal household had all but split into two separate factions; on one hand there was Ekaete who still ruled in her son's name – Olise wasn't too concerned with matters of the realm and was content deferring to his mother – and Jide, who had the backing of the Modakeke and his father's loyal council.

There was no disputing that Ekaete's appetite for power had grown over the years, but much of the kingdom had still not accepted her, and only recognised Jide as the one true ruler. He, however, had been reluctant to take the throne purely out of love for his brother and to avoid the fallout that would precede the fracture of their fragile relationship, but the pressure was mounting for him to claim what was rightfully his. Eventually, the unspoken would need to be addressed. For the time being, Jide sought to preserve the peace as long as he was able.

At the ages of nineteen and sixteen, they had both grown to be fine young men; strong of will and mind and both possessing the strength of good warriors and the character to lead men. There was hardly any time they had spent apart in the years growing up and every day they studied and trained together for hours on end.

Jide was a naturally gifted fighter with effortless skill in both sword and spear, Olise, on the other hand, was more of an intelligent and cunning fighter, honing his skill through hard work and dedication. There were not many men who could beat either of the brothers in single combat, besides the warriors of the Modakeke, who were forbidden to raise arms against the princes.

Nonetheless, many men from across the realm travelled from far and wide to test their skills against the princes in tournaments and training sessions. The boys never lost a contest between them and news of their repute began to spread wings and travel across the lands.

The princes had their first taste of war in the same year; there had been rumours of a foreign tribe of men from a kingdom in the far east that had taken control of numerous settlements on the outskirts of their territory. The councillors on both sides of the throne had advised that peace should be brokered, and an alliance formed in the event that the invaders had designs to cross the borders into the domains of the kingdom. This seemed to be their standard response to any perceived threat of an invasion.

The proposal was rejected by the brothers who, instead, insisted on marching out to display the realm's military strength. They believed that a show of power was the necessary course of action to serve as a deterrent to any overzealous tribe and their argument was backed by some of the other chiefs of the tribes across the realm.

Be it bravado or a desire to make names for themselves, the brothers saw it as the perfect opportunity to demonstrate their quality as leaders and present a unified kingdom against anyone who would consider them weak. In hindsight, a touch of diplomacy would have been the right choice, and perhaps the events that followed could have been avoided, but this was not to be, and the destiny of the brothers was henceforth decided on the field of battle.

Their wishes were eventually granted by the council and a force of two hundred warriors accompanied the princes to confront the invaders. The army was made up of one hundred men loyal to each prince, which included sixty warriors from the Modakeke amongst Jide's retinue. Within a day they were on the march with their eyes filled with visions of glory and their names cemented in history.

After a few weeks' march, smoke was spotted on the horizon, heralding the presence of the invaders. The smoke, which usually succeeded a sacked city in ruin, was clearly within the domain of the princes, which enraged the men of Ile-Ife, provoking the brothers to move their force to intercept the enemy. The captains who maintained order in the ranks had warned against an uninformed attack, but the brothers dismissed this advice, rather choosing to bring the invaders to heel for daring to raid the lands of their father.

Within an hour, the princes' men were bearing down on the foreigners with their blood up and eager for a fight. Unfortunately for the princes, the men they faced were no band of thieves but veteran warriors of many actions, who had travelled through east Africa conquering every city, town, and village in their path. No army or city walls had been able to hinder their progress across the continent and their reputation for savagery was already the talk of legend.

They were led by a ruthless tyrant called Neguse Nirayu who was said to have butchered his own kin to gain sole control of his family's wealth and army with plans to conquer Africa. His empire was built on the ruins of fallen kingdoms gained through force of arms, which he now ruled with an iron fist. He was feared equally by those he led and those he conquered, and his will to dominate had driven him to the point of near insanity with an insatiable appetite for power.

Neguse only had one arm; his missing limb was claimed by a lion, which he still managed to kill, and the pelt of which adorned his shoulders as a reminder of his legend. Despite his impediment, he was fabled to be a master swordsman with the blood of many great warriors on his sword. He also rode a horse as if he was born in the saddle.

Neguse, being the experienced soldier he was, immediately read the princes' intent and rallied his men, who poured out of the settlement like ants escaping a collapsing ant hill, to confront the princes on horseback. The princes had no idea that they'd be facing a mounted hoard, nor did they know that the enemy outnumbered their own men, but they had committed themselves and the men who followed them on this path, and could not be seen to waver in the face of adversity.

Jide stole a quick glance at his brother, whose face tried to mask the fear he felt, but he cast a reassuring smile confirming his resolve. Jide returned the gesture with a curt nod as he braced himself for the slaughter that was nearly upon them.

The experienced captains in the rank saw the overwhelming odds they faced and set about issuing orders to slow the army's advance into a good defensive line, which they managed not without difficulty. Some of the soldiers had already started to waver but words of encouragement were shouted from the first rank, which was made up of the Modakeke.

Jide raised his spear and invoked the gods to give them strength and courage. For the men who could see him, the act was sufficient to inflame their hearts, and they all stood firm in preparation to fight and possibly die with their princes.

When the horsemen were barely a hundred paces away, an order sounded across the lines for the first rank to cast their spears, which was done without hesitation. The spears arced through the air and came down like rain upon the foreigners, killing and maiming man and beast alike.

The felled horses slowed the momentum of the charge as the men behind swerved violently to avoid colliding with their fallen countrymen. The charge, however, couldn't be halted due to their sheer numbers and many more men surged on eagerly, blinded by their lust to claim any spoils to be had. Amongst their rank rode Neguse, wearing his magnificent lion pelt about him and guiding his steed with his knees, whilst wielding a great sword in his only hand.

The second rank of men in the princes' line took up the position of the first and dug the butts of their spears into the ground at an angle supported by a foot, intent on stopping the horses. Men sent their prayers up to their deity of choice and waited. Within minutes, the two armies collided in a great clash of iron and flesh. The fight that ensued was bloodier than any man who survived the battle had ever seen.

The charge swept away a great number of men, but many of the invaders turned away at the last minute, their horses frightened by the sight of the razor-sharp spear points that could impale both man and beast.

The horsemen that miraculously made it through the line unscathed were wreaking havoc deep in the ranks as they slashed about, severing heads and limbs. Through sheer determination, the men on the ground eventually speared those men and drag them off their horses to a violent death.

The princes fought side by side as they had always trained, fighting with such ferocity as if Ogun himself guided their swords, dismembering and disembowelling men by the dozen as if they were mere saplings. For a time, there was no one who could stand in their way, but the sheer force of numbers would eventually tip the balance. It was only a matter of time.

As the fight raged on, Jide took stock of their standing and calculated that roughly a quarter of their force had fallen but the rest of his men continued to hold firm, fighting like demons released from the underworld or men who knew that their fate had been written the moment the fighting began. Men who knew they had no choice but to fight.

He looked over at his brother and saw an expression he had not seen before. At first, he thought it was fear, but quickly realised it was pleasure mixed with excitement. Olise was actually enjoying himself as he killed man after man. He was splattered with blood and guts from head to toe, but most striking of all was the red smile he wore as he went about his bloody work.

The sight deeply unsettled Jide but there was no time to dwell on the matter as he dodged and parried spear thrusts and swinging swords from men intent on claiming his life. Despite the overwhelming odds, the army would not give any ground to the invaders.

They had killed almost twice as many as their own losses numbered, but the surge of horses and warriors carried on. It became apparent that these men lacked the discipline and skill of the men of Ile-Ife, even with the advantage of being on horseback.

They were probably used to armies turning and fleeing from them once they saw their great numbers and the charging began, but not men who trained every day since the ages of five and were anointed with the love and protection of their gods. They would learn by the end of the day, of that Jide had no doubt.

Neguse, realising that he could not simply run these soldiers down as he was so used to doing, ordered his men to spread out to the flanks to encircle them and slowly tighten the circle until they were all dead.

The veterans in Jide's army saw this manoeuvre and immediately went about extending their lines on the flanks, taking down any horseman that tried to race behind them. This infuriated Neguse.

He knew he had the numbers, and yet he could not best this army, he thought bitterly. They must be protected by some kind of divine entity or other to be able to withstand his constant assaults. He looked around and saw many of his men dead and wounded, only realising in that moment how much this small army had cost him.

He let out a shout of frustration and then surged forward, guiding his horse with pressure from his thighs. He would drive through to the heart of this army and take the head of the commander himself, no more time to stay at the back in relative safety; it was time he led by example.

As his horse galloped through the masses, he swung his sword expertly left and right, cutting down man after man. By the time he had ridden one hundred paces along the line, his hand was so slick with blood that he had to stop and wipe it dry for fear of losing the grip on his sword.

Then the sun caught his eye, perhaps from the gleam of a sword, and then he saw two young men in the distance. They both fought like lions, with the fluidity of men who lived and breathed fighting. He was momentarily mesmerised by their movement and balance. They almost moved in sync, as if dancing to a rhythm that only they knew, a dance for the dead that piled at their feet.

They had men who appeared to be protecting them, fighting in close formation, although not moving as elegantly in their delivery of death, but with the skilled efficiency of great warriors, nonetheless. One of the men that fought close to the young men was a huge brute who had the delicacy of a butcher.

He all but obliterated anything that came close to him, splitting man and horse apart with a great sword as if they were made from straw. The corpses mounted up the most around these men, and Neguse knew that this was where he needed to be.

These must be the ones that command the army, *he thought.* These are the heads I require to bring this army to heel. Without a moment's hesitation he called for men to follow him and spurred his horse directly towards the group of men.

Through the melee, Jide saw a man riding towards their position and knew instantly that this man led these foreigners. He could make out a lion's head and furs resting across his shoulders and his bearing was one of a leader. He could tell from the way the horsemen rallied around him as he galloped past, from the way they looked to him eagerly as if he was the saviour come to deliver them. This was surely the man to kill. He turned around and called for Akin to pass him a spear, his own spear lost in the back of an unfortunate horseman during the initial charge.

Akin skewered a soldier off a horse and bore the weight of the man at the end of his spear as he brought him to the ground while the horse cantered away. He withdrew the spear from the dead man's chest, tossed it to Jide and drew his own sword.

Jide snatched the spear from the air and spun it in his hand, angling the broad spearhead in front of him ready to be cast. He had a moment to feel the smooth wooden shaft in his palm, appreciating the balance, before he took careful aim and launched it at the man with the lion head.

The spear soared through the air for a few seconds then came down, striking Neguse's horse high in its back, narrowly missing Neguse's groin. The horse's front legs buckled, and it tumbled forward, throwing Neguse clear. He landed expertly, rolling forward on his shoulder and coming up on one knee.

Neguse had managed to hold onto his sword as he came up, and didn't allow the fall to stop his momentum, but darted forward directly at the line of soldiers, seeking the one who had cast the spear and killed his favourite horse. His men still cantered beside him, protecting his flanks as he ran on.

He reached the line of men and killed the first two who attempted to slow him without breaking a sweat. He was viper fast and had adapted his fighting style to favour his one arm; moving his body like the head of a cobra, striking, retracting, sidestepping and striking again. With the aid of the horsemen who had followed him to the lines, he was able to create some space and suddenly found himself face to face with the man who had thrown the spear.

He was surprised to see just how young he really was, and he almost laughed to himself at how easy it would be to defeat the boy but then, something stopped the laugh dead in his throat. Something in the way the boy stood and levelled his sword, the look in his eye and the undeniable energy about him.

Yes, this boy will be a worthy opponent, he thought with pleasure. A large soldier stepped in front of the young man who exchanged some words and made a gesture that appeared to instruct the soldier to stand aside. This raised the boy's esteem in Neguse's opinion, understanding that the young warrior commanded the respect of these men, but more so, was unafraid to look into his enemies' eyes and face them in combat.

Neguse pointed his sword at the boy and started to walk towards him, flanked by some of his horsemen. His men began to chant his name, which slowly spread amongst the invading army, causing the fighting to dwindle as men strained to see the cause of the shift on the battlefield.

By the time Neguse was directly opposite the young warrior, even the isolated pockets of fighting had come to a halt as men stood transfixed at the confrontation that was about to decide the outcome of the battle.

Akin had wanted to protect his prince and fight the one-handed warrior in his place. He had witnessed how skilfully the man had killed their men with little effort and was under no illusions that this man was a deadly fighter, but Jide would not hear of it. His pride for the prince rose, but also his anxiety.

173

He was sworn to protect him, to serve as his sword and lay down his life for the prince if required. What would become of him if the prince was to be killed before his eyes? What would that tell of his station as a blood-guard if the very blood he was tasked to protect was spilt before his own? He could not contemplate the thought, but Jide had commanded him and he was duty bound to follow the prince's order.

He also understood that Jide needed to prove to his men, but more importantly, to himself that he was worthy of the crown and the kingdom of his father. He reluctantly stepped aside, but tightened the grip on his sword and readied himself to come to the prince's aid if the opportunity presented itself.

The chanting died down as men looked on with baited breath for the first strike to be made; the only sound to be heard was the cries of the wounded who lay in the dirt and the sounds of the vultures circling the battlefield overhead, eagerly awaiting the feast on the bones of the unfortunate.

As Jide prepared himself to do battle something in the crowd of men captured his attention. He glimpsed a girl walking through the crowd who stood out amongst the blood splattered soldiers around him. She wore one length of white wrapper about her chest down to her knees. He narrowed his vision and saw the ghost of a smile on her lips, and suddenly she was gone, lost amongst the masses of men. He wasn't sure if he had imagined it, but he removed the thought from his mind and focused on the task at hand.

Minutes passed as the two warriors gauged each other, and suddenly both men sprang into action, each seeking the advantage to be had in taking the initiative.

Neguse moved like a snake, striking blow after blow, intending to bring the fight to a swift end, but the years Jide had spent training saved his life, adapting to the awkward style of the one-handed warrior after only a few clashes of iron. At first Jide covered the strikes that were aimed at his vitals but once he mastered the rhythm and pace of his opponent, he began to press his own offence, demonstrating his skill and speed. They were well matched, but Jide slowly began to get the better of Neguse and soon dominated the fight.

Both men moved quickly, but Jide's youth and superior training had the slight edge and, after what seemed to be a long contest of skill and finesse, Neguse made a mistake, overextending himself to land a fatal strike to end the fight. Jide seized the opportunity, spinning on the ball of his foot and severed Neguse's arm at the elbow, which sent up a cheer from the men of Ile-Ife.

Neguse looked down at his severed arm in disbelief as it lay in the dirt still clutching his great sword. The attack had been faultless and had taken Neguse completely by surprise. He dropped to his knees as his blood flowed from his arm, painting the soil red about him.

His men were all shocked into silence and, for a moment, no one uttered a word, understanding that before them stood a true warrior greater than the one they followed and greater still than any warrior they had ever known.

Men began to cast aside their weapons and bowed their heads in reverence to the tyrant slayer. Jide's status, in that moment, had soared beyond anything the young prince could ever begin to contemplate, and he knew that the time to claim his place in the world had come. He had earned it through the passage of battle, a right that no one, not even his stepmother Ekaete could deny him.

He scanned the crowd of men seeking out his brother, for he was the only one Jide wanted to share this moment with, the only one he craved approval from. The only person who mattered. His eyes fell upon his brother amongst the gathered men and he knew in that instant that all had changed.

Olise looked back with a blank expression, which slowly gave way to one of disapproval, jealousy, even. Olise believed he was the better fighter and the one deserving of the respect of the realm, but Jide had seized the opportunity and had now elevated himself to a platform Olise could never dream to ascend to.

The bitterness he felt threatened to overwhelm him, so he turned his back on his brother and walked away. Olise's reaction broke Jide's heart, overshadowing everything that had just been achieved. How could he face the trials that lay ahead without his brother? He could not imagine it. He was still lost in thought when Akin gently tapped him on his shoulder, bringing him back to the present.

'You must finish it,' Akin whispered. Then Jide realised that Neguse still knelt before him. The blood from his arm was now only a trickle, and it was clear that he would soon lose consciousness from the blood loss.

Neguse considered Jide's eyes and said, 'Take my head, young warrior, grant me a clean warrior's death.' The words spoken were foreign to Jide, a tongue he had no knowledge of, but he understood the meaning when Neguse leaned forward exposing his neck. Jide moved to stand beside Neguse and said he was a great warrior before bringing his sword down to claim Neguse's head in one stroke.

Before the head even touched the ground, a new chant filled the air. It was one that burned the ears of Olise as he left the battlefield with Dimeji and other men loyal to him. The chant filled his ears and the sting of humiliation welled in his eyes but, through Jide's deeds, the words could not be disputed. These words were now spreading on the tongue of every man on the field, Ile-Ife natives and foreigners alike. The words were "King of Ile-Ife".

SOIL OF THE MOTHERLAND

Weeks had gone by on the road and the young travellers had managed to maintain a low profile without drawing attention to themselves. Enitan's disposition was still sombre for most of the journey, perhaps too used to the comforts of the palace and the privileges afforded a prince of the realm, Ayo thought, but he was adjusting to life on the road and took pleasure in the relative freedom the journey offered and the prospect of adventure.

Ayo had done well to protect him so far but was becoming more and more weary with every mile travelled, and the pressure of his responsibility weighing heavily on his shoulders. However, his duty to the kingdom was bigger than him and had to be seen through at any cost. This was the fuel that drove him on, the invisible hand that propelled him to put one foot in front of the other day after day, through the blazing sun, torrential rain and unforgiving terrain. It was almost a miracle that Enitan had not given in yet. The boy possessed a will that most grown men lacked, a sense of purpose that no child of his age had any right to, but it was undeniably obvious in him.

Ayo had known that something was different ever since they fled the forests of Ife, but Enitan had been unwilling to talk about the events of that day. He had been very quiet for most of the journey, only showing moments of childhood happiness that were a joy to behold but also as fleeting as the birdsong on a sunny morning. The weeks on the road had undoubtedly moulded the boy to the beginnings of a hardened warrior, that and whatever possessed him when anger took him, as it had in the village with the young girl. Again, that was something of a mystery to Ayo, and would most likely remain so. Nothing, however, would change how Ayo felt about his charge; if anything, he felt even more love and protectiveness towards him, and would follow him down whatever path the gods had laid out for him.

The villages they passed through gave way to towns and then to much larger settlements until eventually they came to the land of

Ogun – a city named after the Orisa of war. This was the home of Enitan's mother. From the minute they passed the borders, it was as if a weight was lifted from them, the weeks of travel fell away as if they had been unshackled from a great burden and the anxiety of feeling hunted slowly ebbed away. Ayo was still alert, as they could not really trust anyone until they were safely behind the gates of the palace and in the care of Enitan's relatives.

They would seek out Enitan's grandfather who, despite his age, still ruled the city and surrounding regions with the vigour of a man half his age. It was said that most of the ancient families in Ogun were direct descendants of the deity *Ogun* and the city was named in the god's honour. In return, *Ogun* the god bestowed strength to the families, one of which, queen Lara's descendants, had ruled here for generations. Each of the rulers in that family had lived beyond the age of ninety, which was unheard of in other regions, where the average age of male death was thirty-five.

Whatever the case, Ogun the city was a prosperous place, which didn't lack for anything; the soils were fertile, yielding plentiful crops to support the people, the forests were teeming with wildlife to hunt and the rivers overflowed with fish, so no mouth ever went hungry. This place, as was Ife before it fell, was a place that thrived, full of life and opportunity that was welcome to all.

Ayo and Enitan looked out of place in their ragged cloaks and dust-caked shoes amongst the people here, who all seemed to be very well presented. The women, even the servants, were dressed in wrappers of fine materials with elaborate embroidery and stitching, and the men walked around with exquisitely sewn kaftans and other pieces of expensive attire. There was also a feeling of festivity in the air, as children darted around from house to house barely containing their excitement for whatever was planned in the city. Ayo recognised some of the decorations that had been displayed around the thoroughfare and houses they passed and understood the significance.

'They celebrate the Agemo festival,' he told Enitan, who looked as if he had walked into another world and was as awestruck as a child would be, with his eyes open wide and his mouth salivating with the excitement of it all. His senses were assaulted with the vibrancy and colour of the city; the smell of roasting meats and stewing vegetables made his stomach rumble, reminding him that he hadn't eaten a decent meal in weeks. 'What does that mean?' he asked, watching some of the children running with baskets filled with yams and cassava.

'It's a festival that happens every year around these parts where men dress up as masquerades or Agemos and claim to be possessed by the malevolent spirits that walk the earth. The same spirits that commune with the dead and usher them to the afterlife. They travel through all the towns in this region and the people show them reverence and pray to have good fortunes for the year to come. During the procession of the Agemos through the towns, no man can don a cap and women are not permitted to look upon them for fear of instant death. In fact, the Agemos cry out as they walk that women should avert their eyes, unless they want to be taken along on their journey,' Ayo finished.

Enitan looked sceptical as he digested the words he had heard, but was intrigued none the less. 'So why is it that people seem to be in a celebratory mood if the passing of these Agemos is such a sombre affair? Shouldn't they be dreading the event and wish for it to pass quickly, and not welcome it so?' he asked.

'It is a great honour for the Agemos to come to a town, it shows that the town is of great value to the gods and that the gods in their infinite wisdom consent to the spirits to see the glory of a town favoured by them. So, they celebrate the opening of the gates to the Agemos, and the closing of the gates once the traditional rites are observed and they have departed. Besides, it is an ancient tradition here that is said to have been carried out for centuries, so I don't think anyone would really question changing things now, but rather carry on tradition, as most things are done,' Ayo said.

Enitan seemed to accept this response and did not ask any further questions, but added, with a smile, 'In that case we should make haste to my grandfather before the city grinds to a halt and we are left in the streets to the mercy of these Agemos.' Ayo looked over at the young prince and smiled back, placing his hand on his shoulder, 'You are right, my prince, let us not spare another moment.' With that, they both headed up the street in search of the palace and a reunion with the family Enitan had only ever known as a baby.

By the time they made it to the palace, the streets were almost bare but for a few boys who ran excitedly towards the city gates to glimpse the Agemos, who were by now making their way into the city. The gates of the palace were immense and stood before them in dark timber with overlapping panels of bronze that was intricately detailed, and Ayo wondered what wealth and power lay beyond. The palace was heavily fortified, and any army would have had trouble enough storming it, let alone the city. The design of the fortifications here was very different from those at Ife, which seemed altogether less imposing and more welcoming. Perhaps it was because Ife was the capital city and never in all the centuries had it been envisioned that anyone would attempt to invade it, until now.

Enitan strolled up to the gates, not seeming to be overly impressed by the massive structure, and was about the ring a bronze bell that hung from a post off to the side when the hinges that held the gate in place began to groan with the effort of not being oiled in some time. The gates slowly began to swing outwards to reveal the courtyard within. It so happened that the chief, his grandsire, was on his way out with a small retinue of armed guards to observe the festivities of the evening. Their timing had been perfect. Enitan stepped back from the gates but stood in the centre, anxious to spot his grandsire amongst the men, when a captain in a beautifully designed leather chest plate strolled over to him briskly and shouted, 'Stand aside, beggar, do you not see your lord and chief on the road?'

Enitan didn't appear to have heard him, but was still straining his neck to identify his relative. This must have infuriated the captain, who was now close to Enitan and raised his hand, which held a slim bamboo cane, to strike him. Ayo darted forward and grabbed the man by the wrist before the cane struck.

'Do not dare to lay a hand upon him, fool,' he said calmly. Ayo's grip was iron and the captain's features registered shock, then pain, as he strained against Ayo's hold. 'Think carefully of the next words that part your lips, soldier, if you wish to use your arm again,' he said as he swept back his cloak to reveal his sword, which he touched lightly with his free hand.

'How dare you!' the soldier exclaimed. 'I will have you strung up and flogged raw!' He snarled and tried to use his other hand to reach for the sword at his waist. Ayo twisted the man's wrist upwards, causing him to cry out in pain and drop to one knee, and then Enitan's grandfather stepped forward from the guards who surrounded him.

'What is the meaning of this?' he said, his voice pervaded with authority, while guards flanked him as he walked towards the altercation. 'Who dares to break my peace on such a day as this?' he asked as he took in the scene of his captain down on his knees with his face twisted in pain and the two young men standing over him. Then his eyes met with Enitan's, which stopped him in mid-stride. Recognition suffused his memory as he looked upon the face that bore the delicate but strong features of his beloved daughter. The dark brown-eyed intense stare, high cheekbones and slight cleft at the chin, features he had not seen in years and had feared he would never set eyes upon again. Tears came unbidden to his eyes and his tone softened to almost a whisper.

'Do my eyes deceive me? Can this be my daughter's son? Enitan... is that you?' he asked as he walked over to his youngest grandchild. Enitan, unable to restrain himself, ran over to his grandfather in reply and smothered him in a long and tearful embrace, pouring out all the emotions he'd built up over the past weeks. They remained locked together for a long moment, Enitan sobbing softly into his grandfather's chest, seeking the comfort he had not realised he needed. When they detached, the old chief took Enitan's face in his hands and looked him over with genuine concern and care.

'I believed you all dead. We got the news that the king marched to confront Olise, and in his absence Ife fell, and that my daughter...' he suppressed a sob, 'my beloved Lara, along with all her children, were slaughtered and their remains burned with the palace.' He managed to finish. 'How is it that you now stand before me, my grandchild?'

'I wasn't at the palace when it fell, I was in the forest playing, but I saw the flames. I heard the cries of the people. I felt their pain. Ayo, my blood-guard, spirited me away before we were discovered,' Enitan said, his voice heavy with the emotion of reliving the ordeal his young eyes had witnessed.

His grandfather had a grim look on his face, then turned to Ayo. 'Come forward, young man. You have done well in protecting the prince. You will be rewarded handsomely for delivering him safely to me. Right now, he may be the only heir to the throne. My household is in your debt,' the old chief said.

'Please, my chief,' Ayo said, prostrating himself in front of the old warrior. 'I was merely fulfilling my duty to the prince. I do not require any reward. It is enough to know that he is now safe amongst his kin. It has been a hard journey, and there are still men out there who seek his death.'

The chief nodded gravely. 'I understand, but, as you have said, you are both safe now. You must be weary and famished. Please come in and replenish yourselves. My servants will see to you.' He turned and addressed one of his men. 'Call the servants to attend these young men. See that they are bathed, fed and clothed befitting their status,' he said, before he turned to the captain who had confronted the prince. The man had not moved from where he had taken to his knees, still looking on somewhat bemused by what had transpired.

'Wale, are you just going to kneel there like a confused goat? This is your prince and perhaps your future king. Show him the error of your ways,' he said sternly. Wale recovered from his initial shock quickly and stayed on his bent knees as he had only a moment ago.

'Forgive me, my prince, I had no idea who you were, and I beg your mercy,' he pleaded, extending his sword in its sheath. The gesture was clear. If it so pleased Enitan, he could have taken the soldier's sword and slain him where he knelt for attempting to lay a hand on the prince's person, but Enitan was so drained emotionally and mentally that he just dismissed him with a flick of his head.

'You are a lucky man, Wale. Every day your lungs inhale the morning air you must give thanks to the prince for sparing your life. Even though you are one of my greatest warriors, I, for one, would not have let you off so lightly.' Wale kept his head lowered as sweat dripped from his scalp into the gravel at his feet. He murmured his thanks as the prince and Ayo were ushered off into the palace.

The festival in the city was all but forgotten by those in the palace as the gates were slowly closed to the increasing sounds of the drums and the revelry that would carry on long into the night. The Agemos would make their procession through the town without being overseen by the chief. This would be the first festival in decades that a sitting ruler of the city of Ogun would miss, and his absence would not go unnoticed.

* * * *

The soil underneath his feet was still warm and what remained of the blackened shrubs around him still smoked with tiny embers ignited by the soft wind that blew like a whisper. The field in which he stood was unfamiliar to him and yet he knew it was a place he would come to know intimately. His arms were heavy from the sword and spear he was carrying, but not from the weight of them; that he was used to. It was the same weariness he felt after training for hours on end, but unlike the weapons practice he did in the training yard with Ayo and his brothers; this was different.

The blood on his weapons was evidence that he had been fighting. That and the splatter of red on his arms and armour. He looked around him, bringing his surroundings into focus, and saw nothing but bones, hundreds of them scattered as far as the eye could see. He heard the constant squawking of carrion birds picking what meat remained to be had. The smell of sulphur filled his nose and, overhead, a dark cloud followed his every movement, constantly twisting and changing shape in the wind. Besides the birds, nothing lived in this place; he was the only one, but he dared to venture further into this barren land.

As he walked, he glanced over his shoulder and noticed a black trail of footprints in his wake. His feet were what had scorched the soil. Everywhere he stepped he left a mark like a burning brand in the earth, which spread and torched everything in its path. He sank to his knees, wondering what strange force had possessed him, and cried out in anger. His voice was the sound of thunder sending all the birds away in panic into the sky. He began to cry, and his tears were warm against his cheeks, evaporating before they reached the base of his chin. Then suddenly he felt a presence, and raised his head, but there was nothing there, only his shadow, which seemed odd as it had not been there before. He slowly got to his feet and his shadow followed suit, but it was not his, it was that of a man, tall, broad of shoulder and muscular. From its right hand shone a dazzling light like a bolt of lightning, caused him to shield his eyes against the glare.

A voice spoke to him, a voice he had heard once before in the forests of his homeland. A voice that soothed and empowered him. 'Where you walk, I follow', said the voice in the ancient Yoruba dialect that had been long forgotten, lost with the passing of time but spoken now as clear as day in that deep voice. 'I am your sword. I am your spear. I am the shield that protects you from your enemies, for they will be many.' The words held an unspoken message, one that required some form of acknowledgement of the promises offered. He understood what he must do.

He bent his knee to the ground, bringing him closer to the shadow, which remained standing, and bowed his head in acceptance. As he knelt, the light that glowed in the hand of the shadow began to rise from the ground and emerged from the earth as a constantly shifting glow of energy. It hovered inches from his head for a split second, then burst before his eyes, sending the world into brilliant whiteness.

Enitan let out a cry and woke from the bed on which he lay. He had dreamt the same dream almost every night since leaving Ife, but only now had the dream played out to the end. He finally understood the path that had been laid out for him, the journey he and he alone had to take. His heart was racing, but slowly began to slow as he gathered his thoughts and remembered where he was, safe within the walls of his grandfather's palace.

Clean cloths had been placed at the foot of the bed for him. The smell and dirt of the road had been scrubbed clean from him, and his belly was full of the feast that he had hastily eaten before he fell into a deep slumber. Luckily for him, a feast was always prepared for the festival, so the timing of his arrival was a welcome coincidence. He rose from the bed and got dressed, eager to speak to his grandfather and gather whatever news he might have on the state of the realm and the wellbeing of his father. His thoughts suddenly went to his brothers and the games they would play around the palace when they were younger.

He thought about his mother and felt the bitterness of the fate that had befallen her. The unfairness of his family being snatched away from him was still hard to digest and tears came to his eyes, which he quickly wiped away. He could not afford to be seen to show weakness in front of his grandsire. He had to show strength, as his father would have expected him to. Besides, he secretly harboured the hope that he was not an orphan, and that his father may yet live, as no word had travelled from the east confirming what had become of him. Hopefully his grandsire would have received word.

He found his grandsire along with a few of his allies, rulers of some of the lesser settlements in the region, and Ayo, discussing the current state of the realm. 'It's not good, I fear, but I can't help but feel hopeless and disloyal. I think we should send more men,' one of them was saying, which was met by heated arguments. Enitan approached silently, trying to glean the gist of the discussion before his presence was known, and stopped in the shadow of the large stone arch of the entrance to the room.

'Right now, I cannot afford to send any more men. Half of my strength marched and may never return, plus, with the young prince here, I cannot afford to leave him vulnerable, especially if the worst should happen. You should all do the same. He will need every man amongst us if it comes to that,' his grandfather said. Most of the men in the room nodded. 'Besides, I am your liege lord, so this should not be a discussion at all. I merely give you the opportunity to understand my decision, not to question it,' he said with finality, leaving no room for arguments.

'Is there news of my father?' Enitan asked, unable to restrain himself at the mention of the king. 'Ah, you have awoken, my prince, I see the rest has served you well,' said his grandfather. Most of the men in the room bent the knee showing their respect for the throne, and Ayo had a relieved look on his face. 'You had us worried, my prince,' Ayo said. 'You slept for a day and night; I feared the exhaustion would claim you in your sleep.'

'I feel stronger now, thank you. But what news is there from the east?' Enitan insisted. Most of the men rose and looked at each other and back at his grandfather nervously. 'My grandchild, the last news that has filtered from the east is not good. The king was last reported to be on his way to Benin City, but his forces are greatly diminished. He sent some of his soldiers back to Ile-Ife to learn the fate of your mother and siblings and claim back the throne, but there are reports that those men were ambushed and most of them killed or taken as slaves. As for the king's main army, we've learnt that disease, hunger and desertion has plagued them on their journey, but still he presses on to confront your uncle. That is all we know,' his grandfather said, looking ashamed, as if he bore the responsibility of the misfortunes of the king.

'Then you must send reinforcements to support your king,' Enitan said, his voice raising in anger. Before now, he had almost accepted that all his family were lost to him, but this changed everything, offering him a glimmer of hope that all may not be lost, and the seat of his father could be restored.

'We cannot,' his grandfather said sympathetically. 'When we received the call to arms from the king, we sent most of our best warriors, whose fate is now entwined with that of the king. But I also received a message from the queen that you would be coming, which set in motion a long-standing plan with the throne. Right now, our only priority is your protection, so we cannot risk reducing our forces any more in case Olise decides to send his men this far west. You are all that matters, and we are now duty bound to protect you at all cost.'

'No, you can't leave my father to die, he needs your support!' Enitan shouted. Ayo moved to his side and said calmly, 'My prince, your grandfather is right. If we were to send men east, we would weaken our position and put everything at risk. This is the only choice we have. I am sorry.'

Enitan knew these words to be true, but still couldn't stomach the thought of his father dying in a battle he had no chance of winning. He felt like crying, but he soon mastered himself and looked at all the faces staring back at him. He saw a mixture of emotions on their faces, and could tell that some of them would have ridden if only he gave the word, but he saw the sense in his grandfather's proposal.

'You will need an army of your own, my prince, that is what we are trying to preserve and build for you. Let us see what the gods have planned for us, but know that every man here is yours to command and we will give our blood for yours without hesitation. This is your home now, please find a way in your heart to accept it.'

'Do I have a choice?' Enitan lamented, mostly to himself. 'I do not want to appear to be ungrateful for your protection, grandfather, but how can I live with the thought that I did nothing?' His grandfather walked over to him, placed his hands on his shoulders and spoke affectionately: 'You truly are the child of your mother, selfless and compassionate. I cannot claim to understand how your conscience torments you, but this is the only way. This, my child, is what your father wanted, and I mean to see his command obeyed. With time you will understand. The burden of a king is not one that many men can bear, but you may yet come to realise this.'

In that moment Enitan understood that the path he had been set upon would be a lonely one. Nothing could alter the course of his journey, and right there he decided to cast aside his emotions and all the strings that bound him to his past years of youthful bliss. From now on, he would only look ahead with one purpose, to restore the Adelani family name and re-establish his father's lineage in its rightful place; Ife.

All that shall defy him will burn.

THE CIRCLE

*T*here has always been much speculation surrounding the occult, but not many people actually knew if there was any truth to it. Like most Africans, the people of Ile-Ife were superstitious, with the core belief that with all things, there was a balance; good and evil, light and dark. The world, as we know it, existed in the light, but there was a dark side to our world, the underworld, which we did not know. It was believed that these opposing worlds were ruled by the gods, seated at either side of the balance.

The trickster god, Esu, more widely known as the devil, resided on the side of darkness and Olodumare, the god of creation, presided over the side of light.

It was also believed that some of the gods straddled the two sides of the balance, such as Shango, the god of thunder, who could be a vengeful and wrathful god but also showed moments of deep compassion. Ogun was another one; the god of war who was synonymous with sorrow, hardship and death, but he could also be invoked by the weak and the oppressed.

The matter of the gods was a complicated one and everyone had their own opinions, which were all as diverse as the many tribes scattered across the realm. However, it was not disputed that both sides had an unspoken hierarchy, one that was as ancient as the mountains were old.

Somewhere on that hierarchy of the dark side were the Babalawo and witches. These groups were prevalent across all the tribes. The Babalawo were well known and had no issue revealing who they were and where they resided. As a matter of fact, they dwelled openly in most villages and were seen more as spiritual guardians and native doctors. For the right amount of coin, they could provide to anyone who so sought them a wide range of services, from herbal remedies for all forms of ailments to prophecies, and even offered communion with the dead.

The witches, on the other hand, were a different breed. Only a select few knew for certain who they were or would even dare to know. After the Orisas, or the gods, the witches were feared most in the world of man and were only ever known to be malevolent. The truth was that no one had ever openly claimed to have met or known one. Rather, people speculated or suspected others of being one, but these conclusions were usually prompted by fear, hatred or jealousy, only to be whispered in hushed conversations as rumours that spread like wildfire.

There had never really been any concrete proof of their existence, but rather, the concept of witches was deduced from coincidences and circumstances that suggested supernatural influence that was nonetheless shrouded in secrecy and horror.

Several variations of their possible habits were available, depending on who you asked; for instance, some tribes believed that there was a certain market in the west that was dominated by the witches; traders and customers alike. It was said that if you were to bend forward and look upside down between your legs you would notice that some of the women floated in thin air, their feet hovering above the ground.

No one ever attempted it as it was believed that if anyone was brave or foolish enough to do so, they would feel the force of an almighty slap across their face that would rob them of their senses forever.

Others suggested that if you took a cane to a large banana tree in the dead of night during a full moon, witches would spew from the tree and howl into the night skies like birds released from a cage, taking your sight along with them, and henceforth you would live a life of sickness and suffering.

These were only superstitions that had never been attempted or proven. But witches were very much as real as a heart attack, just not as they were imagined. Not entirely.

Ekaete was one, a very powerful one in fact, and she belonged to a group of seven, whose sole purpose was to bring misfortune on to others and advance their own agenda. Within the group there was a power structure, similar to any hierarchical order. Evil could not even begin to describe those at the top of the order and Ekaete, powerful as she was, had been the last and youngest to have joined the group.

The one who led them was nothing less than a manifestation of pure wickedness. She was known for requesting a severe price for her favour, which was often a life and most likely that of a loved one, and this is the hold she had on some of her own, including Ekaete.

Long before Olise was born, Ekaete had designs of instilling herself at the top of the ruling class of men. She was from wealthy stock, being the daughter of a powerful Igbo lord with mixed Calabar heritage.

She wanted for nothing and was doted on by her father, but by the age of thirteen, her life changed. She had witnessed one of her father's vassals forcing himself on one of the household servants. When she approached her father Chidi on what she had seen, he had dismissed it and responded as if it were the most natural thing, telling her that this is what fighting men did, and for her not to think on it. He further stated that if a man was strong enough to take what he desired without fear of retribution or repercussion then he was entitled to it.

This explanation had shattered her fragile sentiments, which were only crushed further as she got older.

The tribes of the Igbo and Calabar were constantly at war with themselves and others and on several occasions, she would sneak into the hall room on a night of feasting over a victory of some battle or other and eavesdrop on drunken conversations between her father's men on the plunder they had gained from their victories, which almost always included their conquests over the opposite, or as they would refer to it, the weaker, sex. She was appalled to learn that these so-called "spoils of war" were treated as mere commodities to be used, exchanged, traded or discarded as men saw fit.

Since then she had vowed that she would rule these men, but knew she was at a disadvantage due to her gender, even if she was the child of one of the most powerful men in the realm. This is what *drove her to dabble in witchcraft, which all started innocently enough but evolved the older and more experienced she became.*

One day, she was on a trip to a neighbouring village when she was approached by a strange woman. There was something captivating about her, something that Ekaete couldn't quite put her finger on but, nonetheless, drew her in like a moth to a flame. The woman was extremely attractive and seemed to radiate life, but her eyes were old like that of one who had seen enough of the world to understand her place in it.

Ekaete herself was an exceptionally beautiful girl and was the desire of many a noble lord, but she was never approached due to the fear and respect people held for her father. She had no friends and seldom left the company of her household servants. So, to be approached by this mysterious woman only played to her sense of mischief and curiosity.

The woman almost seemed to have read her mind and told her that, with her beauty, she could have anything she desired from the world of man, including absolute power over the men who ruled it, which she deeply craved. She went further to say there were more who felt just like her and would aid her in obtaining her wishes.

The words she spoke were as sweet as nectar to Ekaete's ears, and the more the woman spoke, the more she fell under her spell. Before Ekaete realised it, she was swept away to a place she had no recollection of travelling to, surrounded by women who splashed her with something that appeared to be blood dripping from the tip of horsetail whips which they brandished whilst reciting incantations that held no meaning for her. She desperately looked about her and saw nothing but darkness. Where was she and what was this place that held nothing but shadows?

She was powerless, rooted to the spot, unable to scream out in fear or run away for help, but the longer the incantations were spoken, the calmer she became, and she eventually closed her eyes and gave in to whatever it was that was intended to possess her before falling into a deep trance.

In her dream-like state, images raced through her mind with visions of her father's men and the atrocities they had committed to defenceless women; rape, murder and oppression; men sitting on thrones of gold with female servants and slaves attending their every need. The anger rose in her. All the while, voices filled her head, telling her that she was the one who could right these injustices, for she was meant for a higher purpose, one that would place her above these so-called men. She would accept the path laid before her. She would embrace it.

Her visions began to change and the same men who had earlier been sitting on their thrones of gold and indulging in carnal pleasures began to cower and whimper like infants before her eyes. The women in her vision rose up and took the places of these men, who now grovelled and begged for their mercy, and she stood at the head of these women. Suddenly, hundreds, no thousands of men appeared before her, all with bowed heads and bent knees in supplication and fear of her. This was the world she wanted. The balance had been redressed and restored to the rightful gender.

No longer would women be ruled by men and used for their entertainment and pleasure. The roles had reversed, and she would be amongst the rule makers, feared, powerful and with the ability to alter the course of her own destiny. She would use this authority wisely. However, with all things, there was always a price to pay, one that would be very dear and may cut deeper than she was prepared for.

Ekaete snapped out of her trance and found herself sitting on the floor, still surrounded by the strange women. They had moved closer, tightening the circle, and now bore down on her. Ekaete felt a brief moment of panic, then suffocation but, for whatever reason, she knew she was in no danger. She saw that there was a gap between the women, enough for her to squeeze through and flee from wherever this place was. Then she thought what good that would do her and decided against the idea.

'All that you have seen will be yours if you so desire it. You have only but to take our vows and accept that your fate will forever be entwined with ours,' said one of the women. 'Once you do, there will be no turning back in this life or the next,' she finished. The rest of the women simply stared at her and awaited her response.

'I will accept,' Ekaete said with little hesitation 'But there is something that I would ask of you before–' The woman who had spoken raised her hand to silence Ekaete. 'I know what you desire, child, it is to be viewed as an equal, superior even, to the chiefs of these lands. This is possible for your father and his vassals but not the king who sits the throne of Ile-Ife and all the realm. This cannot be granted.'

'No, the one you think of is beyond our influence. He and his lineage are protected by forces much more powerful than we,' said another one of the women.

'This is what I desire. It is not enough for me to rule Imo and Calabar. If I am to give my mortal life to you, I want more. I want to rule over the entire realm.' Ekaete said with conviction. She knew that she gambled with these women but her natural disposition from her superior breeding and privileged life emboldened her.

There was silence for a while and then one of the women spoke. 'We can grant your wish, but not as you would have it. Although you cannot rule the realm, you could be the instrument for one who can. But I warn you, it will not be a long or prosperous reign, but one fraught with hardship, deceit and betrayal. Five years will be granted to you but, after this, you would sacrifice that most precious to you. The choice is yours.'

Ekaete could not resist the temptation of having ultimate power over the realm, no matter the cost. Whatever consequences they referred to would be dealt with in time but, for now, she would get all that she wanted.

She spoke the vows, drank from their forbidden calabash, a covenant of blood, and became one of them. When the rites were completed, she felt as if she had been born anew, ready to cast aside her old life and begin one that would take her to the throne of a king.

One of the women beckoned her to take her place beside the others, in the space left for her to complete the circle of witches.

SONS OF THE FATHER

The horses careened down the cleared path sending clumps of dirt into the air behind them. Sweat glistened on their backs and their mouths hung open with flecks of spittle from the exertion of travelling many miles without rest. The men who rode the beasts fared no better, weary and saddle sore, but still they rode on, determined to push their mounts to the limits of their endurance.

The great river Benue lay a few miles to their west, marking the border between the realms of the south and the mostly uncharted north; although it was a perilous line they trod, it was a necessary one to ensure the success of their mission.

One of the horsemen still bled from the broken arrow shaft in his shoulder, evidence of the last skirmish with the marauding tribes of these parts; men of no land and no allegiances. The warrior had refused to pull the broad arrowhead free for fear of tearing through more muscle and tissue and rendering his arm useless.

For now, he could still raise his shield and that was reason enough for him to endure the inconvenience, at least until they had ridden free of these hostile lands.

The one who led these men was coated in dirt and dried blood, which concealed his youth but his men, veteran warriors as they were, trusted his instincts and obeyed his every command. He had hoped to have reached the River-lands sooner, but had underestimated the extent of Olise's reach and doggedness to secure all the lands to the east of Benin.

Every settlement and group of men encountered on the road had to be treated as a potential enemy of the throne, and so far, most had proved to be just that, so Adebola had resolved to eliminate them all. He did not want to grant Olise the advantage of bolstering his army with more men to oppose his king. Thus, he had taken it upon himself to serve as the king's blade and hunt down such men on his journey east. Anyone who did not side with the king would only be allowed to serve one master; *Esu* in the afterlife. And he had sent many men there in the short time he had been in the field.

His small force had started off with just four but, along the way, they had gathered a few more soldiers to their cause, swelling their number to thirteen. However, they had lost two along the way in small skirmishes and could potentially lose another; the warrior with the arrow in him, if the wound was not tended to soon and became infected.

Despite this, Adebola had been fortunate to have found real warriors to reinforce his small band of killers, men who had heeded the king's call to arms. However, this was a secondary objective. His main purpose was to reach Imo and the River-lands and rouse what remained of the local lords and chiefs into an army that could reinforce the king's men and march west, hindering any chance of Olise retreating and escaping the king's justice. But he was losing time.

They had intercepted disturbing reports, from merchants and other travellers, of the fighting in the west and, if their words were to be believed, the king did not sound to be faring well. This only made Adebola push himself and his men further, still holding on to the vow he had made to the king and his chief Olusegun.

Adebola's thoughts came back to the present as he noticed a fallen tree some yards ahead of them directly in their path. He signalled for his men to slow their mounts to a trot as he quickly scanned his surroundings. Ever the tactician, he swept his gaze over the landscape; dense vegetation on one side that could easily conceal men, and a ridge on the other side, a good location for an ambush. He gestured for some of his men to fall back and the rest to spread out on the path, which was wide enough to accommodate three horses abreast. He shouldered his shield and drew his sword and his men followed suit without question.

As they approached the tree, two men walked out of the bushes casually as if they were on a morning stroll, only belied by their bearing; they were clearly warriors from the armour they wore and the weapons they both carried. One of the men rested a spear across his shoulder and the other carried a sword sheathed at his side in what appeared to be an intricately crafted leather scabbard inlaid with silver and precious stones. The quality of the men's armour was to a high standard indeed, with interlinking rings of silver and gold across the breastplates. Their insouciant nature didn't suggest violence, but Adebola wasn't prepared to take any chances, so he slowed his men further and advanced with caution.

The man with the sword was younger than Adebola, little more than a boy in fact, but his affectation was one of absolute confidence. He had undoubtedly seen some action from his stance and the balanced steps he took, as if every movement was calculated. There was also something unnerving about the boy's stare as he fixed his hazel coloured eyes on Adebola, rightly singling him out to be the leader of the group.

'Good morning to you,' the boy said. 'You are travelling with some haste, I see. Your horses look like they could do with rest and food, and so do you and your men.'

'And is this why the road has been blocked to us? To offer us a stop for replenishment? Forgive me if I appear unappreciative, but there aren't many hospitable people in these parts,' Adebola replied. His senses told him that there were more men around and he slowly moved his shield across his exposed flank fearing an arrow or spear would fly at any time.

'I have yet to tell you whether I am a friend. That depends on how you answer my next question. Forgive my directness but these are troubled times and, as you have alluded, it is hard to determine between friend and foe. So, I must ask you, who do you serve in the realm?' Adebola was taken aback, because this was the very question he would have put to the boy and his companion. If they were allies of Olise, he would have no choice but to throw caution to the wind and cut them down where they stood, taking his chances with whatever number of men were concealed in the bushes.

This option did not sit well with him, as he had usually meticulously planned every engagement they had been involved in up until this point, but he saw no other alternative. He did not want to needlessly risk the lives of his men, but they had reached an impasse.

He had not the time to turn back and seek another route east, which could take days. Too much was depending on him. The stones had to be cast and left to fall where they may. He chose his response carefully.

'It appears we are of like minds, friend. I understand the importance of such a question considering the dark times the kingdom is currently facing, but we are simple men, nothing but mere vessels for the gods, and we serve whoever they have deemed worthy to rule the lands in which we live.'

The boy considered Adebola's response for a few moments then replied. 'The crown sits on one man's head and no other is more worthy of the burden it holds. This is the decree of the gods. So, let us not mince our words, that king is Jide of the house Adelani. If he is not the man you serve, then I am afraid that you cannot leave this place alive. Friend.'

Something in the boy's tone told Adebola that this was not a mere threat and that he was prepared to act on his words or die in the process, confirming that this was in fact an ambush. He cursed under his breath, knowing that if he had met a real enemy, he most likely would have been facing certain death but, as luck would have it, his purpose was aligned with this strange boy.

He couldn't but admire the boy's bravery; any child, or man for that matter, would have simply turned and fled at the sight of armoured horsemen, but clearly not this boy. His curiosity was piqued.

'I didn't get your name, young man. It would be an honour to know the name of one so brave.'

'My name is of no consequence until you show your hand. So, I ask again, who do you serve?'

This time the boy's hand moved to the beautiful sword at his waist and Adebola glimpsed the scars on the boy's fist, which proclaimed that he was no stranger to fighting. This intrigued him even more. The tall warrior with the spear no longer exhibited a calm demeanour; his shoulders tensed, and his spear had moved into both of his hands, held before him with the broad, razor-sharp head angled slightly forward. These men were undoubtedly very dangerous.

Adebola turned to his men, who looked on uncertainly as their mounts snorted and stamped nervously under their weight. He gave them a signal with his eyes telling them to lower their weapons, which they obeyed somewhat reluctantly, then he turned back to address the boy.

'My name is Adebola and I am sworn to chief Olusegun Lawal, ruler of the Ondo province. I serve only one king, Jide of house Adelani. So now you know my name and my allegiance, will you tell me yours?'

The atmosphere clearly changed as the two figures in the road visibly relaxed. The tall warrior let out a low whistle, and moments later three men emerged from the bushes; two were positioned further back on the path close to where Adebola had halted some of his men and the other had concealed himself just a few feet from where Adebola's horse stood. The men came to stand by the two in the road and Adebola noticed that they all wore similar armour. There was some sort of crest embroidered on their chest, but it was hard to make out under the dirt and dust from the road.

'You have nothing to fear, friend. Will you join us and break your fast? We do not have much, but what we do have you are welcome to share with us.' With that, the boy turned around and started heading off towards a gap at the end of the fallen tree.

Adebola was still puzzled by the whole encounter. The boy had risked his life with only four men, and had not even flinched at the prospect of being outnumbered more than two to one. It also occurred to him that the boy's Yoruba was pristine, as spoken by those with a high standard of education, or royalty, in fact. *Who could he be?* Adebola thought. He called for the rest of his men and they all followed in the boy's wake.

They came to a camp which was mostly obscured by thick vegetation in all directions. Besides the small track that seemed to have been hastily hacked out, no one would have known it was there. Adebola and his people had to dismount and lead their horses on

199

foot along the track and the camp became quite crowded with all the horses and men around, but they all still managed to find a place. A fire had been lit, and for some time, by the looks of it as the smell of roasted meat suffused the air, making Adebola's mouth water in anticipation.

The boy took his seat at one side of the fire, his men arrayed about him like the spikes on a porcupine's back, all bristling with spears. Adebola sat on the other side and his men spread out in a similar manner, eyeing up those opposite and the food before them.

There were several small rodents and a few birds spitted and browned over the fire, and the boy pulled a stick free, took a bite and handed it to the tall warrior at his right shoulder before gesturing to Adebola to help himself. He wasted no time in taking one of the rodents, mimicking the same action as the boy by taking a bite and passing the food to the man behind him.

'So, am I likely to learn your name anytime soon?' he aked, not without humour. The boy looked up and fixed his hazel eyes on Adebola, which wiped the smirk from his face.

'Well, if you must insist. I am prince Niran, son of King Jide,' he said, with no ceremony.

Adebola smiled again and was about to laugh out but he searched the boy's eyes and saw nothing but seriousness there. He looked again at the men behind the boy one after the other. None of them smiled either, all waiting to see Adebola's reaction. There was a tense moment of silence; if any treachery or violence was to occur now would be the time, but no one moved. Adebola noticed again the similar armour on the soldiers; the small tribal marks on the cheeks of the tall warrior. He was most certainly of the Modakeke, of that Adebola had no doubt. So, the boy's words must surely be the truth.

He immediately prostrated himself in front of the boy and his men quickly followed suite. 'My prince,' he said, not believing his luck at finding one of the sons of the great king. 'How is it you have come to be in these parts? There are all sorts of reports coming from

Ife and it's hard to tell which to believe.' All of this while he lay on the floor before the prince.

Niran stood and gestured for the men to rise before he spoke. 'I took a great risk revealing myself to you, but I trusted my instincts. We managed to flee the city before it was razed to the ground,' he said, unable to mask the bitterness in his voice.

Adebola couldn't believe his fate as he stood and dusted the dirt from his cloths and began to tell Niran about the task that had been set him by the king himself.

Niran listened intently without interrupting, clearly hanging on every word spoken, eager to learn any news of his father, but there was no denying the shadow of sadness in his eyes at the mention of the king.

When Adebola had finished, Niran turned to the tall warrior, who had a grim expression, but nodded to his prince.

'I seek to raise support from the River tribesmen and chiefs in the eastern provinces to gather enough men about me to take back my birth right. It seems the gods have designed our paths to cross for this very reason. Will you serve me and join us in this endeavour?'

Adebola didn't need to think twice before he responded. He drew his sword and placed it at the feet of the prince. 'My sword and men are yours to command, my prince. I gave my oath to your father the king, as I would to any of his bloodline.'

The glade was suddenly filled with the sound of many swords leaving their scabbards, as the men behind Adebola followed his example and made their vows to the prince.

'I'm glad for your service. Please eat and rest. I intend to ride in a few hours,' Niran said, looking at all the men who bent the knee before him. He noted that one of the warriors kneeling close to Adebola had an arrow embedded in his shoulder and added, 'Your man will need to get his arm tended if he wishes to fight,' pointing to the big warrior.

The warrior bowed his head respectfully and addressed the prince, 'I can still ride and fight, my prince. All I need is food in my stomach and a few hours' rest.'

Niran regarded him for a few seconds, 'What is your name?' he asked. 'I am Dele, my prince, also sworn to chief Olusegun Lawal.'

'Dele, I am nothing but grateful to have such a brave warrior by my side, but I would rather you see to your wound, if only to ensure that there is no lasting damage. My blood-guard is skilled in such things and can help you.' He called over the tall warrior, who carefully prodded the tender skin around the protruding shaft and gestured for the warrior to sit before pulling out a long blade and placing it in the fire.

'I'm not going to like what comes next, am I?' Dele asked, eyeing the blade in the fire nervously. Adebola couldn't help but laugh. 'You are not afraid to run into a wall of spears, but the sight of a small blade terrifies you so?' he said.

'You do not need to worry. I assure you that you are in good hands,' Niran said to Dele before walking back to take his seat at the fire. An hour later, the shaft had been pulled out and the wound sanitised with a concoction of ground leaves and other herbs, wrapped tightly in heavy cloth donated from one of the men, whilst Niran, Seun and Adebola sat around the dying fire mapping out their route east. The rest of the men busied themselves with checking their gear, and dismantling the camp in preparation to resume the long march.

'This is still the fastest and possibly the safest route east,' Adebola was saying, using a stick to draw a line in the dirt. 'Have you considered which of the chiefs you will approach first?'

'I have an idea but there is still no certainty as to who remains loyal to my father, so we would need to tread carefully,' Niran responded, looking at the circles in the ground drawn to represent the various settlements in the east.

'I think the eastern chiefs will follow you regardless of whether they have sworn loyalty to Olise or not. You have only to proclaim your name and they would all fall behind you. They will never hold any true allegiance to Olise. They've always had bad blood for him, that I am sure of. The River tribes, on the other hand, are a different breed. If they are not loyal to Olise they will certainly be loyal to Ekaete, well, most of them anyway,' Adebola said.

'This is exactly what I fear given her influence; nonetheless, I must still try.'

'Try? You should simply remind them of who you are, and with a force of easterners at your back they wouldn't have a choice but to bend their knees.'

'I would rather they accept me with their own will, and not by force of arms. If I do that it would make me no better than Olise. The River tribes are a proud people with all their unusual traditions and culture, and they certainly don't take lightly to foreign influence. Besides, they have always considered themselves to be outside of the rule of the realm, regardless of how many times my forebears have brought them to heel. I think a little bit of diplomacy would be required to entice them.'

'What do you propose?' Seun asked. 'The way I see it, there are only two options to secure their alliance, either through marriage or a promise of land and title,' Niran finished.

'Marriage I can understand, but land, how so, when they could easily wait for Olise to conquer the west and grant them lands for their continued support anyway?' Seun asked.

'Olise will never grant lands to anyone, especially if he has fought and bled for it. He is a greedy man and, from his recent actions, I deduce that he seeks to take sole control over everything south of the river Benue. A man like that would never want to raise anyone's status for fear that they too, in time, would seek to better their standing in the kingdom and grow bold, eventually threatening his authority. No, he would want to keep every man in their place, always depending on him so he can remain in control.'

'You know a great deal about your enemy, as a true warrior should,' said Adebola, clearly impressed by the young prince's assessment.

'He is my uncle, after all. It would be remiss of me not to understand the man I mean to face; but that is for a time beyond this moment. For now, let us focus on what is in front of us. We have a hard road ahead of us and many a battle to fight, but I feel the gods are with us,' Niran said, looking at both men.

'The gods and my spear,' said Seun, beaming at the prospect of an adventure. This brought a smile to Niran's face, and Adebola's mood was also lifted. 'Right. Friends, shall we take to the road? Destiny awaits us, and I do not intend to keep her waiting.'

* * * *

The crossing of the river Benue had been a perilous one that challenged every fibre of the riders' resolution. At the height of the rainy season, the river was at risk of bursting its banks and flooding entire regions for miles but, over time, the locals had raised, widened and steepened both sides of the bank just for events like this to compensate for the annual increase in rainwater runoff. However, the currents still surged relentlessly, making it almost impossible for the horse's slippery hooves to find purchase on the rocks below the surface in the man-made fords created by the locals to serve as trading routes between settlements on both sides of the border. The crossing points were hard to find in normal conditions as they were constantly damaged by the surge of the river, so finding the passes under acute circumstances heightened the risk to life.

During the crossing, one of the horses had lost its footing and tumbled into the river, which swept both horse and rider away screaming into murky oblivion to be broken against jagged rocks weathered by centuries of water pressure, eventually washing up miles away and their remains eaten by crocodiles and other wildlife.

Only four of them remained, brought closer together from their weeks of travel and shared sacrifices; surviving the elements and attacks from predators, both animal and man alike. The routes beyond the river led them through forests that eventually gave way to miles of desert with sands perfectly intact as if no man had ever set foot on them. Now, as they pushed their horses on through the dunes and unforgiving heat of the northern sun, they had emerged stronger men, more determined and more dangerous than ever.

One of the riders spotted some movement up ahead, a shift in the sands that was unnatural against the otherwise undisturbed mounds of sand in sight, suggesting the presence of men. The rider didn't need to warn his men, they were in perfect synchrony, each rider in tune with the man at his side. Any minute gesture; an angled tug at the reigns, a movement of the head, a shift in body weight, told them all they needed to know. Such was the bond between these men.

Without warning, the four horses leaped into a gallop, throwing up sprays of sand as they split up and raced towards the mounds from different directions. Men began to emerge from the sand, throwing back the mats that had concealed them, all brandishing bows with notched arrows ready to loose. The riders didn't even attempt to stop their mounts but powered on with their shields now held before them. Arrow after arrow was fired at the riders, but they were shot erratically, with no discipline behind them, the would-be attackers being taken by surprise and unable to regain their composure. Most of the arrows went wide of their target, though some got lodged in the heavily layered cow hide shields that protected the riders and their mounts.

Before long, the horsemen were amongst the men in the sand and the killing began. Sprays of blood mixed with the sand, adding colour to the otherwise bland landscape as the bowmen were cut down, unable to flee from the onslaught. It only lasted a few minutes, and suddenly the desert was quiet again but for the occasional sound of wind blowing the sands along.

The horsemen came together, conferred with each other and made a quick assessment of their surroundings before pressing on along the same path they had intended. This time they didn't bother to put away their weapons, for they knew that they had finally reached the land they sought.

From this point onwards, they may need to fight for every mile they crossed, or they could ride unmolested and be welcomed into the bosom of the unknown north, but judging from this initial encounter, things didn't bode well. If there was to be more fighting, however, it made no difference to the men. The one who rode at their head was anointed by none other than *Ogun* himself.

The going was tough and made more difficult with the horse's laborious steps through the ever-deepening sands and, before long, their pace had slowed to a walk. The winds had picked up and the men were forced to wrap their faces with lengths of cloth to shield them from the swirling sands that lashed at them like rain.

They eventually came to a large sand embankment that stretched for miles in both directions, which seemed impossible to cross on horseback. They would need to lead their mounts on foot from this point but, just before they decided to dismount, several men on horses appeared at the top of the embankment. These were the northerners; they were easily distinguishable from the marauders they had previously encountered from the heavy wrappings around their heads and necks. They wore long flowing danshikis in white or tan with leather sandals on their feet. Each man appeared to be carrying bows in leather cases tied to their mounts along with long and slender curved swords at their hips.

At first, there had only appeared to be a handful of them, but slowly more took up position, forming a long line of men. They did not charge down to confront the four solemn figures at the bottom of the embankment, but rather stood and watched silently, as if waiting for a sign or signal of some sort.

The four men at the bottom of the embankment looked on unmoving and prepared themselves for whatever was to come. They didn't intend to give any ground; they had come too far and were not about to be intimidated, despite the greater numbers.

'Your orders, my prince,' said Leke, not taking his eyes off the horizon. 'Let them come to us. It would be foolish to fight uphill and if they choose to charge, their horses could never reach us intact, not in this sand. We will take them on level ground if it comes to that,' Toju replied.

'And if they choose to stay where they are and use us for target practice?' asked one of the other men, eyeing the bows of the northerners.

206

'The wind is against them, and they would just be wasting their arrows; besides, I'm told their attacks are always preceded by a war cry, that's why some people call them the screamers.'

The fourth rider let out a hearty laugh. 'The screamers, eh? Well, if I'm to die here I'd like to go out with my spear in one of their screaming mouths.'

'No one's going to die, not today at least. I don't think they'd wait this long if they did intend to fight us, anyway.' Toju nudged his horse a few steps forward then raised his great grandfather's spear above his head. By way of response, one of the horsemen on the embankment raised his bow. A minute later two men broke from the ranks and started making their way down the steep sandbank with the ease of professional horsemen.

'Look at that, the sand doesn't impede them in the least. Good thing they didn't choose to charge us, eh?' one of Toju's men said. 'Well, let's not get complacent just yet. There is still a chance that this could all be a ruse before they try to slaughter us,' said Toju as he moved forward a little more to meet the approaching men. Leke also kicked his horse forward to stand by his prince while the other men remained behind.

Toju kept his spear raised as a gesture of peace and his counterpart did the same. When they came together Toju noted that he was a handsome young man of an age with Toju with intelligent eyes framed by a soft face.

'Do you speak any southern tongues?' Toju asked in Yoruba, and the man responded back in the same language, fluently, with only a hint of a northern accent. 'Yes, I do,' he said as he inclined his head slightly in acknowledgement.

Both men regarded each other for a split second before the northerner spoke again. 'You are a long way from home, friend. What brings you to the lands of the north, besides eating the sand carried in the wind, may I ask?'

'My name is Toju, prince of Ile-Ife and first son to King Jide Adelani of the south. I seek an audience with the emir, who may be aware of my coming. There are grave matters that I would discuss with him. Matters that carry a degree of urgency, I might add.'

At the mention of his name, the northerner's eyes widened slightly almost in recognition, then he looked back at the other two riders in the background. 'If you are the prince, why is it that you come with such a small escort? I would have expected an army at your back and musicians to precede you beating those funny drums you southerners favour, heralding your arrival! How can I trust your words to be true?' he asked, now looking suspiciously at the sand-caked prince before him.

'He is the prince, and I am his blood-guard. I presume you know the legend of the Modakeke, and are familiar with the marks we bear,' Leke said as he moved closer, confident that no corner of the country was ignorant to his clan's reputation and the deeds of greatness that embodied them. It was also a veiled threat to warn off any thoughts of treachery. The northerner scrutinised Leke for a minute and his eyes settled on the tribal marks on each of Leke's cheeks before nodding approvingly.

'Ah, yes, I see it now. Forgive my rudeness, but it is not every day that we are graced with such esteemed guests. I hope you can appreciate our cautiousness.'

'I doubt anyone from the south would venture this far just to pose as a prince. What would be the point of such an action?' Toju remarked. 'Oh, but it would surprise you, prince of the south, the number of people trying to get an audience with the emir. People would go to any lengths just to glimpse his majesty, and they have started to get more inventive with their claims.'

'And who might you be, if I may ask? I sense some confidence about you, one that speaks of privilege. Not everyone has the liver to talk to me as an equal,' Toju said. The conversation had started to irritate him, and he just wanted to be gone from this desolate ocean of sand and plunge himself into a pool of water to wash the weeks of travel away and rest his weary bones.

'Forgive me, prince, but my name is Usman and, as it happens, I am also a prince, son in fact to the great emir Mustafa

Abubaka. Unfortunately, I am not the first son but one of many. I am, however, a senior member of the royal family none the less, so you will have a fitting escort that befits your station,' the northern man responded, inclining his head once again.

'I am pleased to hear it. I was hoping I wouldn't have to kill you. I rather like your humour,' Toju replied with a ghost of a smile upon his lips. Leke cringed inwardly, hoping that the prince's words wouldn't cause offence and result in bloodshed after all.

Usman looked at his companion, whose expression registered the shock of Toju's words. He then turned back to Toju, stared at him for a minute or so and unexpectedly burst out in a fit of laughter that was loud and genuine. The sound of it was so contagious that even the usually stone-faced Toju couldn't keep a straight face for long and joined in. A moment later, all four men were practically bent over from the pain in their stomachs from laughing; perhaps it was the release of tension that they all needed.

'Oh, by the gods. I can't remember the last time I laughed so. I think you and I will get along just fine, prince Toju,' Usman said, wiping tears from his eyes.

'As do I, prince Usman. I was hoping that you were not all as hostile as the men we first came upon in the sands.'

Usman's expression slowly became serious. 'What men do you speak of?'

'It's nothing, really, but we were welcomed by a group of marauders who sprang from the sands like desert rats hoping to catch us off guard. By the looks of them, I reckon they were just some lowly thieves hoping to waylay easy prey, but they won't be doing that again.'

'You mean you fought these men?' Usman asked.

'Well, I wouldn't call it a fight, if I'm honest, but I killed them all.'

'There have been rumours for many moons of a band of thieves that conceal themselves along the routes to the south, robbing and killing merchants and abducting their women and children for pleasure. That is why I have come here. I was sent by the emir to weed these men out and put an end to their tyranny.'

209

'No need, I have solved that problem for you. Let us call it a show of good will,' Toju said as he returned the gesture of inclining his head.

'A great celebration will be held in your name, my friend. You are truly welcome here. Come, let us not delay any further. The emir must hear of your deeds, he'll reward you handsomely.' Usman clasped Toju on the shoulder then spun his horse around on the spot and started to head back up the embankment.

Leke looked on as Usman and his companion made their way up the slope with the same confidence as riding on a flat surface. 'And we thought that horses could never make such a climb in these terrains. Now I understand why they are called the horse tribe,' he said, shaking his head in wonderment.

'Well, I'm sure if their horses can do it, so can ours. Ok then, lets meet this great emir, and please don't embarrass me on your way up or I'll have your balls,' Toju said as he signalled the other two men to come forward and started to make his way up the slope after Usman.

They travelled for some time, passing a series of strategically placed barracks teeming with horses and soldiers complete with desert settlements that appeared to have been purpose-built to sustain each of the barracks. All the people they passed along the way seemed to know Prince Usman, as they waved and praised him as he rode by.

Children ran alongside the horses with outstretched hands hoping to gain some reward for their efforts, and Usman did not disappoint. He constantly dipped his hand into his purse and produced silver coins, which he threw to the children as they scrambled to fight over their prize, not seeming to care much for their wellbeing as they darted between the horses unheeded.

'You are a popular man in these parts, I see, and quite the generous overlord,' said Toju as he watched yet another group of children and some young men hustle over the fortune in coins.

'Keeping the people fed and happy is the essential recipe required to maintain loyalty and peace in our kingdom. This is something my father taught me, and insists we all practice. That, my friend, is the secret to our prosperity,' Usman replied as he rode on with his near-perfect posture on his magnificent charger.

He continued, 'If ever we needed the people, they would eagerly answer our call in their thousands and lay waste to anything the great emir so much as pointed at, which they would do gladly and without question. Such is the depth of their loyalty, and this fidelity must be reciprocated.'

Toju did not entirely agree with this concept. He had always believed the people were of no consequence and were there only to serve the needs of the ruling class. Toju's father and brother Niran, on the other hand, did not share this view. They advocated putting the people first and giving them the means to thrive. But this had been done to their detriment and was one of the reasons, as far as Toju was concerned, why Ife had fallen.

However, he was not blind to the benefits of having the people at his disposal, and he selfishly thought of his own agenda to garner the support he needed to take back to the south and challenge his uncle. This was his only purpose, and he would see it through no matter the cost. So, he would mask his contempt for the northerners' empathy for their subjects and play the noble prince until he had accomplished his objective.

By the time they reached the city proper Toju could hardly contain his astonishment at what he saw. This place, deep in the harsh deserts of the north was, without doubt, a thing of overwhelming beauty to behold. All the tales, speculations and perceptions associated with the horse tribes couldn't have been further from reality, and Toju couldn't help but notice how dissimilar this alien place was to the land he called home. The wealth of the city was apparent from the quality of the massive wall erected around it that stretched far beyond the edges of his vision, nestling the sprawling dwellings of tens of thousands of citizens. This was the land of the Hausa.

Two magnificently sculptured monuments depicting men on charging horses with raised swords adorned the gates as you rode through, presumably of rulers dead and gone. If the statues were meant to inspire awe, the desired effect was achieved.

Once they cleared the gates, only then did the men of Ife truly appreciate the wealth and strength of this unknown empire. All the houses were built in perfect symmetry from either stone or sandstone bricks, and the favoured architecture of the structures was mostly of a circular design, in contrast to the square and boxlike buildings in the south. Most of the residential dwellings were two or three stories high and laid out in a crude grid format with narrow streets that boasted tall palm trees and other exotic species of wildflowers, which had clearly been planted by man and were not a design of nature in this harsh terrain.

They passed several large open squares that housed fountains or wells at their focal points. There were networks of gutters that were designed around the city, some foul and others supplying fresh water to the houses and irrigation systems for the vegetation and crops, similar to techniques applied in the south, but nonetheless an impressive display of engineering ingenuity. Every other street had a stable, blacksmith or shop and business thrived, from the number of patrons jostling for attention.

The city was buzzing with life as people went about their day, trading their wares, children playing in the street and others just idling in the afternoon sun. The men dressed like prince Usman, but slightly less exquisite, and the women wore wrappers that flowed down to their feet held in place by a knot tied behind their necks and accessorised by an assortment of colourful beads, precious stones or other forms of jewellery.

The wealthy citizens could easily be discerned from the silver or gold bracelets and earrings they wore, and many were accompanied by servants. One thing Toju did notice however, was that there was hardly any sign of poverty, and everyone seemed content with life here.

This was clearly a hub for commerce and the beating heart of the north. Although it did not possess the same charm as the south, with its undulating landscapes, beautiful forests, rivers, diverse ecosystem and wildlife, it made up for those with the beauty of simplicity. Besides the scatterings of satellite cities and settlements, the sight of the undisturbed golden sands that seemed to stretch to the ends of the earth and the disc of the sun hanging in the distance was nothing short of the perfection of the gods' creation.

If Toju thought the city was impressive, he was completely stunned by the sight of the royal palace. It was nothing short of utter opulence; constructed mostly from chiselled and gleaming marble, the palace towers dominated the azure skyline; it was a wonder Toju had not noticed it from outside the city walls. As they approached the impregnable looking walls, horns blared, and the gates swung open to emit a group of screaming riders in royal livery who galloped out from the palace at full speed.

Toju turned to Usman alarmed, who responded with a wink. 'Fear not, they are but an escort. I sent riders ahead of us to announce your arrival. After all, you are a prince of the south and one such as you requires a befitting welcoming,' he said. Toju had a feeling that he was going to enjoy his time here.

A KING, A PRINCE AND A THRONE

The clanging of bells echoed through the city just before the sun was at its highest point in the sky, shattering the brief moments of relative calm. The time had come for the gods to decide the unfortunate souls that would depart from their frivolous existence to forever roam the underworld.

Most of the city's inhabitants had already barricaded themselves in their homes as best they could, knowing that their efforts were probably futile against an army intent on their destruction.

The soldiers, on the other hand, were making every preparation to delay the inevitable and make the task as difficult as possible for the enemies soon to be at the gates; barricades were being erected, pits were dug and filled with sharpened stakes and the battlements were supplied with cauldrons full of heated oil and large rocks hauled from the nearby quarry, ready to be dropped down on any intruders.

Olise stood in his chambers as servants busied themselves about him, fitting him with his armour - leather breast guard with links of bronze plating, arm guards and greaves over the straps of his sandals, while he sipped from a small calabash filled with palm wine.

Dimeji was close by as always, and was silently honing the edge of his great sword with a piece of granite rock, while Ogie was having his wounds cleaned and bound afresh by a young servant with clean linen.

'Gods!' he exclaimed when the cloth was tightened around his torso. 'That bastard was really lucky with that blade of his. If only I could kill him again for the pain he has put me through. Argh!! Take it easy, boy, or I'll hurt you worse than this,' he shouted at the servant who was doing his best to calm his shaking hands.

'Was it not Dimeji that ended him, eh?' Olise asked. 'That may be, but my spear slowed him enough to allow Dimeji to finish him off,' Ogie replied, as he clenched his teeth against the pain.

'You should count yourself fortunate that Dimeji was even there, it could easily have turned out much worse for you. Edem was, after all, one of the most feared River chiefs, and many tales have been told of his skill and brutality, mind you. So, there is no shame in it,' said Olise.

'The only shame I feel is that I didn't make him suffer enough!' Ogie said under his breath.

'Don't worry, you'll have plenty of opportunity to take your anger out on those who would oppose me. By the sounds of it, that could be right now,' Olise remarked as he turned his head towards the window to the sound of the bells in the background.

'I can't wait!' Ogie struggled to his feet, picked up his spear and began to rotate his shoulder tentatively, wincing at every movement.

'Come. Let us see what the day holds for us. It has been a while since I wet my blade. I just hope that Jide is at his best and not too starved to swing his sword,' Olise said with a smile, and began to make his way towards the entrance, followed by the hulking figure of Dimeji and the slightly limping Ogie.

By the time Olise reached the battlements, soldiers had gathered to look out into the field beyond, just as one of the guards on the wall cried out, 'soldiers approaching!' Sure enough, after a few minutes a group of men came into view, walking in single file. There weren't many of them, no more than twenty perhaps, but it was obvious that they were weary from the way they ambled along with their heads downcast as they dragged their feet.

When they were close enough for their features to be distinguished, it became clear that they were Olise's men and not the enemy, and by the looks of their blood-stained clothing, they had obviously been in a serious fight.

'They're our men, my prince,' said one of the guards on the wall. Olise looked closer at the men and confirmed. 'Ah, those are the scouts I sent to infiltrate Jide's camp. I thought them all dead, so this is a welcome sight indeed. Open the gates, I would have their report before they are rested. My brother cannot be too far behind.'

The massive timber gates were hauled open by four men as the soldiers shuffled through as if they had lost the will to live and were being ushered to their deaths.

They gathered just beyond the battlements within the walls, and some of them seemed a bit more alert; scanning their surroundings and casting surreptitious glances at the men beside them.

Olise made his way down from the battlements as he looked over the men, slowly at first and then with rising alarm, as he failed to find a familiar face in the crowd. Something made him stop on the steps and look more closely. The armour they wore certainly bore evidence of a fight, but most of them had punctures to the chest and other areas that should have protected the wearer's vital organs. Surely, these wounds would have been mortal. Then it hit him.

'Close the gates now and seize those men. They are impostors!' Olise roared, and just as the words left his lips, swords, knives and axes appeared in the hands of every man that had come through the gates and they all came alive, springing into action. A group of them detached from the main body of men and immediately went for the gates, killing the guards and forming up in a semicircle in front of it to prevent any more of Olise's men approaching it.

For a few heartbeats, it was complete chaos in the yard as the rest of the intruders drove forward, attacking any solider in sight, most of them caught completely unaware as swords and spears were thrust into unprotected flesh.

Over the sounds of battle and cries of dying men, the bell started to clang once more, alerting the defenders to a new threat. Olise, sword in hand, raced back up to the battlements and, as he came to the top, a moment of fear gripped him at what he saw.

Just coming over the horizon, an army was approaching. He saw thousands of soldiers all running towards the open gates of the city. They moved like wild animals, desperate in their pursuit as if following the scent of blood from a wounded prey. They spread across the blackened landscape like locust as more and more men flowed from a distance. Jide had finally arrived.

'Get those gates closed now!' Olise shouted as he frantically pointed to the army that would soon breach the walls, but as he looked behind him into the yard, he realised that his commands might not be carried out in time.

The men that had made it into the city clearly held the ground. They fought as only desperate men would, with the efficiency of experienced soldiers managing to maintain good order as they gradually advanced through the courtyard, creating more space for the arrival of their king. There were already bodies everywhere, and Olise wondered where the rest of his men were and why they had not engaged the enemy, questioning himself whether some of his eastern allies were purposely holding back to give Jide a fighting chance of taking the city.

Anger rose in him and threatened to boil over as he realised that he could trust no one. He swore to seek out any conspirators and pull them out by their roots, extirpating any further possibility of seeds of deceit being sown amongst the men he had gathered to himself. He would have to get his hands dirty after all, but it made no difference to him. He knew the time would come for him to fight, but had done all he could to dictate the terms.

He turned to the silent figure beside him, sensing his mounting excitement at the prospect of bloodshed. 'Dimeji, take care of those fools at the gates. I want them closed before Jide gets there.' Dimeji cracked a rare smile, all teeth and no emotion, just before he leaped from the battlement stairs and landed lightly with a grunt in the blood-stained courtyard. Several soldiers on the wall followed his lead but took a more cautious approach, choosing to take the stairs rather than the quicker route.

Several of Olise's personal guards now began to pour out of the barracks armed and armoured, ready to add their support in repelling the intruders, for whom it was a losing battle. The shear

217

numbers of soldiers within the wall would eventually overwhelm such a small force, but still the intruders fought on.

These men did not lack in bravery or skill, but they were beginning to lose the previous ground they had so desperately fought to secure and now, they were forced to retreat step by bloody step. They had already lost several of their men and the ones that could still fight retreated to join their comrades at the gates. This would be their last stand.

The fighting had dwindled and now both sides stood across from each other, waiting for the final onslaught. Dimeji pushed his way through the crowded soldiers to stand in front of them and hefted his great sword towards the small force at the gates. They all knew of him and the fear they felt was palpable, but they had a duty to perform and they would not waver. Not with everything that was at stake. Besides, they had only to hold the gates for a few more minutes before Jide brought his army through them to claim back what was his.

'Throw down your weapons. You are outnumbered and can't possibly survive here,' said one of Olise's captains.

'Why don't you come and take them from us, cowards?' replied a grizzled warrior from behind a shield that had been taken from one of the dead. The men beside him laughed, even though they knew that they were unlikely to see the next sunrise.

Dimeji, on the other hand, had no desire to exchange words and started to walk forward. Two overzealous men at the gates broke rank and decided to meet him before he got too close. Dimeji shot forward unexpectedly and as soon as he moved the two men died. With a speed that belied his bulk, he dashed forward and swung his great sword in a diagonal upwards motion, taking the first man, and without breaking his rhythm, his sword arced downwards to take the second.

The remaining men at the gates looked on in horror at the lifeless forms of their companions bleeding out into the soil, fear clearly visible in their widened eyes. They had all accepted that infiltrating the camp and holding the gates was suicidal, but accept it they had, regardless of the consequences. They had all been eager to enact their vengeance on the usurper for his atrocities on their homeland, but they were naïve in thinking that they would not be facing one of the most feared and fabled warriors in all the realm so soon.

The grizzled warrior who had refused to disarm earlier stepped out of the line of shaking spears, swords and shields. He was also a man with a name and would be the king's blade against this adversary.

'You must be Dimeji,' the warrior said. 'It seems that the legends told in your name are true.' Dimeji showed no sign of even comprehending this man's words. 'Well, I'm here to test that legend. My name is chief Rotimi Balogun of Owo and for my king you will die here.' He spoke over his shoulder to his fellow warriors, unwilling to take his eyes off the menacing figure before him. 'Whatever happens here, hold the gates with your life. We can't afford to falter now; your king and the kingdom depends on you. Let us not let the sacrifices of our fallen brothers be in vain.' They all swallowed their fears and gripped their weapons tighter, ready to carry out their final duty to their chief and king. 'On our honour, my chief,' said one of the men, and this sentiment was echoed between them.

Rotimi wiped the blood off his sword and pulled on the axe that hung from his waist. His lips moved as he silently prayed to the gods and, with a last show of defiance, his war cry reverberated through the courtyard as he charged forward to meet Dimeji.

* * * *

Jide's feet, along with those of the thousands of men that ran alongside him, pounded on the desiccated soil, creating clouds of dust that hung in the air as they raced towards the walls of Benin City. His heart beat heavily in his chest and he tried to take measured breaths to pace himself for what was to come. He could see that the gates were still open, and he was determined to make it through before they shut, sealing what could be his best opportunity to take the fight to Olise.

Despite their slightly haggard appearance from the hardships they had endured to get here, the soldiers kept good pace. The moment had finally come for the history of the southern tribes to be etched in stone for all eternity. Jide's legacy and that of his people would be determined here in the soils of Benin. This was the culmination of all the hard miles marched, the innocent lives lost, the cities and villages that had burned and the sacrifices of countless individuals. Jide had vowed not to treat Olise as the brother he had once loved, but as an enemy to everything Jide held dear. Olise's story, and that of those who supported him, needed to be purged from the history of the Yoruba, his tale never to be told and banished in the recesses of time.

Four hundred yards from the gates, the repetitive sound of Akin blowing short bursts of air at Jide's right shoulder gave him reassurance. Jide looked to his left side and saw the smiling face of Adedeji, surrounded by the Modakeke, faces focused intensely ahead, and all visibly eager to breach the walls of the city and carry out the work that they had been put on this earth to perform.

They were the perfect killing machine, the likes of no other amongst the tribes; highly skilled, ruthless and above all, disciplined. However, despite the advantage of possessing a more superior fighting force, Jide knew that the task they faced was one that carried great risk. They were facing a fresh army of greater numbers, well provisioned, prepared and secure behind their wall. Jide's men, on the other hand, could not endure a siege, for they would surely starve at the gates. Their rations were depleted even down to their water, energy and morale was low and the only thing that gave them the will to push on was the hope of what lay beyond the walls. There were no more strategies, no further options. Everything depended on the success of this plan, as it was literally their last attempt at survival.

Three hundred yards; the muscles in his legs had started to ache but he pushed the pain down into the depths of his subconscious, choosing to focus on the ground ahead. He began to go over his strategy once he was beyond the walls; secure the perimeter, neutralise the men on the battlements then spread out into the city. He would spare the innocents – the elderly, women and children, but he would show no mercy to any man who bore arms against him; even though this was against everything he stood for, an example had to be set.

His first child, Toju, had always thought him too lenient. Maybe he was right. Maybe a firmer hand was the right approach and he wouldn't be in this situation right now, but the stones had been cast and the only solution was to shed the blood of his countrymen, for whatever side they chose, countrymen they were.

He knew it wouldn't be easy, Olise had had weeks to prepare for his coming and would have taken necessary steps to ensure that the city was not overrun. The one thing that gave Jide confidence was that his men still boiled with the indignation of the crimes Olise had perpetrated on their homes, families and livelihoods. Each man on these unhallowed fields had been affected either directly or indirectly, and nothing could sate their grievances other than to face the men they held responsible for their pain.

Two hundred yards; his shield was heavy now and the spear in his hand was clumsy, but he propelled himself onwards. He became acute to small details; the stones logged in his sandal between his foot and the soft leather that sent jolts of pain into his leg with every footfall, the constant slap on his thigh from the sword that hung from his waist, the beads of sweat that ran down his back that quickly evaporated from the adrenaline that coursed through his veins.

The gates were clearer now, they were mighty things and one of them suddenly glistened with the sight of fresh blood. His heart lurched at the thought of the men holding them in his name, putting their lives on the line to ensure that their king had a fighting chance.

He thought of Rotimi, the often quiet but humorous chief who had volunteered himself and his best warriors before their plan had even been finalised, risking everything in service to his king and what the kingdom stood for, as all these brave men had done.

His blood boiled at the fate Olise had brought upon the realm through selfish ambition and his hunger for power. This galvanised him and he compelled his legs to move faster, pushing against the pain, the anguish and the onset of fatigue.

One hundred yards; his lungs burned with every breath but still he pushed on. He tried to inhale through his nose and exhale from his mouth to draw as much oxygen as possible into his lungs, to break down the build-up of lactic acid that spread through his muscles like a cancer. But he was failing. And yet he pushed on, not willing to show weakness in the face of the brave men who surrounded him. He would rather his lungs burst, or his legs give out from underneath him, before he gave up.

Adedeji and Akin had moved slightly ahead, flanking him, and slowly the body of men began to form like a spear head as they converged towards the open gates, ready to pierce through. Shields and spears came forward as the men braced themselves for what would surely be a bloody struggle.

'Prepare yourselves and show no mercy!' someone shouted far off to Jide's right. He shot a quick glance at the men closest to him and was greeted by the sight of barred teeth and determined looks. One or two of the men flashed smiles but more held the unmistakable glint of fear in their eyes.

'Guide my right hand and give me strength, protect my mortal flesh and those of the men around me,' Jide prayed to *Yemoja*. Others were doing the same as lips moved in silent prayer to their gods of choice.

Fifty yards; the clash of iron beyond the walls was audible now, accompanied by the screams of dying men. Jide prayed that Rotimi and his men were the ones doing the killing, but he'd be naïve to think that they could possibly survive such a suicidal action. Guilt consumed him once more and the urgency in the movement from his men became palpable, all eager to assist their comrades.

Jide raises his spear, 'For Ife and for our kingdom!', he roared as loudly as his lungs would allow; the cry was taken up by those around him and spread quickly, the cacophony rising to the sky and reaching a crescendo as all the men in the field added their voices to the blood curdling war cries of the men of Yorubaland.

They were within reach now, but the soldiers who manned the walls had their backs turned to the approaching army, preoccupied by the fighting within the wall. However, one or two of them snapped their heads round at the sound of the warriors and began to gesture frantically towards them and the open gates.

Suddenly, the mighty timber gates lurched forward, slowly at first, then they began to pick up momentum and finally slammed shut with a loud boom. Jide breathed inwardly 'No...'

A few minutes later the first wave of men collided with the gates, which only shifted a few inches but held fast. In their desperation, the warriors started to pound and kick at the solid timber; others pulled out axes and began to hack away relentlessly, but in vain, as it would take hours to break through.

The next few moments were nothing short of absolute carnage. Large rocks rained down from the battlements, crushing skulls and maiming men by the dozen. The rocks were followed by streams of boiling black oil that melted flesh on contact, then fire that ignited the oil and sent up a blaze burning all the unlucky men who had been in the front line. More and more men fell, and the air was filled with the sounds of torment and the desperate pleas of men begging for help or the mercy of death's embrace.

'Fall back, fall back!' shouted captains and other officers desperately trying to regain some form of order amongst the disorientated men, but fear had found a home in most hearts at the sight of so much death and a number of soldiers abandoned their courage and desperately tried to flee from the ravenous flames that consumed their companions.

Jide stared helplessly at the imposing gates, now framed in fire and the bodies of his men. He could not understand how the gods could forsake him so and plague him with so much misfortune. He wanted to throw back his head and scream up to the heavens to curse them all. He wanted to sit in the dirt and weep, but even his tears quickly evaporated from the heat. His eyes stung, his throat was dry, and his lungs were singed from the fumes. Worst of all was the scent of burning flesh that filled his nostrils, making it even harder to breathe.

As soon as the first rocks had struck, Jide was surrounded by some of the Modakeke and forcefully ushered towards the back of the lines, his men being too accustomed to the dangers of sieged battles and their duty to protect their king.

The failed assault had resulted in losses of over a hundred men, with more injured, striking a fatal blow to morale and their chances of securing the stronghold. Jide's plan was all but crumbling before his eyes and his grasp on power faded with each fallen soldier.

If Olise chose to stay behind the walls it was only a matter of time before Jide's men starved to death or deserted him knowing that they fought a losing battle.

'All is lost. We have failed you, Kabiyesi,' said Adedeji with a heavy heart. He had been close to the front and only narrowly escaped being crushed by a large rock, but he had been close enough to the man in front of him who hadn't been as lucky and whose blood now decorated Adedeji's features.

'There has to be another way into the city. Any more direct assaults would be suicide. Either that or we turn our tail in defeat, which I don't think is an option,' Olusegun said.

'And how do you think that would go with the men if we were to turn back now? Do you mean to tell me that all our sacrifices have been for nothing? I cannot accept that. One way or another, I will take the city or die in the process.' Jide said with finality.

Most of his chiefs and captains who had survived looked at each other in despair, hoping that someone would magically solve the puzzle they all pondered, but no one spoke up.

'Kabiyesi,' said Akin. 'We have no instruments of siege to breach the walls, nor do we have the luxury of rations or men for that matter, at our disposal. I am not suggesting we flee, but rational thinking must prevail.'

Jide looked at his blood-guard for a moment before he spoke. 'My kingdom is in ruin, most of my people have either been cast to the winds or killed and I have lost the most precious thing of all, my family. Do you think I could simply walk away? All I have left to me are my sword and my spear, and I intend to use them.'

Nothing more needed saying, so Akin averted his eyes and nodded as he turned towards the wall to the distant cries of men still burning.

'This will be the moment that defines us as a people. We were born to these lands; our forebears have bled in these very soils for it and they would turn in their graves to see it in the hands of these traitors. We shall find a way. We MUST find a way,' Jide said, raising his voice so more of the men could hear him.

His words seemed to cut through the fog of fear and doubt. Slowly, the soldiers started to gather to hear their king, getting the attention of their companions who still watched the horrors at the gates.

'Every city wall has its weakness, be it a crack or misplaced stone, there is always one. What of the sewer that takes away the city waste or a source of water that supplies them, something, anything?' Jide continued.

'If we are to wade through shit to get to our enemies I suggest we send our friends from the Ondo province, that place is a shit pit so they should be used to the smell,' said one of the captains. His comment was met with laughter and light-hearted insults. This was good, the officers were attempting to restore morale and it was working.

Jide couldn't help a smile of his own but added seriously, 'If we are to go through shit, we shall do it together. My point is this plight we share is for all of us to bear, not one. Whatever it may be, we shall stand together.'

At this, all the men in earshot let out cheers in defiance, and Akin admired his king the more for his ability to drag a man from the depths of despair and offer a glimpse of hope.

An hour passed and Jide had his men stood in formation at a safe distance away from the walls. They had had no choice but to leave the wounded where they lay or risk more casualties, but every man who survived now burned anew with the desire to take the city and avenge their fallen comrades.

A horn sounded from the battlements and the men on the ground noticed a flurry of activity before several objects were thrown and sent tumbling into the air to land just beyond the remains of Jide's men.

At first everyone thought they were rocks, which was quite unusual, but Jide ordered some of his men to investigate. They did so cautiously but they need not have bothered. What had been launched from the battlements was a message, one that the king would be permitted to receive without the threat of attack.

When the group of soldiers returned to the safety of their lines, it was clear that the flames of their rage had been stoked from the reaction of the soldiers they walked past. They made their way through the lines to where the king stood and when they arrived, he understood.

Cradled in the arms of the soldiers with as much dignity as could be offered were the heads of Rotimi and some of his men, flies already surrounding their gaping mouths and upturned eyes. Jide's fears had been confirmed. A part of him had hoped that if their plan had failed, Olise would have taken Rotimi as a hostage to use as leverage in negotiating a truce or surrender, but his actions had revealed that Olise held no such desire and was determined to end this conflict by the spear.

The soldiers from Owo that had not accompanied their chief were overwhelmed by grief and a vehement desire to avenge their leader as word spread quickly through the ranks of men. Akin and Adedeji simply exchanged looks and began to ready themselves to fight, as they knew that Jide would not sit idly by at this latest provocation from his brother.

'Kabiyesi, please think before you do anything injudicious,' Olusegun implored the king, but his ears were shut to any voice of reason as he stared at the grotesque expression on the head of one of his most trusted chiefs. Picking up his spear, he began to walk towards the walls, followed closely by Akin and Adedeji, the rest of the

Modakekeclose behind. Olusegun still called to his friend, but eventually had no choice but to fall in line with the rest of the men.

Jide came to stand before the walls, which were lined with soldiers armed with spears, but it was obvious from their expressions that they recognised the king, as none of them made any attempt to attack him. They all stood in silence as they watched him walk from the gathered soldiers and despite being in such a vulnerable position, still they did nothing.

'Olise!' Jide suddenly roared. 'Olise! Show yourself.' Only silence followed his request. 'Is this the man you have chosen to follow? One who hides behind stone walls and only fights the weak and helpless? Is this the man you wish to rule your nation?' Jide directed at the men on the wall. Some of them exchanged looks, knowing that Jide's words would surely strike a chord with his enemies. Besides Olise's closest allies, most had questioned his motives and the means by which he set out to achieve them, but fear of his mother had always bound them to him.

'Olise!' Jide continued to shout, 'You claim to be a warrior and yet you fear to show your face? Let it be known that only cowards refuse the call of a warrior. I stand before you with my spear and sword, a king, and you are nothing but a traitor not worthy of the name you carry.'

Within the confines of the city, Olise sat on a stool in the courtyard close to where the bodies of Jide's men had been piled up ready to be thrown over the wall and listened to the rants of his brother. In truth, part of him was afraid of finally seeing Jide, for he knew that, despite the passage of time and the events that had led them on separate paths, he always held a sense of respect, and even love, which could not be extinguished so easily. He was afraid that Jide would see it in him and his resolve would be weakened. That could not be allowed to happen.

'Don't let him goad you into a fight. You should leave them to bake in the sun and starve like dogs,' Ogie said beside him. 'I doubt they'd last a few days. We have nothing but time, the wall and many moons' worth of provisions. When they turn their backs to slip away, we can fall on them like the rainstorm that floods the earth in the rainy season. I see no benefit in wasting our strength on a broken army.'

'I don't think that's a particularly wise decision. Look around you, Ogie. Look at the men about us, see how they avert their eyes. Those are the looks of shamed men. I must hand it to Jide, even in defeat he still knows how to reach the hearts and minds of people. His words have moved these men and if I do nothing, I risk losing them and facing another betrayal just like we saw with Edem,' Olise said, slowly sipping the palm wine that had managed to find its way into his hand. He then stood up, draining the last dregs of the drink before throwing the calabash to the floor, smashing it to pieces.

'It is time for me to claim my throne. This can only end one way, with one king of this realm, and today I will wear the crown. Summon all the chiefs to me this instant,' he said. 'Yes, my prince,' Ogie responded somewhat sheepishly before setting off to round up the commanders.

* * * *

'We cannot hold off any longer or we risk exposing ourselves. As much as I hate this charade, we must be seen to stand with Olise. For now, and certainly before the real fighting starts. When the time is right, we will show our hand,' Zogo said to Nnamdi and Akpan as they watched their combined armies prepare themselves haphazardly in the barracks.

They had been informed of the desperate fighting at the gates and realised that Jide had made an attempt to breach the city. Although they could not be seen to openly support Rotimi and his men, they had agreed to delay joining the effort to repel the invaders and let the scenes of chaos play out, even though it had tormented them to see good men die. They deliberately withheld their joint forces of Igbo and River warriors but now Olise had called on them to attend him and they suspected that he intended to face the king.

'Make sure your men know what to do. Need I remind you what is at stake here, friends?'

228

'They will be ready, Zogo, you have my word,' replied Akpan. Nnamdi just nodded gravely, his mind on the hostages that Olise held. Indeed, plenty was at stake and only the gods knew how the day would end, but the men of Imo were committed to their course and would see it through whatever the outcome.

'Ah, so you have finally decided to join us,' Olise remarked as the Igbo and River chiefs approached the war council he had called in the courtyard. Several of his captains and other chiefs of the realm were already there, all donning an assortment of traditional armour heralding their provinces. 'I was beginning to think you had a change of heart,' he said with a hint of irritation, which Zogo chose to ignore.

'We are here to do your bidding, my prince,' Zogo replied with a bow of his head. An obvious slight, which Olise also chose to ignore given the circumstances.

Olise turned his attention back to the men before him. 'I mean to grant Jide's wish and meet him on the field of battle. I see no reason to wait for the gods to decide our fate, I'd rather be the one to steer it.' This drew some muttered remarks from the soldiers around with some looks of concern.

'However, I'd rather not have to worry about a knife in my back. So the question is, will you fight with me or would you prefer to join our friend chief Edem?' he pointed at the rotting heads that still decorated the ramparts, a stark reminder of how he dealt with traitors. At his side Dimeji stepped forward brandishing his great sword, ready to carry out his prince's commands. Olise looked around at the faces of his chiefs and captains, 'No. No takers? It's settled, then, we fight. Ready your men. We leave the city within the hour.'

'Is that wise, my prince?' one of the Calabar chiefs asked somewhat timidly; 'We have the advantage. To open the gates now would be foolhardy. With respect, my prince,' he added hastily. Olise only looked at him and his silence was answer enough. 'As I said, we leave the city within the hour. I suggest you all prepare yourselves. This conflict ends today'. With that, Olise stood and walked off in the direction of his chambers, with Dimeji and Ogie close behind.

'It is decided, then. Olise means to let the soil flow with blood. *Chineke* will certainly have his fill of worthy sacrifices when the sun sets today. May the gods help us all,' Zogo said in Igbo. Beside him Nnamdi tried to swallow, but his throat was suddenly dry.

SINS OF THE MOTHER

'I see no reason for us to fall out over this. You of all people know that I've never had any designs for the crown, not even with the constant reminder from everyone in the kingdom that it is my birth right. My love for you and the preservation of our bond I place above all else.' Jide pleaded with Olise as they both sat in the gardens of the royal palace in Ife.

Olise tried to contain his emotions, not wanting to show how he truly felt, but he found it hard to stop himself. 'The kingdom belongs to the both of us, we should share it in as much as we share our father's blood. Did we not swear to each other to rule equally if it ever came to this? Instead you expect me to bow and scrape to you as if you are my better? I will not!' he responded, his voice steadily rising in anger.

'What would you have me do? I cannot simply ignore the will of the people, it is them we serve, and they have made the decision, not I.'

'They serve you!' Olise shouted back, 'we rule them, not the other way around. They are only able to exist because we allow it. We hold the titles, the wealth and the resources and they are mere peasants, good for nothing but labouring in our fields.'

'That is where you are wrong, brother. We are nothing without them. They are the beating heart of this kingdom and the source of our strength, and I think they should be treated as such and afforded every respect that loyal subjects demand and desire.'

'What has become of you, brother? Your words are like those of a goat and not the leopard you are. The will of the people is of no significance. Let us rule as we were born to rule. If anyone disagrees, they will simply be removed.'

'We cannot rule in this fashion, brother. All this talk of removing people, what sort of precedent do you think that would set? What would stop the men we entrust to enforce our laws from simply "removing" the people that they don't like? You risk opening a poisoned calabash that would erode the very thing this kingdom stands for. The people would lose all faith in us, and what if they rebel? Have you thought of that?'

Olise banged on the table between them suddenly, sending the horns of water tumbling to the ground. 'Enough of this talk of rebellion! They would not dare raise arms against their sovereign rulers! As far as I am concerned, there is only one law that matters; there are those who rule and those who serve. This is the legacy we must preserve, the legacy of the elite, and not one that benefits the masses. Anything less is weakness.'

Jide looked at his brother for a long time before he finally spoke. 'Brother, are these really your thoughts and your words, or those of your mother? I know deep down you agree with my rationale and I refuse to believe otherwise. Let us be reasonable about this. The last thing I wish is for any of this to affect our relationship. We are brothers and we also swore that we would let nothing come between us, not the kingdom, nor our families. I intend to keep this promise.'

'If you truly meant that then you would heed my words. Think on it, dear brother, but you would do well to think "reasonably". After all, I think you stand to lose more than I.' With that Olise stood from his stool and walked into the palace.

Akin and Adedeji had been attending the prince in the wings at a respectable distance, but stood close enough to hear most of the conversation, and now approached Jide, who sat with his head cradled in his hands obviously affected by the exchange.

'My prince,' Akin said softly, 'No crown is worn lightly, the weight of it can be unbearable and there will be many difficult decisions that come with it, but I can think of no other more suitable.' He hoped to raise Jide's spirits, but he could see that his words had little effect on the prince.

'I never asked for this. I never asked to rule. If I take the crown, I risk losing my brother, and if I do not, I risk losing my people. Either choice I make comes with a price,' Jide said sadly.

'That may be so, my prince, but Olise spoke one truth; there are those who rule and those who serve. You will rule, and he along with everyone in this kingdom of ours will serve. It really is that simple. The council of ten supports any decision you make and the Modakeke will be there to douse any fire that may be ignited,' Adedeji said. His words were clearly directed at Olise and the realisation of the unspoken threat he posed. This was not lost on Jide and he raised his head from his palms to look at his two most trusted advisors.

'I truly hope it does not come to that, but I thank you both for your words. I will think on my decision and make it known in due course. Please, leave me now,' he said, dismissing them. His mind was clouded, and he needed to weigh up his options, but he could not delay for long, as trouble was not far from the horizon. His nostrils were suddenly filled with the scent of rain, which he took as a sign of the storm that was to come.

A month later, Jide was crowned king of Ile-Ife and all the lands south of the river Benue. His coronation was attended by the nobilities from far and wide, all genuinely pleased to have a strong ruler on the throne, one that understood the people, was fair but firm and truly sought the betterment and unity of all the tribes in the kingdom.

The ceremony was similar to those of Jide's father and grandfather before him, lacking some of the rituals and sacrifices that usually preceded the crowning of the Yoruba kings of old. Jide wanted to remain in keeping with the progressive rule of his bloodline, one that recognised tradition and sufficiently honoured the gods, but also one that embraced the diverse cultures of the continually expanding kingdom. Most had agreed with the proceedings but others, specifically those who supported Olise, would see it as an affront to their forebears and would seek to besmirch the name of their new ruler, but they had little success.

The weeks that followed the coronation saw a time of jubilation throughout the kingdom; however, this was marred by a series of unfortunate events, the worst being several attempts on Jide's life.

The first attempt had been during the feast of the crops that was celebrated shortly after the start of the rainy season to usher in the beginnings of the harvesting period. The ceremony was dedicated to Oko, the Orisa of farming and agriculture.

Jide had been in high spirits as he hosted some of the local chiefs in the royal palace when he was approached by one of the servants bearing a skin of palm wine. The drink was offered to Jide when his calabash was almost empty but before Jide had taken a sip from the horn, Rotimi, the chief of Owo, had cracked a joke, which had everyone in earshot doubled over in laughter and fits of hysteria.

Rotimi, in his joviality, had slapped Jide on the back, causing him to spill the contents of his drink all over the table in front of him and on the floor. A stray dog that roamed the palace halls hoping to feast on discarded morsels of food had then licked the dregs of the wine and almost immediately began to yelp and convulse with violent spasms before foaming at the mouth and dying on the spot.

The wine had been poisoned, and every man at Jide's table had run off in search of the young servant who had attended him. The boy was eventually found, but they were unable to obtain any information as he had also drunk from the poisoned wine, for fear of being captured and revealing his fellow conspirators. Olise and Ekaete had been invited to break bread at the feast but had refused the offer, which now raised suspicions amongst the royal court following the events of the evening.

The second attempt had been far more brazen. Jide was attacked by a group of men as he hunted in the forests around Ife. Unfortunately for the would-be assassins, they had chosen the wrong time to carry out their attack as Jide had been accompanied by Akin, as always, and two babas or old timers from the council of ten. Old as they were, the two councillors came from Modakeke stock and were still as deadly as any of the younger warriors. Deadlier perhaps.

The attempt would almost have been laughable if not for the gravity of the implication. The four warriors made an easy job of dispatching their attackers, despite their larger numbers. They had tried to take a prisoner, but the men had refused to be taken alive and

234

died during the confrontation. One thing that was noted was that they were clearly not men from Ife, most likely from the Calabar region from their clothing and southeastern accents.

This deeply troubled the council of ten. Not only did this prove that there was a plot to murder the anointed king but also, it would appear, that the culprits had no scruples about eliminating members of the council.

The time that followed brought about a change in protocol, and more warriors from the Modakeke were used to bolster the security around the palace and accompany Jide everywhere he went, to his annoyance. It was, however, a necessary precaution, as this would not be the last time someone would attempt to cause him harm.

The final time came in the form of a young girl. At the age of twenty, Jide was constantly urged to take a bride to help secure his bloodline, so he had begun to court several girls, often of high birth and at the recommendations of his most trusted allies and members of the council of ten. However, on occasion he would take a liking to some of the local girls that he'd meet to the disappointment of his advisors, but these were never serious relationships, only brief encounters that served to dispel the carnal desires so common amongst the young.

As was customary in the kingdom, following the crowning of a new king, the nobilities and dignitaries from across the realm would travel to Ife to pay homage to their new liege lord for the first few months, and many would use the opportunity as an excuse to present their daughters in the hopes that they would make an impression on the young king.

Jide almost always dismissed the advances he received, but he did find lasting friendships and alliances with a few children of the nobilities, not to mention the love of his life, Lara, though that was almost a year later. However, in the month of his coronation his thoughts were preoccupied with maintaining cohesion between all the leaders within his domain and getting to grips with his new-found powers over everything and everyone south of the great rivers.

On one of the days, Ekaete had come to him unexpectedly and announced that some of her relatives from the noble courts of Calabar intended to visit the capital. This was very odd, as Ekaete never engaged with him directly, always choosing to use messengers, or speaking through Olise.

Jide decided to think nothing of it and agreed to host them, as was expected of any sitting king; he had to be seen to have an open-door policy, especially with the nobilities of the realm.

A week followed and a large contingent of Calabar patricians descended on Ile-Ife. They were all dressed in their traditional finery and had no compunctions about showing off their wealth - gold and silver jewellery adorned all the women and even some of the men wore rings and solid gold bracelets; they rode magnificently groomed horses and even drove their own cattle before them. Not to mention the assortment of traditional items they also brought along, such as coral beads, bronze ware and pottery, some of which they gifted to Jide and members of his household.

Amongst the crowd between the long line of supplicants, Jide spied a young girl who stopped the breath in his lungs. She was tall and slender, with soft features. She had long, thinly braided hair accessorised with beads that hung down to her waist, but her eyes were by far the most astonishing feature she possessed. They were the colour of smoke, charcoal grey, which was highly unusual, framed with long lashes that fluttered every time she looked at Jide. Her lips were full and sumptuous, like ripe peaches, and the upturned corners of her playful smile caused a pain in the pit of Jide's stomach.

He was completely taken, transported into a world were only the two of them existed, all the people around them faded into the background, distorted in his vision, so that only she was visible. In his daydreaming, he forgot his duties and had to be nudged to accept the outstretched hand of the next dignitary in front of him, trying and failing to focus and unable to keep his eyes off this girl.

When it was her turn to kneel before him, his throat tightened, his breath cut off and he was utterly lost for words. All he managed to say after an awkward silence was "welcome", which prompted a raised eyebrow from Akin. There was another glimpse of that playful smile that set his heart ablaze with desire. In Jide's awkwardness he had forgotten to ask the girl's name. The moment had passed, and she was gone, the next person in line had already taken her place and was offering their fealty to the king.

Two days later Jide had decided to visit one of the neighbouring villages on a market day. With the coronation came traders from all over the realm gathered to sell their wares; food and livestock, hides, clothing, pottery and all sorts of ornaments. The city was alive with vibrant colours of materials and the air fragrant with the smells of local produce; it was truly a good day for the capital.

Jide took in his surroundings, pleased at the sight of so much prosperity. The city thrived, and it was a promising start to his first year as king and a sign of good things to come, one that would surely resonate with the people.

He had been under the watchful eyes of a retinue of young Modakeke warriors, in addition to Akin, who shadowed his every move but failed to stop him from colliding with a group of giggling girls as they took in the sights excitedly. One of them was the girl from Calabar. Their eyes instantly found each other, and Jide addressed her straight away, eager to redeem himself and not wanting to miss the opportunity as he had done days ago.

Her name was Aniekan and she was the daughter of a renowned Calabar warrior named Abasi, captain to one of the chiefs of the land. Though Abasi held claim to no titles or wealth, through the strength of his right arm, he had won fame and was celebrated in Calabar land.

Jide had invited her and her family to dine with him at the royal palace, which she accepted without hesitation. It was a great honour not only to be remembered by the king but to be invited to eat with him, one that not many people ever got the opportunity to do.

Aniekan had left the market on a cloud of euphoria; could it be that the most powerful man in the land would be interested in her? She had to pinch herself several times to assure herself that she *wasn't dreaming. She informed her father, who was equally pleased, but reminded her that Jide was no mere man but a king, and tradition had to be observed. She would have to be presented to him through an emissary and accompanied by an entourage of nobles. Abasi then sent word to the royal palace and their request was accepted, somewhat reluctantly by Jide's council as they would have sought a better match for the king, preferably one of high birth. Despite their misgivings and at Jide's insistence, that evening Abasi and Aniekan were seated at the king's table along with other Calabar and Ife nobles.*

Jide had arranged the evening such that he sat close to Aniekan, to the displeasure of his advisors, and over the discussions of trading deals, land disputes and military conquests, the eyes of the two young adults rarely broke apart, to the annoyance of some of the guests, and their hands found each other's under the table. Jide's councillors clearly didn't approve of the match, as the girl was seen as a commoner since her family had no political standing or influence in the realm, even though her father was a famed warrior.

This meant nothing to Jide as the councillors' advice held little value to him; he chose always to defer to the advice of Akin and the Modakeke's council of ten, as they had practically raised him and were the closest thing to his family. Adedeji and Akin had always told him to follow his heart and they once again advised more of the same, so with their blessings he had decided to pursue Aniekan.

They met as often as they could but, at the insistence of her father's chief, she was always accompanied by servants. So, there was never any opportunity of any intimacy between them besides the occasional stolen moment when the servants could be sent away on errands, but that never seemed to allow them much time.

It soon came the time for the Calabar dignitaries to depart, after spending two months in the capital, and both Jide and Aniekan anticipated the day with dread, although they never spoke about it but rather chose to ignore it, naïvely believing that unspoken meant untrue and that all the time in the world was laid out before them.

Over the short period of time they had known each other, their love had grown so strong that neither could bear to be apart from

238

the other, and despite Jide having the power to rule over all his kingdom, he could not find any reasonable excuse to extend her stay in the city, short of asking for her hand in marriage, which even he was not prepared to do so soon. She would eventually leave, and he would have to either find a way in which they could be together or come to terms with the reality of losing her. He was torn but he finally decided that losing her was not an option and he had to tell her as soon as he possibly could and hope that she felt the same.

Through a messenger, he sent for her to meet with him on the eve of her departure in the gardens of the palace. It was a warm evening and the sun was framed in the darkening skies bathing the walls of the garden in a reddish hue that cast long shadows of the iroko trees and wildflowers that adorned the paths within. Jide stood admiring the plants and breathing in the scent of the flowers when Aniekan walked in with one of her servants, a girl who always had a resentful expression.

Aniekan gestured for the girl to stay behind as she hurried over to embrace him. Jide watched Aniekan walk over and followed the curves of her hips, already anticipating the warmth of her body against his. When she drew near he scooped her up in his strong arms, spun her around and held her tightly for a long time.

Neither one of them wanted to let go, and when they finally disengaged, Jide took Aniekan's delicate face in his hands and looked into her beautiful grey eyes that had already started to well with tears. Suddenly her eyes went wide and the sorrow that had been there an instant ago was replaced with terror. She was looking behind him, but as he started to turn Aniekan pushed in front of him and her body went rigid.

Jide was still confused but then he saw that Aniekan's servant was standing in front of them, her chest heaving and a look of shock on her face, then he followed her hand and saw that it held a dagger's hilt, the other end embedded deep in Aniekan's chest. He let out a cry of strained anguish just as Aniekan went limp and slumped to the floor.

The sound of Jide's cry alerted Akin who came charging out of one of the alcoves in the garden, spear in hand. He immediately took in the scene before him and with three long strides bounded towards the servant, who still stood with bloodied hands in shock, and stuck her behind the knees sending her to the ground. The point of his spear was at her throat as he waited for Jide's command, but he was inconsolable. Aniekan had saved his life and taken the blade that was meant for him, she had proved her love for him, and the servant had robbed him of the opportunity to reciprocate.

Jide wept and couldn't take his eyes off the lifeless form of Aniekan as she lay still in his arms and her blood seeped into the soil around them. The gods had been cruel. They had robbed him of a chance at happiness and replaced it with bitterness and resentment. All these thoughts welled through his mind as Akin tried again to get his attention while the servant was trapped under his foot.

Jide eventually looked up at Akin, as if noticing him for the first time and through his tears he whispered through clenched teeth, 'Bring Ekaete to me.' His tone was quiet but menacing and Akin saw only violence behind the tears and bloodshot eyes, knowing too well his intentions.

He sent some of the palace guards that had also been roused by the commotion, instructing them to bring the queen regent to the royal chambers unharmed. They immediately rushed off to carry out his orders. They knew Ekaete would not come willingly; she had a small retinue of devoted soldiers who would protect her. Not to mention Olise's men, who would undoubtedly come to the aid of their prince's mother.

A group of twenty soldiers marched to Ekaete's quarters to arrest her. They were prepared to take her by force if it came to that but hoped that this would not be necessary.

Fortunately, her guards were caught off guard and were quickly disarmed and locked away in cells, while Ekaete's doors were broken down with axes. She was nowhere to be found, so the palace was searched thoroughly. No one had seen her leave and her men swore that she had been in her chambers shortly before the soldiers arrived. It seemed that she had simply vanished.

This, however, was no excuse to give to the grieving king. So, rather than go back empty handed, the royal guards decided to seize Olise to stand in the place of his mother. He was indignant at first, but allowed them to take him willingly enough once he learned the events that had transpired that evening.

He was all but frog marched to Jide, who sat upon his throne in the palace halls, sword in hand across his lap and his clothes still stained with the blood of Aniekan. Akin was with him, as was Adedeji, three other members of the council of ten and some of the Calabar dignitaries, Aniekan's father amongst them standing erect but with a face like thunder.

'Where is Ekaete?' he asked Olise, all traces of his usual warmth lost from his voice.

'Brother, there must be a mistake, I refuse to believe she was involved in any of this,' Olise said, trying to appeal to Jide's judicious sensibility.

'Bring me the girl,' Jide commanded without preamble. She was then dragged in between two guards, her hands and feet bound with thick cords of rope. There were lines across her face and arms, evidence of the flogging she had received at the hands of Jide's men.

'Repeat yourself to the prince. Let him hear your confession from your own lips, so I am not accused of falsifying your words,' Jide said, not taking his eyes off Olise.

'I didn't mean to kill her, my gods, O... forgive me... I loved her.' She burst into tears and sobbed uncontrollably, until she was prompted to keep talking by way of a slap across the face from one of the guards.

'Ekaete came to me one moon ago...' she said through her tears. 'She said I was cursed and that... that my family was also marked by Esu. I had no choice... please... oh, my gods... please.'

Another slap, this time much harder, prompting bouts of fresh tears. Her words came quicker now; 'She told me that only the

241

life of a noble could satisfy the spirits enough to change my fate...oh, my gods what have I done O.'

'How can you believe her? She is obviously lying,' Olise interjected unconvincingly.

'I don't lie!' the girl shouted. 'It's all true, I swear on my mama, I'm not a bad person... gods O help me.'

'Rubbish. This is madness. Why would Mother do such a thing? I can't believe it.'

'It's no secret that she has never wanted me to sit on the throne and you should know of the other attempts that have been made on my life...' Jide said, still watching Olise closely.

'Wait, Jide. Do you truly believe she would mean you harm?' Olise asked, but deep down he knew what his mother was capable of. Silence followed.

Jide only watched him, his expression blank and unyielding like the imposing bronze statues that decorated the halls.

'There must be some proof before you make your judgement, Jide. At least you will grant her that?'

'Show him,' Jide indicated to one of the guards holding the girl, who pulled out a bundle of cloth. It was unwrapped delicately, revealing an amulet that bore the mark of Ekaete's tribe.

She was often seen with such an amulet amongst others that she carried on her person, and it was said that those who held it were protected from harm. Olise had a similar amulet that he wore on a thread around his neck concealed underneath his clothing.

'Were did you come by this?' he asked, his expression now changed as he realised the implications of this finding.

'It was found in the folds of the girl's wrapper. She was beaten when we apprehended her but no signs of it showed on her body. Then the amulet dropped from her clothing and as soon as it did all the marks from the cane appeared on her flesh. There is no way a lowly servant could ever possess such a thing. This belongs to Ekaete, we both know that,' said Jide in a level tone.

'She could have stolen it,' Olise suggested, trying in vain to defend his mother, knowing full well that any argument he presented was flawed.

'Who would dare steal such a thing, and from Ekaete of all people? Let us not play this game, we know that the girl speaks truth,' Jide finished.

'So, what do you intend to do when you find my mother?' Olise asked, but he could fathom a guess at the response he was about to receive.

'The queen regent stands accused of attempted murder. Murder of a king, no less,' replied Adedeji, 'there can only be one punishment'

'And my daughter?' asked Aniekan's father Abasi, 'Is she not deserving of justice?' He obviously was struggling with his own emotions but managed to hide it well, choosing to show his cold warrior face in the presence of his king, and not one of weakness. He would have time to grieve when he was alone.

Jide took his eyes away from Olise for the first time and rested them on Aniekan's father. He was suddenly moved by Abasi's grief, and realised that he had been selfish in failing to understand that his own sorrow would pale in comparison to what this man would be feeling after losing his only child.

'Forgive me, Abasi, I have been inconsiderate. Your daughter certainly deserves justice, and she will have it. You can take the servant. Do with her as you will. We will observe the proper funeral rites for your daughter here in the city, and I will grant you an honour guard to take her back to your homeland at your convenience.

'You are kind, my king, but even though this girl wielded the knife', he indicated the incapacitated servant, 'I hold Ekaete responsible and I will see her pay for her part in it,' Abasi said. He had always held Ekaete's family in contempt, and her father had been responsible for sacking Abasi's town years ago, putting the inhabitants under his yoke. This was the perfect opportunity to mete out his revenge, and he intended to take it.

243

'Do not forget your place. It is a queen you speak of, peasant!' Olise snapped, his own anger now emerging to the surface as he scowled at Abasi, who now turned to face him.

'She will pay for what she has done here, and nothing can stop the inevitable. It is our law; a life for another life, and I will see it fulfilled, I swear it.'

Olise's rage now threatened to explode into violence. 'You dare to talk to me so? One more word from you and I will send you to meet your daughter presently!' Venom dripped from every word he spoke.

Abasi managed a smirk, knowing that he had the right of the confrontation, which had the worst possible effect on Olise. Before another word could be spoken, Olise snatched a spear from the nearest guard to him and drove it into Abasi's exposed throat.

The attack had been so quick and precise that Abasi didn't have time to utter a word. His eyes went wide in shock just as the force of the thrust threw him backwards into some of the other Calabar nobles who stood close by.

'Olise! What have you done?' bellowed Jide, who sprang from his throne and took a step forward but was blocked by Akin and Adedeji, who both held short swords in their hands.

Olise stood over Abasi in his final death throes as he tried in vain to stop the blood that escaped from his throat. He still held the spear and now the guards in the room had drawn their weapons and surrounded him.

'Drop the spear!' ventured one of the guards, but he was clearly not keen on trying to take it from him. Olise took his eyes away from Abasi, briefly hovered over the guard who had addressed him and then finally settled on Jide, who had now pushed past Akin and was walking towards him with his sword held ready to defend himself.

'He insulted me. No one talks to me like that, especially not a peasant. What would be said about us if we allow such behaviour to pass unchallenged? I will not have it! He had no right and he deserved what was coming to him,' Olise said triumphantly.

'Have you lost your mind?! The man was grieving, and you killed him in cold blood, here in my palace! You've just broken centuries of tradition, Olise. Every guest invited under my roof is afforded my protection, and you know that guest rights are held sacred by our people. You have just broken that law. What do you think will be said now of our house?' Jide said angrily.

'I refuse to allow such a lowborn peasant to address me so, or is there not a law on that? I have protected my own honour by my actions, if I'm in the wrong may the gods strike me down where I stand! Besides, who cares what anyone thinks?'

Jide shook his head in sorrow. 'I don't recognise you any more. Put the spear down, or do I have to take it from you?' Olise saw in Jide's eyes that he was prepared to fight him. He paused for a moment then reluctantly dropped the spear that clattered on the tiled floor.

The guards in the room immediately moved closer, but they all glanced over at Jide for direction, still unsure as to whether they could seize Olise as they would a commoner.

'You have brought shame to this house, Olise, and now, you must answer for that,' Jide said sadly. He turned to the Calabar nobles, who huddled together uncomfortably as they looked from Abasi to Olise fearfully.

'People of Calabar. The events of this day are unfortunate. I had hoped for a peaceful gathering of our people, but it was not to be. It was not my wish that such an ending would tarnish such a joyous period in our tribe's history, but the stones have been cast and we must be able to move forward from here.'

Most of the dignitaries only nodded or bowed slightly, as if afraid to talk for fear of getting skewered like their countryman; however, one of them was undeterred and stepped forward to address the king.

'Kabiyesi, the events of today are indeed unfortunate, but I would request that we honour Abasi as you had promised him you would his daughter,' he said.

'Yes, of course. The servant is yours, and I will grant the funeral rites and the honour guard as promised,' Jide replied. 'As for you, Olise, you are to be confined to your quarters until the council agrees upon your fate. I am sorry, brother, but you leave me no choice.'

'Very well,' said Olise with a hint of remorse. He knew that he had let his anger get the better of him and, by so doing, had put Jide's reputation at risk, but deep down, he was saddened that his brother would now have to pass judgement on him. He decided in that moment that he would not fight him, but rather accept any punishment that was given to him. He would have to send word to Dimeji and his men, who would no doubt by now be plotting to storm the king's quarters to set him free.

However, the burning question that was foremost on everyone's mind was the whereabouts of Ekaete. She had orchestrated the whole affair and was solely responsible for the unspoken fracture that now lay between the Yoruba and Calabar tribes. The Calabar would never forgive the loss of their greatest warrior and one of their most beautiful daughters.

They had been denied, or, worse still, not been given the choice of, a life in return for Abasi. They felt that their laws were worth nothing in the eyes of the Yoruba. It was a reminder of the privilege that Jide and his like possessed over the rest of the kingdom, like the taste of bitter leaf on the tongue with no palm wine to dull the sour aftertaste.

The Calabar nobility had insisted on staying in the kingdom long enough to find out the judgement that would be passed on Olise, in the hopes that it would be the death sentence, restoring their pride and faith in their new king, but Jide couldn't guarantee them the justice they deserved. The people's court would decide Olise's fate and Jide had no desire to influence the outcome, giving the Calabar their due. In the end, the nobles left the capital discontent before the funeral rites were performed for Abasi and his slain daughter, purposely snubbing the courtesy extended by the throne.

Even after the Calabar dignitaries departed, Ekaete had not reappeared, nor had she been heard from since the night of the failed assassination. It was rumoured, however, that she had visited Olise several times during his confinement, as some of Jide's guards claimed that on occasion, and always in the dead of night, they would hear him having a heated discussion with what sounded like the voice of a woman, and when they entered the residence Olise would be alone but, peculiarly, he'd be standing close to broken egg shells scattered around the floor.

On the day Olise's fate was to be announced, following several days of failed deliberation between senior figures in the realm, Ekaete was sentenced in absentia and it was death, if ever she was to return to the capital. Olise, on the other hand, was summoned into the closed space of the court hall, a place he would never have imagined he'd be standing, especially on the opposite side of the table. The men who presided over the sentencing were all prominent figures in Ife; the head of the council of ten, Adedeji and his deputy head, the five members of the city council, three of the most powerful chiefs from the provinces and Jide at the head of the court.

Olise was brought before them without his hands bound, which was unusual, a concession only granted due to his station, but he came defiant with his head held high. He had been granted favours that would never normally be afforded a man who stood trial for such a grievous crime, but never in the kingdom's history had a prince been in this position. So, some concessions had to be made.

One of the local councillors read off the charges that had been levied against the prince, which included disregard for the ancestral laws of hospitality, attempted fratricide and treason.

Olise didn't move a muscle as the charges were called against him and never broke eye contact with his brother, who also held his gaze through the proceedings in a silent challenge.

The three chiefs and two of the local councillors called for death, whilst the other three councillors and Adedeji's deputy called for leniency. The vote was left to Adedeji to either condemn Olise to death or balance the scales, opening the final judgement to the crown.

He chose life, so the decision fell to Jide, who in truth could overrule any decision made but chose to let the people's representatives decide.

When Adedeji had cast his vote, Jide's shoulders dropped slightly, signifying his relief at the outcome. He then stood, all this time still locked in a powerful gaze with his brother, and passed the final judgement.

'Olise, for your crimes I will not pass the death sentence on you, a beloved prince of the land, but you will relinquish all your titles and be banished from Ife for seven years. After which time you may return to claim your titles and honour.'

There were grumbles from some of the men present but this was silenced by the sound of the base of Akin's spear rapping against the flagstone in the background.

'You will go to Aba on the eastern fringes of our kingdom to serve out your sentence. I will grant you all your men and servants to accompany you, as befitting of a prince and not a common criminal,' Jide said.

'I suppose I should be grateful to you, and those who do not wish to have my head' Olise said indicating Adedeji and the ones who had voted in his favour. 'However, I should never be standing trial before this council. You have shamed me and reduced me to a pauper and commoner. Me, a son of Adeosi. I will never forgive this affront and I will hold you all to account. And you, Jide, what if they had decided on death, would you have let them take my head? You who are of my own blood?' Jide just looked on with anguish behind his eyes.

'It is you who have brought shame on your name and our tribe,' retorted Adedeji. In truth, he felt no ill will towards Olise and had always held him in high esteem as a warrior. He had hoped that the second chance Olise had been given at life would humble him enough and that, eventually, he would be welcomed back into the bosom of Ife, but it was now clear that this wasn't to be.

'Save your words, old man, the stones have been cast and they have fallen where you have all decided, and not as the gods would

have it. There is nothing more to be said on the matter. If I am now free, I will take my leave to start my new life.'

With that he took a final glaring look at the men seated before him and lingered on Jide for a second. In that moment his expression softened a fraction as he saw the silent emotion etched in Jide's features, but he hardened his heart and turned his back on them all and left the hall.

Jide stood and watched his brother retreat through the large doors of the room and he felt sick to his stomach. He had lost his companion, his brother. One would assume that he would be immune to disappointment by now, as his life had been bereft of the stability of a loving relationship, but it pained him all the same.

Akin came up behind him and placed his hand on Jide's shoulder reassuringly. He was the only man in the world who truly understood him and would never depart from him, only through death.

'You did the right thing, my prince, don't be too hard on yourself,' Akin said softly.

'Yes, but at what cost? Olise is a proud man, we all know that, and we have fouled our relationship with the Calabar. I dare say that this will not end well for any of us,' Jide said, and from the silent response that greeted him, it was obvious that everyone in the room had the same sentiment.

THE GODS RECEIVE THEIR DUE

Jide let the blackened soil tinged with red gravel slip through his fingers. He repeated the action with his right hand, this time holding a clump of dirt pressed between his fingers and smearing it across his cheeks. He looked up at Akin, who came to crouch beside him and did the same.

Just then, the sound of the great timber gates rumbling open caught their attention, slowly followed by the chants of a thousand voices renting the air. Olise had finally decided to answer Jide's call and face him like a warrior. His pride must have been bruised by the accusation of cowardice and he would be desperate to prove the contrary to his men and to himself.

Adedeji walked over, followed by two of his captains, resplendent in their armour, cleaned from all the dust and blood from the earlier failed attack. 'It looks like we'll have a battle on our hands after all,' Adedeji said as he shielded his eyes against the sun and looked towards the gates. After almost an hour of Jide berating Olise and those who followed him, he had decided to move his army back a reasonable distance, but they still maintained the disciplined lines of experienced soldiers.

'It appears that way,' Jide responded. 'Prepare the men. One way or another it ends today.'

'Your will, my king.' Adedeji replied as he walked off, briskly issuing orders to the waiting soldiers.

'You can still change your mind, my king, if this is not what you want,' Akin added as he checked his weapons.

'I wouldn't have it any other way, my friend. I have made my peace with the gods so, whatever the outcome of the day, I am ready. If you are having second thoughts, only say the word and you have my blessings to leave. You can travel back to Ife and find out what has really become of my family and the men we sent to take back our home.'

'You have captains and messengers for that. I'm sure there are capable and willing men that you can send in my stead. My place is by your side, as it was on the day I was bonded to you and so it will be on the day you die. I'm going nowhere,' Akin replied.

'Very well. In truth I can't really afford to lose any more men. We need the numbers and we still don't know the strength Olise holds behind those walls. Let us make our final sacrifices before we face our fate. If we are fortunate enough, we will travel back together.' With that, both men stood and walked towards the gathered army to their rear, where some of the soldiers were already invoking their personal deities to protect them from what they were about to face.

The gates were now open, and the first row of men came into view, ambling out and pushing through the piles of half-melted and maimed corpses to make room for the men who followed behind them.

It was a gruesome task and they made slow progress moving the mangled bodies, as not every man seemed willing to disturb the remains of the dead, believing it to be a taboo, especially for men who had left the world in such a foul manner. Better to leave them where they lay and allow the birds to feast, knowing that by the end of the day only bones would remain.

Eventually, enough ground had been cleared to allow for others to follow, and only then did the men from Ife and the west fully understand the scale of the predicament they faced. More and more soldiers emerged from behind the gates as they spread out across the length of the walls and continued to thicken in ranks.

The various tribes could now be discerned from their coloured headgear, shields and war attire. There were men from Onitsha, Akwa, Amoso, Owerri and Okigwi and the River-lands; Calabar, Bugama, Aba, Okrika and more.

How Olise had managed to swear all these tribes to him still beggared belief, but here they all were, and ready to take up arms against their king, no less. They could only try, thought Jide angrily.

251

He was the true king, and they would have to pry his crown from his cold rigor mortised fingers.

Someone in Jide's army had started to sing. It was an ancient tune, one that was sung by their ancestors on the eve of battle. It was a song that spoke of sorrow, triumph and servitude to the gods, giving them praise and asking for their strength. It spoke of the people, of their culture and their fearlessness in the eye of their enemies. The singer's voice was euphonious, and it carried above the din created by thousands of men and began to spread.

Before long, most of the westerners had taken up the tune, and even Jide couldn't stop himself from joining in. It somehow brought a calm to the men, a calm that descended on them like the replenishing rays from the sun, warming their hearts and quelling their nerves. It was clear that every man who stood by the king had resigned himself to the fate of his gods and would give them their due of blood as demanded.

The opposite army by the gates looked on; some of them would undoubtedly know the song, but to join in would be tantamount to declaring for the true king. So they held their tongues and waited.

The singing went on for about twenty beats of the heart, and then, as if possessed by evil spirits, the men of the west let out a blood curdling war cry in unison, causing some of Olise's men to flinch where they stood. There would be no mercy on this day and blood would flow freely.

Olise stood towards the rear of his men. Dimeji was by his side, as was Ogie, and a few other chiefs from the tribes. His eyes roved the crowd, seeking out Zogo and his tribesmen. Finding him, he tried to judge his state of mind from his composure, but the Igbo chief gave nothing away, only presenting a determined look across the field.

That would have to suffice, Olise thought to himself. He had no option but to trust that the Igbo wouldn't betray him in battle, but he had put in place precautions to protect himself and made a conscious decision to watch his flank, which he shared with his most devoted chiefs.

He then steeled his nerves and gave the order. 'I mean to have the heads of every one of those men at my feet. Bring them to me.' He sneered, and his men came alive like lions released from bondage, let loose to feast on a herd of goats.

The shouts of Olise's men pierced the air as they all surged forward, all but foaming at the mouth in their eagerness to be the first to spill blood. It was a terrifying sight to behold. A large body of the soldiers were slow off the mark and didn't appear as zealous in their advance as others, but still they came.

Never in the history of the tribes had so many men faced each other in battle. It dwarfed the great battles of old fought by their forebears like King Kayode and other great men before him. This day would remain on the lips of many generations to come, and would forever be carved in the stones of antiquity.

'Order! Order!' was yelled down the lines of the westerners, and their spears bristled before them, most held firm and some unsteadily, but all pointed in the direction of the approaching army.

'Now we finally have the contest we craved!' said Adedeji. He had a broad smile as if he was about to greet a long-lost friend and his eyes shone wild with excitement.

'Try not to get yourselves killed, eh?' he said to the men about him. 'Our lives are in the hands of the gods and we know they can be capricious masters,' replied Olusegun with a strained smile of his own. 'One thing I do know is I won't make it easy for Olise,' he managed to say.

'That's the spirit, old man! Let's show these goatherds what real soldiers are made of, eh?' Adedeji said in response.

'I admire your confidence, but I suspect that you already know your fate, eh?' teased Akin, also beaming from ear to ear.

'Yes O. Like I said before, my destiny is to die in the comfort of my bed...' Adedeji started, but was interrupted by Dare, 'Yes, yes. Surrounded by your sons. We have all heard it before,' he said, rolling his eyes and prompting a moment of nervous and strained laughter from the men.

'Come, don't be jealous because I'm favoured by *Ogun*. Besides, my sword might be the very thing that wins us the day,' Adedeji said, his smile even wider now.

'My friends. If you haven't noticed, we have more pressing matters to attend to. Let us concentrate on the task at hand. And may the gods guide your right arms,' Jide said, looking to the heavens.

'Yes, of course, Kabiyesi. Let us make the gods proud and prove our worth if we are to see their kingdom this day.' With that Adedeji took his place at the king's left shoulder with the Modakeke pressed close behind.

The call to ready spears went up and down the lines of men, and those in the front rank set a foot back, poised to launch their weapons. The line had been widened, creating a gap between each man to allow room for the second rank to flow in seamlessly to cast their own spears when the time came.

The enemy was close now, some five hundred paces in front and gaining fast. As soon as they were within range, 'THROW!' echoed down the lines. In an instant, the sun's glow was momentarily darkened by thousands of spears arcing deftly overhead towards the running men.

'SHIELDS!' was the response that followed, but some were too slow to heed the warning and paid dearly. The rain of spears was ferocious, impaling men where they stood, most piercing through the leather hides of their shields to find soft flesh underneath.

Men were struck in the chest, shoulders, through their arms, legs, even though the mouths of some truly unlucky fellows, who had been frozen on the spot by fear and gazed at the deadly missiles in terror.

A second volley was sent in quick succession, this time thrown almost horizontally, taking the lives of many more. Some men were lifted from their feet and sent colliding into their comrades from the impact of the spears, but this did not slow the advance. Jide's men now braced their shield arms and drew their swords, machetes and axes ready for the close quarter combat that would ensue.

For the men on the field, it was almost as if time slowed the moment before the two armies collided, with both sides looking into the eyes of the men opposite them baying for their blood. Every instinct was heightened, and every detail clearly came into focus; sweat glistening on foreheads, faces twisted in hatred or contorted with fear, edges of blades gleaming in the sunlight, the scent of urine and excrement tickling the nose from emptied bladders and bowels brought on by the onset of nerves. Then, all hell was unleashed.

The Modakeke, who had taken up the front ranks, held their shields high when Olise's men struck. The force of the impact numbed arms and bruised muscles instantly, but still, not one of them gave any ground. Each man in the rank lifted his weapon of choice and began to reap souls from the earth. Shields battered back thrusts and kicks as axes and swords darted out in response to sever limbs and land mortal blows. Their discipline was faultless, and when one of them took a step forward, so did the man to either side of him.

The enemy were simply hacking away violently in their desperation to break the wall of shields with no attempt at skill or thought to conserving energy. In truth, a lot of them were in fact farmers, tailors and goatherds; only a few were trained soldiers. It was the opposite for most of the westerners, every movement they made was calculated, measured and paid dividend. In the first few heartbeats, they truly showed their worth and the dedication to their profession.

Bodies began to pile steadily at their feet, hindering the advancing army with every passing moment, leaving Olise's men no choice but to clamber over the wounded and limp cadavers of their fallen comrades to get at the westerners, only to be added to the growing heap of flesh.

Not one of those who lay dead remained whole, most were missing a part of their anatomy claimed by the Modakeke, and they would forever roam the underworld in search of their lost limbs before they would be embraced by their gods, or meander in the perpetuity of *Esu's* dark halls of the forsaken. Be that as it may, the surge of soldiers was relentless and unceasing as they continued to throw themselves at the westerners with reckless abandon. They still possessed the sheer numbers and they intended to crush their foe under the weight of it.

Up until now, Jide's men had suffered no casualties, even though hundreds of the men they faced had been slain. However, their successful performance could not be sustained indefinitely. Soon, the balance would inevitably shift and be left to the mercy of the gods.

The first casualty in Jide's lines was one of the captains in the Modakeke's first rank. He shouldered his shield on his left arm and thrust forward repeatedly with his right. Over and over his sword pierced chests and necks, until one of his opponents grabbed his shield and yanked it violently upwards, dislocating the warrior's arm and exposing his torso.

Almost immediately, a spear found the gap under the shield and went into the open ribs of the warrior, who let out a cry of anguish, but still had the presence of mind to bring his sword round to sever the arm of the man who had stabbed him and bury the bloodied sword in the chest of the man who had tried to take his shield.

His sword was wrenched from his grip as his last victim fell backwards and other men moved to take advantage of the opportunity. The captain instinctively tried to bring his left arm forward to defend himself with his shield, but his arm failed to respond and dangled uselessly by his side. That was all the time required for men to dart forward and cut him down.

As the captain fell, entry was finally being gained to the earlier impenetrable shield wall. The enemy now moved within the ranks of the Modakeke and the fighting intensified. Several of Olise's men had seen the opening and now concentrated their efforts there, forcing the men in the ranks to split and bring their shields round to protect their flanks. Slowly, the formation of the westerners began to disintegrate, and men were forced to fight in smaller groups, which lacked the cohesive power of a single fighting unit, but this did nothing to deter their fighting ability and their will to survive.

Dare was in one of these small groups with some of his warriors. He had taken a wound to his sword arm when the ranks had disengaged and was forced to fight with his left hand, which was awkward, but his men protected him as best they could. A brave warrior from Onitsha leaped over a pile of corpses and landed in the mist of Dare and his men and started swinging his machete wildly. He killed one man and managed to wound another before turning his attention to the chief, who was slow to parry the blow that was aimed at him.

By pure coincidence, Dare's sword was raised just enough to turn the edge of his adversary's blade, but the impact caused his own sword to deflect backwards into his face, cutting him across the cheek. He yelled in pain and kicked out with his leg, catching his foe in the shin, which made him stumble and lose his balance. Just then, one of Dare's nephews, who was also a captain in the army, drove a spear through the man's back, saving him.

Dare thanked his kinsman and touched his cheek. His hand came away dripping with blood, but he felt no pain. It may have been the adrenaline, but he knew it was a nasty cut. He had always been a handsome man, the envy of many in the realm, but he would now wear his scars for all to see, if he were to make it out alive. He looked towards the walls of the palace and saw more and more soldiers running towards their lines. Fresh soldiers, who had not yet entered the fray or tested the strength of their blades. The sight brought on an ominous feeling in his bones.

Adedeji was at peace. He was exactly where he was always destined to be, amid a great battle that would for ever shape the tribes. He thanked the gods for granting him the opportunity to witness and contribute to the making of this history. He fought with his king and kinsmen, and there was nowhere on the gods' green earth that he would have rather been. He was enjoying himself immensely as he performed the dance of *Ogun*, a dance that he had mastered from the tender age of six. Even in his fifties, he still possessed the vigour and tenacity to cross spears with anyone in the realm. Every movement he performed was a dedication to *Ogun*, and every soul he took was a personal sacrificial offering to his most beloved deity.

Most of his trusted commanders were arrayed about him, with Jide and Akin in the centre of the press. Their spears darted out over the shoulders of the men in front of them, inflicting mortal wounds with every stroke. Their only respite was to adjust their grips on the smooth, blood-slick shafts.

Adedeji struck again and again, but this style of fighting bored him. He was eager to move out of the relative safety of the formation and face the enemy unrestricted. Only then could he show his true skill at arms. He tapped Jide on the shoulder and pointed with his spear at the horde that still approached them from behind the men they were already engaging, having to shout over the din of clashing metal.

'We need to press forward, Kabiyesi. Our position is too exposed here. Let us move to greet those men on the advance before they have the chance to overwhelm us.'

Jide retrieved his spear from a man's eye, who died screaming, then strained to look over the men in front of him. He made a quick assessment of the numbers and looked towards the gates to judge the distance. It was hard to determine through all the fighting figures and the corpses that littered the field, but he had to decide quickly. The fighting had pushed them offline from the city gates and they would have more ground to cover to reach it, but he knew the gates were their best chance of survival.

'Very well, but we move diagonally in that direction.' He indicated with his spear. 'We need to signal the men to do the same and widen their lines, so we are not flanked.' A warrior who stood to the right of Jide in the front line heard the king's plan and looked to his peers either side of him before gesturing with his head and then taking a step back. The gap he left was immediately closed by the men who had been beside him, communicating only through experience.

The warrior now turned to Jide and knelt. 'My king, let me take your command to the men,' he said, looking up at Jide expectantly.

'You do understand the risk you face? There's no guarantee that you'll even make it across to the closest men,' Jide said, looking at the nearest group of warriors locked in a desperate struggle over to their left.

'I do, my king, but there is no guarantee that any of us will leave this field. I can only try, but I go willingly,' the warrior replied.

'You are a brave man and you do our tribe proud. May the gods make you light of foot and protect you to carry my words. Tell the men that my raised spear will be the signal to advance.'

'Your will, my king,' the warrior responded, and didn't waste a moment. He tested the shield on his arm and moved off to the edge of the tight circle of men locked in a fierce fight. Tapping the shoulder of one of them, words were hastily exchanged and within minutes they had switched sides and the warrior was sprinting off through the cluster of fighting men, hopping over bodies and slashing wildly but skilfully at anyone who stood in his way.

Jide watched as the warrior darted through the throng and made it with relative ease to the next group of men, stabbing a few men in the back to gain entry to the circular formation. Within a few moments, the group began to edge slightly closer to Jide's position, acknowledging that they understood his intent.

The same warrior then detached from this group and headed to the next line of men, fighting all the way and not stopping long enough to get entangled in any serious skirmish.

He dodged spear and sword strikes that were aimed at him, deflecting with his shield and sword, and slashing as he ran. He moved with the eloquence of one of those acrobatic performing masquerades of the villages, so lithe was his figure and deft was his hand. He reached the next group of men unscathed, and the word was spread again.

The warrior repeated this mad dash across death's obstacle course several times, working his way across the field and down the lines. Jide's warriors now heeded the message and set about appointing one man amongst them to look out for the king's signal or watch for when the others began to move.

Once again, the warrior attempted to reach the next group but, as he broke away, a spear from one of the enemies caught him under his raised arm, knocking him sideways off his feet and screaming to the ground. Within minutes, men were stabbing down at him as he withered in the dirt, killing him instantly. Jide did not see him fall, he was far beyond his vision, but he had kept his word to his king and his sacrifice had not been in vain.

Jide raised his spear, let out a cry and his men began to advance. Other groups of men saw the spear and followed their king. Soon, all Jide's warriors were wading across the sea of chaos desperately fighting towards the gates.

The going was slow and brutal, with men literally throwing themselves against Jide's men to stop their progress. To make matters worse, the ground was saturated in blood, trampled human organs and excrement, not to mention the piles of limbs and corpses, making it treacherous underfoot. Men who lost their footing were hastily impaled where they lay on both sides of the army.

The sound of war was deafening. Jide could hardly hear the grunts of exertion from the men beside him, let alone those some paces away. Men were dying all around, some screaming out in rage and some in torment, as they soiled themselves before leaving the land of the living.

The Modakeke held firm and didn't seem to have lost too many men, but the same could not be said about some of the western warriors from the other tribes, which he noted as he scanned the groups of men that pushed through to his position. He sent up a quick prayer to *Yemoja* to protect all his people and grant him the strength to fight on. That was his only desire. His only option.

Something grabbed at his leg, and he looked down to see one of his warriors crying out in delirium, a long rope of intestines trailing from his open stomach. Jide couldn't assist him and guiltily pulled his leg away from the grasping fingers and prayed for a quick end to the warrior's suffering.

Without warning, the strain of the press slowly began to ease off. It appeared that the enemy had finally assimilated Jide's tactics and decided to make a stand rather than throw themselves at his army headlong. They had discovered far too late that the lustre that accompanied the name of the Modakeke was not a thing of fantasy. This pace suited the fighting style of Jide's warriors, however, and the true strength of their hand would soon be revealed.

'Spread the line!' Jide called, catching a flash of teeth from Adedeji and Akin. Now the two warriors could be unleashed to wreak havoc on their foe. Immediately, Akin positioned himself in front of Jide and started cutting men down as if taking a cutlass to long grass. It was a sight to behold as he sidestepped and slashed back and forth, knocking swords and spears aside almost with disdain and severing limbs by the dozen.

Not wanting to be outdone by Akin, Adedeji moved forward and began his own onslaught, showing the very reason why he alone sat at the head of the Modakeke. He was perhaps one of the deadliest warriors in the realm, despite his age. His attack was unnaturally fast, and his sword was a blur of grey metal as it cut through wood and leather and bit into flesh. He killed four men in quick succession and continued along the same line slaughtering and maiming as he progressed through the ranks.

Before long, Olise's army had started to lose ground as the Modakeke warriors and the other tribes of the west increased their ferocity, inspired by the example Adedeji and Akin had set.

Jide instinctively moved to the side as an axe spun past, narrowly missing his ear, and stopped in the forehead of one of his warriors behind him. The man dropped without a word with the axe embedded between his eyes and another man moved into his place, yelling bloody murder at the sight of his fallen peer.

Just then, a group of four men from the enemy line broke away and started in Jide's direction. They must have noticed the glint of gold in his armour, seen the craftsmanship of his weapons and knew it was the king. They almost tripped over themselves to get at him.

Without even thinking, Jide hurled his spear towards them. It caught the closest man in the chest, who was thrown backwards and died with a look of surprise frozen on his face; the razor-sharp spear point had pierced the soft leather of his armour, splitting bone and finding his heart.

The remaining three carried on undeterred, brandishing their swords and spears and bearing down on Jide. He ripped the sword from the scabbard by his waist just in time to take the edge of the sword from one of his assailants. He had performed his defence in one fluid movement and followed through with a shift in his weight as he brought his own sword down from the guard position and sliced a deep gash in the man's thigh, shattering bone. He was rewarded by a yelp as the man fell onto the spear of the warrior who had been at Jide's rear.

As he turned to face the other two, the one with the spear thrust it forward, but Jide bounced it off his shield, raising it up and forcing the man's attack offline, leaving his stomach unprotected to take half the length of Jide's sword.

Still he moved, covering himself on his left side where the last man swung down at him with his sword. Jide withdrew his weapon from the dying man's stomach and spun low, his shield held at shoulder height, protecting his head, and lobbed off the leg of his final opponent below the knee. As the man realised he was missing a leg and started to flail and fall forward, Jide, still moving, arced his sword in a circular motion and brought it down on the back of the man's neck, severing his head as he passed him.

His momentum drove him into his next opponent, a huge brute, presumably from the River-lands from the elaborate painting on his shield and colours of his crocodile skin armour. The man held a long-handled axe with a pointed tip, which he jabbed at Jide like a spear. His attack was blocked effortlessly on Jide's shield and he leaped up, driving his sword over the warrior's shield and through the gap between his neck and shoulder. The warrior dropped like a sack of yams, and Jide moved to his next victim. He was suddenly filled with a sense of immortality; gone was his fatigue and his fears, and every man who dared to stand before him was cut down.

'Will someone please explain to me why our men's advance has slowed? They should have overwhelmed Jide's warriors by now!' Olise yelled indignantly to no one in particular. 'If they do not seize the advantage of our numbers Jide's men will break through and soon be upon us at this rate! I am surrounded by fools.' He could barely believe what his eyes beheld. Despite the thousands of warriors he had committed to the field, Jide was somehow holding ground, gaining some even, bringing him slowly within reach of the walls. *The very walls that his head should be adorning,* Olise thought furiously.

He contemplated retreating to the safety of the city for a split second, which he dismissed almost as quickly as the thought had crossed his mind. He couldn't yield Benin to his brother, considering the long and bloody road he had taken to get this far. No. He would stay his course no matter the outcome. He would rather see all his warriors dead and the city burned to the ground before he'd allow it to be taken from him.

He tried to calm his nerves and prevent his anger from clouding his judgement, knowing that Jide would probably anticipate this from him, as he was always prone to anger. *Battles were fought not only with the strength of the iron in your hand, but with that of your mind too.* Remembering the words of their tutor. If ever there was a time to use his mind, this was it. He could not afford to make any impulsive decisions, not now.

Dimeji stood at his shoulder hefting his great sword. He could tell that the big man was impatient to spill blood from the way he continuously released and tightened his grip on the pommel, tendons of muscle bulging and flexing in his arms and biceps. Ogie, on the other hand, was more composed, despite his injuries. He stood with the base of his spear planted in the ground, watching the fight calmly, assessing the tide of battle and evaluating potential advantages to be had.

Olise had sensibly held back most of the Igbo warriors and some of the lesser tribes as a reserve force, in addition to his personal guards of some three hundred men, but it was becoming apparent that he would soon have to commit all his resources, and soak his own blade in blood.

Turning to one of his captains, he said, 'Send for Zogo to attend me. I believe it is time for him to prove his loyalty.' The captain sprinted off like a horse that had been whipped into motion, only to return minutes later with Zogo and his cousin Nnamdi in tow. The Igbo chief's face was dour, already guessing at the summons and knowing that he would be sent to reinforce the main army as a test to his fealty.

'Prince Olise?' he said, his tone dangerously verging on the line of hostility. Olise chose to ignore it. 'Ah, my good chief, it seems that I am in need of your warriors presently. As you can see, some of our tribesmen are finding it difficult to follow simple instructions and sweep the field clean of the intruders. I will have a competent man taking the reins. I want you and two hundred of your finest warriors to support those laymen,' he finished.

Zogo looked over at the battlefield and then back to Olise. His plans had been at risk the moment Olise had deliberately sent Akpan and the River-land warriors into the first charge, separating the two largest armies amongst the tribes he commanded. It was the obvious choice to make after Edem's treacherous actions. If Olise still feared dissention amongst his ranks, the Igbo and the River tribes would be the most likely candidates. Besides, Zogo would have made the same choice in Olise's position. He could but begrudgingly admire Olise's prudence. Now, Olise was seeking to separate the Igbos further by sending Zogo into battle, leaving the bulk of his men behind at Olise's disposal. If this was to be the case, Nnamdi would have to lead them in his place, and maybe their plans could still be salvaged somehow. This would be the only consolation.

'If you insist, Prince Olise. I would have Nnamdi take charge of my men in my stead, he would–'

'That won't be necessary.' Olise cut him off abruptly. 'Nnamdi will remain by my side. Iboro here will take command of your men,' he said, indicating a stout muscular warrior from Abia, one of his trusted commanders. 'He is as capable a man as any and he will join his own men with yours to serve as the rear guard.'

Zogo could hardly believe what he was being told. If he were to follow these orders without offering a molecule of resistance, any hopes of reviving the already waning flames of his stratagem would fast be extinguished.

'Prince Olise,' he began, 'I don't think this is a reasonable idea. Let Nnamdi take command of my men. We are a proud people, and with so many of our brothers being butchered in the field, only a leader from our tribe could possibly reach the hearts of the men sufficiently enough to spur them into action,' he said, and then adding as an afterthought, 'Not to cause offence to Iboro here, who I'm sure is a capable commander as you have said.' Iboro just nodded his head with a grunt, dismissing the backhanded compliment.

Olise watched Zogo closely as he spoke and remained silent for a few seconds after he'd finished.

'No,' he said simply after a while. 'Nnamdi will remain by my side until we are forced to join the battle. If your men need further incentive to obey my orders, tell them to look towards the city walls and upon the ramparts,' he said, sweeping an outstretched hand in the direction of the grotesque heads with their hollowed eye sockets and drooping jaws, with flies and vultures jostling for what little flesh remained on them. 'Tell them that will be their fate.'

Bastard! Zogo thought bitterly. Olise had outmanoeuvred him at every turn, he had ensured that every possibility of betrayal had been neutralised, leaving no stone unturned. He was truly a cunning adversary, and for the second time, he felt a sense of begrudging respect. He knew that if he were to refuse the direct order his position would be compromised, not to mention all the warriors around Olise who eyed him suspiciously as they gripped their weapons. It would only take one word from Olise to set them on him like ravenous dogs on a cornered rat. He wouldn't stand a chance, and had no choice but to acquiesce.

'So be it,' Zogo said eventually, not even attempting to hide his disappointment. He glanced at his cousin Nnamdi, who looked just as despondent as he felt. Nnamdi however, set his jaw and gave Zogo a curt nod. 'May *Chineke* go with you,' Zogo said to his kinsman in their native Igbo tongue before he turned and headed towards his waiting warriors, already expecting to be called to test their mettle.

Zogo could only hope he wouldn't be forced to cross spears with Jide. If he did all would truly be lost, and he feared that the tribes would never recover from the fallout. Furthermore, the unified country that Jide and some of his loyal chiefs had aspired to would remain but a dream and wither away like a dying flower deprived of the sustenance to allow it to bloom.

Olise watched Zogo as he joined his men. He still couldn't dispel his mistrust in the Igbo chief, who seemed to want to oppose his every command. He always knew that sooner or later he'd have to deal with the pompous chief, and the opportunity to do so seemed to have presented itself. Olise could only hope that he'd be able to turn the opportunity to his advantage. But he would have to tread lightly, as Zogo could still turn the tide of battle if he were to join Jide's forces and turn his spears towards the city. He would have to watch him closely.

Turning to Ogie, he whispered to him, ensuring that Nnamdi was not within earshot, 'Take fifty of my guards and follow Zogo. Don't let him out of your sight, and if you feel he is about to betray us, kill him.'

'He wouldn't be foolish enough to try such a thing. Not with his cousin here and his young whelp of a son in bondage at Aba, would he?' Ogie asked with a raised eyebrow.

'I can't take any chances. He wields great influence. Perhaps more than any of the other Igbo or River chiefs in the land. Sometimes you must take the head of the snake for the body to fail,' Olise said.

266

Ogie just inclined his head in reply and walked over to the ranks of Olise's guards on the wings to relay the prince's orders. Before long, the group of the black-clad warriors detached from the amassed body of Olise's men with Ogie at their head and marched towards the Igbos, ready to reinforce their comrades locked in bloody combat.

'I fear this battle will take longer than I had hoped it would, but by all the gods, when the fading light of the sun fails to illuminate this accursed field, I will wear that crown and proclaim my rightful place as the king of the tribes,' Olise said as he looked on and witnessed the true nature of his countrymen; to kill and to conquer.

FOLLOW ME

Spoken words always find a way to travel, whether over land of harsh terrain or rivers of great length, they always manage to traverse great distances and spread like a pestilence. Faster, it would seem, than racing horses or pigeons bearing messages. Such was the case for Niran's coming.

In just a matter of days, word of his exploits had taken on a life of their own, embellished by travellers and foes who had encountered him along the road or through word of mouth. Niran's journey to the eastern provinces had not, however, been an easy one. It had been wrought with bloody skirmishes, failed robberies, and even the odd assassination. It was said that the prince rode with a thousand men that roamed the land like vengeful apparitions, cleansing it with spear and fire wherever their feet trod.

The truth, however, was an altogether different tale. Niran did now ride with many more spears at his back, but they were not nearly as many as the rumours suggested. In fact, they were just shy of two hundred men, with most of the newcomers joining his ranks along the way, having previously failed to answer the call to arms from their king or escape the forced submission of Olise. Their excuses had varied, from not believing in fighting for a king or prince they had never met, to not having the resources to make a meaningful contribution and spilling their blood in a land that was foreign to them. However, the presence of a living and breathing descendant of the throne was reason enough to rouse them and grant purpose to their otherwise uneventful existences.

Not all those who bolstered Niran's numbers had been real warriors. Some of them had only ever been in minor tribal clashes, or wielded their machetes in anger, but whatever skill they lacked they made up for in enthusiasm and the will to prove themselves in the eyes of the prince. The veterans amongst the men, however, made up over two-thirds of the small force and served as the spearhead that forged through the eastern landscape.

Messengers from Niran's growing army always preceded him, moving from one settlement to the next proclaiming his arrival and giving the people the opportunity to renew their fealties to the throne or face the consequences. This, however, was only the secondary objective. Primarily, the advance party served as scouts tasked with gauging the ambiance in the towns and cities, assessing their defences, weaknesses and the strengths of what armies remained.

The townships and cities that remained defiant were dismantled if they held no strategic value, with their inhabitants displaced or sworn to the prince in the presence of their gods, while others were quickly subjugated and left under the control of Niran's trusted men to govern in his name. Many of the settlements were devoid of warriors, as most had travelled west to support one of the warring factions. Niran had seized upon this opportunity and, within a matter of days, he had managed to secure a large region in the east with a network of spies and local militia that answered only to him. His influence had continued to spread as had word of his success, which encouraged more gates to open before him. Now, deep in the heartland of the Igbos, he would finally encounter those who held true power in the region, and the nobilities of the land.

As he had done for every town he now controlled, he sent forth his scouts to a city called Nsukka, which was under the rule of a minor faction of the Chidozie family. His men rode through the city gates demanding an audience with the chief or whoever sat in his seat, expecting that the chief would have marched west. The city officials had appeared genuinely interested in their message and had immediately arranged for the scouts to see the chief, who as it happened, had not left the city and retained a skeleton army to protect the city's interests while the fighting men were away. On arrival at the townhouse of the chief, the scouts were set upon, arrested and bound in ropes. He then sent out a message of his own informing Niran that his scouts were being held captive until he came in person to deliver whatever message he had. Niran had pre-empted this very response but rode to the city nonetheless with only a dozen of his warriors accompanying him.

'This is suicide, you do realise that?' Adebola was saying for the third time, failing to conceal his agitation, as their horses cantered towards the city gates. 'The thing that bothers me even more is that you don't seem concerned about this ambush, because that's what we are going into you know, an ambush.' Niran only looked over his shoulder and offered Adebola a conspiratorial smile.

'Correct me if I'm wrong, my prince, but we don't have any idea how many warriors remain in the city,' Adebola added, also looking to Seun for some reassurance, but the tall warrior only shrugged his shoulders as if he didn't have a care in the world.

'We are merely going to have a reasoned discussion with the chief, nothing more. I see no cause for concern,' Niran said, but Adebola wasn't convinced.

'I wish I shared your optimism, my prince, but it's hard to stay calm when we're walking into a pit of snakes. If this chief has the liver to imprison your messengers, who, I might add, came to him under peaceful terms, what do you think he'll do when he's got you behind his gates without an army to protect you?' asked Adebola as he peered into the distance at the looming gates of the city.

'The Igbo are a proud tribe; perhaps prouder than us Yoruba, and some of them may consider it an insult that I have chosen to speak through an emissary rather than in person. What it does tell me is the character of the man. He considers himself important, but doesn't feel he is treated as such by his peers. He is brave, but not considered a threat, and more importantly, not foolish enough to openly dismiss an extended hand that may benefit him. We can use such a man to our advantage; of that I am sure,' Niran said.

'I hope you are right, my prince, otherwise we'll be in a very precarious predicament,' Adebola said.

'The prince's instincts have brought us this far, have they not? If I didn't know any better, I'd say you still have doubts that he can unite the tribes,' Seun said, looking sideways at Adebola.

'No. Of course I have no doubt, I only advise caution. We still don't have absolute certainty of those who are genuinely under Olise's hand and those who merely follow him out of fear, witchcraft or whatever else he holds over them,' Adebola replied.

'Be that as it may, this is something I must do. I cannot afford to show weakness to the men I intend to lead,' said Niran and, with that, Adebola knew not to push the subject any further, but to prepare for whatever awaited them in the city.

By the time they reached the city, a contingent of Igbo warriors stood waiting to receive them in full armour, as if expecting a confrontation, but they were courteous enough and gave Niran the respect due a prince. Some of the warriors regarded him with reverence, surprised that one so young could be behind all the talk that had captivated the region, while others treated him with a hint of suspicion. Niran scanned the streets that snaked away from where they now stood as his men dismounted and young boys hastily accepted the bridles to their horses and placed skins of water in their hands.

One of the Igbo warriors approached Niran awkwardly, not knowing the correct protocol to address a prince of such esteem. He first attempted to kneel, before deciding to prostrate himself, to the amusement of Niran and his people.

'Stand. There is no need for formalities right now. Please take me to your chief,' Niran said in heavily accented Igbo, saving the warrior from further embarrassment.

The warrior stood but could not bring his eyes level with the prince's. 'Thank you... erm... my prince. Apologies. Chief Emeka has insisted on you and your men... erm... leaving your weapons with my men... I'm sorry, my prince,' he fumbled, still not able to look Niran in the eye.

'Absolutely not! We will do no such thing,' countered Seun in fluent Igbo, 'You expect us to simply hand over our weapons when you hold our men hostage?' He let out a cackle. 'Let's not waste any more time here. Lead the way,' he finished with a look that spoke volumes.

271

The warrior looked as if he would have sooner preferred the ground to swallow him where he stood, and Niran couldn't help but feel a little sorry for the man, so he was willing to compromise. Only slightly.

'We will leave behind our shields and spears, but nothing else.' Even though every man in Niran's retinue had an assortment of weapons hanging from their waists, some more than two. 'We mean your chief no harm, you have my word, provided no harm has come to my scouts.' The last sentence was delivered with a slight touch of iron to show that he was willing to revert to violence if the circumstances demanded it.

The warrior swallowed hard and looked to his companions, whose faces mirrored his own, fearful and befuddled, then he looked back to Niran.

'Ok, my prince... but can I ask that... that some of your men remain at the gates?' He asked uncertainly as if expecting the sharp end of a spear as a reply.

'You are beginning to test my patience. We have ridden a long way and I'd like to conclude this business as quickly as possible. If you haven't noticed, time is of the essence. Now show me to your chief.' Niran had hardened his expression as he fixed the warrior with his hazel eyes. The man all but stumbled backwards and ordered his companions to form up on either side of the westerners before hastily marching them to the chief's townhouse.

Chief Emeka was a solid man in his mid-forties, his skin weathered from years in the sun, but he also had a vitality about him that boasted a lifetime of fighting. His arms bulged with muscles and veins, and coarse black hair clung to his shoulders and chest like an ape. Niran noticed an old scar that cut across the muscle of one thigh diagonally, an old war wound perhaps, and the way he stood unevenly balancing most of his weight on his other leg. Niran realised that this may be why Emeka had remained in the city and was not off fighting in the west.

His eyes darted around nervously as he looked from man to man, failing to conceal his anxiety at the sight of their weapons; he would punish the guards for failing to carry out his instructions, if he still lived after this meeting.

'Prince Niran,' he said without preamble. 'Forgive me for not kneeling in your presence, these old legs do not permit me to bend much these days.' He indicated the old wound he bore.

'The false courtesy I can forgive, but the abduction of my men is a different matter. Bring them to me now before we continue this conversation any further, I would see them with mine own eyes and know what treatment they have received at your hands,' Niran replied, not breaking eye contact with Emeka, who after a few seconds of an intense stare down, looked away and turned to one of his men. 'Bring them,' he said before turning back to Niran.

There were a few moments of tense silence as Niran and his men, who all had their hands close to the handles of their weapons, stood across from Emeka and his men, awaiting the captured scouts. All the while Niran never broke eye contact as he studied the man in front of him. Emeka did the same, but his confidence was not absolute, Niran noticed, and he seemed more uncomfortable with every passing moment. Eventually, Niran's men were brought from wherever they had been held, still with their wrists bound but otherwise unharmed.

'Release them at once,' Niran said in a tone that demanded no argument. Emeka's men immediately cut the captives' bonds without even looking to their chief for his consent. Once this was done, the scouts moved to stand by their prince.

'I see you have not treated them unkindly. A wise decision, but I sense that this was only a ploy to get me here. Now that you have my full attention, tell me what it is you seek from me?' Niran said, not once having broken his gaze on Emeka.

'Young prince, you are mistaken. I think the question is, what is it you seek from me? I have heard your message and the talk of the people. I know of your triumphs and the peoples you have won to your cause, but you are too late. We cannot offer you an army, most of our men are shedding their blood for your uncle, probably as we speak, and from what I hear, your homeland has been laid to waste. What could you possibly offer us that Olise has not done already, I wonder?' Emeka said, showing a trace of the young fearless warrior he had once been.

'That may be so, but I am aware of the plight your people face. I know that your sons are being held in Aba. I know of the heavy taxes Olise has imposed on your tribes that threatens to compromise your ability to feed your citizens, not to mention the supplies that you have been required to send to him to sustain his armies to the detriment of your own people. Let us talk plainly, you have no love for Olise, so why fight for a monarch your people despise? If he does succeed in taking the throne, what makes you think he won't hold your children indefinitely to guarantee you remain under his rule? Is that the life you would choose for your people? To live in fear and oppression? There is an alternative, and this is what I offer you,' said Niran.

'And what is it you offer exactly? From what I can see, I don't think you are able to offer us anything. You hold claim to no lands, wealth or even a decent army. Olise has taken that from you. Besides, what makes you think I won't just put you in ropes right now? I'm sure Olise would pay handsomely for the head of one of his nephews.'

Niran only smiled and briefly looked to Seun, who inclined his head slightly in response. 'I think you are forgetting to whom you speak. You say I hold no wealth or lands, but I do. For as long as I draw breath every piece of land south of the great rivers for as long as your eyes can see belongs to my family, and as for an army, I may not have the men to rival Olise's forces, but given time the tribes he has amassed will be insignificant. You see, I anticipated your response and I have already sent word ahead to every town and city between here and the River-lands. Most have already pledged their spears to me.'

'You lie! I would have heard from my tribesmen if any Yoruba emissaries passed through my territories!' Emeka said angrily.

'And what makes you think they were Yoruba? Did you really think I'd risk my life in your homeland without first securing the path ahead of me? There is much you will come to learn of me, Emeka, if you are wise enough to accept the opportunity I extend to you.'

'Ha! Do I have fool written across my face? You really expect me to believe this story of yours? You are desperate and your sweet words do nothing to appeal to me. Guards!' Emeka roared and his men took an uncertain step forward.

Adebola was the first to draw his weapons, and a few others in Niran's retinue followed suit, as the metallic sound of swords leaving their scabbards reverberated in the confines of the reception room of the townhouse.

However, Niran, Seun and the other warriors from Ile-Ife had barely flinched or appeared the least concerned. Niran then raised his arm to Adebola and gestured for him to lower his weapons. He then addressed Emeka again, and his tone was severe; gone was the amicable prince, in his place stood the warrior, the liege lord and, perhaps, the future king.

'You dare to raise your weapons against me? I see that you are indeed a fool and you would put your pride before your reasoning. Let me explain, a pact has been in existence between the king and your tribesmen since long before the current conflict even started. A pact that was sworn in blood between all the great tribes of the west, east and the north. Your clan-lord, chief Zogo and my father the king had anticipated the events of the past months, and Zogo instructed the senior members of his house to pledge their fealty and to protect the prince when the hour comes. This was not made common knowledge to all the chiefs in the province as it was known that some would undoubtedly wish to betray the king out of selfish ambition even before the demand for hostages by Olise. You have just proven yourself to be one of them.'

'More lies! Zogo would have informed me, I am a chief in my own right, a respected warrior. There is no way I wouldn't have been brought into his confidence. I refuse to believe that!' Emeka roared.

'You still doubt me? Even the men who serve you do so only at the behest of your clan-lord, and will turn on you if I but give the word,' Niran said, his expression one of stone. 'I will grant you one last opportunity to swear your spear to me, but know this; refuse and I will have no choice but to execute you. I cannot afford to spare the lives of traitors, that was the mistake my father made, and I will not fall into the same trap, but there is no need for any blood to be shed.'

Perspiration dripped from Emeka's brow and he looked even more uncomfortable as he shifted his weight between his legs. 'Your words do not scare me, young prince, you are in my city and in my house, surrounded by men loyal to me. You should not have come here spewing your lies and, for that, you will not leave here alive!'

Niran's expression softened only a fraction but it was one of sorrow. 'Very well.' Turning to Emeka's guards, who covered the exit and lined the walls of the townhouse he said, 'Take him.' Immediately, all the spears in the room were pointed at Emeka, who looked on in bewilderment, then shock, which finally gave way to fear.

'W-what are you doing? Azuka, Uche? Have you all gone mad? I'm your chief!' he stammered. One of the men he called upon, the same warrior from the gates, only bowed his head slightly in shame. 'I'm sorry my chief, this is the will of chief Zogo and we are sworn to see it through. Put him in ropes.'

'Unhand me!' Emeka exclaimed as he was grabbed and roughly ushered towards the entrance. He struggled, but was quickly subdued and bundled away kicking and shouting.

'Even I have underestimated you, my prince,' Adebola said, sheathing his sword and axe as they watched Emeka being dragged off. 'I see there is much that I didn't know; have I not proven to be trustworthy?' he asked Niran.

'If I have learnt anything over the last moon, it's that some plans are better unspoken. I am sorry, but I assure you that you have my trust,' Niran said. 'We still have a long road ahead. There are a few of the Igbo that remain loyal to Olise, and it is these men who I need to root out, just as we have done here today. Also, we still have

276

the River tribe to contend with. That will certainly be a much more difficult task to overcome. I have invited the Igbo chiefs we can trust here to Nsukka to hold court with me. This is their land, after all, and I would welcome their thoughts and support before I move further east.'

'Will you really execute this Emeka character? His body language suggested that he was conflicted. There is no doubt he is a proud man and ambitious, but there is no telling what a man would do to protect his family. If Olise was to catch wind of what has transpired here, he could order the hostages to be killed. I don't want to be presumptuous, but are you prepared to have such a thing weighing on your conscience?' Adebola asked.

'To do so, he'd have to send his men through some of the towns we now hold, and there is no way a message would get past us without me hearing about it. We hold the passes through the east now, so we control the flow of information. Rest assured I have considered this possibility. Once the nobilities of the province are gathered all will be revealed. Right now, we need to secure the city and place our men amongst the warriors that remain here. Summon one hundred of our warriors, we have much to prepare for.'

As evening drew near, many of the chiefs and vassal lords had gathered outside Emeka's townhouse, where they were received by Niran, who had chosen to hold the meeting outside in the large compound of the residence. His choice of location had not been without reason, as Niran still had his doubts about some of the men who sat before him.

Ever the punctilious one, he had concealed warriors around the premises who could come to his defence if one of those present had an ulterior motive for being here and decided to deal a hand of treachery. Niran and his men still wore their armour and carried daggers, but Seun wore his sword at his waist, as was expected of a blood-guard. The visitors, however, were made to relinquish their weapons before being admitted to the presence of the prince.

Fires had been lit around the compound with rags dipped in animal fat and tied to the ends of long sticks driven into the ground and the faint scent of burning meat wafted into the air. The men that had gathered were mostly elders, too old to wield a spear, but most were accompanied by at least one strapping warrior who watched over their lords and the prince's men with a keen eye.

'Chiefs of Imo, thank you for making the journey today as I know you have all risked a great deal to be here, but before we discuss the matters at hand I would welcome you to break some kola nuts with me and share in my palm wine as tradition demands,' Niran said courteously as he indicated the tributes that had been laid out in the centre of the gathered men. The kola nuts, which were placed in leaves, were split between the men as a symbol of friendship, and the wine shared as dedication was given to their respective gods; *Olodumare* in the case of the Yoruba and *Chineke* for the Igbo.

'Your grasp of our tongue and culture does you great honour, my prince, but what is most pleasing is that despite the troubles that have befallen the realm you have managed to make it through to stand before us unharmed. Your estimation has gone up in my eyes and I am happy to serve such a man,' said one of the gathered chiefs.

'You honour me, chief Ikenna, and I am glad to see that there are still men in the realm that the throne can rely upon even with everything that has transpired. As you all know, my father the king had cultivated a deep friendship and trust in your clan-lord chief Zogo over the years and had prepared us for these very circumstances. I am aware that some of you have had little choice but to send your warriors away to fight for Olise, thus maintaining the pretence, but I have summoned you in the hopes that you have not forgotten your vows to the throne, which I am now required to call upon.'

'Our vows to your family have not changed, even if appearances suggest otherwise. Zogo and the chiefs who accompanied him west were merely dancing to Olise's drums until an opportunity to aid the king presents itself, this has always been made clear to our tribe and a few trusted chiefs from the River-land who are allied to us. With that said, I only speak for my own house, but I am

278

sure the chiefs gathered here would also agree, yes?' asked another one of the elders to murmurs of agreement from the rest of the men.

'It gladdens my heart to hear this and I can assure you that your loyalty will not soon be forgotten by the throne, in this you have my word,' Niran replied.

'What of our children who are being held captive by Olise? We are putting their lives in jeopardy. This is something that cannot be overlooked so easily. Many of the sons held are heirs in the tribe, and some are sole children to their parents. How do we explain this to our wives and our sisters? Are we to tell them that we're prepared to sacrifice the children for the sake of the realm? They have suffered enough; many of our young men will not return from this conflict, and some mothers are too old to bear another seed, so we should preserve the lives of those we still can,' One of the elders remarked, and many of the men acknowledged his argument.

'Chief Achike, I understand the difficult position that you and many of your tribal lords face and I am taking steps to ensure that all those taken are returned to you. I have not been idle the last few days, as you well know, but what you don't know is that I have already sent a reasonable portion of my men to Aba. Word from my scouts has already filtered back informing me of their progress and, gods willing, my forces will be ready to take the town by sunset tomorrow.'

Niran had their full attention now, and most of them chattered amongst themselves bemusedly and excitedly.

'How is that possible?' asked Ikenna. 'We have received no such reports of warriors travelling south. How can you possibly conceal a force without us knowing?'

Niran only smiled. 'It pleases me to know that if my men have managed to evade you all, then so it will be for Olise's spies, but I can assure you that I offer you no falsehood. You see, the only way to get a small army across lands undetected is to hide them in plain sight. They travelled as merchants, traders, even beggars, and they all went separately in small groups, never using the same route or crossing paths. By the time the sun rises tomorrow they will converge on the town of Ikot-Ekpene, where they will join the local militia, who have sworn to aid me in this endeavour, before finally moving to Aba. I also know that the garrison in Aba is ill prepared to defend against a coordinated attack, not to mention that they are dependent on food supplies from the neighbouring town of Umuahia, another settlement that I have managed to secure, albeit silently. The men of Aba are expecting their monthly supply late afternoon tomorrow, and this is when we will strike. Once they have gained the walls and after night falls, they will open the gates to the rest of the men and take the city.'

The chiefs looked on dumbfounded, some shook their heads in disbelief and others just starred open mouthed at the news they had just received. 'Wonderful...' said Achike. 'How you have managed to plan and execute all of this under our noses is beyond me. You are truly your father's son and a man worthy to follow,' said Ikenna.

'Again, Ikenna, you honour me, but I consider it my duty to put the safety of my people above everything. After all, what is the purpose of a monarchy that cannot protect its subjects? But I would request something in return, and it is something I do not ask lightly,' Niran said, looking at all the gathered men in turn.

'What would you ask of us, my prince?' said one of the elders expectantly.

'I would ask only one thing, that you all swear your spears to me. You will forsake all your promises to Olise and Ekaete and support me in ridding the realm of their influence. This is all I require from you,' he replied.

'And what of Emeka?' asked another elder, who had remained quiet throughout the conversation. 'We all know he is an ambitious man, but he belongs to the Chidozie family and is a distant relative to our clan-lord himself. I do not condone whatever plot he may have been concocting, but I would ask that his life is spared.'

Niran considered this for a moment before responding. 'Emeka is an unrepentant traitor and he would have me in ropes right now, or worse, have my head in a sack on its way to Olise as proof of his loyalty. I cannot allow such a man to live. Zogo will understand the necessity of my action, even though it is a difficult one to swallow, but I have decided on this and intend to see it through. If it makes a difference, I will not make him suffer as he deserves, but I will grant him a swift death.'

The gathered men all exchanged looks and some conferred between themselves until finally Ikenna spoke for the collective. 'If that is your will, we must accept it. I hope that this proves to you that we are for you, my prince, and we will follow you wherever your destiny leads us.'

With that, each of the men stood and took turns in renewing their vows to Niran in the presence of their gods. Once the oaths had been made, Niran outlined his proposal to march on the River-lands and the chiefs promised to send what resources they had to support him, which he accepted thankfully.

'This meeting is concluded. I thank you all for your understanding, and I will call on you soon, but for now you should go back to your provinces, so no further suspicion is aroused – and remember, what has occurred here today is to remain between only those who are gathered here. The rest of the realm will learn in time.'

They all bade him farewell as they left the compound, leaving Niran alone with his guards. Adebola approached him with a look of veneration plastered on his face.

'I almost don't believe what has happened here tonight. You do realise that now you effectively have sole dominion over the east, except for the River-lands of course, but in one fell swoop you have dealt an almost fatal blow to Olise's grip on the region. You truly are an inspiration, my prince, I don't think I have seen anything quite like this.'

'Please, I am merely doing my father's bidding, he would expect nothing less,' Niran responded. 'Let us hope that the gods favour Toju in the north as they have done for us here, then we will truly see your father's legacy fulfilled,' said Seun.

'I pray it is so. Only time will tell, but this is only the beginning, and we still have a long struggle ahead of us. The River tribes will not be as easily convinced, of that I am certain.'

The following morning, as the cockerel hailed the rising sun, Emeka was brought out to the compound of his townhouse, where he was forced to kneel in front of Niran, who was seated on a stool opposite him flanked by Seun and Adebola. He was offered an opportunity to make his peace with his gods, but he chose rather to use his last breath in directing his vituperation at the prince. Niran allowed him this last show of defiance, but once the spittle in his mouth ran dry, he was forced down onto a block of wood and his head was parted from his body, just as the sun crested the roofs of Nsukka.

THE SCENT OF RAIN

The sun hung blood red in the distance, an ominous sight for those who had lived through the nightmare of what had been one of the darkest days in the history of the tribes. It was almost as if the sun bled for the many souls that had, only a few hours earlier, drawn breath, but now lay still across the barren landscape. Dark clouds interspersed with the evening's red glow roved the skies overhead, ushering in what was likely to be a heavy storm that would saturate the soil with the blood that had been spilt, paving the way for more to flow.

With the approach of the evening and the failing light of the sun, both armies had retreated to the relative safety of their lines after hours of unrestrained bloodletting, which had inflicted heavy casualties on either side of the divide. The bodies of the fallen had been left where they died, the survivors were too exhausted to even offer prayers for their slain companions, rather choosing to preserve their energy for the next wave of fighting. All this, in the name of two men. How did it come to this? How was it that despite Jide's ambitions to unite the tribes and create a nation that would rival any known to history, all had unravelled like a thread pulled from a cloth until the pattern in the fabric was lost, undistinguishable and eventually reduced to a pile of loose string in the dust. All this Jide pondered as he stood and overlooked the battlefield, a reminder of the wickedness in the hearts of men.

The carrion birds were feasting and the sound they brought along with them sent a shudder through his skin. The constant squawking and flapping of dark wings amongst the broken weapons and bodies was like a mosquito in his ear, worse still was the sound of flesh torn from bone as the hungry birds devoured the banquet that had been laid out before them. The sound of dying men still haunted him and he struggled to distinguish between the sounds and sights in his mind's eye and the reality of those who yet lived on that field of horrors and pleaded for an end to their suffering. He could not

283

escape the scent of death that hung heavy in the air along with the coppery taste and smell of congealed blood that clung to his skin like a lover's embrace.

It brought tears to his eyes as he searched the skies for an answer. 'Is this our fate, for us to kill each other to preside over a hollow kingdom? Is this pleasing to you?' he asked softly with his head raised to the heavens. 'Why do we have to suffer so? All these lives lost, and for what, so that my brother can claim *my* birth right? I would sooner give it to him just to bring an end to all this bloodshed, I would sooner lay down my crown...' His emotions threatened to overwhelm him, and he had to force himself to remain composed. ' *Yemoja*, I beseech you. Forgive me for my past indiscretions, for not heeding your word. I implore you to deliver our people from this threat to our very existence. Guide me now, I beg of you.' A crackle of thunder in the distance was the only response he received, and more dark clouds moving across the horizon.

He stood there for a moment longer waiting for a message, a sign, anything, but received nothing. Then he finally decided to slowly make his way back to his camp and his bedraggled warriors, wiping the tears from his eyes and, in the process, smudging the dirt and dried blood that encrusted his handsome features.

As he walked through the camp, his despair deepened; looking at his men, most had taken a wound of some description, some minor and others serious or mortal. It was clear that many would not make it through the night. Men lay about the camp bandaged or with open wounds that festered and oozed pus, attracting flies, accompanied by groans of pain. Some had taken it upon themselves to serve as field medics as they went about applying ointments and improvised herbal remedies they had managed to forage from this desolate land.

No one had bothered to erect tents, men had simply collapsed in exhaustion wherever they could find a relatively flat surface, and only a few had managed to build miserable excuses for fires in the evening breeze, knowing that within a few hours the nightmare would start all over again. The sight was nothing short of a defeated army; resignation was etched on the faces of many, who probably contemplated the reality of not witnessing the next sunset. If the battle didn't kill them, starvation surely would, with food supplies dangerously low and very little water available to quench the thirst of the parched warriors. Getting beyond the walls was now their only chance of survival.

He eventually came to where his chiefs and commanders were seated, talking in hushed voices, tending their wounds, sharpening their weapons and some already fast asleep, taking advantage of what little time remained to them. All activities ceased the moment they noticed him, as he sat heavily on a straw mat cushioned with cow hides that had been laid out for him. Like the warriors in the camp around them, every one of Jide's commanders sported a new scar, some hideous, like Dare, who outdid everyone with a massive gash across the cheek exposing part of his gums and teeth, and Olusegun with several lacerations on his arms. Only Adedeji seemed to have come out unscathed, looking as fresh as if he had just emerged from a river, bathed and refreshed, with his body glistening with sweat.

They had all seen the king's expression, so no one spoke but rather looked at each other and silently urged the next man to part with some words of wisdom or humour to lift the mood. In the end Jide broke the tension. 'Dare, you really need to get that wound tended,' he said, looking to his old companion. 'Yes, Kabiyesi, I've already sent for someone to stich it up, but apparently all the tailors in the army have been killed,' Dare replied, trying his best not to laugh at his own joke for fear of the pain that would follow.

The men sitting around started to chortle and soon burst out with laughter. 'That's bad news for you O, you look terrible,' said Akin. Until now, no one had commented on Dare's gruesome disfigurement, but it was now fair game to all. 'Indeed, your wife will definitely turn to a younger village boy now, and I wouldn't blame her,' said Adedeji, to more laughter.

'Let me know if you decide to drink some of that palm wine, so I can place my horn to your cheek and collect what doesn't reach your throat,' said another of the captains.

'Please, please don't make me laugh, talking is painful enough,' Dare said through clenched teeth.

A ghost of a smile briefly crossed Jide's face but was as fleeting as the evening breeze. 'I know you try to lighten my mood, which I appreciate in this dark hour, but we cannot forget the day behind us nor ignore the one ahead of us. We have lost too many men, including almost a quarter of the Modakeke, with many more wounded. It will be a mountain of a task holding against Olise's men, especially with the Igbo now joined to the ranks. It almost seems impossible.'

'I know you say that, but was it only me that noticed that the Igbo contingents seemed reluctant to engage? They had so many opportunities to weaken our position but failed to take one of them. Surely their reluctance to commit must mean something. Hope, at the very least?' asked Olusegun.

'That may be so, but even without the Igbo we are still outnumbered. We fought well today, and I am sure that our enemies will be even more wary of testing our spears come the morning, but they still have the numbers. All it takes is for them to outflank us on both sides and we'll be overwhelmed. I'm not sure how much longer we can fight with our lines spread so thinly,' Adedeji replied.

'That is the only formation that is viable given the circumstances. Anything else would leave us too exposed,' Akin pointed out. 'There is no choice but to keep pushing forward until we are in the shadow of the walls,' he went on. 'Unless...' said Dare, speaking low and trying not to move his jaw too much, causing everyone to lean in slightly to hear him. 'Unless we send some men under the cover of darkness to look for a way around Olise's men and lay in wait to take them in the rear when the main army attacks?' he finished.

'That would be a good idea but, knowing my brother, he'd have posted guards all around the perimeter. So, to get past them, our

286

men would probably have to travel a good deal wider, and they'd never make it into position in time before the fighting starts tomorrow, I fear,' answered Jide.

'Then we simply fight. We have no choice, besides turning back, which isn't an option. We just have to fight and leave the rest to the gods,' said Adedeji to the downcast faces around him. No one spoke, they all knew the likely outcome, but more so, they knew their duty to their king. Eventually Jide nodded grimly. 'You are right, Deji, that is exactly what we'll do. We will fight. Get whatever rest you can, and some food if there is still any to be had. Tomorrow will not be an easy day for us,' he said and, with that, he lay back on his mat and almost immediately fell into a fitful slumber.

Hours later Jide woke with a start to the sounds of crickets in the charred undergrowth and a multitude of snores of varying decibels. He was surprised he had managed to sleep at all but was quickly reminded of how fatigued he was from the aches in his joints and the throbbing behind his eyes. All his commanders were there, as comfortable as they could be on their mats laid over the hard earth. Akin was next to him, with his hand resting on the pommel of his sword, as he tended to sleep. In the distance, Jide could see the fires from the city, and envied the warriors behind the safety of the wall, fed, comfortable and secure, while he and his men were reduced to sleeping rough out in the open like beggars.

Suddenly, a flash of white caught the corner of his eye and he turned his head, only to see a girl standing a few feet away from him wearing a white wrapper with embroidery that shifted like the clouds overhead as she looked directly at him. The hairs on the back of his neck and arms prickled and his heart raced but there was something familiar about her, it was a face that he had seen before. He couldn't focus his mind as if he was suddenly wading through a mist seeking purchase on anything to stabilise him.

The girl continued to stare at him and then slowly began to turn, until she was facing west and started to walk away through the crowd of sleeping warriors. After covering a short distance, she looked back at Jide almost as if beckoning him to accompany her. He did exactly that. He also took his sword along with him, more out of habit than a feeling of threat, and he followed behind keeping a reasonable distance between the two of them whilst trying not to step on one of his sleeping warriors.

As he followed, all the sounds of their surroundings seemed to fall away, until the only noise that cut through the eerie silence was the gentle rattling made by the coral beads she wore about her. Soon, Jide's surroundings also faded away into a blur until all he could see was the gently swinging braids and the swaying hips of the girl in front of him. Her movement was mesmerising, clearly that of a confident woman and not of a girl, and he was compelled to keep following.

After what seemed to be an age, the girl came to stop on a rise in the landscape. Standing on the mound, she turned towards him and awaited his approach, all the while appraising him with her stare. The hairs on the back of his neck stood out again as he moved tentatively towards her. He stopped a few yards away from her and immediately felt the urge to take a knee, but his own sense of authority prevented him from doing so.

He waited for her to speak, and then it hit him, this was the girl he had seen in the forest all those months ago when he visited the seers in the forest of his hometown. He was certain that she had also visited him in his youth on the day he was proclaimed king on the battlefield, and she had haunted his dreams, all of which came flooding back to him in vivid detail.

'Who are you...' his words came out in a whisper, already guessing the answer before it was confirmed. 'You know who I am, King Jide,' the same deep and stentorian voice. He immediately fell to the ground and prostrated himself.

' *Yemoja.* You have come to me in my darkest hour. I bless your name,' he said, pressing his forehead into the soil. 'Do not think I am here to deliver you, King Jide. You failed to heed my word when I tried to warn you, or do you forget? Have I not always watched over you? Have I not always given you your heart's desires; your crown, your kingdom, your family? Instead, you turned to the *Babalawo,* men who are not even worthy to touch the ground I walk upon. Those charlatans are in Ekaete's employ, and the offerings you gave them only weakened you and everything you hold dear. Your fate was sealed upon that very act.'

Jide remembered the items he took along with him that day, and almost as if she read his mind she responded to his thoughts. 'The palm wine tapped from your lands signified the toil of the people of Ile-Ife; the blood from the maiden of your household signified your birthed allies and those who serve you; and the hair bound in the iroko leaves signified your roots and your bloodline. All were destroyed in that cauldron, and so they intended it to be in life.'

Her words were like a spear to his heart. He had been a fool to trust the *Babalawo* despite his misgivings, but he had let his anger towards his brother blind his judgement, for which he was now paying dearly. He remembered the last tribute he had taken with him and was almost afraid to ask, but he had to know what it meant. 'And the kola nuts. What did they represent?' he asked with a shaky voice. She watched him from behind her dark haunting eyes, but he dared not raise his face to her, and she replied, 'The breaking of the kola nuts signified the division of your kingdom.' That which was happening before his eyes.

His worst fears had been confirmed; the gods had forsaken him and there was nothing more he could do but accept their will. He had lost everything and had been left empty; devoid of emotion and almost of fate. He had nothing left to lose. He slowly began to rise but changed his mind and stayed on his knees with his head bowed. 'If this is the fate that is designed for me, who am I to fight against it? I will accept it willingly, as any man must. I can only hope that my humility stands me in good stead with the gods, even though it has been late coming,' he said.

Yemoja watched the king for a while before she spoke. 'King Jide, you have always been a devout man and one with great dignity and honour, which has put you in good standing with the gods, especially with me. I swore to protect you from the day you opened your eyes to the world, and I have always done so. However, you did not undertake the final sacrifice that was asked of you. The white ram

289

the *Babalawo* asked you to slaughter. That at least stands for something, but the gods must be appeased for your disobedience, and they will receive their due. I will not, however, leave you completely forsaken, my child, for you have suffered plenty in this life. Some things I can undo, but others, you have no choice but to accept.' A glimmer of light offered along the dark path Jide trod was all he could hope for, it was all that he deserved.

Akin and Adedeji frantically searched the faces around each fire for their king, asking questions of every man they came across. So far, no one had seen the king and the sentries that had been placed around the camp swore that no one had passed by them, so Jide had to be somewhere close. They had initially feared that Olise had chosen to strike in the night and had sent men to kidnap Jide, which would immediately force the army into submission but, as the hours passed, this scenario became more unlikely, as word would have filtered through by now if such a deed had been perpetrated.

As they searched the grounds, they came across a path leading away from the camp back in the direction they had marched days ago. Akin, who was a natural hunter, had noticed a trail of disturbed dead leaves and one set of depressions in the soil, marking the footfall of a man from the size of the indentations. So, with swords in hand, they padded along the narrow path until the ground started to rise and eventually opened out on to a clear patch of land. There they saw the king sitting with his folded legs beneath him and his head bowed, and they immediately rushed to his side.

'Kabiyesi!' Akin shouted, unable to hide the panic in his voice as he hooked an arm under Jide's and gently raised him to his feet. Jide's eyes snapped open, as if he had suddenly awoken from a deep sleep, and looked between the two faces looming above him. His eyes were red rimmed and the bags under them stood out, but he was alert and lucid.

The lines around his brows furrowed as he looked to the skies and noted the receding darkness hailing the approach of dawn. 'There is much to be done, we have little time,' he said, hurrying his speech. 'Adedeji, I want you to take twenty of your best men, men you trust with your life, and head west to the lands of the queen, that is where you are needed.'

Adedeji looked to Akin, then back at the king, confused. 'Kabiyesi, I don't understand. My place is by your side. You can't expect me to abandon you now in your hour of need!' he said as his heart started to beat faster.

'I don't have time to explain, but this is my command, and you will follow my orders,' Jide replied sternly. It was clear that Adedeji was almost close to tears, something that neither of the other men had ever witnessed, or thought possible, for that matter. Adedeji opened his mouth to protest, but the king raised his hand, silencing him before he spoke, this time speaking to him softly as a mother would do to soothe a child.

'I know this is a difficult thing to ask of you, but much has been revealed to me this night, my friend, and I have seen the fate of our people. I do not expect you to understand, but I do require you to obey me. If there was another way, I would surely have chosen it, but there isn't. One thing is certain, that you are destined to die an old man as you have always reminded us, and even though you are old, today, my friend, is not that day,' he said with a sad smile.

'Kabiyesi, I have known you all of your life just as Akin has. All the Modakeke are bound to you by blood. How can I, of all men, be given such a command to turn my back on you? I have as much right to protect you as your blood-guard, and you would deny me this? Everything in my life has led me to this very moment; to stand by your side in this pivotal time of our history. Sending me away now would only rob me of my life's work and my true calling.' Adedeji spoke sadly, but from his disposition it was clear that he was not planning to challenge the king further.

Akin, who had been silent while he assimilated the king's words, then turned to his oldest ally and placed his hand on his shoulder. 'Adedeji, in all the years we have served the throne you have never questioned the king's judgement, which has always been sound and not without thorough consideration. If he requires you in the west, you know deep down that that is where you must be. As much as it hurts my heart to utter the words, this is the right thing to do.'

Adedeji looked deflated. He sheathed the sword he had been holding and stood there for a long moment without saying a word. Jide and Akin allowed him the time to process it all, and then he knelt in front of the king. 'If that is your will, my king, I will see it through. You have my word.'

'It gladdens me that you trust and accept my judgement. Let us not waste any more time, my friend, and may the gods go with you and protect you all of your days,' Jide said, his words weighing heavy on him as he struggled to part with one of his most trusted men. Before Adedeji turned to leave, the sound of drums, followed by horns, echoed across the field, drawing all their attention to the direction of the city.

'The gates are opening. It appears that Olise wants to end this conflict sooner than I had hoped.' Jide then turned to Akin. 'It is time to embrace our fate, Akin. Destiny awaits us,' he finished, as they all headed back to the camp, which was already stirring into life.

* * * *

Olise pointed to the sky overhead. 'Before the sun reaches its peak, I want this thing over. Look at them. They are defeated men, even if they don't know it yet. It is up to you to show them. No more disappointments; get it done!' he said to the chiefs who had survived the day before, as he snatched his sword from a waiting attendant. His captains had gathered at the gates as soon as the first cockerel had crowed, proclaiming the arrival of dawn. Many of his trusted men had been slain, and he had no choice but to promote others to stand in their place, but the core of his inner circle remained; Ogie, Dimeji, Iboro and a handful of Igbo and River chiefs, including Zogo, Nnamdi and Akpan.

Akpan, who had been part of the first assault, had only narrowly escaped with his life under the relentless spears of the Modakeke warriors. He had tried to rein in his men behind the lines of some of Olise's warriors, but those men had all fallen to the superior warriors they had faced, leaving no buffer between Akpan's tribesmen and the men of the west. He had then been forced to fight defensively, mostly retreating, which resulted in him losing a great many warriors.

It was an almost impossible position to be in; he awaited an opportunity to turn his own spears on Olise as he and some of the Igbo chiefs had planned, but to do so, he would need to have the support of the Igbo warriors, who Olise had intentionally separated, preventing the two tribes from joining their strength. It was almost as if Olise had pre-empted this very scenario and was doing his best to prevent it from happening. Until such an opportunity presented itself, he was forced to fight and kill the very men he would sooner support, and risk dying himself. He hoped that the gods would show him favour today, but he couldn't ignore the feeling of helplessness that had slowly started to consume him.

When Olise had finished his poor attempt at motivating or, rather, intimidating his men, he turned his gaze on the Igbo and River chiefs. 'Akpan, today I grant you the privilege of leading the army into battle. I hope you understand what a great honour I have bestowed upon you. See to it that you weaken our enemy's front line, then I will send in the warriors from Okrika and Aba to support you.'

Akpan stole a quick glance at Zogo and Nnamdi to his right, who both tried their best to appear apathetic, but failed miserably. Olise read all of this, and the corners of his mouth curved in a sneer, but it was gone as quickly as it had appeared.

'Do you have any objections to my command? Or do you fear to lead the army from the front? I truly hope not, but if you would rather stay in the back ranks, I can easily find someone more befitting to lead your men,' Olise suggested, but before he could say more Akpan responded, 'I will do it,' more aggressively than he had intended. 'I would only ask you send in the reinforcements as soon as we are engaged, my prince.'

Olise's features suddenly lit up. 'Oh, I will, don't you worry. Zogo, I will have you follow behind the first wave of reinforcements.

Ogie will accompany you as he did yesterday. Nnamdi will remain with me. Now, let us begin, my friends, we have the remnants of Jide's tattered army to crush.' With that he left the commanders and started making his way towards his own personal guards in their black-clad ranks, followed by Dimeji and Iboro.

Nnamdi lingered for a few minutes, clearly trying to convey some sort of emotion, but forced to restrain himself in the presence of Ogie and the other commanders loyal to Olise. In the end, he turned to Zogo and said in his native dialect, 'All will be well, cousin, *Chineke* is on our side today.' The two men gripped each other's forearm for a few seconds before Nnamdi turned to nod at Akpan, then followed in Olise's wake.

'I hope you actually intend to fight today, chief Zogo, we can't afford a repeat of your half-hearted efforts.' Ogie said as he looked into the eyes of the one called *the Black*. 'Those men,' Ogie continued, pointing at the amassed men of the west on the other side of the field, 'are like cornered animals, and they will fight as such, twice as hard, so we need to be the aggressors this time around.' Zogo only looked at Ogie in silence and didn't bother to grant him the privilege of a reply before turning his back on him and heading for his own men. Ogie stood there for a moment and thought to himself that he would have to kill this pompous goat once the dust had settled, and he would relish every moment of it.

Less than an hour later, Akpan and the Akwa-Ibom warriors were arrayed in the shadow of the city walls as they bore down on the westerners. Similarly, Jide's men had already taken up formation beyond the thousands of bloated bodies on the other side of the field. The carrion birds seemed to sense what was coming, as hundreds of them took to the sky, temporarily abandoning their meals. A solitary vulture remained perched on a heap of bodies as if silently challenging the men.

It flapped its large black wings several times and let out a series of raspy grunting calls before joining the other birds in flight. Some of the men who had seen the bird took this as an omen and made signs to their various deities to protect them, and then the rain started. It came as drizzle at first, then it slowly began to increase in intensity. The rain did, at least, help to dampen the scent of corruption that infused the air, but it would be a great hindrance once the bloodshed started in earnest.

At Jide's command, Adedeji had taken twenty men and marched west, while the rest of the western tribes formed up around their king and prepared to face their countrymen for what might be the last time. Despite their dishevelled and malnourished appearance, the determination in their eyes had not wavered, and every man among them burned with a fire anew to carve their names in the stones of history and leave behind their mark on the world for future generations to write songs about.

Akpan gave the order and his men started to advance. They moved carefully at first, trying their best not to disturb the bodies that littered their path, but they need not have troubled themselves, as the living and the dead would soon be intertwined in sorrowful embrace before becoming one with the earth, as all men are destined to be.

Jide thrust his spear in the direction of the city and his men poured forward to meet the advancing enemy, summoning every ounce of energy that was left to them. There was an urgency about their momentum, each of them eager to claim victory or meet their gods; either way they welcomed an end to it all.

Shields were battered and wrenched aside as spears and swords ripped through soft tissue and muscles. Within minutes, Jide and Akin were amid the fighting, cutting down everything in their path, and the remaining Modakeke warriors, now only a fraction of their original number, wrought fear in the ranks of the enemy as they positioned themselves about their king and obliterated their foe. The westerners did in fact fight like cornered animals, but deadly ones, nonetheless, knowing that this was possibly their last stand, and everything they had done in their lives had led to this very moment. That very determination drove them on as they continued to cut a bloody red line through the mass of warriors before them.

Jide had asked the men of Ondo to remain behind until Olise had committed all his warriors to the fight, in a bid to retain some of their strength, but this was a dangerous gamble and a taxing one on the westerners who now crossed swords and spears on *Ogun's* stage. It was as if a fire had been lit under their feet, the way they drove back their foe with furious force. For every one of Jide's men who fell, four of Olise's followed him into the afterlife. The men from Akwa-Ibom and Aba lacked the grit to face the westerners and, after a short and bloody clash, Jide's men began to gain ground and inch ever closer to the walls of the city.

Akpan was desperately fending off two warriors who attacked him like demons released from the bowels of the underworld. He desperately used his shield as a club and repeatedly bludgeoned one of his adversaries while struggling to use his sword arm to parry blows from the spear of his other assailant. It was obvious that he had a slight advantage, as the men were clearly drained physically, but the skill they possessed was undeniably their only means of survival. One of his attackers, frustrated by his failure to subdue Akpan, made a fatal error in his footing as he thrust his spear forward and overextended his reach. Taking advantage of the man's disbalance, Akpan sidestepped and rammed his shield into the man's face, causing him to stumble. One of Akpan's men then stepped forward and drove his sword into the falling man's head, which burst from the other side of his temple, killing him in an instant. The second warrior, undeterred by his companion's death, darted past Akpan and killed the man in retaliation but, by so doing, exposed his back to Akpan's sword, which came down on the warrior's skull and split it open.

Akpan was appalled that he had to kill men he should ally with, but he had little choice, for the moment, and had to endure and fight on or become a victim himself. It was obvious that these men knew nothing of the plans the men of Akwa-Ibom had struck with the Igbo. He turned back to the battlefield and his heart stopped for a split second. Standing a few paces ahead of him was the king, with his blood-guard close by his side, both covered in the blood of his clansmen.

The king's eyes appeared vacant, void of emotion as he dispatched the men that separated them, and then their eyes locked. Akpan's throat went dry and he was aware of the sweat that began to run down his forehead. He dropped his shield as he tried to address the king, but the noise of battle swallowed his words, so he began to shout, 'I AM WITH YOU, MY KING! I AM WITH...' a piercing pain seized him for less than a second, and then, nothing.

Jide feared that he would soon be faced by his vassals on the field and now standing before him was Akpan, a good chief who had always paid him homage through the years with his loyalty and courage, and was possibly the only River chief that the king truly trusted. He saw his eyes register something akin to relief, and he could have sworn that he had mouthed the words "I am with you", just before his head was parted from his shoulders by one of the westerners.

Jide had watched Akpan's body tense, while his head spun in the air, and crumple to the ground still grasping his sword and shield. He died as any true warrior would have wanted; in combat, and Jide spared him a moment before moving forward, knowing that many more would follow Akpan in death on this day, but now was not the time to mourn.

Akpan's death sent a ripple through the ranks of the Akwa-Ibom warriors and their cohesion was lost almost instantly. The advance had completely halted and the men in the front rank had already started to turn their backs and cast their weapons aside, seeking the safety of the wall. They didn't get far, as the press of the men behind them blocked their retreat and drove them back into the spears of the westerners. It quickly became a massacre, with Jide's men pushing further into the ranks of the enemy, slaying those who tried to flee like goats to the slaughter. The ground beneath their feet was sticky with mud and blood, which further impeded movement as the onslaught continued.

'I am surrounded by imbeciles! Look at those cowards, see how they flee like rodents. I see that I have to get it done myself. Iboro, Etido, Odafe, inform your captains that we will join the fight.

No more delays, we must crush this army once and for all!' said Olise as he watched so many of his men fall on the field.

'Is that wise, my prince, to commit all of your men so soon?' asked Iboro.

'Are you questioning my decision? Or are you also afraid to fight this false king?' spat Olise.

'No, my prince... it's just that there is still time for the men to rally. Maybe we should send in more of our reserve forces first before we-'

'Shut your mouth! I said get your men ready, now! Enough of this nonsense. If it means committing all our men, so be it. Now get your men into position immediately!' Olise roared, leaving no room for argument.

'Yes, my prince.' The three chiefs took off at a run to gather their troops as Olise turned to Dimeji and Nnamdi: 'Let us see where your loyalties truly lie, Nnamdi. I hope I will not have to kill you myself. Come, it is time to earn your place in my future kingdom.'

Ogie saw the frantic movement of the warriors behind them and knew at once that Olise was planning to move the entire army into position. Olise must have seen the chaos on the field and decided that this was the final straw, knowing his patience was already running thin. This worried Ogie as he knew that the prince was easily driven by anger and his irrational tendencies. Ogie would have to see to it that Olise was not compromised and he didn't put himself in any unnecessary danger. He would have to ensure that the enemy was weakened enough for Olise to land a crippling blow. It was now time for Zogo to prove which side of the balance he stood on.

He turned to Zogo. 'It's time, chief. We should position ourselves on the right flank of the enemy, they seem weakest there,' he said, pointing at the thin line of shields and spears of the westerners, 'Olise is bringing the whole army down to bear and I suspect he'll aim to strike directly through the centre line and sweep up any remnants as they go along.' Zogo was watching the fighting intently, he was clearly unsettled by something he had seen, and concern was etched across his features with his mouth hanging open slightly. He contemplated a great risk. 'Chief Zogo! Are you even listening?' Ogie shouted, and Zogo came back to the present and looked over his shoulder at Ogie, evidently unimpressed by the tone used to address him from someone he considered so far beneath him.

'You would do well to mind your tongue, peasant. Don't for once think that your elevation by Olise holds any water with me, or any of the chiefs in fact. You are still nothing but a low-born dog in my eyes and you wield no authority here.' Every word from Zogo seeped with pure malice that chilled Ogie's blood as if he was plunged into a freezing river. It was clear that Zogo had not derived the name *the Black* only from his skin tone. Some of Olise's guards who stood close enough to hear the threat moved closer to Ogie, hands tightening around spears and pommels. Zogo's men did the same, and now both sides eyed each other nervously, waiting for the word from their respective leaders to cover the soil in red. As if the tension of the raging battle was not scary enough.

Ogie knew that if he was to give the order, he'd be one of the first to see the gods as his fifty men were clearly outmatched by Zogo's four hundred-odd warriors, so he raised his hands in capitulation. 'I mean no offence, chief; I'm only reiterating the orders which we are both obliged to follow. Any moment now all the tribes under Olise will be at our back and they will swallow up everything in their path. I simply suggest that we are not engulfed by the tide when it arrives but seek to position ourselves where we can benefit the army, not hinder it.'

Zogo watched Ogie from under his furrowed brows; gone was the usual calm and controlled chief, and in his place stood a conflicted and dangerous man. He turned back to the mass of fighting figures scanning the right flank that Ogie had mentioned, then addressed Ogie again, this time in a slightly less threatening tone. 'Very well. We'll move to flank them on the right side, but you and your men will lead the way.'

Ogie didn't particularly relish the thought of having Zogo's men at his back, but he was consoled by the fact that Olise would soon join the fighting and reinforce his rear. He looked to one of the senior officers in his ranks who probably had the same thoughts as him, but he agreed anyway.

'Fine. We'll take the lead in this, but we must hurry.' He gave the order and, within minutes, the black-clad guards were skirting the battlefield to the far-right line of westerners locked in combat with some warriors from Okrika.

The men of Okrika were dropping fast, and suddenly spears came flying in Ogie's direction, impaling many around him, one narrowly missing his shoulder, forcing him to duck and roll forward onto his back. He sprang up, spear in hand, and launched it at the nearest man, but his old wounds sent pain through his arm and back and started to bleed again. His throw came up short and struck the floor inches from a group of the western warriors who came charging to meet him. Still in pain, Ogie drew his sword and prepared himself, but the westerners stopped dead in their tracks with confused looks on their faces.

'Come on, you cowards!' Ogie roared, spittle flying from his mouth then a scream from the warrior beside him pierced his ear drums. At first, he didn't understand what he was seeing; the head of a spear had sprouted from the man's chest, then he fell face first into the mud exposing the length of the shaft that had taken him squarely between the shoulders.

Turning, he heard more cries, and realised that Zogo had begun to slaughter his men from the back. Olise's fears had been confirmed, Zogo had been a traitor all along and the same would go for Nnamdi. He frantically sought a way out, but he was surrounded, trapped like a rat between two cats. The westerners moved closer cautiously now, shields and spear tips dripping blood pointed towards him, then he stood alone, the last of his men writhing in the mud.

Zogo walked towards him, wiping his blade on a length of cloth wrapped around his arm. 'This is where it ends for you. Make your peace with your gods.' Zogo's voice held the same cold edge as it had earlier.

'I knew you were a traitor. I should have killed you when I had the chance,' Ogie spat as he nervously looked from Zogo to the men creeping up behind him.

Zogo stopped cleaning his sword and raised an eyebrow. He sheathed his blade and spread his hands in a welcoming gesture. 'This is your chance dog, make the most of it.'

Without a second thought Ogie lunged with his sword, but he only caught air as Zogo effortlessly spun away from the extended length of iron. Ogie moved quickly, spinning his sword in a sideways arc towards Zogo's head, but he bent backwards, the blade narrowly missing the tip of his nose.

Ogie came in again, this time cutting downwards and yelling at the top of his lungs. Zogo easily moved from side to side, dodging each strike remarkably quickly for a man his size. 'Is that the best you can do? I told you, your elevation means nothing to true warriors,' he said, and landed a heavy kick to Ogie's stomach, winding him and sending him to his knees. Ogie's hands squelched in the mud as he desperately tried to retrieve his fallen sword, but a sandaled foot held it fast, pressing it further into the mire. He looked up just in time to see a dagger plunged through his left eye and deep into the back of his skull. Zogo turned to meet the eyes of the westerners who had halted some paces away watching the events unfold. He raised his fist to them and roared 'FOR THE KING!' The chant was taken up by his men and slowly spread to the westerners. It invigorated them, breathed new life into their weary bones, giving them the strength to take the fight to Olise.

Then a new sound filled the air. It started as a low rumble, then increased to a deafening cacophony of horns and voices; it was the sound of thousands of men charging towards the westerners. Olise had joined the fight, and with him came death.

Jide's shoulder was badly bruised from the blows he had taken on his shield, but he had painted the mud red with the blood of every man who was brave enough to face him. The rain slightly impaired his vision, but it also gave him a slight edge as it lashed diagonally at his back and into the faces of the approaching enemy.

Akin had remained at his right shoulder protecting his flank, a bulwark against the sea of men who desperately tried to claim the greatest prize of all; the king's head.

Most of Olise's men lay dead or wounded and Jide had also taken on more casualties, but with every man that fell more ground was being taken by the westerners. Then horns sounded, proclaiming the arrival of yet more enemy warriors. This was it, the moment that Jide had anticipated; Olise's anger had finally forced his hand into committing all his resources.

'Send for Olusegun, now!' he bellowed to one of his men who watched wide eyed at the fresh wave of soldiers coursing towards them. He recovered himself and raced back through the mass of westerners to alert the old chief and the men of Ondo.

'That's Olise,' Akin said, pointing to a cluster of black-clad warriors in the centre of the press. 'He's finally decided to get his hands bloody.'

'Yes, indeed he has. Are you ready, my friend?' Jide asked his oldest companion. Akin just smiled, his eyes burning with the fire that not many warriors possessed. 'I was born for this very moment. Whatever happens here, I stand with you, Kabiyesi.' Jide loved Akin more than anything in that instance. He knew that he'd follow him down to *Esu's* dark halls if only he'd ask, and that thought alone gave him strength.

'Kabiyesi!' someone shouted off to his left. 'Kabiyesi...' the warrior said trying to catch his breath, 'the Igbo... They've joined us... Chief Zogo leads them.' Jide had been expecting this news, which couldn't have come at a better time. 'Excellent. Now we can end this. Order the men to get in position.'

Within a few heartbeats, the entire line of the westerners, now reinforced by the Igbo, locked their shields together and stared down the charging enemy, and the slaughter continued.

A SONG FOR MOTHER

As the battles raged on in the east, most of the cities in the far west chose to remain in blissful ignorance of the suffering of their fathers and sons. Regardless of their forced disposition, there was no mistaking that never in the history of the tribes had the landscape been so emotionally charged, rife with the uncertainty of what impact the tribal clashes would have on the realm for at least a generation to come.

In the city of Ogun, the residents went about their days as best they could. In truth, many had purposely chosen to enjoy the peace and freedom that they still possessed, and to live in the moment knowing that all could be snatched away in the blink of an eye, if the gods deemed it so. This was a unique quality in the tribe; to find happiness in everything until happiness itself could no longer be granted, regardless of circumstances – poor or rich, able bodied or disabled, blessed by the gods or forsaken, this was the single attribute that defined them as a people.

However, the atmosphere was different behind the palace gates. Here, the war was real enough, and every preparation was being made to ensure that when the tides of war came, those who held power in Ogun would not succumb to it. Chief Kola, Enitan's grandfather, had continued to send word to all his vassals and allies across the western provinces and had gradually begun to build the makings of a considerable fighting force, albeit an ageing one.

Men from Oyo in the north, and the outer settlements of Lagos in the south, had answered his call and sent whatever resources they had to support the chief, which was made up mostly of older warriors, as the young men and those with great names had already followed the drums east. When word spread that a son of the king yet lived, the men filtered into Ogun in their numbers. These would be Enitan's loyal subjects, the men that would stand at his side to take back the realm in the name of the Adelanis.

303

The responsibilities of a ruler of men did not come naturally to a boy of twelve, but with the guidance of Kola and Ayo, Enitan was taking to the role as would have been expected for a child of his pedigree. He attended every summoning of the chiefs and elders, and he turned out to be a precocious student in the art of warfare. He learned to read men of power and distinguish between the wise and the idiotic, the loyal and those seeking advancement, and all the while he trained with spear and shield, sword and dagger, axe and throwing knives. His fragile body hardened, his hands became calloused from hours spent in the yard, and his mind sharpened keener than any blade.

One hot afternoon, after his morning practice, Enitan had decided to tour the city of his mother, immerse himself in the culture of the people and learn their ways, which differed from those of Ile-Ife, and Ayo had relished the opportunity to explore the world beyond the palace gates. They had manged to slip out undetected, adorning non-descript attire that would pass them off as locals, and headed for the market square which, as was the case in most of the villages, towns and cities, was the focal point of the people and where everyday life resided. Wale, the captain of the palace guard who had formed a close bond with Ayo since their initial altercation, had also accompanied them. He was a native of the city and had volunteered to serve as their guide and protector.

Enitan was fascinated by the market, the local produce; from the carcasses of trapped exotic animals on display to the ingenuity of the goods stores; leather goods and all kind of animal skins from snakes to crocodiles, fashioned into sandals, sword scabbards, belts and so much more. He marvelled at the resourcefulness of the people, how they found opportunity to create a living through almost any means, and how they thrived.

These were his distant relatives. These were his mother's people. It saddened him to think that his mother, Queen Lara, had once walked these very streets. He could see that she would have been happy here until the duty of her birth took her away to Ife, away from her comforts and everything she knew. But such was the curse of high

304

birth, especially for women, to be used as pawns in political games to secure alliances, broker peace or settle feuds. However, Lara had been lucky, she had been betrothed to a man she not only respected but one she truly loved with all her being, a union that would stand the test of time and transcend death; this consoled his heart.

As he walked in his mother's footsteps, they came upon a great white mahogany tree that grew in the very centre of the city amidst the market, under which a man in ragged clothing resided. He was clearly mentally challenged from his incoherent muttering, uncontrollable laughter and constant scratching. He was severely malnourished, and his skin was cracked and begrimed with dirt. Flies tracked his every movement and his eyes shone wild in receding sockets. He laughed without provocation, but everyone seemed to ignore him as if he was a part of the surroundings.

'Who is that?' Enitan asked Wale.

'Don't mind him, he's the local crazy man, every city around here has one,' he responded dismissively.

'There isn't one in Ife. Not that I know of, anyway. Does he need help? Perhaps some food or water?' Enitan asked innocently.

'No. The local priests feed him every few days, but I wouldn't go near him if I were you O, unless you want faeces thrown in your face. That's what he's known for,' Wale replied.

'How did he come to be like that?' asked Enitan intrigued, having never seen a person so afflicted before, too used to his sheltered life behind palace walls.

'No one knows for certain, but he was once a respectable man, a merchant as it happens, and quite a prosperous one, but also very shrewd, stingy and with a reputation for taking advantage of people to gain his wealth. Rumour has it that he once visited a market in Sagamu, some miles from here, where he came upon a beggar asking for alms. He refused him and told him that if his hands and legs still functioned, he could find work and accused him of being lazy and a burden on society. The beggar then said to him that he had been seeking work for a year, but no one would hire him because he was not a native of the region, and that he was forced to beg not by choice but out of necessity. The merchant then responded that those were nothing but excuses and that if he were a beggar, he'd have found a way to raise his status in the community within a few months. It's thought that the beggar concluded that the merchant was a man who valued his self-importance too highly and decided to punish him for his arrogance. The beggar then made a simple request for the merchant to pick some flowers that grew around his feet and pass them to the beggar so he could enjoy the beauty of the gods' creation. The merchant was enraged that such a lowly individual would have the nerve to ask him, a well-respected man, to forage in the dirt like a child. The beggar somehow convinced the merchant that a simple act of kindness would see his fortunes grow if only he could humble himself and undertake a seemingly menial task for an unfortunate soul. The merchant finally relented but, as he bent to retrieve the flowers, he was said to have looked between his legs towards the market and suddenly reeled as if he had been struck and began to lament inconsolably. He never returned to his senses after that day. That was over fifteen years ago.'

Enitan could not help but feel pity for the man, but it seemed that the gods were punishing him for the wrongs he had committed in his life. He wondered if the punishment was proportionate to his sins and his thoughts drifted to his uncle and the crimes that he had committed against his family and the kingdom. Would the gods punish him just as harshly, or worse?

Ayo tugged at Enitan's sleeve, breaking into his thoughts, and urged him to follow: 'I think we should move on, my prince, besides it's unsightly to stare at those less fortunate.'

'Yes, yes. There is still much to see of the city,' Wale added, and he and Ayo turned to leave. Enitan noticed that the mad man was no longer muttering to himself but, instead, was watching him intently. He returned the man's gaze for a short while and, just as he was about to leave the man started pointing and shouting at the top of his voice, 'You... his hand is upon you! I see it, I see the fire that surrounds you... and your shadow... it is his! No... no... he has come for us. He's come to burn us all! Spare me. Spare me!' he yelled, now attracting the attention of passers-by, some of whom began to look nervously from the mad man to Enitan.

Enitan looked on, confused, until Wale walked up to him and gently guided him away. 'I told you, he is mad, let us leave before you are recognised,' he said. The man was still screaming, and now weeping like a child, and rolling around in the dirt as if he had been set alight and desperately tried to extinguish the flames that consumed him. His screams could still be heard as the three men rounded the corner and lost themselves in the throng of people.

Ayo pondered the mad man's words; it could not be a coincidence that the man had been in fear of his mortal life after setting eyes on the prince. There was certainly something strange about the whole encounter, but he just couldn't bring himself to striking up the conversation with Enitan. *What harm could it do, though?* he thought, and then decided he'd broach the topic when the right opportunity presented itself.

Time passed and Enitan had started to get a good sense of life in Ogun. The city was split into two distinct sections. The city above and the city below, as they were referred to by the people – ilu oke and ilu isalẹ, in the native tongue of Yoruba. The palace was built in the city above, along with the homes of the prominent and affluent residents. There was also a barracks and a blacksmith.

The city below was where life truly resided, it housed the market and the square – which was really a circle of cleared land, where people of all walks of life gathered to trade and socialise. Women sat outside their houses chatting, some pounded cassava in huge mortars in pairs, while men were hunched over boards of Ncho or drank palm-wine and other, stronger concoctions, like ogogoro – distilled from fermented raffia palm tree juice. Chickens and dogs roamed the streets freely and the sounds of children's playful laughter was all around them. This brought a smile to Enitan's face, remembering days passed with his brothers, and a sudden pang of sorrow and suffocation gripped him.

'I would rather see beyond the city walls and feel the peace of the forest,' he said to Wale. A smile tugged on the corner of Ayo's mouth as memories of his own came to him. Enitan had always loved the forest and the tranquillity it offered. He would often stay out for hours on end playing with his brothers, hunting or just basking in the beauty of nature. Weeks behind the palace walls had clearly been a drain on his morale, and an opportunity to feel the soft grass beneath his sandals would be a welcome distraction for the prince.

From his expression, Wale was not convinced that it was a good idea, but before he could object Ayo intervened. 'The fresh air would do us all some good, and to get away from commotion. I'm sure the chief would agree with this.' Wale still looked unimpressed but shrugged his shoulders. 'I suppose so, but we must return to the city before sunset. The forest is not the best place to be after dark.'

They passed through the rear gates of the city, which were less well manned than those at the front, and made their way along the paths that had been cut through the bushes. Wale led them to a rise that housed a shrine dedicated to *Ogun*. There they met several people who made offerings to the god and prayed to the bronze statue that had been created in his image – the war god was depicted in full armour with a mighty machete in one hand and a hammer in the other.

'Why does the god hold a hammer?' Enitan asked Wale. Before he could reply, a priest of the shrine suddenly appeared at their shoulders and answered the question enthusiastically. 'That is a very good question, young man. Besides being a fearsome warrior god, he was also known to be a great blacksmith and is also referred to as the god of iron. It is said that he moulded this city with his mighty hammer and forged the iron used to create our weapons.' The old priest said excitedly, clearly having told the tale a thousand times, 'It is also believed that when he first arrived here from the heavens, the world was nothing but an overgrown bush, so he turned into a great machete and cleared the land, paving the way for this great city, and when the settlements were established, he led the tribe through many wars and conquered far into the west; that's why we give him great honour.'

'That's quite interesting. He must be a great god,' Enitan replied as he gazed upon the statue. 'Indeed, he is. You look quite familiar, young man. Do you have relatives here?' the priest asked as he looked at Enitan, who then tried to conceal his face. 'Ah, yes. You look surprisingly like Queen Lara. Actually... your face is almost identical...'

'She is... she was my mother,' Enitan said sadly. 'Wait. If she's your mother...' the priest immediately dropped to his knees, as did everyone that overheard the conversation. 'My prince. I offer you my deepest condolences. I was heartbroken to learn of the fate of the queen and the people of Ile-Ife. We have prayed for their souls and those affected by the war in the east,' the priest said, showing genuine concern and sorrow.

'I thank you for your kind words, and please stand, I'm still not used to this kind of attention,' Enitan said, feeling self-conscious. 'We are honoured to have a prince of the realm amongst us. I do hope you are comfortable here. You are certainly safe. I for one do not condone violence, but the people of Ogun will protect you as you are one of our own,' the priest said.

'I am grateful. You said I look like my mother; did you know her?' he asked curiously.

'Oh, I doubt you'd find anyone who didn't know her. She was much loved by the people, with the kindest of hearts and one of the strongest of wills. She often visited this shrine and always provided great tributes to the god, and gifts to the priests here. I was privileged to have known her as a young girl and later as a beautiful woman. She also had a mischievous side, always getting into trouble with the chief,' the priest said with a smile as he visited memories of a distant time.

'When she was of an age, your grandparents were continuously frustrated with her antics; she refused to wed or even entertain the advances of many suitors who travelled from far and wide to win her heart. The kingdom almost went to war on one occasion, when your grandfather promised her to the son of a great chief in the south, which she naturally refused. Ah yes, the queen was a rebel, but that all changed when she met the king your father. He was a dashing monarch; charismatic, handsome and said to be the greatest warrior of his time. He was here on a royal visit and had decided to go hunting with your grandfather. Queen Lara had also requested to accompany them, which was most unusual for women, but, as I said, she had a mind of her own. Apparently, with her own hands, she killed a leopard that was known to have been stalking the forests for months, killing the farmers' livestock. The king was so impressed not only by her beauty but also by her bravery and her skill with the spear that he asked your grandfather for her hand in marriage on the spot, while her spear was still wet with the leopard's blood.'

'I've heard this story,' Ayo interrupted. 'My father was one of the Modakeke who accompanied the king,' he said proudly. 'I always thought it was just a tale he liked to use to entertain the children.'

The priest inclined his head to Ayo in acknowledgement before he continued. 'No O. It's not a tale at all. Anyway, as was expected, Queen Lara refused, and quite forcefully, not wanting to become an ornament in the royal court and lose her freedom. Your grandfather was furious, but he loved her so much that he was prepared to risk the wrath of a king just to honour the wishes of his only daughter. But he need not have worried, it only made Queen Lara more desirable in the eyes of the king, and he pursued her relentlessly for many moons, travelling back and forth to win her over, which he did, eventually, but not without difficulty.'

'I've never heard about this before. I always believed that the marriage was arranged, as was the usual custom of our people,' said Enitan, amazed at what he was hearing.

'Well, it was afterwards, but not in the traditional sense. On one of the king's trips, it is said that he had gone to the river, not too far from here, when he heard that Queen Lara was there with some of her maids, fetching water. The king then offered to carry a pail of water on his head like the women if Queen Lara would agree to visit him in Ile-Ife. She didn't believe that a king would lower himself and do such a thing, until he started to strip off his regal attire. She immediately begged him not to do it and agreed to visit the capital.

Most think that she fell in love with him in that moment. No king would ever stoop so low as to carry water like a servant! She saw that he was a humble man and one of great dignity, a quality none of her other suitors had ever possessed. After a time, the marriage was arranged in the traditional fashion.'

Ayo whistled to himself. 'Imagine that, the great king Jide with a pail of water on his head. That is some story,' he said, smiling to himself. Then he looked over at Enitan and saw the smile on his face, the innocent look of a child who was completely submerged in the story of his family. He had not seen the boy in such high spirits in such a long while, it brought joy to his heart to witness it. Unfortunately, Enitan had had to grow up faster than his years because of the position he was in, and moments like this were extremely rare, so Ayo wanted him to soak up as much of it as he could.

At Enitan's request, the priest went on to tell more tales of his mother and all the adventures that she had in her youth that had been the stuff of legend around these parts, giving Enitan the opportunity to get to know another side of the mother he had loved so dearly. He held the stories as close to his heart as he could, because these stories, and his memories, were all that he had left.

Before they knew it, the sun had started to dip towards the horizon, and Wale insisted that they return to the palace before a search party was sent out to look for them. Enitan thanked the priest profusely, promised he'd return soon with tributes for the shrine and left with Ayo and Wale.

As they descended the slope that led to the city, they heard horses and men, so they decided to conceal themselves behind some trees and observe the procession of men undetected. Soon enough, several riders came into view on big horses, followed by warriors on foot, approximately thirty men, singing as they jogged along with short spears and curved swords on their hips. The colours of their attire and the tribal marks on their faces denoted them as warriors of the Iwoye tribe, from the fringes of the far western border, great warriors and master hunters, loyal to chief Kola.

'It looks like more men have answered your grandfather's call. At this rate you'll soon have an army that could rival Olise's. It won't be long now before we are ready to march on Benin and take back what is yours, my prince. That will be a grand day indeed,' Wale said excitedly.

'Come, let's make haste to the palace. They may have come across some news from the east. I'd rather hear it first-hand, if there is word of the fighting,' Ayo said as he watched the last of the foot soldiers hurry along and slowly become obscured by the trees and bushes of the forest.

It was dark now and they picked their way through the path in the forest. Wale was cursing under his breath for having left so late, and was clearly uncomfortable being in the forest after dark, but at the same time he insisted that they tread carefully to avoid stumbling on the uneven surface and potentially breaking an ankle, or veering off the beaten track and winding up deeper in the forest. So, they walked cautiously along the path with the tall trees of the forest on either side of them looming overhead like silent sentries.

Just then, a light caught the corner of Enitan's eye. He turned his head to see a young boy, perhaps the same age as him or slightly older, bearing a torch and dressed with an arrangement of leaves tied around his waist and genitals that served as a loin cloth, standing some paces away from them amongst the trees of the forest. The light from the torch revealed white skin, as though he was rubbed in chalk, with large eyes and cracked red lips. Around his neck, he wore a string of what appeared to be cowrie shells, which hung down to his chest, rising and falling with every breath he took. Enitan called out to Wale, who was in front, and pointed the boy out. When Wale saw what had attracted Enitan's attention he went rigid with fear.

'We need to leave now!' he whispered in a voice laced with fear. 'What is the problem?' asked Ayo, who already had a dagger in his hand ready for a fight – he always relished an excuse to test his skills.

'That boy.... he's not of this world,' Wale said, clearly shaken.

'Nonsense. It's just a boy. Granted it's strange that he's in the forest at this time by himself, but he's probably thinking the same about us,' Ayo replied, placing his dagger back in the leather sheath at his hip, already dismissing any danger.

The boy with the torch stood watching them for a moment, then turned, extremely slowly, all the while maintaining his gaze on the trio, before finally walking away in the opposite direction.

'What's that way?' asked Enitan. 'There is a graveyard, just beyond the tree line. There have been numerous unexplained sightings of lone children around there after dark, and no one dares to venture even close to the periphery of the burial ground at night. We must leave now, my prince. It is bad enough that we have seen the boy, it's an omen. We should count ourselves lucky that he did not mark us.'

'Mark us with what?' asked Enitan dubiously.

'Mark us with a curse,' Wale said as he made the sign of *Ogun* to protect him.

'Don't be silly. You don't really believe all that, do you?' Ayo asked, but then he wasn't so sure himself when he heard the words out loud, as there were things that he couldn't explain about his own charge, Enitan.

'Believe what you want but everyone around here knows of the danger. They say that they are the children of the spirit world, those who die at childbirth or in their early years only to return to the family and do the same repeatedly in a continuous cycle of life and death, bringing sorrow and misery to the parents. I'm leaving right now; you can stay here if you want but I'd rather escort the prince out of here to the safely of the city,' Wale said and turned away and hurriedly sought out the path that lead to the city.

Ayo and Enitan continued to trace the flame from the torch as it burned further into the distance and illuminated the surroundings, and then the light suddenly vanished, plunging the forest back into darkness.

WHEN THE HEAVENS WEEP

The westerners were losing ground from the relentless pressure exerted by Olise's men. Thousands of sandals splashed and slipped in the churned-up earth mixed with blood, desperately trying to find purchase while the rain pounded down on them unabated.

Jide had taken on a great number of casualties, and his numbers had continued to dwindle as the tribes under Olise persisted in the slaughter of their fellow countrymen. There had been a moment of respite when the men of Ondo, led by chief Olusegun, joined the fighting, successfully launching a counterattack on the flanks of the enemy, which sent Olise's men into disarray. Many had fallen in the bloody clash that ensued, but the surprise did not last long. The knowledge that Olise himself and his devil, Dimeji, were on the field infused bravery, or rather fear, into the hearts of his men, granting them the presence of mind to regroup and the courage to inflict a counterattack of their own, sending Olusegun onto the back foot and forcing him to retreat, driving him further away from the main body of Jide's army.

Now, the two groups of westerners fought in isolation, desperately trying to fend off the enemy and avoid being engulfed by the tide of men baying for their blood. They held firm, considering the odds against them, but fatigue was now playing a leading role in this play of survival, while each man continued to dance the dance of the warriors' embrace on the stage that *Ogun* had set for them.

The Modakeke warriors who yet lived did their best to protect their king, granting him moments of rest to catch his breath and tend his severely damaged left arm. The bruising that had started on his shoulder had now spread along the length of his arm, which was delicate to the touch and felt like *Shango's* fire every time he took a blow on his shield. One of his men had given up part of his clothing to wrap around the king's arm and serve as a cushion to soften the blows, but this had not been very effective, so Jide had eventually stripped the cloth from his arm and flung it into the face of one of the enemy, obscuring his sight before impaling him in the chest.

He had been forced to discard his shield and draw his ancestral dagger; now armed with two lengths of iron, he repositioned himself behind a shield bearer, attacking over the man's shoulder like a cobra released from its basket. Akin was still at his side, protecting his right flank, and if he was fatigued, he showed nothing of it, only the face of a determined warrior. He stood strong and killed everyone he crossed swords with, and most of the enemy had started to avoid fighting him as soon as they saw the work he did. The same could be said for Jide; however, he was a much greater prize, so caution was cast to the wind and men continued to throw themselves at him in the hope that one of them would get lucky and down the king of the tribes.

Chief Dare was close by with his island warriors, who were putting up a good fight. They were, in truth, probably the best fighters on the field after the Modakeke, and they proved their worth tenfold in their ceaseless efforts in repelling the enemy. The chief had tied a length of cloth around the lower half of his face to conceal the horrific wound he had taken, which had worsened over the course of the fighting. The cloth was soaked in blood, but he had refused to fall back and fought twice as hard as the men at his shoulder.

He had been disheartened to learn that Adedeji and a contingent of Modakeke had been sent west, reducing their already waning strength, but he knew that the king would not have sent away the head of the Modakeke without good reason, so there was nothing left to do but accept the decision and fight on until the battle was won or he fell to an enemy spear.

He had lost some key members in his command, including his nephew, who had been drawn away from the protection of the shield wall amidst the chaos and was quickly set upon by a group of Amoso warriors. Dare had managed to fight his way to his dying nephew's side in time to hear his last words; thanking Dare for the opportunity to stand by his side and beginning a heartfelt message for his mother, Dare's younger sister, but he perished before he could finish his message. Dare had instructed some of his warriors to retrieve the body and carry him to the back of the lines while he and some of his best warriors had engaged the perpetrators, wiping them all out, including the rest of the Amoso warriors they fought with.

His mood darkened as the fight wore on, considering the prospect of breaking the news to his sister, but it dawned on him that his own life wasn't guaranteed with the persistent barrage from the enemy. For every man they killed, three took their place, each more aggressive, more bloodthirsty than the last.

He looked across the battlefield and saw that many of the enemy forces were pushing towards Olusegun's position, like hyenas converging on a weak prey, and his heart lurched in his chest. Making a quick assessment of the distance between himself and the Ondo chief, he made a snap decision.

'They'll be overwhelmed in no time,' he shouted to one of his most senior officers, 'Get a message to the king, tell him that I will reinforce chief Segun's numbers, but I'll need some support. Take half of the men with you, I'll take the other half.'

The officer looked in Olusegun's direction, and saw a large force moving on his position. 'My chief, it's suicide. You'll never make it there in time, and if you do, you'll be cut off from the rest of the army!' he said clearly worried for his commander.

'That is why you must go now and get more men from the king. I can't let the chief die out there if I can help it. These are my orders now go!'

The officer was clearly torn but he knew better than to question his chief. He could do nothing but salute him. 'Your will, my chief. *Olodumare* protect you.' With that he hurried off.

His personal bodyguards and trusted vassal lords understood the risk, but he could tell that they would follow him anywhere he commanded. 'Let us do this thing. On my command tell the men in the front rank to cover us, the rest of you will come with me. Speed is key, so only the most agile will carry shields, the rest of us will take the spears.

316

Breaking cover, Dare led half of his men towards the enemy's far lines. With a short axe in one hand and a sword in the other, he ran headlong into the first group of men. They did not expect the sudden charge and were caught off guard. Taking advantage, Dare slammed his axe into the shoulder of the first man who was too slow to raise his shield, shattering his collar bone on impact, and was rewarded by a howl of pain. Without slowing, he drove his sword forward into the man behind him and shouldered a third out of his path. He could sense rather than see his men behind him and pressed forward deeper into the enemy ranks, both arms swinging and slashing bare flesh as he moved. *Hold on, old man, hold on,* he thought to himself as he pressed his attack.

* * * *

Olusegun deflected a spear thrust across his centreline and grabbed it with his free hand before bringing his sword down and splitting the shaft in two. He turned on his front foot and drove the broken spear into the head of the man who had attacked him, dropping him dead instantly. Before the man had even hit the floor, more men were already lunging at him. He managed to dodge one with a feint, but had to cover a blow from a second, which he did with ease. He slashed downwards at the man's legs and felt his sword bite into soft tissue and bone; reaching out, he grabbed at the man and swung him around, using him as a shield, just as the first man he had avoided spun and thrust his sword into his companion. Olusegun wasted no time in pushing the impaled man forward into the man who had stabbed him, sending both to the ground, the sword driving through the wounded man and punching out of his back.

Olusegun leaped forward, impaled the man trapped under his comrade and turned around to face the next warrior. The fighting had persisted in this fashion for some time; fast-paced and brutal, and it was starting to take its toll on the old chief. He thought to himself that battles were a young man's game, and his entire body ached. He hadn't been in battle such as this in years and, although he was as fit as most of the younger warriors, he couldn't deny the weariness he felt deep in his bones.

His men fought as they retreated, but they were losing men fast. They had found early success landing a surprise attack on the flanks, killing many and granting the king precious time to press forward his own attack as the enemy was forced to deal with the breach in their flanks. However, the numbers were against them and after a while the enemy had reinforced their lines, sending Olusegun back and further away from the king.

His thoughts suddenly went to Adebola somewhere in the east. He hoped that the young warrior was still alive and had been fortunate enough to reach the provinces and convince some of the lords to come to the king's aid, but he knew that any such help would never come in time, if at all. He looked to the men who fought alongside him, saw the desperation on their faces, wounded, fatigued, losing hope. Someone barged into him with a shield, stunning him for a second. He fell through the air and landed hard on his back, dropping his sword. Some of his men moved quickly in the space in front of him, offering protection, and were immediately confronted by heavily armed warriors from the River-lands.

He turned onto his stomach and scrambled through the mud, looking frantically for his sword, which was just out of reach of his searching hands. He found a discarded spear and snatched it up before rolling onto his back just in time to see one of the River-land warriors who had made it through his men. The man came in fast, then his eyes went wide, seeing the spear that came up from the mud angled towards him. He tried to pull back, but had already committed himself and ran straight into the spear, which took him beneath the chin, stopping him dead in his tracks. Olusegun was showered by the blood that flowed from the wound and he yanked the spear to the side, tipping the dead warrior over.

He pushed himself up onto his elbows and looked around for another weapon. Finding his sword, he rolled over to retrieve it and another one of his warriors was by his side fending off another man. 'Get back to the line, my chief, I'll cover you!' the man roared over the din. Olusegun rose, wiping the blood from his face. He looked to the men in front of him; two were already down and the last three were struggling.

Moving to the side of the warrior who had just come to his aid, he went around him and hacked at the leg of the man he was fighting, then rammed his sword upwards into his torso. 'Help those men!' he said to the warrior, pointing towards the group in front. 'I'll bring some of the others forward to support you.' He didn't wait for a response and was already making his way towards the rear. He ran as fast as his old legs could carry him, shouting at the top of his voice to more of his men to halt the retreat and stand to fight.

Some of them stopped, heeding the call from their chief, but a few carried on in their retreat, broken men from the horrors they had witnessed. *Cowards!* Olusegun though bitterly, but he stood his ground. Spinning round, he saw that all the warriors who had been covering him were down, and now the enemy was pushing forward directly towards him. He looked over in the direction of the king and noticed a group of westerners were fighting their way towards him. This lifted his heart, but he knew deep down that they'd never get to him in time.

He looked to the sky and felt the rain on his face just before he shouted at the top of his voice and charged forward to meet the enemy. Some of his men followed, he heard their war cries behind him, felt their energy, then he was fighting again. He wielded his sword wildly, parrying, stabbing, hacking away, blood drenching his arms and splashing into his face. He killed one man, then another, wounded a third and then screamed out in pain.

He had been struck, but his brain couldn't register where the pain was coming from. He saw another warrior coming towards him on his left and raised his arm to meet the man's falling axe, but his sword wasn't there. His hand had been hacked off at the forearm. He looked down in disbelief just as a spear impaled him in his side, jolting him.

The axe followed, cutting deep into his armour, splitting open his pectoral muscles and throwing him onto his back. He turned his head in the fetid mud and the last thing he saw was the sandals of his men splashing towards him.

* * * *

'My king!' Zogo shouted as he came to stand by Jide's side with a group of Igbo warriors. 'Forgive my lateness; I would have come to you sooner if I was able, my king. Olise has dogged my every move since I arrived in Benin. He is quite the paranoid and, dare I say, precautious man, but not without good reason, I might add,' he said with a smile.

'It gladdens me to see you here, chief, your presence serves us a great deal. I can't begin to imagine the risk you have taken to stand with us. You have my deepest gratitude,' Jide replied. 'How many men are with you?' he asked.

'I have just over four hundred warriors. We lost a few on our way to you, unfortunately, but more of my men are held under Olise's command. I had hoped that chief Akpan's men would have granted us all the support we need, but it seems that isn't the case. Do you know what has become of him?' Zogo asked, already dreading the answer.

'Chief Akpan has fallen,' Jide replied gravely. 'He was trapped between my forces and Olise's warriors, I believe men from Onitsha and Okigwi. He was in an impossible position, hemmed in and unable to turn his forces against the men at his back, and would have been slaughtered in an instant. He chose to stand his ground and pay the ultimate sacrifice, but I know he would have aided us if only he had the opportunity. He died bravely; I saw it with my own eyes.'

Zogo's heart felt tight in his chest; he had known that Olise had purposely placed Akpan in harm's way amongst warriors who would be ready to cut him down the moment they detected a whiff of deception. He could not let his friend's sacrifice go unanswered and swore that his sword would taste the blood of Olise, or at the very least, those he held dear.

Akin then appeared from the mass of fighting men in front of them, holding a bloodied sword and a battered shield. His features were grim, but his face broke into a broad smile when his eyes rested on Zogo and the men standing behind him. 'Ah, chief Zogo. You took your time,' he said as he dropped his shield and clasped the man's forearm.

'I was otherwise engaged, my friend, but I'm here now,' Zogo replied, returning the smile. 'I'm happy to see that you are still going strong. I see your appetite for war has not quenched,' Zogo said, looking at Akin's stained sword.

'Ah, you should know a leopard never changes its spots. So, what news do you bring from the city? Has Olise got anything more in store for us?' Akin asked. 'Nothing but more warriors and a desire to see your heads mounted on poles. He has committed every warrior under his command to the field. You have certainly gotten under his skin, my king,' Zogo replied amusedly.

'And what of Nnamdi, I don't see him here. Is he...?' Jide asked looking towards the rest of the Igbo warriors.

'No, no my king. Nnamdi lives. Olise is also holding him for assurance of my loyalty. I suspect he'd be amongst the throng right now. Gods willing, if he survives, he will stand with us and perhaps spur the rest of my men to turn their spears when they see me standing with you,' Zogo said hopefully.

'And so shall it be, Zogo. So shall it be. I would see to Olise now, let us go,' Jide said, indicating to his shield bearer to advance into the knot of fighting men before them. Zogo drew his sword, looked to his warriors and chanted their war song, and they responded with extra zeal, all lifting their weapons to the sky in salute to their god *Chineke,* before joining the tide to wreak havoc on their enemies.

Zogo placed himself and his men to the left of the king and immediately careened past the line of Modakeke warriors in the front rank holding the enemy line at bay. He carried nothing but his sword, which was all he needed. He struck down men with an ease that marked him as the epitome of a warrior. Two of his men were at his shoulder, big and brutal with large axes and curved reinforced wicker shields. As one, they broke the line of soldiers in front of them, shattering shields, breaking swords and spears, and sending heads tumbling through the air.

The combined strength of the Igbo and the Yoruba was a sight to behold, their ferocity unparalleled as they cut across the field. Even with the odds stacked heavily against them, they inflicted more damage in that moment than what had been done over the course of the whole campaign. However, Olise's men were not backing down, they came on in their hundreds and died fighting for a prince they feared but clearly did not love.

Jide took up position behind his shield bearer, still trying to conserve his strength, but he could feel that they were gaining some ground and his heart was lifted. He looked over to his right and saw Akin, thoroughly enjoying himself as he fought three men at a time, and he wondered if they could turn the fight around. Suddenly, the man bearing his shield exploded in a fountain of blood that splattered everywhere, covering Jide. His eyes were thick with the man's blood, causing him to lose his sight momentarily as he leaped backwards trying to comprehend what had just happened. He wiped his face with the backs of his hands, bringing his vision back into focus. What he saw was something you'd expect to see only in nightmares, but this was no dream and his eyes did not deceive him.

The warrior who had been protecting him had literally been split in half from his shoulder all the way down to his groin. The two halves of the man's body fell away revealing a great sword wielded by the one often referred to as *ejo* – the serpent. Dimeji had found him.

Dimeji's eyes narrowed at the sight of the king and his scarred, blood-splattered face contorted in what could be described as a mixture of hatred and excitement. Jide had been anticipating this confrontation, and now that the man stood in front of him all his wariness and pains were cast away like a snake shedding its skin. He gripped the pommel of his sword tighter and reversed his grip on the ancestral dagger. Bending his knees slightly, he shifted his weight and prepared himself to fight and then, with a speed that shocked him,

Dimeji leaped over the corpse of the halved warrior and swung his sword at Jide's head.

Dimeji's movement had been so fast that Jide only had a split second to react. He took a step back and weaved his head clear, the sword just missing the top of his scalp by inches. As he dipped under the swinging length of iron, he moved forward, placing himself on the left side of Dimeji, and carved his dagger across Dimeji's ribs, drawing a red gash where his blade had touched. Dimeji, who had disdained donning his torso armour for this special occasion, didn't seem to have even felt the wound and was already turning his blade in an arc, tracking the king's movement. He struck again, but this time Jide moved to meet him and took the edge of the great sword on his own. The sound of the clashing swords sent an echo through the field and both men felt the strength of the other before disengaging and striking again.

This time Dimeji brought his sword swinging downwards from a high guard; Jide deflected it easily, fouling Dimeji's balance, and he scored another cut on his attacker's sword arm with his dagger. Dimeji only barred his teeth, in what may have been a smile, before lunging again. Jide prepared to parry the blow, but something had caught Dimeji's eye and he changed his course at the last minute, leaping to the side, avoiding another sword that was aimed at him.

Akin's smile couldn't have been wider as he placed himself between the king and Dimeji. 'Kabiyesi, I hope you will not be offended if I take this fight. This man is too far beneath the attention of a king; don't soil your blade on such an abomination, let me kill this one for you,' he said over his shoulder at Jide. 'Very well. I would find his master; he cannot be too far behind,' Jide replied.

'I will be with you momentarily my king, once I cut down this accursed brute,' Akin added, and leaped into an attack on Dimeji. Their swords met and sparks flew, sizzling in the rain. Akin chose to see every blow Dimeji threw at him, not wanting to use his speed. This was a fight of strength and dominance. Two blood-guards fighting in defence of their lords. It was a fight that would echo through the ages, one of prowess and the right to be called the most feared warrior in the tribes.

Men on both sides of the fight spread out, giving the blood-guards a wide berth, not wanting to get caught up in the clash of iron. Some watched in awe and paid for their lack of concentration with a spear in the guts; others continued to fight, taking advantage of the moment of inactivity by their opponents. One unfortunate warrior was slow to move and the parried attack from Dimeji's sword chopped half of his foot clean off as the sword was deflected to the ground. After that, the circle around the men got bigger and the fighting around them began to slow as more men started to take notice of the clash of these two revered names in the tribes.

Back and forth they swung at each other, parrying each attack, striking and dodging as they circled each other. They continued in this fashion for some time and none had the better of the other, both seeking weaknesses and flaws only to find that their skills were a match.

Dimeji attacked with a flurry of jabs, wielding his sword as if it weighed next to nothing, sending Akin back towards the knot of warriors. Dimeji was extraordinarily light on his feet for a man of his bulk, though this only excited Akin the more as he blocked each strike and looked for an opening, but there was none to be had. Dimeji covered himself well, turning his body with every movement of his arm and leaving little room for exposure. A warrior from Aba who had his back turned to the fight was kicked by one of the westerners into the path of Dimeji. The man stumbled backwards, trying to regain his balance, just as Dimeji was moving in with another attack. Akin saw the stumbling warrior and moved clear, positioning himself outside the reach of Dimeji's blade.

Before the warrior could correct his footing and avoid colliding into Dimeji, the great sword came swinging horizontally, hitting the warrior in the waist and cutting through him. The man let out a terrified scream as his upper body hit the ground. Looking at his lower half, he began desperately trying to gather his trailing intestines and push them back into the opening of his stomach before dying in the process.

Akin took advantage of the moment and pressed his own attack, coming in low, swinging for the legs, which Dimeji managed to avoid, and then another sweeping slash towards his chest. Dimeji caught the second strike with his sword as Akin turned towards him and rammed the pommel of his sword in Dimeji's face, causing his nose to explode and rocking his head back. Dimeji took a step backwards as he swung his sword wildly to fend off any further attacks. He touched his ruined nose as blood streamed down his chest. This was the first time he had felt pain in years. Only exceptionally skilled warriors had ever managed to land a blow on him, but all those men had died at his hand, and now he had two new scars and a disfigured nose all in one fight. He was enraged and, in that moment, he saw red.

With an ear-splitting cry Dimeji vaulted towards Akin, bringing his great sword upwards from a low guard position. Akin was prepared, he moved to the side and brought his own sword down two-handed, hard on the edge of Dimeji's blade, and knocked it out of the giant's hands. In the same movement, Akin rotated his hips and swept his sword sideways towards Dimeji's mid-section, but he was too close and Dimeji, as quick as a viper, moved into the swinging sword and grabbed Akin's hands on the pommel. The blade wrapped around Dimeji's left bicep, opening another gash on the thick cords of muscle.

Dimeji, still gripping onto Akin's hands around the pommel, turned his back into Akin, shifted his weight and threw Akin over his shoulder hard into the mud. Akin landed on his back, knocking the air out of his lungs from the force of the throw, but he managed to hold onto his sword. He rolled to the side as a huge foot stomped into the ground where his head had been a moment ago. He came up on one knee holding his sword in front of him, completely covered in mud that dripped from his body in thick clumps.

Dimeji had retrieved his sword and now brought it down hard, intending to cleave him in two. Akin raised his sword over his head just in time to take the full impact of the blow, which pushed his own sword down into his shoulder, smashing his collar bone and shearing off part of his ear. He yelled out but pushed through the pain, drove himself upwards to his feet and turned, causing Dimeji's sword to slide off his own towards the ground. Akin summoned all his strength and punched Dimeji in the jaw, dislocating it and breaking his hand for his efforts. Dimeji's head rocked sideways violently, and the brute spun away holding his jaw, which hung loose, in his free hand. He began to make grunting and wheezing sounds as blood dripped from his open mouth into his hands and onto the ground, pooling at his feet. He breathed uneasily as his mighty shoulders went up and down in great bouts.

Akin took up position once again and tried to wrap his broken fist around his pommel, but pain lanced through his hand when he moved his fingers. He was forced to fight with his left hand, as the pain in his shoulder intensified, which didn't bode well for him. He changed his stance, bringing his left leg forward, while his sword was raised across his body protectively.

'I give you credit, serpent; you are much better than I had expected. It seems that some of the rumours about you are true after all. But this will be your last fight, I guarantee it. I hope you have made your peace with *Esu*; he will receive your damned soul shortly!' Akin said, gritting his teeth as he took a step towards his opponent.

Dimeji said nothing; he couldn't have even if he wanted to, his jaw had been shattered in several places by the blow, and all he wanted now was to tear Akin to shreds.

Akin tossed his sword in the air and caught the grip reversed, with the blade pointing towards the ground, as he darted forward. He spun his sword in two quick successions with a right and left stroke. The first, Dimeji blocked, but he misjudged the speed of the second, which cut across his bare chest, spraying blood. Akin stepped in and twisted his waist, levelling his sword for a third stroke. He intended to use his momentum to decapitate Dimeji, but the giant recovered quickly. As the sword came in, Dimeji spun away from it, used his sword to knock away the tip of the blade, which left Akin open, then chopped downwards striking him in the pelvis and shattering the bone. Akin's leg buckled on impact and he screamed out in pain.

Just as he was falling, he twisted his body around, so he would land on his back and swept his sword upwards. The blade took Dimeji in the stomach and travelled up inside his ribcage, piercing his heart. Dimeji's eyes widened and he let out a muffled cry. He dropped his sword and grabbed at the blade handle protruding from his stomach, but his energy seeped away almost instantly, like a fire doused with water, and he fell on his side. His mouth moved and an unintelligible word passed his lips before they stopped moving. Akin saw the life leave his eyes and let out a sigh of relief. He tried to move, but couldn't; his pelvis was in pieces and he knew he would never walk again. He began to weep as his blood escaped into the ground. *What use was a blood-guard if he could not protect his king?* he thought angrily.

Some of the Modakeke warriors immediately rushed to his side, while others took up position in front of him, deterring anyone who tried to finish him off as he lay there. They dragged him, screaming in agony, to the back of their lines and all the while he shouted, 'Protect your king! Kill them all!'

Jide had seen Akin fall and his heart stopped in his chest. He wanted to run over to him, but his eyes spied a glint of gilded armour. He took a better look, and standing some paces away was his brother Olise. Both men stood rooted to the ground, not having seen each other in almost twenty years, and a flood of emotion washed over them. Jide had not thought that the sight of his brother would conjure up so many feelings, and it was plain to see that this was reflected in Olise's expression. It was almost painful, that the love that they had once held for each other was evidently still there, be it buried below years of damaged ego, resentment and the blood of the many innocents that had led them on this path, that love had always connected them.

Nnamdi was close to Olise, and so were a few of Olise's captains and trusted men, but most had been transfixed on the fight between Dimeji and Akin, and had not noticed the king. Zogo suddenly came to stand by Jide's side. He saw that the king was staring intensely ahead and followed his vision to see Olise and his cousin standing not far from them. He let out a cry to his cousin Nnamdi and, with that, the moment of peace that the two brothers shared was shattered. Olise's features darkened at the sight of Zogo. He had been deceived as he had suspected. All his misgivings had been confirmed in that moment, and he was glad he had followed his intuitions and separated the Igbo forces.

'You treacherous black bastard!' he cried out to Zogo, before he looked to Iboro and gave him an almost imperceptible signal. The man immediately moved behind Nnamdi, and a sword suddenly burst through his chest. His eyes went wide with shock and blood traced a thin line from the corner of his mouth. The sword retracted as fast as it had appeared and Nnamdi sank to his knees, watching Zogo with pleading eyes before falling face first into the mud, dead.

'NO!' Zogo roared and rushed forward without a second thought. His shout alerted a few of the men standing around Olise and they all moved to protect their prince. Within moments, Zogo was fighting off six men in his desperation to reach Iboro or Olise, it was hard to tell. Zogo's two warriors with axes immediately went to the aid of their chief and several other Igbo warriors, and a ferocious fight ensued as both sides tried to butcher the other. Meanwhile, the two brothers eyed each other, locked in a fight in their minds as they slowly began to approach.

'Brother.' Jide said when they were within a spear's length of on another. 'Brother.' Olise replied. 'I hope you are proud, all this blood is on your hands, and for what? So you can lay claim to a throne that doesn't belong to you? Do you hate me so that you'd see the kingdom burned just to get what you want, or is it still Ekaete that pulls the threads?' Jide asked.

'Mother has nothing to do with this. It is between you and me, dear brother. Did you really think I'd forgive you for the way you wronged me all those years ago? Stripping me of my titles and my honour. Humiliating me like a mere peasant?'

'You were free to return after seven years! You knew that, but you chose to extend your banishment and spit in my face after the mercy I showed you. They wanted your blood, Olise. I went behind the council's backs and convinced Adedeji to vote in your favour, something no king should ever do. I betrayed my own laws to save your skin and you repay me with treason? How dare you stand there and accuse me?' Jide spat.

'You wanted me out of the way so you could rule the realm as you saw fit. I have as much right to the throne as you. We share the same blood and my mother was favoured! Our father announced my ascension to the throne before he died; it should have been me sitting there, not you!' Olise shot back.

'That is another one of Ekaete's lies. Listen to yourself, see how she has poisoned you. Our father would never have made such a statement when he already had an heir.'

'It matters not anymore. I will take back what is mine and build my own kingdom in the ruins of the old. You can gracefully step aside or die; the choice is yours.'

'I would have given you anything, brother, but your arrogance must be tamed. Come and take it if you can,' Jide said, raising his sword towards Olise.

'Have it your way. Brother.' Olise lunged at Jide in an instant and their swords struck, bringing them close together. Jide brought his dagger round to stab Olise in the neck, but he only found air – Olise danced away from the blade as if he had pre-empted it.

They came together again, striking high, low, then high again, and each time their swords clashed in the same position. They circled each other slowly as they watched every movement; the placing of their feet, the shift in weight, a twitch in their muscles. Both had trained together for many years in their youth and it seemed that their fighting instincts had remained in sync even with the passage of time. Each man read the other as easily as charcoal scratched on hide. None could best the other, but both had learned some new tricks over the years that had defined them.

Olise swung high, Jide dodged it and jabbed low, Olise withdrew out of reach and came in again. Jide spun clear and returned with another strike of his own, but again there was no contact. This carried on for a few heartbeats, until both men jumped back to appraise the other.

'I've missed our sparring, brother. It has been a while since I fought anyone with half the skill I have. I see you have kept your edge keen,' Olise said, almost convivially. 'Save your words, speak with your blade instead!' Jide replied as he came in again. This time he feigned right and changed direction at the last minute, attacking to the left. This caught Olise by surprise, forcing him to twist his body away from the swinging blade, so that it ripped across his chest plate and the point of the blade sliced across his sword arm. Jide moved in as quickly as a cobra and struck low, stabbing his dagger into Olise's leg.

Both blades came away clean. Jide looked at Olise's arm and leg in shock – there wasn't a scratch, nothing, not even a mark where the blades had touched. 'The prophecy was true. What kind of witchcraft have you got yourself into?' he said more to himself than his brother; his tone was fearful. 'The kind that will see you dead!' Olise spat as he pounced at Jide.

He deflected Olise's attack, which caused both men to collide and fall to the ground in a tangle of limbs. Jide scrambled from beneath Olise and, rammed his dagger as hard as he could into the space between Olise's neck and the shoulder straps of his armour. The blade struck but found no purchase, as if stabbing stone, the force of the strike twisted Jide's wrist and the dagger fell from his grip as he stared in shocked horror at his brother.

'Did you think it'd be that easy, brother? Did you really think I'd go against you without taking precautions? I am protected for as long as I have this amulet on my person, no weapon created by man can harm me,' he said, pulling the thread around his neck clear from behind his chest armour to reveal a small brightly coloured stone wrapped in dark string.

Suddenly spears were thrust towards Jide, ready to strike down and slay him where he lay. Olise's men had surrounded him and awaited the order to end his life right there in the mud outside Benin.

'It's over, dear brother. The crown is mine. Tell your men to lay down their weapons or I will have you killed like a dog for all to see. I would rather you live to see me seated on the throne, but you will die if you give me reason. It is over.'

Jide smiled sorrowfully. 'You may take the crown, but you will never take the name of the king nor possess the essence of one. Do you truly think the realm would accept you? You who choose to rule with wickedness, treachery and witchcraft? No brother, it can never be over, not while I draw breath.'

Zogo was close by, holding the severed head of Iboro, a look of total despair plastered on his face as he looked in the direction of the king. His axe-wielding guards were still beside him, as were several Igbo warriors, but many more lay in the mud unmoving. Jide looked to him and then over to the miserable remains of the Modakeke warriors moving to his position.

He had known that his reign would end, but he never thought it would be like this. Most of his allies had been killed, and his army was in tatters. He could only hope that the words spoken by the deity *Yemoja* would come to pass.

He thought about the rest of his family, his tribesmen, all the warriors who had given their lives for him and for their belief in the realm, created for all to prosper and to live in harmony. He thought of his kingdom, burned to the ground, all the displaced citizens that would be taken as slaves, if they hadn't already been killed. He thought about his father, King Adeosi, his grandfather, King Kayode and all the great Adelani kings before him. How they would be turning in their graves to witness this day.

But he was still the king and he would remain so for as long as the blood of his ancestors flowed through his veins. He closed his eyes, felt the soft drops of rain on his cheek, then let out a defiant shout to the westerners, 'FIGHT FOR YOUR KINGDOM!' All his warriors echoed his cry and surged forward, ready to lay down their lives for the king they loved so dearly.

A spear butt came crashing down into the side of Jide's head a moment later. Pain shot through his head and neck and his vision burst into brilliant brightness, just before the darkness embraced him.

PRINCE OF TWO KINGDOMS

The vaulted ceiling held beautifully painted murals depicting men in battle. One side showed warriors on horseback draped in regal finery; gold and silver inlaid armour, immaculate white flowing kaftans and scarfs that wrapped around their necks and chests. An army of bowmen followed, with hundreds of shafts flying overhead. The other side depicted men in what appeared to be simple tunics or loin cloths, barbaric looking men who carried oddly shaped spears and swords. Many lay on the ground with arrows all about them from the opposite army. This told a simple story; the royal houses of the north were of a divine order and the men they fought, presumably anyone foolish enough to challenge them in battle, were seen as nothing short of savages.

This was the impression that Toju had deduced from the images as he stood in the throne room awaiting an audience with the great emir Mustafa Abubaka. Prince Usman stood by his side, as did Leke and three other northern princes, half-brothers to Usman, all washed and scrubbed clean, clothed in appropriate attire ready to see the emir. They had recently returned from a skirmish with an army of marauding northerners, killing most of their number and capturing a handful of survivors, now destined for hard lives as slaves. This had been the six successful battle that Toju and Usman had led since his arrival in the north months ago, and he was fast building a reputation for himself.

Every so often, Usman, who had rarely been far from Toju's side since his arrival in the north, would flash him a smile like a pupil eagerly waiting praise from a teacher, but today they had earned the praise they were about to receive. The marauders they had crossed swords with had been a great threat in the region, pillaging and laying waste to many settlements, but Toju had put an end to that. Not only had he broken them, he had defeated their leader in single combat, killing him in front of all his men with almost no effort, which served as the catalyst to their destruction.

Toju had proved his worth tenfold through his bravery and his prowess, earning accolades from many of the noble northern lords who followed him in battle, giving him the nickname 'fearless one'. Now, he was about to be honoured by none other than the emir himself. An audience with the emir was no small thing, only the greatest of lords were permitted in his presence, and only if it was related to matters of great importance or grave concern to the land. Normally, the emir's first-born son and heir to the north, Prince Danjuma presided over most matters, but he would only serve as a translator today.

Danjuma had the makings of a great ruler when the reins of power would eventually be handed over to him. He was a handsome man with feminine-like facial features, inherited from his mother, slender of build but compact and muscular from his time spent on the field and on horseback. Undeniably a fearsome warrior, commanding the emir's vast armies and the hearts of all the nobles in the land. He was respected as much as he was feared and was known as 'destroyer of dreams' for the way he utterly crushed the ambitions of his enemies. He held no mercy in his heart for those who dared to cross him, and he did not suffer fools gladly. However, despite his cold demeanour, he was a man of great principles with unyielding love for his family and his motherland, but what he respected above all were true warriors, and he had come to accept Toju as an equal.

Horns blared from a corner of the room announcing the emir's approach, and all those present tensed nervously. Danjuma walked in first, followed by two of the emir's bodyguards, then the man himself walked behind dressed in an elaborate gown that flowed down to his feet, covering him almost entirely. His head was wrapped in many folds of cloth, which wound around his neck, like the men in the mural, and the air of power that surrounded him was unmistakable.

He seated himself on a pile of cushions that had been laid out on a dais; Hausa royalty disdained thrones, much preferring to remain close to the ground and almost at eye level when they held court, so they could look directly into the eyes of those they addressed. The bodyguards took up position behind him and Danjuma sat in front of the emir to his right.

Toju had only seen the emir twice since his arrival and only one of those was directly in his presence, shortly after his arrival in the city. The other time he had just spied him from a distance. He noted again how healthy the man looked, despite being in his late seventies. Maybe it was the many wives and servants he had at his beck and call that kept his appearance youthful, or perhaps it was the wealth he possessed that kept him in the bosom of luxury.

The emir spoke softly, almost as if the effort of talking was beneath him, but his face held a friendly expression as he studied Toju before him. 'His excellency greets you and thanks you for attending him today', Danjuma translated in fluent Yoruba with only a hint of an accent. Toju's grasp of the native Hausa tongue was rudimental at best, only King Jide and Niran understood and spoke many of the languages of the other tribes.

'You honour me, great emir.' Toju replied as he inclined his head slightly to show his respect. The emir spoke again at length. 'His excellency says that your bravery has not gone unnoticed and that you have proved yourself to be a man of great dignity. You will be rewarded handsomely for your deeds in supporting our lands.' Danjuma finished, also inclining his head at Toju, acknowledging him.

'Again, please accept my thanks. I am truly grateful, but I would like to speak freely if it pleases his highness.' Toju waited for Danjuma to translate, and the emir raised an open palm in a gesture permitting Toju to speak.

'Your excellency. I have been in your city for some moons now and my time here has been nothing short of an inspiration and pleasure, however, I would sooner return to the south. I made a promise to my brother, Prince Niran, that I would find support here and join with him in winning back our inheritance. I have bled for these lands and showed that I stand with you as an ally, but I cannot forsake my people. With your permission, great one, I would respectfully request an army to accompany me back to the south to regain my father's lands.' Usman looked at Toju, knowing that this day would come eventually, but still looked surprised at the request.

The emir looked on pensively as Danjuma translated Toju's words, and sat for a while assessing the young prince before he spoke. 'His Excellency understands your plight, but he is concerned that he could potentially offend the gods if he were to grant your wishes. He says that his father, the old emir, had promised King Jide long ago that no arms would ever be raised against a descendant of king Adeosi. It is your uncle you wish to confront, is it not? And he is a son of king Adeosi.'

Toju was devastated. This was the first time he had learned of the pledge that had been struck between the two nations. He knew that there were ties that bound the north and south but never had his father mentioned it; presumably he didn't anticipate that this situation would ever arise. He felt bitter knowing that all the months he had spent here, establishing relationships, garnering favours and embedding himself within the aristocracies of the north had been for nothing. The gods had played him a wicked hand and all he could think of was his brother and how he had failed him.

Noticing Toju's despondency, the emir spoke again for a time. Whatever he said caused Usman to take in a breath and then cast an expectant smile towards Toju. Danjuma raised an eyebrow and had an uncertain expression, but he translated, nonetheless. 'His excellency thinks he may have an alternative solution to your dilemma. He says that although he cannot break the promises of his forebear, you can.'

It was Toju's turn to be uncertain and confused. He had a funny feeling about where the conversation was going but he waited in silence for Danjuma to elaborate more on the emir's words.

'He says that if you were recognised as a prince of these lands, you would be free to wage war in your own name, being a prince of foreign blood, to right a personal injustice done to you. The only way you could be a part of these lands would be if you were to marry a daughter from these lands. One that would be befitting of a prince of your status, but more importantly, one whose dowry could be an army, perhaps, one that was sufficient to support you in your endeavours.

'The emir proposes that you marry his second daughter, Habibah; she is of an age with you, some years younger perhaps. This, he thinks, is a better alternative than going back to the south empty handed. It would surely satisfy all parties, would it not? You would have an army of your own to command as you see fit, but you would also be bound to our great house, and your bloodline would never be able to turn their spears on your adopted people.' He finished.

Toju didn't know how to respond. He had known that he'd have to sacrifice something to gain the support of the northerners, which he thought he had done by defeating some of their enemies and winning them new dominions, but to agree to such a request was a great deal to ask, and one he was not entirely sure he was prepared to accept.

'Your excellency... I... I am overwhelmed that you would treat me with such honour. I must admit that I have never once considered the prospect of marriage and raising a family. My true calling is that of a warrior. This is all I have ever known and, since leaving Ife, I have been consumed by only one desire, to bathe in the blood of those responsible for breaking my family and my kingdom. I will not insult you by simply accepting your proposal just to resolve my problem. I would only accept if I know in my heart that I will do right by your daughter, the princess, and not bring shame to your name. I suppose what I am trying to say is that I would respectfully request that I have some time to consider your proposal. This is not a matter that can be made in haste, as you will understand, Your Excellency.' Toju finished.

When Danjuma had finished translating Toju's words to the emir, to everyone's surprise, his face brightened with a beaming smile as he spoke to Danjuma. 'His excellency says that you are truly an honourable man and that he was right to have brought you into the royal confidence. He understands your misgivings and sympathises with you. He will grant you seven days to consider his proposal and make a decision. He does, however, assure you that regardless of your choice, you and your family will always be afforded the same hospitalities promised to you, but know that if you were to accept, you would not only have the wealth and means to take back what is yours but you would also be recognised as a prince of the north and welcomed as a son into the arms of our great house and be rewarded as such.'

The emir turned to Usman and his other two sons who stood with Toju. Some words were exchanged that sounded good natured, which was evident from their excited tones. After a short while, the emir rose from his cushions and gave Toju a final smile before making his way to the entrance he had come in from, his bodyguards following close behind.

Danjuma lingered for a moment until the emir had left the room. 'He regards you very highly indeed for him to make you such a generous proposal,' he said to Toju. 'He wouldn't give most men a say in the matter, but would simply expect them to obey his command. The fact that he has given you the choice speaks volumes.'

'As I said to the emir, I'm deeply honoured. I truly am, but you understand that this is a lot to digest, and marriage is not something I'd want to take lightly. I've never even met Habibah. We could turn out to be as incompatible as oil and water!' Toju said.

Danjuma let out a chuckle, 'Do you southerners always have to over think things? From where I stand, it is a simple choice, ride back to the south with an army at your back, or with the men you came with. Plus, you'd have a beautiful wife on your arm as a bonus. She really is beautiful, my father's greatest jewel in fact. Many men have vied for her hand, but none have ever been considered worthy enough in the eyes of the emir. It seems he considers you worthy,' Danjuma finished with a sly smile.

'He speaks the truth, prince,' Usman added. 'But what he didn't tell you is that she is a free spirit, fierce and passionate. Almost like you in some ways, though much better on the eye.' Usman winked, prompting laughter from the other two princes.

'I'm glad that you can laugh at my expense. In truth, the thought of entering a union terrifies me more than the thought of riding into battle against a thousand warriors. Maybe if I were to meet her that would help my decision,' suggested Toju.

'That will not be possible,' Danjuma responded flatly. 'In our tradition, you only see your wife on the day of the wedding. It cannot be any other way, I am afraid, and I'm sure that the emir would insist as much.'

'Well, that certainly helps things,' Toju answered, rolling his eyes and prompting more laughter from the princes.

'I'm sure you'll choose wisely. I would expect nothing less from a son of the fabled king in the south. Besides, having us as your brothers can only be a good thing, no? I might even consider riding south with you when the time comes. I've heard great things about your lands and would like to see them for myself. Not to mention the battle you intend to wage. What northerner doesn't relish the opportunity to test his skill?' Danjuma said as he patted Toju on the shoulder before following in his father's footsteps.

Toju watched the heir to all the north recede through the arched doorway before turning to Leke, Usman and the other two princes.

'Tell me honestly, Leke, what do you make of all this?' he asked. The blood-guard rubbed his stubbled chin as he often did. 'It wouldn't be such a bad thing if you went along with it. You'd be joining two of the greatest nations known to the tribes, a feat not even your great grandfather King Kayode was able to accomplish, one that he coveted avidly through all the years of his conquests in the north I might add. You would be the only legitimate crowned prince of all the lands either side of the great river, a title that would be passed to generations after you. No one before you has ever wielded such influence.'

'Well, that's one way to look at it. But I'd be bound to another. Not able to live my life as I see fit. Not able to go to war as I please without having to consider the thoughts and feelings of another,' Toju lamented.

'Is that what truly bothers you? Look, come what may, there will always be battles to fight. That is just the nature of our people.

Besides, no one can tell a northern prince what to do, least of all his wife,' one of the princes said.

'Brother, you talk as if you do not know Habibah,' Usman replied, then continued. 'Don't get me wrong, my brother's words are true, most men rule their household with an iron fist but, somehow, I don't think this would work with my sister. What I do know is that if she is taken by you and you by her, all this discussion will be irrelevant. And, who knows, maybe a strong woman is what you need to sate your desire for war. She might make a better man out of you.'

'Somehow I doubt that. What I do know is that I have a lot to think about.' Just then, Toju noticed one of his guards who had accompanied him from Ife pacing agitatedly just beyond the arched doorway opposite the throne room from where they had all entered. Leke had also spotted the man and they all went out to meet him, sensing something was amiss.

'Well? What is it that has you behaving as if someone has lit a fire under your feet?' Toju asked as he approached the guard.

'My prince, the news is not good,' the man replied, clearly having trouble trying to find the right way to phrase his message without evoking the wrath of the prince. 'I was in the market and came across a merchant who had travelled from the south. He spoke of a great battle, the battle for Benin, as he coined it, between the king and the prince. The way he tells it, a great many souls were lost, and the earth is still saturated with their blood. The king's army was almost completely destroyed, and he was taken prisoner by the prince.'

'My father lives?' Toju asked astonished. Up until now, he had assumed him dead. To know he could still be alive filled him with some hope. He no longer had an option; he needed an army.

'That is not the worst part, my prince.' He hesitated. 'The battle happened almost two moons ago. The merchant travelled many lands before he arrived here this morning. The gods only know what has transpired between now and then. Apparently, Olise has declared himself king, but for him to do so, there can only be one sitting monarch.' The warrior's words were plain enough for all to understand; he needed not to elaborate further.

340

Toju was silent for a while, head down, eyes closed, and hands balled up in fists by his side. His hopes were shattered. Usman was about to talk, offer words of condolence perhaps, but Leke's subtle gesture dissuaded him. They all waited in silence for the prince to say something. Anything. Then he raised his head, eyes burning with a desire that Leke knew all too well; the look that Toju wore whenever he intended to shed blood.

'This message has forced my hand. I need that army the emir promised if I am to punish those that aided in my father's demise. And I will send every one of those traitors down to *Esu's* fiery halls, this I swear on *Ogun's* blade. I will accept the offer of marriage. I only hope that this union can be made soon, so I can ride back and correct the wrong that has been done to my family.' Toju's fists shook as he spoke and the veins on his arms stood out, threatening to escape from beneath his skin. Rage consumed him, and the darkness deep in his heart slowly began to resurface. His time in the north had seen an assuaging of his famously ugly temperament, and his short-lived good nature evaporated like droplets of rain on leaves in the sun after a storm.

'My prince...' Leke ventured, 'Are you sure you don't require further time to consider your options? I know this news is upsetting, but don't make a rash decision driven by anger. I will follow you whatever path you take, and I will always trust your judgement in all things, but please think about it.'

Toju didn't need any more time, in fact he had run out of time in his mind. 'It is decided. I will marry the princess. There is no need to dwell on the matter. Usman, inform the emir that I accept his offer and would see the marriage tied at his earliest convenience.'

Usman looked from Leke to Toju, but chose not to protest or offer his own advice. 'Very well, prince. I will see it done.'

* * * *

To Toju's frustration, northern weddings were never minor affairs, but required great planning and preparation, especially considering the significance of the day; the joining of two great nations, a landmark of unions that had never before been witnessed by the tribes.

The ceremony was carried out over five days, each filled with lavish banquets and the exchange of rare and exotic gifts. Nobles from all over the north travelled to pay homage to their new warrior prince and the promises of support and allegiances were unending. The groom was required to present gifts of his own to his new family, but the emir had decreed that all the lands Toju had taken and the defeated lords he had brought to heel through the strength of his sword arm were enough to pay for his daughter's hand ten times over. The celebrations had seen countless cattle slaughtered, sacrifices and offerings to the gods, and the flow of palm wine and burukutu; the Hausa alcoholic drink of choice, never seemed to cease.

The groom was also obliged to perform several tasks of strength and cunning, wedding games as they were referred to, with the other princes and renowned warriors of the land to prove his manliness and worthiness of such a coveted prize. They rode wild horses, displayed skills in archery and wrestled, amongst a host of other activities, in which Toju, to the annoyance of his peers, bested everyone. These were all formalities really, but the emir was a stickler for tradition and wished to see their rites observed before he handed over his most adored child.

Toju acquainted himself with the emir's wives and younger children, of which he had so many he had lost count. He met the men of power and made mental notes of their strengths, weaknesses, noting the trustworthy, the power hungry and the dangerous. He met a great many people over those days, and he committed all to memory. The one person he was eager to meet, however, was nowhere to be seen. Every day, he scanned the faces of the crowd hoping to spy his wife to be, but she had been kept away from the festivities in preparation for the main wedding day.

On the morning of the fifth day Toju found himself very nervous, a feeling he was unfamiliar with. Leke had tried to reassure him as best he could, but every passing hour brought on more anxiety about the unknown aspects of what lay ahead of him. Under normal circumstances, the families of the bride and groom would meet with their entourages to observe the final rites and exchange their pledges of unity, but as Toju had no relatives to support him the emir had kindly paid his bride price the day before, gifting him with the army he had wished for.

Two thousand warriors, armed and horsed, rode towards the palace gates, following their procession through the city, which had been met with the customary and celebratory high-pitched screams from the women and raised swords and bows from the men, all wishing their new prince happy married life and prosperity. Toju had ridden through the streets like a conquering king returned, and his normally cold heart swelled with affection for his adopted people.

His men stood impressive in their head wraps, flowing kaftans and polished leather sandals. Oiled bows rest on their horses' flanks beside wicker baskets filled with newly fletched arrows of white feathers. Curved swords and daggers hung from leather belts on each man's hip and gleamed in the morning sun. Toju had led the procession on a magnificent black charger; a gift from Danjuma, who had spared no expense in sourcing the stallion, which would have cost a small fortune.

The other men from Ife had also been gifted beautiful horses from the northern princes, which they rode with pride at the prince's side, beaming from ear to ear at the adoration of the crowd. As they neared the gates of the palace Toju dismounted, and was followed in by his people from Ife and five men from his newly acquired army. They were met by the emir's sons, all seven princes of the north, Danjuma standing foremost. Toju embraced each of them in turn before being allowed to pass the threshold, and the sight he saw took his breath away.

The palace court looked exquisite; wild flowers had been arranged all around, finely woven mats covered most of the gravel floor, large portions of the grounds were draped in colourful yards of cloth held in place by long pieces of timber to shield against the sun, casting multi-coloured hues around the court that enhanced the harmonious look of the scenery.

The emir was there, as were his wives and children, with some prominent figures of the land, elders including the emir's marabu, who would officiate the ceremony. And next to him was Habibah. She was veiled in a thin transparent cloth of fine embroidery, standing tall and elegant. Her hands were decorated with swirling patterns of henna and her wrists were adorned with many thin bracelets of gold and silver. Toju's heart quickened as he approached her. He had to control his steps and try not to stumble, but he brought himself to his full height and walked over with his head held high and his chest out.

Northern wedding ceremonies would normally see the groom in a white flowing gown, but Toju had refused to wear one, instead donning his armour, which had been polished to a high sheen with animal fat. He intended to be wed as a warrior, a not-so-subtle statement to his wife-to-be.

When he reached her side, he caught a whiff of a flowery scent that evoked some hidden emotion in him, but he kept his composure. The marabu began the ceremony, performing his duty, which lasted several minutes, deftly.

Once the words were said, the right hands of the couple were joined. Toju couldn't help but notice how soft and delicate she felt against his calloused palm. More words were spoken and, finally, he was asked to unveil his bride and look upon her face for the first time. His hands trembled, but he controlled his nerve and reached for the veil. He set it behind her head gently to reveal a smooth flawless face. She was the most beautiful person he had ever seen, and in that instant, everything changed.

WALK IN THE SHADOW OF RUIN

Ile-Ife. A land once the jewel in the crown of the south. The focal point for art, culture and history. Abundant with life; hunting, fishing, trade; and home to a proud and ancient people. A sacred land fabled to have been founded by *Oduduwa* himself, passed to his offspring and eventually entrusted to mortals favoured by the gods. These very mortals would later begin the lineage of kingship and go on to build a palace surrounded by a magnificent city, all in dedication to *Oduduwa,* maintaining the traditions that were handed down to them, which formed the cornerstones of their being and the very foundations on which they stood.

Now, this once hallowed land was nothing but a vast graveyard, haunted by ghosts. Those who had lived through the sack of the city were reduced to slaves, treated no better than animals of burden. Such was the fate of *Oduduwa's* people. The god of Ife must have wept to see his creations so beset with misfortune, but he was a god who never intervened; rather, he left man to his own devices, unlike some of the other gods who chose to influence the hands of men to do their will. Unfortunately, all the men sworn to preserve this land now fed the soil, and those who remained were lost souls, broken men from the atrocities they had witnessed when the fire and spears came for their homes and families, never to be whole again.

All this, Jide had seen as he was forced to march through the ruin of his homeland on what used to be the city's thoroughfare. After he was taken in the battle for Benin, what remained of his army had been decimated almost to a man. His capture had emboldened Olise's forces and they swept the field like a mighty flood flowing downhill, engulfing everything in their path. Jide's allies had fought bravely, refusing to abandon their king, but their efforts had been futile. One by one they fell, taking many with them down to the halls of the underworld, but unable to slow the inevitable tide of violent death.

Olise had ordered the heads of every man with a name of note to be mounted on spears and joined in the ominous procession through the ruins of the city. Olusegun, Nnamdi, Akin, Dare and a host of others who had sworn to protect their king now watched over him through unseeing eyes.

Intended as further mockery and a twist of the blade of humiliation that pierced the heart of Jide, Olise had insisted that the king was clamped in chains of gold wrought especially for his prized capture, restraints suitable for one thought to be so great, as he was paraded through the streets like a sacrificial goat on a leash. Jide sobbed openly at the sight of his home, which he had not seen in many months, and some of the surviving citizens wept with him to see their king so reduced.

Some had tried to approach him, but were driven away with canes that left marks on their bodies, their new overlords only too eager to have an excuse to dole out punishment. They learnt their lesson quickly, and soon no one made any further attempts to step forward, but just stood where they were and lamented at the unjust treatment of their king.

It was, however, a bittersweet moment for Olise. Though he had won the seat he had so desperately sought, his triumphant homecoming had been tainted by the sight of the city. He knew that it had been razed but he hadn't expected it to be so absolute. He'd visualised the streets lined with thousands of people bowing at his feet and cowering in fear of him, but what he was greeted with were handfuls of defeated and dishevelled people, mostly women and children, who all but ignored him and rather directed their attention towards their beloved king. What had he expected, leaving lowborn scavengers with the task of securing such a prize of a city? He should have known that without a firm hand to guide them they'd only seek to take advantage of the chaos to pillage, kill and burn unrestrainedly. He thought how he should have left someone respected in command, which only reminded him that he had lost two of his most trusted men; Dimeji and Ogie, who had joined the thousands of dead that littered the barren fields of Benin, not given a proper burial but left for the birds and other scavengers.

Who could he possibly trust now? He was certain that the men who surrounded him only indulged him for the favours that he could grant them, and he still had to bring a few of the tribes to heel and get them to accept him as their new ruler. He was under no illusions that the road ahead would be hard, but he still had his mother and the influence she wielded, which he required now more than ever.

But he hadn't come to Ife just to gloat; the main reason he had chosen to return to the capital was to be crowned here, as his father and all the kings before him had been, to stamp his legitimacy. He wanted to bring back the traditions of the kings of old and take his seat in a rebuilt city, one constructed to his own likeness, and that is exactly what he did.

It had taken a year of forced labour by the previous inhabitants and captured warriors to rebuild the city stone by stone from the rubble and debris of the old. A city built stronger and even more opulent than it had been in honour of the usurper. Olise had levied taxes, which he called the "king's taxes", on all the provinces to pay for the new city, which were so exorbitant that they not only funded the rebuild, but also filled his personal coffers. The request was highly unpopular but could hardly be refused, which only served to increase the resentment towards the new monarchy. Olise wanted Jide to live to see the crown laid on his head and had erected a cage for him outside the palace walls, which was guarded day and night by warriors. Still in chains of gold, he was displayed for the world to see; the defeated king.

He was fed scraps and only managed to survive due to the meagre rations donated by the people, when the guards allowed it. Besides malnutrition, he was otherwise unmolested. The humiliation of being a prized possession was enough, and crowds gathered daily to show solidarity to the man who was loved by all. He became a shadow of his former self, gaunt and unkempt, but defiance still burned in his eyes and he stood tall in his cage like a leopard, declawed but still deadly.

Efetobo, who had somehow survived the massacre and now found himself at the right hand of Olise, the status to which he had aspired for as long as he had been a councillor, oversaw preparations for the coronation. Olise had handpicked his own kingmakers, men who would proclaim his ascension to the throne legitimate and favoured by the gods, leaving no room for dispute by the locals and nobilities of the realm. These men were essentially the ones who would place the crown on his head.

However, the event had been a thing of controversy and mixed opinions even within his newly formed government, in particular because of his insistence in having human sacrifices dedicated to the gods for their blessings, as was done in times of old. A practice that had since been abolished by the Adelani bloodline. The sacrifices would require six people - three men and women, and the king-to-be would be marked in their blood and crowned as they passed into the afterlife. The first Adelani ruler had detested the act, branding it an antiquated tradition, but Olise wanted to set himself apart from his ancestors, paving a way for his own line, one that would speak to his perceived greatness.

And so, his request was granted, more accurately obeyed, and six random unfortunates were taken against their will from different parts of the kingdom. Unbeknownst to Olise, one of the maidens taken for this purpose was the daughter of a prominent chief from the city of Ekiti, just north of Ife. The chief had served in Jide's army and was amongst the many dead, so the elders had no choice but to pledge their fealty to the new ruler of the realm, whilst harbouring their contempt, as did most of the kingdom. The daughter, Fadęke, was widely considered to be the chieftain of the Ekiti people, since the chief had no other heirs and, although it was an unprecedented appointment, her father was so revered that the people had insisted that the future chieftaincy should come from his bloodline. Fadęke, on the other hand, had no such desires and preferred to live a life of relative freedom away from the politics of leadership.

One night, she travelled from her city, intent on meeting with her friends from one of the neighbouring villages as she often did. She chose not to use a torch to light her way out until she was clear of the city, to avoid being spotted by the sentries. As she ran through the forest, she had stumbled in the darkness and fallen down an embankment, striking her head, which rendered her unconscious.

Some of Olise's soldiers happened to be on their way to Ekiti to collect the king's tax, when one of the men, who had gone deeper into the woods to urinate, came across the prone figure of Fadẹke in the undergrowth. Mistaking her for a common peasant or run-away servant, she was bound, gagged and immediately taken back to Ife before an alarm could be raised about a missing girl.

Fadẹke and the other people kidnapped from various corners of the realm for the sacrifice, were thrown into the dungeons and left to languish for days while preparations for the coronation were being made. None of them had an inkling as to why they were there or what fate awaited them, and they found comfort in each other, hoping that their abduction had been one big mistake that would all be put right.

The day of the ceremony came, and the six of them were dragged from the pits, lashed together with ropes, with cloths thrown over their faces. They were marched out to the courtyard of the palace to beating drums, the scent of burning wood and the murmurs of many people, and their anxieties increased. When the cloths were removed from their heads, they faced a large crowed of gathered nobles and prominent figures in the realm.

A group of men in the crowd were pointing at Fadẹke. She could not understand why at first, as she was still bewildered by the scenery and the circumstances that had led her to this place. Suddenly, recognition registered in her features. They were her people, elders from Ekiti invited to bear witness to the crowning of the new king. A few more people in attendance started to gesticulate animatedly, names were shouted, Fadẹke's being one of them, and

349

several men in the crowed attempted to push forward to reach the captives. They were immediately set upon by Olise's guards and most were forcibly restrained then removed, arrested and destined for imprisonment or a flogging for having the audacity to interrupt such a sacred ceremony.

And there stood Olise, dressed in a white wrapper tied around his waist. His chest was bare but for the amulet that hung from a thread around his neck. His body was knotted with muscles, declaring his status as a warrior, but he bore no marks or scars as most of his peers did. His expression was both stern and arrogant at the same time, like a man about to receive something that had belonged to him all along. He kept glancing over to his right at something. Fadeke followed his gaze and saw a man locked in a cage some paces away. The man appeared bedraggled, with a bushy head of hair and beard streaked with greys, but the look in his eyes was like thunder, stark and penetrating, as he watched the ceremony intensely.

Suddenly Fadeke and five other men and women with her were ushered towards posts that had been erected in a semicircle not far from where Olise stood. They were tied to the posts with their hands above their heads, and then the reality of her predicament dawned on her. There would be no escaping what was about to happen. No waking up from this nightmare. Some of the others started to cry, some prayed and some, like her, just looked on in silent terror.

The kingmakers stepped forward, holding Olise by both arms, and guided him to stand in front of the six figures with his back to them and the crowd of people. They started to intone words theatrically, which sounded distant to Fadeke's foggy mind; the drums beat and one of the kingmakers produced a circlet of gold and some other precious metal. He held it aloft for all to see as he addressed the people in attendance and then, one by one, the offerings were given to the gods.

Fadeke watched in horror as an executioner professionally went about slitting the throats of the men and women to her left. He waited for each person to bleed out and cease their final death throes before moving onto the next one. One of the kingmakers held a calabash to catch the blood dripping from the dead, and another smeared it on Olise's forehead and chest. This was repeated after each kill. Some of the captives tried to turn from the blade, but it was pointless.

Some screamed uncontrollably, only to be silenced a moment later, gurgling their final breath. She would be the last offering to the gods. She watched the man beside her shake violently, his blood streaming down his chest, then she felt a warm sensation on her legs and realised she had wet herself. She looked around desperately, hoping that someone would call out to stop what was happening and save her in these final moments. She hoped that *Aganju*, her revered deity, would open the grounds and swallow all the men who intended to harm her, but none of that happened.

When the man beside her stopped moving and his blood had been collected, the executioner walked in front of her. She looked into his eyes pleadingly and saw the unmistakable glint of sorrow there, then her eyes were drawn to the bloody blade in his hand, as he raised it to her neck. There was a flash of pain, sharp at first and then dull and throbbing. She gasped, desperately fighting for air, but none came to her, and she vaguely felt the warmth of her blood running between her exposed breasts. The sounds of the drums and shouts receded into the distance as she faded away. Her blood filled the calabash, then the kingmaker repeated the ritual of marking Olise with it, just before the circlet of gold was placed on his head to more beating drums. The ceremony was complete, and with Fadẹke's passing, a new king emerged.

* * * *

Olise's crowning rippled through the kingdom with dissent trailing in its wake. Most were sickened by the reports of human sacrifices and the treatment of some of the dignitaries who were in attendance; however, these sentiments were not expressed openly, and fear remained the overwhelming emotion that prevailed in the

351

lands. Olise's influence over the provinces was almost absolute, and his first act as ruler was to systematically seek out those who harboured notions of rebellion and crush them utterly.

Ekiti was the first city to bear the brunt of his iron rule, as word of Fadęke's death had ignited a fire that burned in the hearts of the citizens. Spies had reported rumours of a potential uprising and Olise had responded by sending an army to detain all those in power, along with their allies. He installed puppet leaders in their seats and garrisoned the city with his warriors, quenching the flames of revolt before they had a chance to mature. The arrested dignitaries, including relatives of the late chieftain, were executed without trial and their heads adorned the walls of the city as a deterrent to those who would consider turning their spears on the new king.

Olise carried on in this fashion, replacing the heads of principalities with those he favoured, leaving few remnants of the old hierarchy. Soon, the ruler south of the great river came to be known as the king of heads, a testament of the number of these he had claimed over the course of his reign.

His new subjects were not the only problems he faced; Jide, who remained in his chains of gold like a prized pet, was still the biggest stone in his sandal; secretly he served as a beacon of hope to those who silently plotted in the shadows, seeking to redress the balance of power. Ekaete had pleaded with Olise to be done with Jide, knowing that for as long as he lived the people would always look to him, and never truly accept Olise as king.

Olise knew this to be true, but couldn't bring himself to order the death of the one person he admired, and had once loved above all. That was until word began to spread of an uprising in the east. There were whispers that a man claiming to be from the royal bloodline; a prince, some said, led a mighty army that had taken control of most of the provinces in the region.

Even more disturbing was the news that Zogo the black had survived the battle for Benin and had ridden to his homeland to join forces with this so-called prince. When these reports filtered down to Ife, Olise had immediately dispatched scouts to the east in the hope of gathering further information. He also sent some of his warriors south to his estates in Aba, with orders to eliminate the hostages he held there, punishment for the Igbo chiefs' betrayal. Months went by, and none of his men returned. This infuriated him.

He sent out larger forces, under the command of hardened veterans, ruthless men who he knew he could rely upon to deliver the king's justice. Time passed and word was finally received, confirming that the east was in turmoil. Battles had been raging for months between the Igbo and southern tribes, mainly led by Calabar, and the death toll was said to be in the thousands. Little information was gleaned about the so-called prince besides the fact that he was young and had proved to be extremely resourceful and tactical, winning many battles.

In a bid to preserve his interests in some of the wealthier provinces, Olise had commanded his warriors to secure the borders to the east of Onitsha and to the south of the River-lands, but the battles threatened to spill over the imaginary lines of territory and drift further west. Worse was the risk of the kingdom being fractured into separate dominions if the victor of the battles so chose. Olise had no choice but to take drastic actions to ensure that his grip on power remained as his mother intended, so he heeded her counsel.

Jide's body was failing him. Hunger pangs came in waves, constantly plaguing him, and yet his pride would not allow him to beg for more nourishment like a peasant. The people of the city still fed him when they could, but there was no denying that he was slowly wasting away in his cage. With every passing week, the chains that bound him weighed heavier, and most days he lay on his back to preserve what little energy he had left to him, although for what purpose he knew not. He was losing hope.

The sound of movement from the ring of sentries who watched over him night and day caught his attention. Debilitated he may be, but his senses were far from diminished, heightened if anything. Mental conditioning and focus had been the only thing keeping him sane, as he constantly walked the threshold of madness, being confined for so long. A year in a cage would have turned most men into little more than animals, but not Jide. He was from unyielding stock, and he was determined to show just that.

The sentries parted to admit someone. He could just make out the silhouette in the torch light but, as the figure came into view, he now saw the cold features of his brother. Olise.

'And what do I owe the pleasure of this visit?' Jide asked. 'You haven't so much as set foot here for months. Just how long do you intend to keep me on display like a caged beast to wallow in my own waste? Is your ego not stroked enough, or do you wish to demean me until I am broken?'

Olise's expression softened a fraction to see the image of his brother. Gone were the compact muscles, the handsome groomed appearance, the domineering air of authority. What he saw was an impostor, a gaunt shell of a man not worthy to have ever been called king. It would be a mercy, a last act of kindness, he thought to himself. His mind was set.

'I am here to tell you that you will see the blade once the sun crests the mountains tomorrow, brother. Make peace with your gods,' Olise replied with a touch of sorrow in his tone. 'I never wanted this, but you left me little choice. It must be done for the greater good of my kingdom.' He stopped.

'*Your* kingdom? Listen to yourself. After all these years it is still Ekaete's tongue that speaks through you. When will you ever stand for yourself rather than cling to the folds of her wrapper like a child desperately seeking the teat?'

'You know nothing of what I am capable of! How could you, after you turned your back on me all those years ago. So do not presume to know my mind or the decisions that I alone must bear! I wanted to extend you a courtesy, to spare you from further humiliation, and yet you insult me. I suggest you ponder what little time you have left, brother. It is over.'

'I have nothing to ponder, brother. Do you think I fear death? I knew this day would come, though I thought it would be sooner. In truth I died on the battlefield a year ago and have since accepted that I'm on borrowed time, purgatory if you like. I've

354

embraced my destiny. I dare say I yearn what is to come because I know I'll be in the arms of those I love while your "kingdom" and all you think you have accomplished will burn before your eyes. Mark my words, he who laughs last laughs the hardest.'

'Well there'll be no laughing for you tomorrow, that I can assure you.' Olise turned his back on Jide and started to make his way back towards the sentries, deliberately taking his time, hoping that Jide would make a last bid for freedom and plead for his life, but he said nothing. When he reached to within a pace of the guards, he looked back to see Jide lying down with his eyes closed.

'Farewell, my brother,' he said as he walked back towards the palace.

The hours stretched as the night sky gradually shed some of its darkness, and Jide took in every moment of it. He felt more connected to his surroundings than he had ever been; the soft night breeze that cooled his brow, the sounds of crickets in the grass, the mixture of scents carried on the night air, and the stars as they receded with the passing night. He had never really appreciated how numerous they were, scattered across the sky like the sparkles of sunlight that reflected on open water. The image that filled his vision was truly a thing of beauty.

As dawn approached and the first signs of light started to appear, Jide noticed a group of people shuffling towards the guards. It was not uncommon for him to receive visitors bearing alms in the form of food and water, but there was something out of place. There were three of them wearing multiple layers of clothing, which was most unusual, as the day promised to be sweltering. It was as if they were trying to camouflage their identities.

Two of them were big individuals, their bulk barely concealed under the layers of cloth, presumably men who worked the fields. Or warriors. The third was slight of build and oddly familiar. He walked with a limp, and from the way he guided him gently towards Jide it was plain to see that the bigger of the other two held this one in high esteem.

Most of the sentries were asleep or trying to stay awake as they leaned on their spears and against trees, so no challenges were issued when the three visitors passed the through the line. For some unknown reason, the closer they came, the more Jide's anxiety began to rise. This was unbecoming of his character; why would his emotions stir so in the presence of his subjects? He would soon find out.

As they got to within a few paces of his cage, the two larger visitors stopped, but the smaller figure amongst them took a few precarious steps forward, obviously struggling to walk steadily on his damaged leg. A hand shot out from under his robes to brace himself from falling and Jide's eyes were drawn to the small and delicate hand, not that of a labourer or a warrior; more like... a woman's hand. His breath caught in his throat.

She pushed back the cloth concealing her face, and tears began to stream down Jide's cheeks unabated.

Lara.

He couldn't trust his own eyes, and for a split second believed that his imprisonment had finally robbed him of his senses, but at the same time he was too scared to close his eyes lest she vanish like an apparition, confirming that she was only a figment of his imagination. Until she began to cry softly, sorrow, relief and anger mixed in her expression.

'Do my eyes deceive me? Is that really you, my love?' he whispered. She stepped closer and reached out to touch his cheek. The feel of her skin sent a wave of emotion through him, almost unmanning him in an instant. All the time he had spent in the cage, the torment, humiliation, depravation, he had stood tall, unbreakable – but the sight of his beloved wife destroyed all of that with a touch.

'It is me, my love, I am here. What have they done to you?' Her sobs intensified as she looked into his eyes and felt his wasted body through the bars of the cage. She yearned to hold him and be consumed by him, cocooned in his embrace beyond the reach of the world.

'I thought you had perished. They said you all burned with the palace. How did you survive all this time?' A hundred questions rushed through his head, but there was little time. Between sobs, she told him how she had managed to escape the assassins and the flames that ravaged the old palace. How Ogogo, Taiwo and two others had fought their way through with her and managed to flee the city amidst the chaos. How she had come close to dying from the wound she had taken, and would have done so, but for the kindness and medical attention received from some townspeople who had also fled the carnage. She told him how she had managed to travel to Ibadan, a town due west of Ife, and shelter there for months, eventually planning to journey further west to her father's homeland of Ogun. Until rumours had started to spread that he was alive and captured in Ife.

'I could not go anywhere without coming to see for myself. Even the slightest possibility of you being alive was reason enough to risk everything,' she said as she wiped her face dry of tears, only for more to replace them.

Jide spoke through his own tears: 'My love, you risk too much being here. I can't bear to think what Olise would do if he were to discover you. That would destroy me. You must leave while there is still time.'

'How can I? I took a vow and I am bound to you in this life and the next and gladly accept whatever fate the gods have planned for you. I thought I'd lost you forever and I refuse to turn my back on you now!' They held each other as closely as they could, given the restrictions of the cage between them.

'Listen to me, Lara. If you live there is hope. It makes no sense for both of us to die here. My fate is sealed but you, my love, will be needed when the time comes. What of our sons? They could be out there somewhere!'

'Toju and Niran were with me when the soldiers came and I sent them away, but there is no telling if they escaped. Enitan was out in the forest at the time and I have heard nothing. I fear he is...'

she trailed off, plagued by sadness and unable to bring herself to utter the words.

'Go west. Trust your instincts, as you always have. Seek your father and all will be well. But go now, I beg you. No matter what befalls me, my heart is content now that I have seen you. The gods have given me that much. Now, please go. If you love me, obey my wishes.'

A cockerel crowed in the distance and some of the guards began to stir. Ogogo and Taiwo looked around nervously, and then at each other, their hands moving below the folds of their cloths ready to reveal their weapons, no doubt, and paint the soil red.

'Go now, my love. I implore you.' Jide pleaded and gently began to remove Lara's hands from his face and arm. His actions broke his heart, but it was necessary. She stood there trying to muffle her sobs but didn't offer any resistance.

'I will always love you,' she managed to say. 'And I love you,' he replied through his tears, just as Ogogo approached and guided her gently away, bowing his head at his king in respect. As she left, she glanced back several times until they were beyond the line of guards, now all awake. When she was out of sight, he broke down and cried uncontrollably, his sorrow overwhelming him, but he was also gladdened that he had seen her again. He thanked *Yemoja* for this gift.

As the sun rose over the mountains, five guards came for him, released him from his chains and marched him to a secluded part of the palace. He was made to kneel in the soil and place his head on a tree stump that looked to have been cut only a few hours ago. He called on *Yemoja* once more, thanking her for his life and begging her to receive his soul, just as the axe came down. His blood seeped into the reddish-brown soil of Ife, becoming one with the land of his forebears.

Thank you for taking the time to read my book. I sincerely hope that you have enjoyed it as much as I enjoyed writing it. I am excited about sharing what I have planned for the Fractured Kingdom Series. In the meantime, if you can spare a moment to leave a review, your feedback would be most appreciated. Thank you for your continued support.

Subscribe to my newsletter at www.de-bajo.com/books for updates, character artwork and sneak previews on the upcoming books in the Fractured Kingdom Series.

Printed in Great Britain
by Amazon

82570560R00212